PENGUIN BOOKS

Nicole Alexander is a fourth-generation grazier, and the business manager of her family property. She has a Master of Letters in creative writing and her novels, poetry, travel and genealogy articles have been published in Australia, Germany, the United States and Singapore.

She is the author of nine other novels: *The Bark Cutters, A Changing Land, Absolution Creek, Sunset Ridge, The Great Plains, Wild Lands, River Run, An Uncommon Woman* and *Stone Country.*

T0363343

Also by Nicole Alexander

NICOLE ALEXANDER

The Cedar Tree

PENGUIN BOOKS

PENGUIN BOOKS

UK | USA | Canada | Ireland | Australia
India | New Zealand | South Africa | China

Penguin Books is part of the Penguin Random House group of companies
whose addresses can be found at global.penguinrandomhouse.com

First published by Bantam in 2020
This edition published by Penguin Books in 2021

Cover photography by Drunaa/Trevillion Images (main image) and Zerbor/Shutterstock (tree)
Cover design by Louisa Maggio © Penguin Random House Australia Pty Ltd
Typeset in Fairfield LT by Midland Typesetters, Australia

Printed and bound in Australia by Griffin Press, an accredited
ISO AS/NZS 14001 Environmental Management Systems printer

 A catalogue record for this
book is available from the
National Library of Australia

ISBN 978 0 14378 686 3

penguin.com.au

❧ Prologue ❧

Kirooma Station, far west New South Wales, 1949

Stella came from over the mountains. From a place battered by the lash of the wind and buffeted by the lifting soil. It was a snake-etched, empty environment; one stretched and hollowed out by fragments of cultures that had once fought for its ownership, the winners unaware that nature, not stubborn perseverance, would decide their fates. White men had died traversing the interior tracks that the black people called home. But in a place where fortitude came second to knowledge, it was stupidity that kept most searching ever onwards for a portal further into the Great South Land.

Stella's homestead had faced north-east. It had stared defiantly from the New South Wales–South Australian border across hundreds of kilometres to where people who were closer settled lived underground and mined for pretty opals, and where great pastoralists had once walked wagonloads of firm-packed wool bales to the Darling River to be transported to market. There was water. But they saw little of it. Most of what flowed beyond their grasp terminated in shallow lakes and flood-outs in the northernmost stretches of the Strzelecki Desert. It certainly wasn't all gibber plains and sand dunes; there was some good country among the useless. Stubby bushes stooped by nature sustained life, and among

1

the best of the acreage there were familiar trees, but it wasn't the promised land. In high summer when the westerlies arrived, there were days when Stella only had to open her mouth to taste salt on her tongue.

Her home of old was a space unlike any other. One littered with the echo of endless sighs that seemed to stretch far beyond the land that engulfed her married life. She had left a baby in that fierce land's grasp. One who might have survived, had circumstance and distance not prevented it. Her husband, Joseph, also remained there, buried deep in the red heart of their property where the dingoes and crows couldn't molest him. He belonged to that place. It had been his land, after all. Not once, not even at the very end, had she been unkind enough to tell him that the only thing he really possessed was a futile dream. Endings, no matter how painful, are no time for reproach. At least not of the verbal kind. Instead, the homestead haunted her that last day as she trailed through rooms, dragging furniture across floorboards, throwing clothes into suitcases, sorting through a life lived in the shadowlands. She was sure that the salty dunes edged a little nearer the day she drove away.

❦ Chapter 1 ❧

Richmond Valley, 1949

Now Stella was in this new place of waterways, crops, swampy lands and flood plains. Her eyes glazed over at the greenery, the brimming rivers and the concentration required for the undulating, twisting roads. She drove past fluffy trees with bushy crowns and papery bark and a sign that advertised the selling of tea-tree oil. She pressed the brake pedal and pulled the station wagon to the edge of the road, slowing to a stop. In the shade of a proud tree, she dug in the soil, squeezing the earth until it gummed together in her palms. She looked back towards the hills and the spring haze that blurred the scene in a whitish mist and breathed in hot, moist air. It was seven years since she'd left to go inland. Stella supposed the eastern coast hadn't changed much in her absence. She was the one altered. Her mind and body would forever remain braced for the dry, hot winds of the past, for the bulging dust storms that sought out man and beast, and the emptiness of that old life.

On her left was an expanse of tall, tropical grass. The fields of sugar cane that charted her course to the fork in the road were in various stages of growth. Some of the paddocks were cut off close to the ground. Other stands of cane had sent up new, bright green stalks. Green. The shade of life. The colour of most grasses and leaves, of some fruits, like limes and avocados, flavours she could barely recall. Stella stared at the simple cane shoots, and the strip of grass on the verge of the road, and considered the warp and weave of this new place.

She got back into the vehicle and checked the scratchy directions noted on the piece of paper sitting on the seat next to her, then looked back out the car window. Separated by a patch of burrs, two postboxes served as property signs. They were positioned on either side of the road just before it split into two. One of the letterboxes bore her married surname, O'Riain. The other had been vandalised, the words unreadable. In the rear-view mirror an indignant Watson stared back at her from his cage. The bird cocked his proud head sideways, his expressive sulphur-yellow crest rising in annoyance.

Her brother-in-law Harry had said that his house was less than two miles from the gravel road. Stella wished it were another twenty miles, or even thirty. Four days' driving had not lessened her unease. The car and trailer she towed jolted over a buckled ramp where a no-trespassing sign in red lettering hung at an angle. Stella drove past a turn-off that led to a double gate, behind which were what Stella guessed were the work sheds, while the road she followed ended directly at the front of the house. She followed the narrowing track and parked the station wagon to one side of the carport, near where a clothesline tilted ominously.

Stella carefully unclenched her hands from the steering wheel and wiped her palms across the skirt of her dress. To think she'd been married to Joe for seven years and only now was she visiting his family home.

'I'll be back for you,' she said to Watson, opening a window for him.

The bird averted his dark eyes in reply.

Dust flew from the rear of the vehicle as she opened the boot. The contents had shifted during the journey. Stella surveyed the assortment of belongings and then dragged out two suitcases. She ran her eyes over the remaining items and righted a large globe of the world, which had fallen on its side. She tucked her handbag under an arm and lifted the suitcases, setting her eyes squarely on the building before her. The sun-blistered walls of the old timber house were yellowish in colour. Someone had painted the gutters without sanding back the original shade and brown patches showed through a more recent coat of grey.

Stella swallowed, feeling the air catch in her throat, then she stepped up onto the open veranda and, placing the suitcases on the timber boards, knocked on the frame of the screen door. A sweetness hung in the air, reminding her of the caramel tart she used to make for Joe. She rapped on the door again, and when no one answered she started wandering along the length of the veranda.

'Stella?'

The voice was weak. Stella called out a response, her vocal cords scratchy through disuse after the long days of solo travel. She peered through each of the four gauze-covered windows, moving carefully so as not to trip on the buckled veranda that, like the house, was built flat on the ground. The wall was of tongue-and-groove pine like her old home and she ran her hand against the weathered timber until she came to the last window.

'Hello,' said a woman's voice.

Stella lifted a hand to her eyes. It was almost impossible to see anything through the flyscreen. 'Are you Ann?'

'You must be Stella.'

'Yes,' she replied.

'Let yourself in. My bedroom is at the end of the hallway.'

Stella returned to the front door. She propped it open with her foot and pushed the suitcases inside. The door closed loudly behind her. She was standing in a narrow passageway. Through an open door on her right was a kitchen with mint-coloured benchtops and wooden cupboards. From where she stood, every surface appeared to be covered with unwashed dishes, glasses and

5

saucepans. Something crunched underfoot as Stella crossed the floor and entered the adjoining sitting room. It was in a similarly messy state. A trail of ants were making their way across the coffee table and up the side of a bottle of red cordial. Newspapers were scattered on the sofa and armchairs and an old roll-top desk and filing cabinets were crammed along a wall. She found herself hesitating, caught in the clutter of someone else's life.

The end of the sitting room led to another hallway. Stella walked its length slowly, studying the photographs that hung in a row, one by one. She recognised her brother-in-law Harry, and assumed the slight woman beside him was his wife Ann. She looked nice. Four children featured prominently. Three boys and a girl, the tallest boy dressed in a uniform. The other people were strangers, like most of her husband's family.

There were two doors on each side of the hallway and the last on the left was open.

'Hello?' called Stella.

'Come in.'

She entered tentatively. A woman was propped up in bed, a mass of pillows framing her. The sheet was moulded to her body so that her legs appeared long and skinny beneath the material. A table had been dragged to one side of the bed, and on it were magazines and books, a jug of water and a plate of uneaten, curling sandwiches. The bedroom was stuffy and smelt of stale air, and it was just as untidy as the rest of the house. Clothes were strewn across the floor while flies buzzed about a chair that had a sheet draped across it.

'So then, you're here. I'm Ann.' She smiled.

'Hello, Ann. I'm Stella.' The woman lying before her was fair-haired and pale-skinned, a frailer version of the person in the photographs. Stella guessed her to be in her mid-fifties, a good decade older than she was.

'It's nice to meet you,' said Ann. 'I can't believe that it's taken so long.'

Stella was unprepared for this moment. She knew that she

should be grateful. She had no other options, at least not ones that came with a home and employment of sorts, however these people were strangers and they must have wondered at her ready acceptance of their offer. They probably assumed she had nowhere else to go – which was true as far as her immediate future was concerned.

She brushed hair from her face in an effort to tidy it, recalling the sugary tea spilt on her dress, and ran a hand over the creases. The car had been her bed. It was four days since she'd showered. Cleanliness had been replaced by a terrible need for action, to pack her belongings, leave her home and simply drive. And now she was standing in her sister-in-law's bedroom, suffering the inspection of a woman she'd never met before.

'You're very Italian,' said Ann finally, as if she'd been searching for conversation in the absence of any help from Stella.

'That's because I am,' replied Stella, immediately wishing she'd not been so abrupt.

'Of course.' Ann smiled apologetically. 'I'm sorry about the state of the house. I've not been able to do anything since the accident. I don't know if Harry explained what happened.' She paused and, when Stella didn't interrupt, continued. 'I was on the ladder cleaning out the gutters. It was the simplest thing. One minute I was bucketing leaves, and the next I was backing away from one of those nasty black spiders. I woke up on the ground.' She gave a brief laugh. 'It was just like any ordinary day.'

'They always are,' said Stella, wincing at how formal she sounded. 'Quite ordinary.'

Ann stayed silently expectant, however Stella wasn't quite ready to reciprocate with her own story. She was still trying to make sense of the changes in her life.

Finally she asked, 'Where are you injured?'

'It's my lower back. The pain is excruciating. I've damaged three discs. If I lie still, it's not nearly half as bad. But I'm getting better. I couldn't move at all the first week. Now I can just manage to make the pot.' She glanced at the sheet-covered chair. 'Harry cut a hole in the upholstery and wedged a bowl in it. Sorry. Don't think I'm happy with the arrangement. I'm not used to living so basically.'

Stella thought of the walk to the long drop at Kirooma, with its plank of wood and three holes of different sizes. While Joe was out bush tending his sheep, living on silence and greasy mutton chops, a chamber pot had been a welcome alternative to the deep pits in the garden.

'It's been terribly hard on Harry,' Ann continued. 'It's harvest time here. The worst time to be laid up in bed.' Ann stopped again, as if she were waiting for Stella to reply.

Stella gave a slight smile, feeling foolish at her inability to chatter along.

'Well, you'll be wanting to settle in. You can take the first room on the left. It belonged to my eldest, Lyn, but she's long since married.'

Stella gave a grateful nod, both for the welcome and the lack of fuss. She supposed any queries regarding her own situation would come later – not that she had any plans that she could share, not yet. 'I don't want to impose, but I do have a few bits of furniture. Nothing much. A lamp and a table. A rug. Odds and ends. I can leave them in the car unless there's somewhere I can store them. And there's a cockatoo,' she added.

Ann pushed herself up a little higher in the bed, her already pale face turning white with the effort. 'A cockatoo.'

'I couldn't leave him behind.'

'I forgot. You've come straight from the property, haven't you? A long drive, I'd imagine.'

'I can leave the furniture in the car. It doesn't matter.'

'No. Don't do that. I'm pleased you've brought some things with you. It makes a person feel more at home. Anything in Lyn's room that you don't need you can put next door in Paddy's room. He's trying to be a banker in Sydney, much to his father's annoyance. He came home for a few months after he was demobbed, but he was too restless to stay.'

'It's just you and Harry, then?' queried Stella, pleased that she'd actually been capable of asking another question.

'Good heavens, no. The twins, Bill and John, still live with us. They work at the sugar mill and help out here when they can. They keep long hours during harvest season so you'll hardly see them. Sometimes they stay overnight in town. But if they intend on being home for dinner, they'll let you know.'

'Oh, dinner?' said Stella.

Ann sighed. 'I knew Harry wouldn't go into detail. I'm afraid you'll be doing more than just helping me until I'm up and about again. There's the house of course, which I'm sure is in a dreadful state. My boys have never been known for their cleaning abilities. The garden, like most, needs constant attention now we're heading into the hotter months, then there's clothes-washing and, of course, the meals. I should warn you, the three of them have large appetites. You'll have to keep an eye on the tea. We're lucky if we have enough to make it through each week. I thought they would have ended rationing by now.'

Cook, cleaner, carer. Ann was right. The extent of Stella's duties was more than she'd anticipated.

'Is that all right?' asked Ann.

'I wasn't expecting—'

'I'm sorry.' Ann drew up the sheet, fiddling with the top hem. 'Country homes. There's always so much to do.'

Although Stella hadn't considered her role beyond that of tending to Ann's needs, she realised that it was impractical of her to have believed that her tasks would have been limited to that of carer, and yet it irked her that Joe's family assumed that she'd be happy to do whatever was asked of her.

'You can put your bird on the rear veranda if you like.'

'Thank you, Ann, for having me here,' Stella said cordially.

'Keeping busy. That's the thing, Stella, during difficult times. It's always helped me. And I'm sorry – about what happened.'

'Thank you.'

'Now, you might empty my pot for me. The bathroom is just down the hall.'

Stella walked around the bed and, uncovering the chair, carried the pot out of the room, the flies trailing her. Harry had been remarkably plain in his speech across the telephone line when he'd told Stella of Ann's accident and offered her a bed in exchange for help in caring for his wife.

Perhaps she'd been a little too quick to accept.

⊰ Chapter 2 ⊱

The knock at the door startled Stella. She'd been lying on the bed, staring out the window at a dusky sky. A dim light hung low through the trees. The angle suggested it wasn't a star, but something else. A vehicle perhaps, or torchlight. And that smell. The air was sweet. It was a scent at odds with what she was used to. Usually the night air carried with it the smells of the sheep yards, of urine and manure, a tangy sharpness that seeped into clothes and hair and wafted about her husband like unwanted cologne. At the sound of a man's voice Stella rubbed her eyes and sat upright. The light disappeared.

'Joe?' she called. He'd always been late. Always driving around at night, checking on something. Nature has its own rhythm, he'd tell her, it doesn't work nine to five. And neither did he. Joe had had no sense of time. To him, the demarcation between night and day was, if anything, an annoyance to be tolerated. Her husband was always prepared, ready for anything. If there was a weed, he'd take to the hoe until he'd chipped the life from it. If one of his beloved sheep contracted a disease, then there was a chemical to eradicate the liver fluke or tapeworm, or one of the many other issues that might affect his livestock. When the blowflies attacked them, he would painstakingly clip away the sopping wool to reach the flesh-feeding maggots. There was a dreadful necessity to his persistence at times – he couldn't let go, even for a moment. He was addicted. Obsessed. Joe was a proud landowner and he wasn't letting nature or anything else ruin his domination.

The voices were clearer now. It was a man and a woman. She listened to their muffled conversation. She'd already hung her clothes in a large cedar wardrobe and slid underwear into a drawer that held a porcelain doll. The clothes on the toy were age-worn, the face, with its eyelids that flicked open and shut, crazed by heat. This wasn't her home. It was another family's life, not hers. And as of today, she was staff.

From outside on the veranda came Watson's familiar cry. '*Hello*,' he called. '*Coming back, coming back. When. When.*'

The knock sounded again and the door to the room opened. A man appeared. He flicked on the overhead light and Stella scowled at the sudden brightness.

'Stella. Hello. Ann fell over. She couldn't see where she was going in the dark. You're here to help and she can't be left alone. I told you that on the phone. She said she called out for you.'

Her brother-in-law's voice was deeper in person. It was seven years since their last meeting, at her wedding.

'I'm sorry,' she said. 'It was a long drive.'

Harry's shoulders were squared as if expecting an argument, perhaps even seeking one. She knew the stance – it appeared to be genetic – but at least here was a man who spoke his mind, and immediately Stella respected him for this simplest of attributes.

'If you don't think you can help out like we discussed you better let me know,' said Harry.

'I've just arrived,' she reminded him, squeezing back tears that had little to do with Harry's presence. She was thinking of Joe, of what she'd once hoped for and what she now faced in his absence. 'We're doing each other a favour, Harry.'

She was careful to emphasise his name. There had been two rules that her mother had enforced from an early age: one, don't let yourself be yelled at and two, don't be taken for granted. That last rule had not been so easy to achieve – at least, not where her husband was concerned.

Harry stood in the doorway, much like a shag on the edge of a drying dam, trying to decide whether to take a step closer or not. He'd grown older. They all had. But the sixteen-year age gap between Harry and Joe seemed more pronounced now. She counted the years. Joe died at forty-two, which meant Harry was in his fifty-eighth year. He had the same freckled skin as her husband. The same full face and rounded jaw. The same thin-lipped tightness that suggested a temper, except that in Joe's case he'd seldom let anything out. That was the problem. It was hard to build a life with a man who rarely spoke, except for the basics of sun and sheep and the price of wool.

'Reckon you'd have an attitude, being Italian,' said Harry.

It was the second time that day that her ethnicity had been raised. Stella bit away the retort forming in her mind.

'I'd appreciate a meal. I'm burning one of the fields tonight. If you leave it in the warming oven, I can eat it later when I come in.'

'Fine,' said Stella, but her reply was wasted. He'd already departed.

When a door slammed somewhere in the house she walked across the hall to Ann's room and apologised.

'It's okay. I get impatient and Harry doesn't mean to be so abrupt.' Ann tipped out a pill from a medicine bottle and swallowed it with a sip of water. 'He feels guilty about the accident. I'd been asking him for the last three months to clean the gutters.'

'I always cleaned ours,' said Stella, trying to find solidarity with the woman, and failing miserably.

Ann regarded her steadily before screwing the top back on the medicine bottle. 'We both know this is an awkward situation. Harry and Joe never did understand each other.'

'Why is that?' asked Stella.

'Myriad reasons,' Ann said flatly.

Stella waited for her sister-in-law to elaborate, however Ann was reading the label on the bottle.

'Can I get you anything?' Stella picked up the dried sandwiches sitting on the table.

'Some scrambled eggs would be great. Can I ask about your own family? We thought you would have gone straight home to them until you got yourself sorted. I mean, it's not like I don't appreciate your coming to help us . . .'

Stella wasn't sure if she'd ever be able to satisfy Ann's curiosity. Their lives were as distant in experience as the miles that had been between them. 'Harry was worried about you. He said that you needed help,' was all Stella said.

Ann nodded at this, accepting the answer. But her face betrayed the slightest trace of disbelief, as Stella excused herself from the room.

⋘ Chapter 3 ⋙

Stella had met Joe seven years earlier at Woodburn, a sleepy town further along the Richmond River that was only a short drive to the south-east of Harry's cane farm. She'd travelled there from Sydney with her parents and younger cousins, Angelina and Carmela, to visit New Italy, the settlement her grandparents had arrived at in 1882, having survived the Marquis de Rays expedition. The mad Frenchman had promised a group of Italian colonists from Veneto some land at Port Breton in New Ireland in the South Pacific. Stella's grandparents had paid the idiot 1800 francs in gold for a new beginning. In the end, the passage returned only starvation and death for many, before eventual salvation for the luckier ones in New South Wales.

The visit to New Italy was the idea of Stella's mother, Dona, who wished to visit her father's resting place, but the daytrip to Woodburn was unplanned. Joe had been carting sheep and was parked nearby when Stella and her cousins, ice creams in hand, decided to stretch their legs. She still wondered at their meeting. Had it been mere coincidence or fate?

She and her cousins took one side street and then another until they reached the edge of town, where sheep were being unloaded into a small set of yards. Specifically, one large woolly sheep with twirling horns. A man was standing in the rear of a truck trying to push the animal from the crate off the back, down a make-shift ramp and into a timber pen. Stella and her cousins stood watching, tongues stuck to their ice creams. The man braced his legs and leant down so that his head nearly contacted the sheep's rear end. He groaned under the effort and gave an almighty push. And another. And another.

'Come on,' he said loudly, his body nearly parallel to the ground.

With no warning the sheep moved. Not slowly and deliberately but with the quickness of an animal intent on escape. It jumped from the vehicle and ran down the ramp into the pen. The man fell, disappearing from view.

Stella, Angelina and Carmela glanced at each other and burst out laughing.

'Go on, then.' Carmela elbowed Stella. 'He looks like your type, and you aren't getting any younger.'

'Who said I had a type?' Stella replied.

'What are you waiting for?' said Angelina. 'You've been complaining for the last three years—'

'—ever since war broke out,' continued Carmela, 'that you'll die an old maid if something isn't done about Hitler very soon. And now you're presented with a living, breathing, un-uniformed species of the male variety and you stand there like—'

A hand appeared on the crate and the man pulled himself up. He swore at the ram and began brushing his clothes.

'All right.' Stella licked the ice cream that had dripped onto her hand.

At the spinsterly age of thirty, marriage was becoming an issue for more than just her parents. But it wasn't that she was fussy, simply that she had a certain kind of husband in mind. One who didn't come attached to a grocery store, milk bar or used car dealership.

'We've got ten minutes before we have to meet your parents, Stella,' Angelina reminded her.

'Clock's ticking,' said Carmela.

The man jumped from the rear of the truck. Noticing the three girls watching, he gave them a nod.

'Are you all right?' called Stella, walking towards the truck, her cousins following. Gooey clumps of manure stuck to the soles of her shoes as she moved to within a couple of feet of the yards. The sheep bashed against the railings of the enclosure.

'Don't get too close, he can get a bit obstreperous if you do.'

Stella took a step back from the sheep pen and the man came to her side. He was moon-faced, copper-haired and tall. Taller than anyone in her family, who were prone to being on the plusher side and barely able to make five foot five inches according to the aged scribblings on the kitchen doorway of her childhood home.

'Obstreperous,' she repeated. Angelina and Carmela giggled.

'It means—' said the man.

'I know what it means,' said Stella.

'He doesn't like being trucked,' the man continued. 'He should be back home in the paddock.'

'Then why isn't he?' asked Stella.

'Because I can't use another ram. By rights he should be winning prizes at the regional shows but the war's stopped all that. I have to sell him. Don't you think he's a fine animal? Look at his conformation; the body. His strong head, the horn placement.' He deftly hurdled the railing.

'Well, go on,' whispered Carmela. 'Look interested.'

Stella threw the ice cream over her shoulder, and moved closer to the pen.

The man walked up to the ram and carefully spread the fleece on the side of the animal's body until bright white wool showed. 'Twenty micron. Soft and white.'

'How amazing,' said Carmela, stringing the word out so that by the time she'd finished, it meant the opposite. She hooked an arm through her sister's and dragged her away.

'Sorry, they're not really sheep girls,' Stella apologised.

'No worries.' He rubbed the animal's back, closing the wool he'd displayed.

'You like sheep,' Stella commented.

'I like anything of beauty.' He jumped the railing and held out his hand. 'Joe O'Riain. You're not from around here, are you? Otherwise I'd offer to buy you a drink.'

'Stella Moretti, and I'm with my family.' She gestured to where her cousins were now waiting at the end of the street. She was pleased by his interest, however also a little wary of his forthright nature. 'We're visiting New Italy.'

'Have you got family there?'

'Used to,' Stella told him.

'Where are you from?' he asked.

'Sydney.'

'I go there a bit.'

'Really?'

'Sure.' He smiled.

Stella allowed herself to enjoy the harmless flirtation. It wasn't hard. Joe's pleasant nature showed itself in the laconic way he leant on the railing.

'Are you going to enlist?' She already knew of young men who'd done so voluntarily, although there was talk that by the middle of the year conscription would be introduced. She reminded herself that there was every likelihood this man would soon be lacing up soldier's boots and joining the Citizen Military Forces.

'Not if I can help it. Someone's gotta keep the country running,' said Joe.

'I suppose. How many sheep do you have? Thousands, I imagine.'

He pursed his lips. 'Twenty,' he admitted, a self-conscious blush rising on his neck. 'Twenty head. I'm off a cane farm a bit further north.'

'So, this is like a hobby?'

'At the moment. But not forever,' he added.

Stella knew nothing about cane or farming and even less about sheep. If there'd been more time, she might have liked to learn, if only because the teacher was very easy on the eye.

'Stella, we have to go!' yelled Carmela.

She looked over at her cousins. 'I have to go.'

'Can I call you when I'm next in Sydney?'

'I suppose.'

He opened the door of the truck and rummaged on the dashboard. 'I've got a pencil somewhere here.'

'Stella, come on!' Carmela yelled again.

'I'm coming!'

'Here it is,' Joe said, handing her a notebook and pencil. 'Can I have your telephone number, please?' he asked.

She wrote down her name and number, and then added her address.

'I'll see you later, then,' he replied.

'Sure.' She smiled goodbye, then turned and walked off to meet her cousins, not even bothering to take a final glance over her shoulder at the man she'd so freely given her contact details to.

Stella never expected to hear from him again. Certainly she never dreamt that Joe O'Riain would be knocking at her door only three weeks later.

≪ Chapter 4 ≫

It was evening by the time Stella carried the washing outdoors, ducking from the mass of insects flocking around the light above the screen door. She switched the station wagon's headlights on and, with the line illuminated, hung Ann's clothes out to dry. Back inside the house, she poured a glass of the wine she'd brought in from the station wagon, cut a wedge from some cheese she'd found in the fridge and walked back into the cool of the night. Turning the headlights off, she sat on the bonnet of the car. The patient was asleep and Harry's dinner in the warming oven, as requested. Only a few hours had passed since her arrival and it already felt like a month. On the horizon, a flare of red and yellow rippled across the night sky. The scent of the blaze was strong. It hung in the air, replacing the familiar dryness of her old home with the tang of smouldering paper.

She watched the fire until the redness diminished in size and was finally extinguished. It was as if the black of the atmosphere had suffocated the flames, smothering the unruly beast until all air was gone from its body. It was many years since she'd been surrounded by so much colour and it stung her to think of what she'd endured, of the things an individual could become accustomed to, and of what a person could be driven to do. Stella drank the wine and then angrily threw the glass to the ground, where it smashed into pieces.

Some time later, vehicle headlights appeared on the road leading to the house. They bounced around, following the uneven surface as the car approached. Stella slid from the bonnet and gathered up the shards of glass as the truck swung sideways, spotlighting first the clothesline and then her before stopping. Harry stepped into the halo of the porch light.

'How did it go?' asked Stella tentatively.

He paused, as if not expecting her to speak, let alone comment on the day's work. 'Good. It was a good burn. At one stage I thought it might have got away from me. There were a couple of floaters that caught fire to the western edge, but the wind dropped and I had the water cart nearby so I got a handle on it pretty quick.'

She followed him indoors, placing the glass in the rubbish bin, and waited as he washed his hands at the kitchen sink. 'Do you have a drink before dinner, Harry?'

He dried his hands on a towel. 'A beer.'

Stella fetched a longneck bottle from the fridge and a glass from the cupboard and set them on the table where Harry was now sitting. His clothes were flecked with ash and he smelt strongly of smoke.

'You don't need to wait on me,' he told her, taking the top off the bottle and pouring the beer.

Stella leant against the cupboards. Crossed her arms and then uncrossed them.

'And you can sit down, you know.'

She helped herself to another glass of wine and joined him at the table. Outside, insects bashed against the flyscreen. He downed the contents of the glass as if it were water. Stella noticed the red tinges in the day-old growth on his cheeks and thought of Joe.

'Did you bring that?' He nodded at her drink.

'Yes.'

21

'Our grog not good enough for you?' he asked.

'I don't drink beer,' she replied.

'Fair enough.' He took a long sip. 'There's probably a bottle of red in that cabinet.' He pointed. 'How was the drive?'

'Long.' Ann's earlier fall, it seemed, had been forgotten.

'That washing you did. Waste of time. It'll be covered in ash from the fire. The women never hang clothes out when we're burning.'

'Oh,' she replied, a little deflated.

'Well, you're not from here, are you. You were a Sydney girl. I remember Joe telling me when you two first met that your ancestors were part of the same mob that fell for that dodgy French fella's settlement scheme.'

'The Marquis de Rays expedition,' said Stella.

'That's the one,' said Harry. 'And what about your parents? What line of business are they in?'

'They have a café and a greengrocer's,' said Stella.

'Good business?' asked Harry.

'I guess. I became a typist straight out of school.'

'Yeah, you never looked like the sort to be waiting behind a counter.'

'And what sort do I look like?' Stella asked, not sure if she was being complimented or condemned.

He cleared his throat. 'It was a big risk back then, your family sailing all the way from Italy.'

'No greater than your family coming here. Joe said that your father arrived here in the 1860s from Ireland. He must have had a good selection of land to choose from, getting here so early.'

Harry drank some more beer, his swallowing loud in the quiet room.

'You have a nice farm. What size is it?' Stella was trying to make amends for the difficulties of their earlier meeting, however her brother-in-law snorted in response.

'It's not big enough.' He peered at her over the rim of the glass, his blunt gaze more suited to someone who'd just been provoked rather than praised. 'I never could understand why Joe went out west. Bastard of a place.'

'Joe wanted to run sheep. A person goes where they have to. Where there's opportunity,' said Stella, finding comfort in the level of wine in her glass. After all that had occurred, she still felt the need to defend him.

'We could have had two cane farms by now. It's good country here,' said Harry.

'But not good for sheep.'

'It's the wrong climate for them. Cattle, he could have run some cattle. I would have been prepared to let him do that,' admitted Harry. 'Forty head in the river-bend paddock. That's what I offered him. We haven't got the grass for a larger number.'

Joe once told her that he couldn't work with his brother. Listening to Harry, Stella wondered if his bossy nature hadn't been one of the causes for the rift between them. They were similar – driven to work, to succeed. She imagined the two of them side by side, pushing, cajoling, striving to be the best. It made her wonder what they may have been able to achieve if they'd shared a single ambition. She recalled Ann's words, about how the brothers' relationship was far from close. A confirmation of what she already knew.

'What did you two fall out over?' she asked quietly.

'I don't remember. It was a long time ago,' replied Harry.

'Sure you do,' she probed carefully. 'You and Joe rarely spoke after our wedding.'

Harry took his meal from the oven and sat down again. 'It's unimportant.'

'Do we owe you money?'

'"We"?' he queried.

'You know what I mean,' she replied, more tightly than intended.

'Stella, just drop it.' Harry tasted the meal, and then, cutlery gripped in one hand, he added salt to his vegetables, shaking the container vigorously. 'Don't you cook with salt?'

'Never,' she replied adamantly.

Harry raised an eyebrow. 'Well, I like salt. How's Ann?'

'Asleep.'

'I told her to leave the gutters alone. That I'd do them when I had a moment. She's the most impatient person I know. Everything has to be done yesterday. I've got enough problems keeping up with today.' He cut into one of the chops, sawed at the meat and chewed quickly. 'So, you said when we spoke on the telephone that you were nearly bankrupt. You either are or you aren't.'

Stella hadn't wanted to share the news about Kirooma's financial troubles, but she had to tell someone and her parents' predictable lecture on her poor decision-making was not an option worth choosing at the time. She already had enough regrets. 'The bank has taken over Kirooma Station. I could have tried to sell it myself, but it seemed easier to pass it on to them to handle and apparently there's someone interested in purchasing the property. There won't be much left over from the sale.'

'Made a fortune and then lost it, eh?' said Harry, the side of his face distended from the hunk of meat he was chewing.

'We never made a fortune,' said Stella quietly.

Harry scratched at the stubble on his cheek. 'Do you have anything? Apart from what you brought with you. Any money?'

Stella thought of the furniture she had dragged from the homestead along the cracked concrete path. The red dirt outside the back gate that had banked up against every item like stubbornly persistent waves. A screeching Watson. Odd tables and chairs. A standard lamp and boxes of books. Their wedding gifts. The terrestrial globe from the library. She'd taken what she could, loading them into the trailer and then sold some of the belongings to second-hand shops along the way in exchange for fuel money. Any profit was a bonus.

Harry waited for an answer. She could have lied. 'I have about one hundred pounds until the estate is sorted. Everything was in Joe's name.'

'Boracic, eh? Well, there's a bit to do around here until Ann's up and about again, but I can't pay you. As I said on the phone, this gets you out of a spot and us as well.'

'I don't know how long I'll be able to stay for, Harry. The bank's frozen our account.'

'Debt does that to a person,' said Harry matter-of-factly.

'The bush does that to a person,' countered Stella, beginning to take offence at her brother-in-law's attitude.

'You people hardly lived in the bush. The bush is scrub and trees and wildlife. The type of place where there's a better than average chance of scratching out a decent living. But Joe never settled for what was right. He refused to be a part of anything. He set his sights on his own little kingdom far away from his family and he chose a property on the outer limits, where barely a woody plant could grow. There was nothing there.'

Stella thought of the life she had carved out of Harry's 'nothing'. There were orange trees in the homestead garden now. A band of lawn outside the kitchen window that she'd prided herself on keeping green. And a well-trodden dirt path leading from a garden tap to her cherished tomatoes. It wasn't much. Lawn, trees and a few vines, and land, surrounding them like a never-ending moat. Stella had never quite made it to the outer reaches of what they'd once owned. No one would ever understand what it was truly like at Kirooma Station. No one.

She finished her wine and stood, clutching the back of the chair. 'Well, there's something out there now, Harry. Two graves.'

Her brother-in-law set his knife and fork down on the table. 'He never should have taken you there.'

Stella stemmed the trembling in her voice. 'Maybe I shouldn't have agreed to go.'

'He would have gone regardless, Stella. He loved you, but—'

'I know.' She swallowed the pain that threatened to embarrass her. 'He loved his sheep more.'

Harry considered her. It was a deep-seated stare. Not the kind his wife had subjected her to at their first meeting, where a woman sums up another based on her exterior – face, clothes and the styling of her hair – but the kind that probes beneath the surface of the skin, where the object of scrutiny knows that an investigation is underway that delves into their heart. Stella held the eyes of the man opposite. She may have been shattered by the recent past, however she was not quite ready to fall.

'My father's first cousin, Brandon, loved sheep,' Harry finally said.

'Joe told me that.'

'Did he now? And what else did he share with you?'

'Only that Brandon and your father Sean had a disagreement,' said Stella.

Her brother-in-law cleared his throat noisily, as if the word 'disagreement' barely did justice to what had occurred. 'Let me tell you about Brandon. My father told me that Brandon herded sheep in the hills of the old country for a bastard Protestant while the rest of them grew potatoes and cabbages and tried to forget their hunger. There's a story that's told of a winter that was especially cruel. One of those sheep would have fed both families for weeks, but Brandon would have none of it. He guarded that glorious meat like it was his very own. Tied a bell about the neck of the lead wether to keep track of the flock's wanderings, probably slept with them for all I know. 'Course, to be fair, if he'd slaughtered one and been caught the worst would have occurred – they'd have been evicted, the lot of them – but my father Sean went hungry. And starvation can't tell the difference between right and wrong. The sheep herd remained intact, if you're wondering. My grandfather and Great-Uncle Liam ensured it. Later on they joked that not one sheep ever went missing under Brandon's watch. He was an honest man, in the beginning.' Harry paused. 'That's where Joe inherited it, this obsession with sheep. I can see no other explanation that would make him turn from the family business and become fixated on something that the rest of us knew nothing about. The genetic strain that lodged itself in Brandon somehow managed to worm its way into my brother's blood. That, along with a nose for opportunity. But I'm not telling you anything that you aren't already aware of, Stella. Joe never bothered who he trod on in the pursuit of his goals.'

Harry glanced at his meal and rested the cutlery sideways on the plate. He appeared to have lost his appetite.

'I think you're a little harsh,' said Stella. 'It's true, Joe was ambitious. But I don't think that's a bad thing.'

'That depends on what you're willing to do to obtain your prize. People like Joe – and Brandon – don't see the world through another person's eyes. They simply don't have that perspective. They'd rather see it from their own viewpoint, because that's all that is important to them. How their decision-making affects other people doesn't really concern them. I loved Joe, he was my brother, but I haven't liked him for a very long time. Anyway, I still can't understand why Joe left us, but he had Brandon's blood in him and that's the only explanation I can think of.' He lifted the empty beer glass, peering into the bottom as if searching for a reply.

Stella sat back down. 'Maybe you should tell me what Joe did to disappoint you so much.'

Harry ran a charcoal-blackened fingernail around the rim of the beer glass.

'I know very little about your family, Harry,' Stella continued. 'Joe and I were married so quickly and once we moved to Kirooma, well, life out there overtook us and Joe never was one for idle chat.'

'Perhaps it's best that way. Dredging up the past isn't going to change things.'

'You told me about Brandon,' she persisted.

'Yes.' He stood up, pushing out the chair with the force of his legs. 'I did. I thought it might help, hearing that Joe's father's cousin was a shepherd, but I see I was wrong. Brandon was my father's best friend, but he threw everything dear to this family into the mud. And Joe did exactly the same.'

❧ Chapter 5 ❧

County Tipperary, Ireland, 1864

He was still a child, really. One only intent on getting home to warm himself by the fire for a moment or so while the rest of the family were working in the fields or at school. It was late morning, early spring. Slate sky. Snowmelt in the hills. Biting wind. Fourteen-year-old Brandon turned up the collar of his jacket and trudged homewards, the turf softening underfoot. The greening of the plains was not yet completed. Winter brown still mantled the distant grasslands and skirted their thatched cottage, where a slight twist of grey from the chimney suggested the fire needed fuelling.

They lived by the seasons and by the grace of Mr Macklin, whose sheep Brandon shepherded for a good part of the year. Another five lambs born overnight and more due to drop by this afternoon would please most owners. However, their landlord was a moody man and, on occasion, as sour as rotted cabbages, with scarcely a single expression crossing his features to let a person know where he stood. He would be expecting a better lambing, an increase in the number of twins at least. Brandon decided to wait until tomorrow before telling Mr Macklin about the new births. The day was too fine to be seeking out the ruin of it.

His father, Liam, was inside the thatched cottage, one leg slung over the edge of the table, his finger tapping his thigh. Brandon noted immediately that the fire in the hearth was licking at a tally stick. Its length was filled with notches, each one representing the use of the old language.

A scraping noise drew him to the corner, where his stepsister Maggie had pushed aside the stool she'd been sitting on and was stepping into the light.

'Oh Maggie,' said Brandon. The cuts on the tally stick suggested she'd received a whipping as punishment and been sent home early from school.

'What?' She tossed back long red-brown hair, the thick lengths crinkled by continued plaiting, and stared at him, her dark eyes widening.

'Why do you do it?' he asked.

'What gives them the right to tell me what I can speak? I'm Irish, not English. I hate school anyway.'

'No you don't.'

'Oh really?' She moved towards him, her fists rounding. She'd always been prone to sudden anger.

'Maggie. Stop it.' His father's mouth was settled in a grim, defiant line, which was unusual for a man whose frame was bent and bowed by the burden of living. Brandon noticed the cut above his left eye. The blood from it had caught in the dense eyebrow beneath and hardened there.

'What happened?'

Liam gave his son a curt nod and walked out of the cottage.

Brandon looked to Maggie but she hunched her shoulders. 'I don't know anything.' She flicked her hand. 'Well, go on then.'

Brandon kept by his father's side, silent. Speculating on the injury. Anticipating the direction in which they were headed, knowing the Rock of Cashel was five miles away. On the right, in a little less than two miles at the end of a well-used path, Brandon's Uncle Fergal lived. They stepped over the rocky mound of a wrecked cottier's house, frightening three quails sheltering on the leeward side. The small, round birds lifted into the air, and then dropped back onto the ground a short distance away before scattering into the grass.

Liam O'Riain marched on, unspeaking. He covered the next mile and the next, right past Brandon's uncle's farm, without breaking his stride. Brandon undid the buttons on his jacket. His father was keeping up a fine pace.

'I have to get back to the sheep.'

His words ignored, Brandon tailed his father up the side of the hill, their boots slipping in the springy new growth. He grew worried as the crest was reached and the downwards slope presented itself. And still they kept moving, crossing another rise. The land swelled in size as they climbed and then grew small again on the leeward side, another mound blocking the country ahead. It was strange enough to have an unspeaking father, but it was their destination that bothered Brandon the most. He'd been here before, of course, with his cousin, Sean. But only once before with his father, and there was good reason for that.

They finally stopped at a crumbling stone wall. His father sat on its edge and stared into the distance, pushing an anxious thumbnail back and forth along the length of a trouser seam. Others rarely came here with his father. And everyone knew not to disturb him once he was here. This was the place Liam O'Riain visited when disaster befell the family. It was here that he thought on their problems. Deaths. Failed crops. Bloodsucking rent-gatherers. The types of disasters that made Brandon wish for the comfort of his sheep. The wind blew strong and fierce and he shivered with its arrival. Although the day had grown bright, the distant ruins were outlined starkly against the sky.

He'd grown up in the shadow of Carraig Phadraig, the Rock of Cashel. A huge limestone monolith, crowned by ancient ruins that

30

rose from a broad plain known as the Golden Vale. It was rich, fertile land – if you held enough of it. But the O'Riains were poor and even the pagan gods that his stepmother, Cait, prayed to were of no help to them.

'We once had fifty acres in my father's time. Fifty acres. Such a tract of land you never did see, Brandon. We grew potatoes and cabbages. And we had sheep and cows. There was an old milker and my mother would spoon the cream off the top of the pail and slop it into our bowls. I think back now to those wondrous years and try to make sense of where it all went. It's impossible, of course, for change can sneak up on a man, and it only takes a handful of bad times to make the good curdle. And there's been plenty of bad times.' He knuckled an eye and the folded skin at the bottom of the socket drooped severely so that pink flesh showed. 'It's been a slow, hard slide into poverty.'

'Father?' Brandon had never heard his father speak this way. It unsettled him.

Liam brushed his palms together. 'Which is why things must change. We've hardly enough land left to keep one family.'

'But we've five acres, Father. Uncle Fergal says a man can do much with five acres.'

'Not anymore.' He rested his elbows on his knees and then dropped his hands between his legs.

Brandon was sure he hadn't heard correctly. It was true that the small amount of wheat they planted had come to nothing, but he'd helped fill the cart with the last potato and cabbage crop and while the harvest hadn't been a great success, he'd thought his father pleased with the result. 'Was it him that hit you, then?'

'Macklin? No. It was your uncle.'

Brandon started at this revelation. 'Uncle Fergal? But why?'

His father looked him square in the eye. 'I'm marrying Maggie to Tobias Macklin.'

Brandon blinked twice. 'What? How can you? He's an old man.'

'With an eye for a pretty girl,' said his father.

'She's a child,' said Brandon.

'She's nearly thirteen. And clever. She'll learn quickly, whether she wants to or not, and she'll carry his children easily, just like her mother. He'll forgive us this year's rent if we agree.'

'I can't believe you would do such a thing,' said Brandon, his voice rising. Maggie was only a year younger than him. They'd grown up together. Treated each other as brother and sister, though there was no shared blood between them. The thought of losing her made his heart pound.

'Why? Why wouldn't I? She'll be well cared for. And we'll have the chance at another crop. An opportunity to put extra food away for the winter. We've been in arrears for the last two years, Brandon. Nearly everything we've made has been used to pay off debt. To be fair to Macklin, there's been plenty of times in the past when he could have thrown us out. But this time Lord Huntley has increased his rent and so in turn Macklin must increase ours. We need a year's grace. Otherwise we'll be evicted.'

Brandon stood and kicked hard at the wall with the toe of his shoe, grimacing at the sudden pain.

'The days of small tenant farmers like us are disappearing. The big landholders want to run more stock. That's where the living is to be made. Not with the likes of us when we can't afford to pay our dues and we're sitting on valuable pasture. This is why Macklin wanting Maggie is a blessing. It's given me more time.'

'*More time?*'

'I have other children to consider. Including you. Anyway, as far as Maggie is concerned, there is nothing for her here. No work, and the prospect of marriage is unlikely with the numbers of young men who have left. That leaves the church, a vocation that's as far removed from Maggie as anything could be.'

'You're only willing to be rid of her because she's not your daughter,' Brandon said, raising his voice even more.

'And you are as wrong as a person can be, son. I love Maggie as if she were my own. And it's for that very reason that I have to consider what is best for her and for everyone else in this family.

I know this is hard for you. Why, I remember when the two of you were wee things huddling by the fire holding hands. You're like peas in a pod, despite the bickering that goes on between you, but I'm telling you, Brandon, I have made my decision and it's for the best.'

Brandon chewed on his father's words. Hours earlier he'd spread his fingers across a ewe's woolly stomach, feeling the bulge of life within. He'd grasped the legs of the lamb stuck in its mother and, with a gentle pull, watched as the newborn had fallen to earth. He felt his anger dwindle to confusion as his father rambled on. Liam was enthusiastic, he'd give him that. Keen to be rid of his stepdaughter. Caught up in a plan that he believed would benefit everyone. Especially himself. Brandon hated him at that moment. The way his eyes grew starry-bright, his hands waving about as he uttered things about Mr Macklin's good nature that he could scarcely know. The way he almost smiled. Like one of Cait's all-knowing pagan gods. Brandon turned towards home, ignoring his father's calls. His own family had become like the potatoes and cabbages they plucked from the soil at harvest time – commodities for the rich to buy.

⋘ Chapter 6 ⋙

Brandon found his cousin at Uncle Fergal's cottage. Sean was wielding a hoe with savage strokes, the tilled earth flying up about his legs. His mutterings came out muffled and fast, as if he were layering prayers, one on top of the other, after a particularly lengthy confession.

'You've heard,' said Sean, not halting in his work.

'That your father bashed mine? Yes.'

Sean leant against the wooden handle. 'That's not what I meant.'

'I know. I'm pleased Uncle Fergal hit him.'

Sean wiped at the sweat dripping from his nose and Brandon recalled the past winter; the two of them shivering over a shared bowl of cabbage in his uncle's cottage. Sean never resented Brandon coming to his home on the nights his stepmother's bad humour got the better of her, even though it meant less room and food for everyone.

'I can't believe it. That turnip-nosed cretin Macklin.' Sean speared the hoe across the ground.

Brandon looked at his cousin, who at seventeen seemed a full-grown man, and shook away forming tears.

34

'If I'd been your father I'd have given Macklin a taste of my fist. What man barters tenancy for a young girl? And what happened to the bastard's first wife? For all we know he could have worked her to death,' Sean stated fiercely.

'This is Maggie we're talking about, damn it.' Brandon kicked at the freshly dug earth, suddenly overwhelmed with anger at his helplessness. 'Damn it! Damn it! Damn it!' He kept on yelling until Sean took him by the arm and dragged him across the field.

'Here take this.' Sean sat a rock in Brandon's palm. 'Take aim and throw it.'

'Why?' Brandon asked, panting.

'It's better to let the anger out. It'll make you feel happier,' said Sean.

Brandon gripped the stone and pelted it low and hard.

'Doesn't that feel good?'

'Not really.'

'Come on,' said Sean.

They moved together over the grassland as they had as boys, picking up rocks and tossing them into the air, frightening grouse and quail, their actions replacing the unspeakable truth that Maggie was to marry an old man against her will.

'Does Maggie know yet?' asked Sean.

Brandon thought of his stepsister sitting on the stool, the tally stick on the coals. 'I don't think so.'

They reached the stony spine of another cottier's house abandoned during the famine and sat in the shade of the tumbledown wall. The sky was banded blue. Ribbons of colour grew dark and low in the south where, three miles away, Mr Macklin's house was visible.

'She won't go quietly,' said Sean. His deep-set eyes reflected his worry.

Brandon gave a sad smile. 'No, she won't.'

Sean started balancing rocks one on top of the other. 'I'll never forgive them.'

'Who?' Brandon felt tired now, all energy spent.

'The English. And men like Macklin, who work for them. This is *my* country, as it's yours. But a man can do nothing here. You write your business on the side of your cart in the old language and you're fined. You snare a bird or a rabbit on Macklin's land to feed a hungry child and they'll put you in chains.' Sean turned to him. 'Do you know why my father punched yours? Because Macklin's a *Protestant*.'

'I know that,' said Brandon. 'But that doesn't matter, compared to the marriage.'

'Have you gone daft in the head? Of course it matters,' said Sean loudly. 'That's the only thing that matters. He'll try to make her forget her teachings. Fill her head with rubbish.'

'That will never happen. Maggie's not one to be told what to do,' said Brandon.

'That's true enough, I suppose.'

So engrossed had they been in their discussion they'd barely heard the horse's hooves approaching. Suddenly, as if conjured out of their anger, Mr Macklin appeared before them on a chestnut horse. Brandon got to his feet immediately while Sean slowly lifted his head, chose a large rock from the pile and rolled it between his palms.

The horse whinnied and backed up. Mr Macklin, heavily built and thickly bearded, gave them a cursory glance as if they barely warranted acknowledgement. He scanned about and beyond them, taking stock of the countryside and then narrowed his vision back to the two young men. The mare arched her neck and, as he loosened the reins, the dark cloth of his suit showed clean white shirt cuffs.

'And have my sheep learnt to fend for themselves, Brandon O'Riain?'

'No, Mr Macklin.' Brandon felt a tightness grip his stomach.

The landlord turned his head one way and then the other. 'Then what are you doing here?'

'Nothing,' said Brandon.

Next to him, Sean cleared his throat and spat loudly on the ground.

Mr Macklin's forehead creased. 'If a man does nothing with his time then you have to wonder at his value. Don't you agree? A man's prospects are important. Your stepsister would agree with me, I'm sure.'

The landlord had meaty hands. Brandon was tortured with a vision of those same stout fingers roaming Maggie's body.

'She's too young,' he called, his legs bracing with anger.

A whip hung from the saddle, coiled and waiting. He expected Mr Macklin to reach for it, but instead the man simply laughed. It was a strange sound, made all the more unusual because Brandon had never heard it before. He assumed Maggie was the cause for the change in Mr Macklin's disposition. He looked to Sean for guidance. His cousin was throwing the rock up and down, catching it in the palm of his hand.

'She *is* too young for marrying,' Sean agreed.

Mr Macklin's expression remained unchanged. 'It was a decision made between Liam O'Riain and myself and it has nothing to do with you. Either of you,' he said pointedly.

Sean slowly got to his feet. 'And wasn't it just to your advantage, bartering my cousin for a year's rent? Taking a child instead of waiting for—'

'Payment due,' Macklin finished. 'Or, should I say, *overdue*. You lot gripe like you're owed a living, but you're not. We all work for somebody, boy, and no man should be expected to carry a family for free. A farm that can't pay its way is no good to anyone, least of all the family living on it. Consider that, young Brandon, while you sit and whine about your stepsister. Would you rather be evicted? This country is pockmarked by the pits of the dead. I'm doing you all a favour. Her as well. Or would you prefer that she spend her days with you sorry lot?' He patted the horse's neck.

'Better with us than the likes of you.' Sean took a step forward.

'Sean, don't,' Brandon warned.

Sean was quick to anger and thought nothing of ending an argument with his fists. But this was a battle that they had no chance of winning.

'I'll have her converted to the one true faith within a year of bedding her,' said Macklin, with a sly smile.

'Maggie will lie to your face while keeping her religion, and you won't know the difference,' yelled Sean.

'You think that simple child will choose the supposed Vicar of Christ over the welfare of her family and that of her own? If she is that dull-witted, then perhaps I'll have to beat the sense back into her. There's nothing like a length of leather on a young filly for the teaching of obedience.'

'You bastard,' said Sean slowly.

'I praised the Lord the famine came to Ireland,' Mr Macklin snarled. 'I only wish that it had killed more Catholics.' He tugged on the reins and the mare responded immediately, turning and beginning to walk away.

'Damn Protestant Irish!' Sean yelled after him. He aimed the rock and threw it. The stone struck Macklin in the back of the head and he fell from the mare to land heavily on the ground. The horse, untroubled by her master's fall, trotted off to stand a few feet away.

'Saint Patrick, what have you done?' whispered Brandon. He couldn't move. Could barely speak.

Sean hesitated and then slowly crept to Macklin's side. He walked around the body and gave the man a kick, then another, before rolling him onto his back. One leg was twisted beneath the other. An arm flung sideways, as if in a final gesture. Sean squatted and then placed an ear to the man's chest, held a finger near his mouth.

'Gone,' he said quietly.

'Gone? You mean *dead*?' Brandon walked quickly to Sean's side. Together they stared at the landlord. 'He can't be.'

'He is,' said Sean. His eyes had glazed over, whether from fear or satisfaction, Brandon couldn't tell.

Brandon backed away. A terrible sickness was beginning to spread from the pit of his insides.

Sean was now searching the man's pockets. He retrieved a silver fob watch and matching chain, and swung the timepiece back and forth so that it swayed like a pendulum.

'Put that back!' Brandon shouted.

'Why? He'll not be needing it.' Sean tucked the items in his pocket and then wiped his hands on his trousers as if the action would cleanse him of both deeds, murder and thievery in a single afternoon.

For a long time, they stared at the body on the ground. It wasn't as if they hadn't witnessed death before. Open caskets. Wakes. The old, the young, the sick. But this was different. Sean had done this, and Brandon was a part of it.

'If I was a girl I'd start wailing,' commented Sean. 'Him lying there, unwashed and unprepared to meet his maker. Well, a good cry would bring the evil spirits in and take his black soul to where it belongs.'

'We should leave,' said Brandon. If there were evil spirits about, he wasn't staying to greet them.

'What about the horse?' asked Sean, rolling Macklin back onto his stomach.

'What *about* the horse?'

'It's valuable.' Sean caught the mare grazing nearby and led it back over to Brandon. 'I'm keeping it.'

'You can't even ride,' Brandon said.

'Neither can you. I'll hide the horse and then go and see Jamie Gallagher. Jamie's a nationalist, like his father was. He'll see us right,' Sean replied.

Brandon halted but then followed Sean, who had started to lead the mare away at a fast walk. Irish Republicans, a stolen horse and a murdered landlord. Brandon imagined what lay before them if their current course wasn't altered and felt his stomach drop.

'Just let the horse go free,' he pleaded.

'No. Not when I can sell it. We could use the money.'

'Sean, please,' said Brandon.

'No. I'm not listening to you, Brandon O'Riain. Why should I? When we were cold and hungry last year you couldn't even bring yourself to take one of those sheep that you guard with your life.

One miserly sheep to feed us through winter.' Sean increased his pace as the mare broke into a trot.

'And if I'd been caught? What then?' Brandon demanded.

They reached the remains of another cottier's house and Sean led the horse inside the roofless dwelling, wedging the reins in the stonework of the collapsed chimney.

'Are you willing to wreck our family's lives?' Brandon asked.

'It'd be better if we don't tell a soul,' said Sean. He seemed almost calm now. Excited, even.

Brandon shook his head.

'Did you hear me?' said Sean. 'Come on. Let's go.'

Brandon's home was less than a half mile away. It sat in a narrow cleft ringed by the rising and falling ground. He walked towards it determinedly, feeling the fear of what lay behind, until his walk became a run. Sean kept pace next to him.

From within the cottage's dim interior the outline of Brandon's father appeared as he and Sean approached.

'Whose horse was that?' said Liam to the two boys. 'Don't stand there quiet like you've no idea what I'm speaking about. I saw you leading it into the Dohertys' old place.'

Maggie came to the door. 'What have you done?'

'Shush up,' Liam told his stepdaughter. 'Brandon, get yourself inside this instant. You as well, Sean.'

Brandon and Sean sat at the table as ordered, while Maggie dropped the dense leaves of a quartered cabbage into a pot of water.

Liam spread his hands on the scrubbed tabletop. 'Tell me and be quick about it.'

'We saw Macklin,' began Brandon, his voice trembling. He didn't know how to continue and he turned to his cousin.

'There were words.' Sean leant nonchalantly back in the chair. The timber creaked with the movement. 'I threw a rock.'

'It hit,' said Brandon, scarcely able to believe what he was saying.

'And?' asked Liam.

Brandon looked at Sean and then back at his father. The magnitude of what they'd done pierced his conscience, and he stuttered as he spoke. 'Father, he's dead.'

The room was silent. Liam eyeballed his son and then Sean. 'Macklin is dead. Is that what you're telling me.'

Brandon nodded. His mouth was dry.

Liam dropped his head to his hands.

Suddenly Maggie flung herself at Sean, hammering at his chest with her fists. 'You stupid, *stupid*!' Brandon captured his stepsister in his arms and held her back while she struggled.

'Stop it, Maggie!' Brandon told her.

'What if someone finds out?' said Maggie. She struggled free of Brandon and sat in a chair. Brandon kept a firm hand on her slight shoulder.

His father appeared stunned. He lifted his head and rubbed at his brow and spoke uncertainly. 'Then it will be bad. Very bad.'

'They should run, Father. They *must* run. Otherwise we'll all be caught up in this. We'll be thrown out. Evicted.' Maggie began to cry.

'Shut up, girl, and let me think.' Liam considered the three young people before him and then slammed his palm hard on the table. He turned to Brandon. 'An accident. That's how it will seem. Sean, as you threw that rock it's you who will take the mare back tonight under cover of dark. Leave her close to where Macklin lies and pray to Saint Patrick that none of us are given blame.'

'Surely there is a way to turn this to our advantage. There's money to be made here,' argued Sean.

Liam screwed up his eyes until they were tight and small. 'And how, boy, do you think that can be achieved when a man is murdered? Do what I say, and *do it quickly*, for there's only one penalty for this crime and they'll have no hesitation in hanging you both by the neck until you're dead.'

❧ Chapter 7 ❧

The morning following Mr Macklin's death, Brandon woke after a restless night and crawled over the top of his three sleeping younger brothers, placing his feet carefully so as not to disturb Maggie and his younger half-sister Sarah on the bedding next to them. In the main room was his stepmother, Cait, who had wrapped a shawl about her chemise. His father cradled Elsie, the youngest. There was water boiling over the fire, and the room was stuffy with the smells of smoke, yesterday's boiled cabbage, of too many people and not enough washing of skin.

Maggie appeared a few minutes later, carrying Sarah on a hip. She drew up a chair and faced Brandon, sullen and accusing, as he splashed icy water on his face from a bucket. His father passed baby Elsie to Cait and, taking his trousers from where they were folded over the back of a chair, stepped into them.

Arranging herself near the hearth, Cait pulled at the chemise so that her breast fell out of its flimsy covering. She spat on her hand and rubbed at the nipple and then squeezed it, teasing the baby with a few spots of milk before Elsie took hold. The youngest boy, Dennis, crawled from where he slept and, with a whine, rushed to his mother, clinging to her knee and crying for milk too. He wore a dress, a cast-off from Maggie.

'I think the boy should be in trousers, Cait,' said his father. 'He's seven years of age, and no good to me outside in that.'

'No. If he's breeched too soon the fairy-folk might come for him. He's the last of my boys so they'll be watching careful, like. Waiting for the opportunity.'

Brandon sighed at this talk, a little too loudly. There were times when he saw far more sense in the Christian religion, where people lived and died without the need to dance around shadows.

'You blow your hot air, Brandon O'Riain. But see if the worst doesn't happen when you ignore the ways of the fairies,' warned Cait.

His two other half-brothers, Marcus and Michael, entered the main room, arguing.

'It's too early for your bickering,' chided their father. Brandon dried off using his shirt tail, pausing, as did his father, when a noise came from outside. It sounded like footsteps.

Liam gave his son a meaningful look. He'd sworn Maggie and Brandon to secrecy, so that not even Cait knew of the previous day's disaster. Then he'd had words with Brandon, making him swear on all that was good and holy to never tell Maggie that Macklin was to be her intended. Although his father was convinced that she would blame herself for any sufferings that followed, Brandon doubted that he'd ever want Maggie to know that he'd married her off.

'Someone's coming,' said Liam.

'Who would come a-knocking at this hour? When we've not even had time to rub the crust from our eyes.' Cait yawned.

The door flew open, the latch breaking under the strength of the kick. A young constable stepped into the cottage holding a pistol. He waved it vaguely about the stunned room. The baby's suckling was the only noise and the constable glanced with disgust at Cait as she shoved aside her frocked son who'd latched on to her other nipple. Behind him, Sean was visible. He sat on a horse, his wrists bound, nose bloody, cowed but unbeaten.

'Constable Swift. What's this?' asked Liam.

'Sit down and don't pretend ignorance, Liam O'Riain. Sean's been caught with a bag of coin such that three generations of your lot would never see. He spends a lot of time with your son, doesn't he?' He waved the gun at Brandon, blond hair falling across his brow.

'They're cousins,' answered Liam.

'Ribbonmen, more likely. I'll not see the start-up of you rebels again,' said Constable Swift.

'They've nothing to do with that lot, and it's a long time since we've seen their like around here,' said Liam, his voice steady.

'I'll be the judge of that. Brandon O'Riain, you're to come quietly,' ordered Swift.

'Constable, you know us for honest people. My son's a good boy.' Liam pleaded his case with outstretched arms.

'Then he'll not mind coming into the village and explaining what he was doing with Sean yesterday afternoon,' explained Swift.

'Is it a crime to be out and about with his cousin?' argued Liam.

'It could be.' Swift held up a silver fob and chain. 'We found these in Sean's pocket. A pretty piece for a poor man to have.' He beckoned to Brandon.

Brandon's heart began to race. He swallowed noisily, his mouth and throat suddenly dry.

'Mr Tobias Macklin has been found dead not three mile from his house. His horse is missing, and this here watch belongs to him. You can see by the initials scratched into the back of it. I say you two killed your landlord, sold the horse and were saving the trinkets for later.'

'I told you, I found it,' protested Sean from outside.

Swift laughed and grabbed the front of Brandon's shirt.

'Leave him alone!' Liam shouted. He leapt to his feet, only for the constable to strike him on the shoulder with the butt of the gun.

The children screamed and began to wail. Cait backed into a corner of the room, hugging the baby.

Brandon yelled out in anger, lowered his head and charged at the constable. He hit Swift's midsection, pushing him across the room, where his body hit the wall with a thud.

The pistol flew from the constable's grasp towards Maggie, who snatched it up. There was a sudden bang and a shriek as a bullet narrowly missed Brandon and hit the constable in the thigh. Swift groaned and slid to the floor.

Brandon turned in the direction the shot had come from and met Maggie's stunned expression. She carefully placed the firearm on the ground and then edged away from it.

Outside, the horse had startled at the gunshot and Sean, having lost his balance, had fallen to the ground with a thud. He got to his feet with difficulty and, staggering inside the cottage, saw the wounded constable.

'Let him bleed,' he said.

Brandon helped his father to a chair and then, detaching the keys from the policeman's belt, unlocked Sean's cuffs.

'What have you done, you stupid girl?!' yelled Cait, the baby howling in her arms.

'Leave her be, woman, or it's you that will be on the striking end,' Liam told his wife calmly.

Cait gave the baby to one of the children, who were huddled against a stone wall. Her expression traced a thoughtful line between anger and possible retaliation. 'It's your blood that's in them, Liam. O'Riain blood. Tempters and traitors and troublemakers, the lot of them.' She picked up the gun and sat it in the middle of the table. Then she backed away and folded her arms across her chest. 'I never should have married you. We'll be evicted before the day is out.'

Brandon crouched by Constable Swift, who was now slumped against the wall. Blood was pooling onto the ground from the gunshot to his thigh. 'I'm sorry. It was an accident,' he said.

'You'll hang for this,' Swift muttered, clutching at his leg. He was only a few years older than Sean. His face was turning the colour of the ash that littered the hearth in the mornings.

'None of us meant any trouble,' said Brandon. The pooled blood was darkening as if it were being forced from the deepest recesses of the man's body.

'Get him out, lad,' ordered Liam.

Brandon hooked his hands under Swift's armpits and dragged him outside. Sean followed close behind. Behind them, a bloody trail seeped into the frosty ground.

'He'll die,' Sean told Brandon, his satisfaction at this prospect clear. 'Did you hear that?' He leant over Swift so that their faces were inches apart. 'The blood will pump out of you just as fast as if you were pulling water.'

'That's far enough, lads. Leave him be and come here,' Liam barked.

Sean snarled as he followed Brandon back inside the cottage. Maggie was on all fours near the blood-stained floor, digging up the packed earth with a trowel and throwing it on top of the wet floor. Brandon could see her hands were shaking.

'Now what?' yelled Cait, above the howls and tears of the younger children.

'You must go,' Liam said calmly to Brandon and Sean. He turned to meet Maggie's dazed stare as well. 'You must *all* go.'

'We can't. You'll be blamed,' argued Brandon. 'The constable said someone saw Sean and me together. Word will get out.'

'It always does,' Cait added gloomily.

'Better one than three. Come here, Maggie.'

Maggie rushed to her stepfather's side, crumpled to the floor and rested her chin on his knee. 'I'm so sorry, Father.'

'I know, lass. It was an accident.' He stroked her hair slowly. 'You must go with Brandon and your cousin, girl. It's for the best.'

'No, Father, no!' Maggie lifted her head. 'I won't do it! I won't leave you! Who's to know what I did? He'll die, won't he?'

Liam tried to offer a soothing smile. 'You *must* leave, girl.'

Maggie flung her arms about her stepfather and began to weep. 'But please, Father, no one needs to know what I did.'

'Shush now, little Maggie. Everything will be all right. Brandon and Sean will see to that.' Liam looked to his son and nephew, his face passive, calm, however Brandon noted the trembling at the corner of his father's mouth. Although his heart refused to acknowledge what was happening, his head took control. In response, he found himself agreeing, although he wondered at the pact. Things were still too raw for him to comprehend what he'd just been entrusted with. He was only fourteen and the fear he felt at leaving home outweighed everything that had occurred since yesterday.

He realised with unwanted clarity that he'd been waiting for his father to speak again, hoping for guidance, for he knew Maggie was now his to safeguard, but his father appeared just as unsure as he was. With that knowledge Brandon understood that no one could help him. From now on, he would be the one making the decisions. The thought terrified him.

Liam gently shook Maggie off, rose and placed a hand on his son's shoulder.

'You can never come back, lad.' He directed his next words to Maggie and Sean too. 'If you do, only death will be waiting. You must go far away and make a new life.'

Never. Brandon's knees buckled at that single word. 'But nobody knows what happened,' he reasoned.

'And you think they won't guess in a heartbeat? Macklin's death will be on everyone's lips by noon and Constable Swift will have told others about why he was coming here this morning.'

Liam led him into the corner of the room. His father's fingers pinched him to straightness and they hugged, Brandon feeling the bone structure that contained a strength he'd never noticed before.

'Maggie will do better with you two,' his father whispered. 'She can't stay here. They'd likely arrest her for her connection to Macklin, for he's sure to have told someone of our bargain. Never tell her what part she played in this, Brandon. Never let Maggie know how I bartered her for a year's grace. She will blame herself for this fine mess and hate me for the doing of it, and there is nothing worse than a child's disappointment in a parent. This I do know.'

'You've brung the devil on us, Brandon,' Cait hissed. 'Brung him on as if you opened the door and called him in.'

Brandon wanted to tell his stepmother that it was a pity that the devil hadn't taken her instead. As the insults continued, he ruffled Dennis's and Sarah's hair, nodded at Marcus and Michael, then slowly took his coat from the peg on the wall and met his father's eyes one last time. 'I'm sorry.'

'It wasn't your fault, son.' Liam nodded through the doorway to where Sean was rifling through the dying constable's pockets. 'Better fifty enemies outside the house than one within. Sean will not change. He cannot. There's too much hate in him.'

'Father . . .' Brandon wanted to say that he loved him, but the words wouldn't come.

'Enough. There's plenty to be said, but none that really needs saying. I know what's in your heart. Now drag Swift around the back. I'll tell your Uncle Fergal what's happened and ask him to help me get rid of him.' He beckoned to his stepdaughter. 'It's time to say goodbye, girl.'

Maggie cried and hugged her stepfather, and then walked to her mother, still sniffling.

'Find a good husband,' said Cait, her hip cocked sideways where the baby perched. 'Not one with a ready-made family. And don't be forgetting how hard I've worked over the years.'

'Yes, Mamaí,' said Maggie, solemnly kissing her on the cheek.

Brandon watched from the door as his stepsister said her goodbyes to her siblings. Maggie shuffled across the room and then launched herself at their father one more time, gripping him so tightly that Brandon was forced to prise her loose. She shrugged free of Brandon's grasp and briefly held his gaze, and in that single look he saw the pain that came with their forced leaving, and he knew she blamed him squarely, despite Sean's guilt.

Maggie was waiting outside the cottage with only a shawl when Brandon and Sean returned from hiding the dying constable. Her eyes were puffy and red, her back ramrod straight.

'I hate you both,' she said.

'Hate us you can, Maggie,' said Sean, 'but I'm more than happy to have a fair shot on a foul night.'

'I didn't mean to shoot him,' she replied tearfully.

'But you did,' replied Sean. 'And now you're just the same as us. A murderer.'

'Sean, for pity's sake, let her alone,' said Brandon.

He looped an arm about Maggie's waist and dragged her towards the hills. She struggled and complained, yet he managed to keep her moving away from the only home they'd known.

Although his own eyes stung and his chest ached, Brandon held tight to Maggie. They walked until the sky darkened and grew light once again, and the hills and valleys that appeared in front of them were as unknown as the new life to which they were heading.

≪ Chapter 8 ≫

Richmond Valley, 1949

The night proved long and troubled. Stella lay awake recalling what Harry had told her – that Joe had disregarded his family in the pursuit of ambition and in the doing retraced the footsteps of a dishonourable ancestor, Brandon O'Riain. It was difficult to comprehend this tenuous family link. Harry and Joe's father, Sean, had passed many years ago aged in his seventies, and she assumed that his cousin Brandon was also long dead. Yet he was still talked about. This man who had once been a shepherd in Ireland. She wondered if Brandon had fretted for the flock in his care as Joe had. If he too had cursed when the tally was short while counting the mob into the yards. If it pained him, as it did Joe, to see the grasses wither with cold or heat. If he was once as attuned to the sick and the maimed and the need to ensure that the flock was not pushed too hard when walking them, as Joe had been. Perhaps Brandon had also stayed awake at night when danger neared, readying to take on poachers, while thousands of sea miles away, in another century, his descendant armed himself against wild dogs in the fringe lands of Australia.

Stella opened her eyes to the grey smudge of dawn and wiggled a little in her niece's bed. She could say nothing of these rambling nocturnal thoughts to Harry. He bore a grudge towards this simple sheepman of the past, and seemed keen to reduce Joe's complex personality to a convenient comparison to a long-dead relative.

She dressed quickly and, leaving Ann to sleep, headed to the kitchen. Morning light filtered through the house and she stopped at one of the photographs hanging on the wall that she'd briefly glanced at the previous day. There was a grainy black-and-white shot of two boys with their parents. She recognised a teenage Harry and assumed the baby in the dour-faced woman's arms was Joe. Stella had never seen a picture of her husband as a child before and at the sight of this innocent baby she felt a stab of pain. She drew her eyes away. Next to mother and child was a stocky, slab-sided man who even with the tread of advancing years appeared more than capable of handling himself in a fight. The resemblance to Harry was remarkable. This was Sean, Stella was sure of it.

A chair scraped. Men started laughing. Stella glanced in the direction of the kitchen and, not quite ready for the onslaught of conversation, escaped out onto the veranda.

Watson was awake, his yellow crest rising as she approached. She was yet to be forgiven for taking him from his home and subjecting him to a jolting car ride, and she supposed that the table on which his cage was perched was also unsatisfactory.

'Pretty boy,' she said softly. He edged away from her in response. His nails curled around the perch and he stretched out his white wings so that the lemon meringue of his underside and tail feathers was visible. 'I'll try to find you a bigger cage,' she promised, although at this early stage Stella was loath to ask for favours.

The back garden was a shady area filled with shrubs and native trees. Stella walked among the plants, stopping to turn on the sprinkler that watered the vegetable plot. Carrots and late potatoes filled the rows, as well as tomatoes. Stella sniffed at the vines, gently pressing the skins of the ripening fruit and then lifted her gaze to the house and its surrounds.

As she walked, she slowly got the feeling that someone was observing her, however there was no movement or sign of anyone, not from the house or garden nor from the land that stretched out beyond the fence to the distant mountains. She shook the thought free and continued exploring.

A tall cedar tree acted as a focal point at the bottom of the gently sloping lawn, and she walked towards it, surprised that the grounds were so extensive. The further she walked the more unkempt the garden became. It was quite overgrown in places. A straggly, fragrant hedge partially concealed the garden fence along one side. Stella tripped on something and found herself standing on a large tree stump that was cut close to the ground. She scraped the dirt off it, dragging her shoe across the concentric rings that marked each growing season, until the edges were revealed. Then she stepped out the diameter, whistling as she counted twenty feet. There were other stumps scattered around. Some were a good five feet in height, others had been hacked off closer to the ground, the axe marks still visible. All were enormous.

She walked through the woody maze trying to visualise the area as it had once been, a place thick with large cedar trees. The point of cutting them down was lost on her. Particularly as the remaining stumps made the area unsuitable for lawn or garden beds and a grouping of stately timber would have done much to cut back on summer's western sun. Beyond the stumps, the lone remaining cedar tree she'd first seen at the top of the garden stood in the middle of the fence. The wire boundary edged the tree's massive brown girth on either side but stopped short of reaching the timber. Stella tilted her head back. The cedar stretched to a height that she guessed was well over one hundred feet. Large spreading limbs were crowned with new season's growth, reddish leaves and white-petalled flowers.

She leant across the large buttressing roots and ran a palm over the knobby bark. The base must have been close to thirty feet in diameter. She walked about it, marvelling, wondering at its age, growing ever more aware of the tree's enormity. This tree had been needed, appreciated, saved, while around it, fanning out from its base, lay the timber labyrinth of others not worthy of life. It was as if those trees, cut down in their prime, were sacrifices, offered up to protect this tree.

On the cedar's trunk, a few feet above her head, initials were carved within a roughly scored circle. Stella traced each letter slowly, reading the ragged S, O and R.

Sean O'Riain.

A dog barked on the other side of the fence and ran towards her, attempting to stick its nose through the series of small hexagonal wire holes almost certainly erected to keep the kelpie out. Stella spoke softly to the animal who obediently quietened, its head angled to one side. Beyond, the hills were green-blue in the morning light. Pinkish cloud unfurled to hug the distant slopes. Again a prickle of unease ran down the length of her spine. It was back. That feeling of being observed.

Stella moved further along the fence, the dog quietly trailing her on the opposite side. A building suddenly appeared through the trees. She stopped and stared. It sat slightly lower than Ann and Harry's house due to the gradual incline of the ground and was a distance away, perhaps less than a quarter mile. The house was far larger than the one she currently inhabited, but not quite as roomy as the old homestead at Kirooma, which echoed when a person walked through it. Joe once said of their home that when he coughed, it coughed back.

This building was two storeys, with large oblong windows on the second floor and the type of fretwork that suggested wealth and age. Stella thought of the distant light that she'd seen through her bedroom window the previous evening and now knew its origin. It was strange to be in an environment where there were other people so close by; where neighbours' lights could be spotted in the dark and a simple exploratory walk could lead to their homes. On moonless nights at Kirooma, she'd kept a garden flare lit, which could be seen through the bedroom doors that had opened onto the veranda. It was a small but crucial act of defiance against a land that had the ability to swallow her whole.

Here, there were other people only a hair's breadth away. The knowledge of strangers' lives being lived so nearby chipped away at the steely resolve that had closed around her over the previous years. She found herself wiping away tears as she walked back to the house.

'*Who's a pretty boy*,' called Watson.

Stella saw Harry approaching.

'You brought a bird with you?' Harry's hands were on his hips, his elbows angular below the rolled sleeves of his shirt.

Stella patted her face, hoping that all evidence of her tears was gone, and walked towards her brother-in-law. 'His name is Watson and he belonged to Joe.'

'*Pretty boy, pretty boy*,' Watson repeated.

Harry frowned, the humour lost on him. His glance took in the fence and the house beyond. 'I wouldn't wander down there too often. It's a bit overgrown. There could be snakes.'

'Who lives over there?' Stella asked.

'We don't mix with them,' said Harry.

'But who are they?' she persisted.

'People you don't need to worry about. Now come inside. I want you to meet the twins.'

Stella considered mentioning her suspicion of being observed, however Harry was already walking ahead. She reluctantly followed him.

'I took Ann some tea and toast,' said Harry.

'Oh. Right. Sorry. I'll be a bit more organised today.'

'Good. Ann said you had some furniture with you, so the boys unpacked what was in the car. They're just finishing putting it in your room. We couldn't fit everything in so I parked the trailer in one of the sheds. You'd get some handy cash for that if you wanted to sell it.'

'Thank you.' Stella was taken aback by this act of helpfulness. Perhaps they'd misread each other. 'I hadn't thought about selling the trailer. I mean, I'll need it when I leave.'

'For what?' asked Harry. 'Some of that stuff you've got piled in it could be valuable. If you're after cash, then I'd be selling it. I don't

54

know much about antiques but there'll be some wealthy old cove about keen to buy. Just a thought. If things get tight.'

'Sure. Thanks.' He certainly seemed more amicable this morning. Not quite friendly, but at least the frosty tone of yesterday had lessened.

They reached the house. Harry stepped up onto the veranda and thumbed at Watson, who was chewing the cage bars as if he were a lifer at Alcatraz. 'We'll have to find him a bigger cage. You can't keep him in that.'

'Joe used one of the old meat-houses at Kirooma,' Stella told him.

'Well, I can't convert a building for a bird, but we'll figure something out,' said Harry.

'I appreciate that.'

Harry opened the door and she followed him inside.

'So who are those people?' Stella asked again, gesturing beyond the end of the garden. 'It's a very impressive-looking house.'

Harry pivoted on his heel. 'I told you. We don't speak to them.'

Stella flinched at the sudden anger in his voice. She knew the subject should be forgotten but she couldn't stop herself. '*Why* don't you speak to them?' she asked quietly.

The air in the hallway was warm, the heat of the day already growing. Harry gave her a hard, appraising stare, similar to the one he'd employed the previous evening. It was clearly an expression he was used to drawing on, except that at this moment it appeared as if he was trying to decide what should be shared and what not.

'Let's just say we had a boundary dispute with them a while back. We haven't spoken since. It was quite—'

'Hostile,' she offered, when it was clear Harry was finding it difficult to explain the situation.

'Bad,' he stated, ignoring her. 'Very bad. No one wants another fight to brew. All right?'

'Okay,' said Stella. First Joe and now the neighbours. It seemed her brother-in-law wasn't averse to arguments.

Harry strode down the hall to the kitchen. Stella sighed and followed him.

The kitchen was now filled with Harry and his two sons. Long limbs and broad shoulders crowded an area that had seemed so spacious the previous evening. The boys' talk stopped on her entry and chairs were scraped across the floor so that she could pass. Harry did the introductions. Fraternal twins Bill and John were the youngest of the O'Riain children at twenty-five years of age. Bill took after Harry, and Stella could see a lot of Ann in John's slighter build.

'G'day, Aunty Stella.' Bill winked. 'How you going?'

'Well. Thank you.' She took over the toast-making from John while Harry sat down to finish the remains of his breakfast, which appeared to be equal parts sausages, eggs and fat.

'We'll be in for dinner tonight,' said John.

'That'll be a change,' Harry quipped.

'I couldn't come at another pub meal,' replied Bill.

'Did you hear that, Stella?' said Harry. 'You'll be cooking for three.'

'Four,' said John. 'You forgot Mum.'

'Four,' repeated Stella.

'Five,' said Bill, 'unless you don't eat.'

'I eat.'

'Just checking,' said Bill, with a grin.

'Put everything in the warming oven and we'll have it when we get back. Right. I'm off then. By the way, your Aunt Stella has a cockatoo out the back and I need a decent cage made for the bird. All right?' Harry gulped down the rest of his tea then disappeared outside. The screen door slammed noisily behind him.

'A cockatoo. Another job,' said John, with a distinct lack of enthusiasm. 'I suppose we can put some chicken wire around that old A-frame and rig up something next to one of the sheds.'

'You draw it and I'll help build,' said Bill. 'See you.' He took a piece of buttered toast from the plate Stella placed on the table. 'Hey, Aunty Stella, nice to finally meet you.' He gave her a kiss on the cheek and the door slammed for a second time.

'Thank you. You too,' she called after him.

'Aunty Stel. Take a load off.'

'Take a—' She looked at John dumbly for a moment and then, selecting a yellow mug from the cupboard, poured herself tea and sat down at the table.

'I was sorry to hear about Uncle Joe.'

'Yes.' Stella clasped the mug between her fingers. This boy was the only one in the house to express remorse over Joe's death. People were a strange lot. Some were quick to offer condolences and others chose to ignore the tragedy. Stella wasn't sure which reaction she preferred. It was challenging enough navigating the situation without being faced with the simple fact that death made others feel uneasy.

'I told Dad we should've all gone out there, after it happened.'

'He told me it wasn't possible what with the harvest and everything,' said Stella, watching as John stacked the breakfast plates, pushing them to one side. In the end, she'd been glad they'd not ventured westward. It had been difficult enough in those final days without dealing with Joe's family.

Many kind people had arrived unannounced at Kirooma after Joe's passing. Stella should have been grateful. For the food and the house-cleaning. For the men driving out to check bores and stock. For Father Colin, who'd alerted his troops like the commander of an army and descended from Broken Hill with a handful of his scattered flock to tend to one of his wounded. However these visitations were from people she scarcely knew. All Stella had wanted to do was crawl into a dark corner and hide from what had become of her life, while they, with their good intentions, were committed to restoring a sense of order and normality to a property that was already beyond it.

'There's always something going on here. Planting cane. Burning cane. Slashing cane. Carting cane. Crushing cane,' said John. 'I keep telling Dad that he can't let it control his life, but cane *is* his life. If we planted him he'd probably grow a decent crop.'

'He's like his brother,' said Stella.

'I liked Uncle Joe,' said John. 'He used to take us fishing. The last time we went down to the river it was the day after my sixteenth birthday. I'd been given a new rod. Well, it wasn't new. It was Dad's, actually. Then it fell off the back of the truck on the way home and broke in half.' His face deflated, as if the loss were only recent. 'I was pretty angry when I heard Uncle Joe had got engaged and was buying a sheep property and moving away. I blamed you.'

'Me?'

'Yeah. Bill and Paddy and me all thought it was because of you that he left. But of course, you weren't the reason.'

'Joe loved sheep,' she replied.

John picked at a piece of gristle in his teeth. 'Yeah, he did.'

She hazarded that what Harry had refused to discuss the night before might well be known to John, perhaps the entire family. 'Did your father ever mention what he and Joe fell out over?'

Her nephew edged his chair back from the table. 'I better get going.'

'John, my husband is gone. If there's something I should know then I'd appreciate it if you'd tell me.'

In time, the frown line between John's eyes would be as deep as Joe's she thought.

'Uncle Joe never told you?'

'About what?'

A fly was buzzing around the table and John flicked at it with a tea towel, becoming instantly absorbed in the insect's looming destruction.

Stella thought of her and Joe's wedding in Sydney. Her parents, being against the union, had refused to attend, leaving the guest list decidedly small. There were her friends and some family, including Angelina and Carmela. Harry had been present, while Ann had stayed at home to care for one of the twins who'd contracted glandular fever. As for an argument or dispute of some kind, Stella couldn't recall a single one, but neither had there been any communication with Joe's family after they'd moved to the property.

'I know your father and Joe fell out when Joe left the Valley, but was there something else, John? Religion, perhaps? Did Joe tell your father he was an atheist? He was prone to joking about the Catholic faith at times, but surely Harry knew that deep down Joe was a believer,' said Stella.

John carried the plates to the sink. 'All I'll say is that Uncle Joe did the wrong thing. Dad said he put his own needs above family loyalty, and I doubt he'll ever forgive Uncle Joe for that.'

He gave her a look of commiseration and then walked outside to pull on his boots. Stella heard the crunch of gravel as he stepped from the veranda. She clutched the cup of now-cold tea and thought of Joe, the man she'd loved and married, and the older brother, whose lack of forgiveness hinted at something inexcusable.

✖ Chapter 9 ✖

Sydney, 1942

'Great news,' said Joe, the day after their engagement was announced. 'I signed the contract this morning for a one hundred-and-forty-thousand-acre sheep property in the far west of New South Wales. What do you think about that, eh?' He lifted his beer glass, in salute to his news.

They were eating takeaway fish and chips on the cramped balcony of her one-bedroom unit on the third floor of a red-brick building that ran to a busy corner on Sydney's New South Head Road. It was a Saturday afternoon and the noise from the traffic made it difficult to hear.

Stella was positive that she'd misheard. 'Did you say a sheep property?'

'Yes.' He took her hand in his. 'You'll love it.'

Stella drew her hand free. 'I don't understand. I thought we were going north. That's where your family farm is. When on earth did you decide to buy a property? And with what?'

Joe topped up her wine glass from the bottle of Chianti on the table. 'I'm not interested in sugar cane. I want to breed sheep. You know that.'

'Yes, but Joe—'

'I never said we were going back to the Valley,' he told her plainly.

'And you never said that we weren't,' she argued, feeling bewildered. 'You told me that's where your family's roots were. That the O'Riains had been there since the 1860s, very soon after they'd emigrated from Ireland.'

'Time for a change then. So, have you rung your parents to tell them our news?' he asked.

'Tomorrow,' she said as brightly as she could. The mention of her family reminded her of the dreaded task that lay ahead. Their engagement wouldn't be received well. It was a hard decision to go against the traditions of her family and marry outside their circle, but she had chosen love. A love that now confused her.

'As long as you know what you're doing, Stel,' had been Carmela's reply when Stella told her of the engagement.

It hadn't exactly been the excited response Stella was hoping for.

'You were the one that was keen for me to speak to Joe that day at Woodburn,' Stella had reminded her.

Staring at Joe now, she wondered if she knew what she was doing. Joe had spoken on numerous occasions about his work at a rural merchandise store and the small block of land he leased for his sheep. Was it so wrong to have assumed that they would move there?

'You've never even invited me to visit your home,' she complained.

'I always come to Sydney. Anyway, you were only up in the Valley a few months ago,' he said, referring to their first meeting, 'and you'll meet Harry at the wedding.'

'Don't you think we should have discussed this together? Where is this property, anyway? How far away is the far west of the state?'

'Not too far,' said Joe vaguely.

'However could you afford it?'

Joe smiled encouragingly. 'Timing. Everything is in the timing, Stella. Kirooma Station has been listed for sale for quite a while. It's a gift. An absolute gift.'

'There's probably a reason for that,' she interrupted.

'What? Now you're a rural property expert?' he said sharply.

She hadn't seen that before. The sharpness; the glitter of confrontation. The moment of awkwardness lingered long enough for Stella to realise that it was she who would have to apologise. 'I'm sorry. Please go on.'

He gave her a dismissive glance and began picking at the remains of the battered fish sitting on newspaper in front of them.

'Please, Joe,' she encouraged.

'This is exactly the reason I haven't told you about this before. Everyone's so damn negative.'

'What did your brother have to say?' said Stella.

'I haven't told Harry yet. I plan to after the wedding. I hope he'll be supportive.'

'Harry doesn't have to live out the back of Woop Woop. We do.'

'Well then maybe we shouldn't be getting married,' he countered.

Stella stared at him. 'You don't mean that.'

'Sometimes I wonder if you're cut out for the type of life I want.'

His words were again said sharply. Stella reached for the pack of menthol cigarettes on the table and lit one, inhaling with sudden need.

'I thought you were giving those up.'

'You're still drinking beer and you know how I hate the smell of it,' she countered.

In the street below a car honked and a man yelled out in response.

'I don't know how you can live here. A man can barely think with all this noise.' Joe walked inside and sat on the sofa.

Stella decided not to pursue the matter, at least not at that moment. The fact that he'd purchased property without even discussing it with her was more than cause for worry. It suggested her opinion was unimportant to him, and, at worst, that he considered her willing to go along with whatever he decided. Joe's attitude was new to her and it dulled the thrill of the previous day when he'd lowered himself to one knee and proposed.

What was she to do? Walk away because he'd cut her out of a major decision, one that in the end would probably benefit her as well? Hadn't he promised to provide her with a home and a decent income? The diamond on her finger was small, but she'd wanted it – and its giver. So she found herself joining Joe on the couch and reaching for his hand.

'Our first argument.'

'Not good,' he replied stiffly.

'So, then.' She elbowed him playfully in his side. 'Tell me about this property you've bought. How did you manage it?'

'I have my contacts, and a good bank manager.'

'But there's a war on,' she argued.

'Exactly. The British contract covers Australian wool for the duration of the war and one clip after. Wool is *the* fibre, Stella. That's never going to change. I can't lose. This is my chance.' He took her hand and squeezed it.

'*Our* chance,' she corrected.

'That's what I meant.' Joe left her side and walked about the room, his raw energy filling the living area so that the space appeared to shrink. He wasn't seeing her; his expression was one of remoteness. She knew at that moment Joe was in another world and she felt almost inconsequential to his needs.

When Joe was away from her, back in the Valley, Stella liked to envision him in the paddock with his sheep. The sun belting down. Shirtsleeves rolled high. The bushman's tan on his arms, face and neck, like a tidemark from his outdoor life. She could almost conjure up the sweet scent of hay as he cut the twine on a bale and handfed one of his rams. Now, as he stood in the centre of the room, she saw how restricted he appeared, as if the unit couldn't hold him. The man before her was not the bricks-and-mortar kind. Stella wondered where he might lead her if she let him.

'Harry was an Anzac,' said Joe. 'He was at Gallipoli.' He met her stare, returning from whatever place he'd just inhabited. 'I always wondered what it would have been like to be there, Stella. To be one of the brave. A hero. One of those men who battled

63

incredible odds.' He placed his hands in his pockets and then, just as quickly, withdrew them. 'Every year I think of him marching on Anzac Day and imagine the cheering crowds and I wish with all my heart that there was some great event that I could be involved in. Some way that I could follow in his steps and be tested, as he has been tested.' He sat on the chair opposite her, his leather boots leaving a smudge of dark-brown polish on the floor.

'You're not going to enlist?' she asked with trepidation.

'No, I'm not,' said Joe adamantly. 'There's only one war hero in this family. Besides, I'm thirty-five years old and about to be married. While I don't have any issue with being conscripted into the Citizen Military Forces, I'm safely outside the government's reach.'

'Good,' said Stella. 'Because I wouldn't let you go without a fight.'

Joe's expression was like that of a child just given a lolly. He sat back, contemplating the floor as if the answers to humanity's greatest problems could be found in the woody knots at his feet.

'When I was eighteen I took my swag and headed inland on foot. People gave me odd jobs along the way. And I learnt to do things that I never would have had the opportunity to do if I'd remained on the farm. The first thing I did was grow a beard. Harry was a stickler for a close shave. It took a while,' he admitted with a smile. 'I spent a lot of time in the bush, camping out, educating myself about the different trees and grasses, collecting beetles and bugs, stick insects, cicadas, dead spiders. I wanted to understand how the tawny frogmouth could stay so still during the day that he appeared like a fallen branch. Why ants don't always bite. How butterflies sip nectar. I guess I was trying to understand where I fitted in.' During his speech his face had grown animated, as if he were reliving every moment of those years.

Stella smiled at him, toying with the not-unpleasant thought that, in his unbridled curiosity, he was part child.

'You'll think me strange,' said Joe.

'Not at all,' said Stella.

'I ended up in the north-west of the state on a sheep property for eighteen months. Mr Wells, my employer, was frank and honest. He took people on merit and though I worked for him and called him Mister or Boss, I always felt like an equal.' Joe leant forwards in the chair. 'You see, Stella, we were battling the weather and bad sheep prices, side by side. It made no difference that I came from a family of cane farmers and he was a wealthy grazier. If Mr Wells thought himself better than me, he never said anything or acted that way.'

A brief quiet followed. Stella wondered if he was waiting for a response but realised, from the unaffected tone of Joe's words, that he wanted nothing more than for her to understand the substance of what he was sharing. So she said nothing, simply nodding for him to continue.

'During the worst of it, when his wife had to shovel dirt from the dust storms off the veranda, we fed the sheep still living and shot those soon to die. There was something grand about what we did on that property. The way the business survived through sheer persistence. From the first week I arrived to the day I left, my opinion never varied of Mr Wells, nor of what he was trying to achieve. Feed his family, clothe the nation and be damned the obstacles that got in his way. It was a noble way to live. I read something about the Anzac spirit not long after I'd left Mr Wells. The words that were used in the newspaper were ones like "endurance", "courage" and "humour", and it made me think that those things could still be found. Not in the Valley, where people hold their grudges like they tend potted plants, but in the bush. The real bush. That's when I decided where I wanted to be. The path I would take. So, you see, it's not that I intentionally cut you out of the decision-making, Stella. It's simply that I have to go where I'm called. And it's the bush that calls me.' He came over and sat beside her again. Kissed her on the cheek. 'Harry doesn't understand. He'll never understand. He'll hate what I'm about to do.'

'You mean buying the property?'

After what he'd just shared, it was a complete reversal to find Joe suddenly so guarded. He finally offered a hesitant yes in answer to her question, but Stella knew that something else troubled him.

'What's the matter?' she queried.

'Harry holds grudges,' Joe replied. 'Always has. Probably always will. Our father was the same. I don't want to be like them.'

'And you won't be. You are your own person, Joe.'

'I want to do great things with my life as well.'

'And you will, but what if I'm no good at living on a sheep property?' Stella said quietly. 'I'm a city girl, Joe. I go to the beach and eat banana splits and I drink Chianti on the weekends.'

'And you love me,' he added.

'Yes,' she said. 'But country people are different. They're used to that kind of life. I'm not. I'm thirty years old. I worry that it will be hard for me to adapt.'

'But you *do* love me,' he persisted, squeezing her knee until she laughed and brushed him away playfully.

'You know I do.'

'Well then, the other things don't really matter, do they?'

'But what if I don't fit in?' she argued.

'We're not going to some fancy party.' He stroked the silver cross at her neck and then pressed his tongue to the hollow at the base of her throat.

Stella had not expected to think so much when Joe was with her. But with everything he did, the way he touched her, the places he chose to concentrate his efforts, her own desire was inevitably blighted with questions. Why did he always push her back on the couch so that her head was angled uncomfortably? Did he enjoy squeezing her breasts or was it done for her satisfaction and, if so, should she murmur or moan? And how far should she allow his interest to wander when at that very moment he was struggling to remove her knickers. They weren't married yet. What if she let him have her and she became pregnant? What would people say? She was Catholic. So was Joe. It was a sin to have sex before marriage.

A bulge was pushing up into her. She struggled a little and they fell from the couch to the floor.

'Joe, we shouldn't,' she said.

But Joe was single-minded. 'We're engaged. What can it matter now?'

'It matters a lot.' She spoke into his neck, her words muffled. His belt-buckle flapped hard against her thigh. A boot scraped her shin.

'Joe . . .' she repeated.

But it was done. He was inside her and she had not the courage to ask him to stop, for, finally, there was pleasure for her as well.

❧ Chapter 10 ❧

Stella carried a reminder of that afternoon for more than a week afterwards in the form of a bruise on her leg. Every morning she checked her reflection in the mirror before heading off to her typist job, expecting to see a change. No woman could experience what she had without some singular mark exhibiting the fact to the outside world. She had been infused with love, and this awakening gave her a sense of joy that in the past she'd associated with entering a cathedral. That comparison was undoubtedly a sin. However, to her surprise, afterwards she remained quite blandly herself. Apart from the bruise, there was nothing to declare the sanctity of the moment shared with her husband-to-be, and it was something of a disappointment and a relief to realise that no one had any idea of what had occurred in a third-floor flat on a quiet afternoon.

She studied her womanly proportions. Her olive skin. Spent a good half-hour rolling her dark hair into a complicated bun that swirled like spoon-curved butter about her head. She had prayed to the Virgin for forgiveness for her transgression and spent long hours in confessional with a priest, who seemed more interested in detail than repentance. She had sinned, but if there was no sign of a child before the wedding then her fear would change to happiness and the secretive pleasure she'd enjoyed could be pursued all over again without reproach.

Her fingers brushed the purple discolouration in the shape of a lily that spread across her thigh. She tried not to dwell on Joe's decision to purchase the sheep property without discussion. Decided that it was far better to be with a man who knew what he wanted, one that was prepared to be tested, than another who chose a vocation for simplicity, or worse, lack of forethought. Joe O'Riain wanted a big life. There was a mythic quality to the way he explained his awe of the bush and now he owned a portion of it. A noble run of ancient lineage, far removed from the existence either of them knew.

Stella glanced through the narrow window to the street from the typing pool on the lower-ground floor. Her fingers flowed effortlessly across the keys as people walked past the office. Only briefcases, women's hemlines and children were visible from where she sat, providing a ceaseless view of moving feet. She had learnt to angle her chair throughout the course of the day to ensure she received as much of the streaky rays of sunlight that the window would allow. It had pleased her once, this manoeuvring of seat and desk. Now the stripy light seemed petty, and her chasing of it futile. The clack of her nails on the typewriter keys was an annoyance.

'I suppose you won't bother with any of us once you're married.' Jordan Vincent was one of the older women at work. A slight and bony spinster, she stepped in front of Stella, effectively blocking her from joining the other girls as they filed from the office for a quick cigarette outside before their usual morning tea-break.

'What do you mean?' said Stella, ignoring the pulling of faces by the departing women over Miss Vincent's shoulder.

Miss Vincent shrugged. 'You and your pleased smile. You'd never know there was a war on.'

Stella tried to walk past but Miss Vincent blocked her. Everyone knew Miss Vincent entertained aspirations of becoming the typing-pool supervisor, however ten years had passed without a hint of promotion. She dealt with her disappointment by exuding superiority whenever she had the opportunity. 'You always struck me as a young girl with few prospects and limited intellect, but I see now that you've quite the ambition.'

'Because I'm getting married.'

'Your parents own a café, don't they? I heard you call it a "greasy spoon" to one of the other girls yesterday.'

'I was only joking.'

'Were you?'

Stella hesitated. Miss Vincent had made her sound mean and ungrateful, when her comment had actually been inspired by anger at her parents for refusing to accept her fiancé or her invitation to the wedding.

'Trying to fit in, are we? But what's the point? Once you've married you won't bother with your old friends. Do the girls know that while they're all scrabbling together their ration coupons to help with your wedding day that you're desperate to leave them behind? I've seen you roll your eyes at the trainees and daydream out the window while the rest of us are working and worrying about the war. But the war wouldn't be causing you one bit of sleeplessness. You're not even Australian. In fact, you Italians are our enemies.'

'I'm Australian. My family came here last century,' Stella replied indignantly.

'That's not so very long ago, compared to some of us. I've seen girls like you come and go. Marry up, down, sidewards, but not all of them have been quite so smug on announcing their engagement. Be careful of leaving your past behind and aspiring to greatness. Marriage is never the perfect vision young brides imagine.'

Miss Vincent lifted her chin in conclusion, as if the slight elevation helped stress her point. The older woman unfurled a *Daily Telegraph* from under her arm, pushed a typewriter to one side and spread it on a table. 'The 1941–42 wool clip is expected to total 3,590,000 bales,' she read. There was a corresponding picture of a well-dressed man in a yard full of sheep.

'Mr Pollard told you.' Stella had pleaded with the section manager when she'd given her notice not to tell anyone of her and Joe's plans to go west.

Miss Vincent placed her hand on a hip, particularly cheerful. 'Think you're *special*, don't you. With your overseer, cook and governess for when the little ones come, and your husband *safe from doing his duty*.' Her particular word emphasis suggested that she held a low opinion of those who considered themselves better than others. She snatched up the paper, curled it into a tube and placed it in a rubbish bin. 'It's worth remembering, dearie, that once you're out there you'll be in the middle of nowhere.' She left the room.

Stella waited a few seconds and then, retrieving the paper, began reading. It was true what Miss Vincent had said. People were making good money from wool. She now had every reason to believe that buying the property was a sound idea. Stella perched on the edge of the desk, a warm sensation settling within her. She looked to the plaster ceiling and then back to the oblong room realising at last the constrictions of the world she inhabited. Ahead lay a new home, fresh opportunities, family and staff. Miss Vincent was wrong about her, on so many levels, but on one score she was right. She would leave the small world they inhabited and never return. For she was soon to be a grazier's wife.

❧ Chapter 11 ❧

Richmond Valley, 1867

The tree was massive, perhaps one hundred and sixty feet high. Brandon wedged the pole into the cut in its trunk and hoisted himself up onto the narrow, wobbly platform, balancing like a circus performer. He was standing thirty feet above the ground. The air was so hot and humid that he almost believed that if he pushed against it, it might well press back. Sweat trickled down into his eyes.

For the last few months, he and Sean had contented themselves with smaller specimens near the river, ones that could be easily felled and floated downstream to be sold. There was a pile of their branded logs hidden away on the fringes of the forest, waiting for a summer flood to move them. Why he had felt compelled to go exploring he couldn't explain, except that he suspected that this hill, much like the depths of the forest, contained pockets of timber that other cedar-getters would avoid due to the difficulty of removing the precious wood from the rough terrain. So he and Sean had bashed their way uphill through the scrub, their efforts leading them to this very spot, where they'd found a tree so mighty it was impossible to walk away from. It was like discovering a gold nugget.

Brandon hacked at the vines and creepers that twisted about the trunk, careful lest they recoiled. A weak breeze rustled the surrounding foliage and, as if engulfed by the thickness of the forest, quickly dropped away. They were in the Big Scrub for the second year running. A strange name for a place that grew the tallest, thickest trees he'd ever seen.

He waited for Sean to join him, listening to his cousin grunting as he heaved himself up onto a separate horizontal piece of timber thrust into a notch on the opposite side of the tree. Behind them, a narrow track showed the path they'd slashed through fallen saplings, tangled vines and brush to reach their target. In front of them lay the thoroughfare they'd readied for when the tree would fall. They'd cleared away the smaller trees they'd already felled, piling the timber on either side of the thoroughfare. An understorey, once thick with ferns, palms and spikey bushes that scratched and drew blood, had been obliterated by saw and hoe.

Luck was with them, as the tree crowned the side of a hill. There were only two ways down: a straight fall to the bush below or a gentle slope that led to the bottom. If they managed to shoot the log along the concave track they'd carved into the soil, there was a chance the great tree would follow the safer path to the base of the hill. Brandon reckoned the top of the fallen tree would be just short of the cliff's edge when it fell.

Sean's hand sought balance against the scaly bark. 'It won't work, you know. And if it doesn't we'll never be able to clear a road to get the bullock team up here.'

'We can saw planks out of it,' said Brandon. 'And then snig them down.'

'Stubborn. You've always been stubborn.' Sean gave a grunt, smacking his hand against the tree's girth. 'Are you sure this is the narrowest point?'

'It's about ten feet in circumference. A good twenty feet less than the bottom of her. Ready?' Brandon swung the axe, making the first undercut on the side the tree would fall, the impact reverberating through his arm and shoulder and down his spine.

Balancing on the opposite side of the tree, Sean followed immediately, then Brandon swung again, and soon the area echoed with the rhythmic *thwack* of iron on cedar. Woodchips flew outwards and the air grew thick with the strong woody fragrance. They kept at it until the cut was deep and wide. Big enough for a man to lie in. Then, having confirmed the direction in which the tree was to fall, they began cutting on the opposite face of the axed trunk.

'You think this'll be the end of our cedar days?' asked Sean when they stopped for a rest.

Brandon immediately thought of Maggie, left behind in town. 'Yes.'

Sean pulled the axe clean of the cut and stopped. 'A person shouldn't stay in one place,' he said. 'That suggests a man's comfortable, and no good can come of that. I want to keep moving as we have the past three years. I don't want land or that life again. Not when a man can simply cut a tree and be done with blight and starvation.'

Since leaving their old life in Ireland Sean had come to embrace their wandering to the point where Brandon knew he grew restless after a week or so in one place. It was as if he feared putting down roots, wary that they may well be dug up again.

They were young men – Brandon seventeen years old, Sean twenty – and they only had each other. And Maggie. She was the reason Brandon wanted to stop roaming. His stepsister needed a proper home and he'd made a promise to their father that he would care for her. Not that his oath had come to much yet.

'We have to think of Maggie. It's not fair dumping her in the nearest village for months on end while we're cutting.' Brandon swung his axe. He was only being partially honest. It pained him every time he said goodbye to her, and for a long time his dreams had been consumed with worry for her safety. Quite simply, he missed her.

'She's always got extra coin, should she need it. Besides, Maggie's nearing sixteen. Your little stepsister is almost a full-grown woman and pretty soon she won't be needing either of us.' Sean grunted as he followed with a rapid axe strike.

'Yes she will,' said Brandon.

'You worry about her too much.' Sean tugged the axe-head from the tree. 'We should have stayed with Hackett's men. It's easier in a team.'

'They're troublemakers, with nothing to show for their work at the end of a season,' said Brandon.

'Perhaps, but they're Irish and a people should stay close together.'

When the back cut was finally completed, the tree gave a fierce crack. The men dropped their axes to the ground and, as the ancient cedar began to topple, they quickly clambered downwards, springing from board to board like monkeys until they reached the large buttressing roots and jumped to the earth. The decapitated tree crashed to the ground, destroying lesser timbers, scaring birds and animals, until it landed with a shudder on the floor of the forest, the crown just shy of the cliff's edge.

Brandon and Sean lay next to each other as their lungs steadied. They'd jumped the last six feet and were sprawled on the ground, each silently hoping for the felled tree to gather momentum and plough a course over the cliff.

The gap in the canopy spilt sunlight onto their forest-pale faces and sweaty, bare torsos – Brandon, dark-haired and brawny, his body toned by axe and saw so that he looked as old as, if not older than, his cousin, and Sean, red-headed, and twice Brandon's size. When it came to his cousin, Brandon ignored what others could not: the bulky frame and ginger hair, the square face that matched the brutish edge that his words and deeds possessed.

Next to him, his cousin scratched at the mosquito bites that covered their bodies from time spent by the river.

'And now we've cut it,' said Sean, 'how do you *really* think we're going to get it out of here?'

There was a loud snap. Then a fracturing noise echoed about them as the great trunk began to slide. Freed from its woody anchor, it rushed forwards, down the manmade corridor of cleared scrub, before veering sharply to the left and shooting out in the wrong direction over the top of the cliff.

They scrambled to their feet and trailed the airborne length of timber at a run, bracing their descent on the surrounding trees until they were standing on the edge of the precipice. The momentum of the timber had speared it away from the grooved path and the gentle slope beneath. It landed at the base of the cliff, accompanied by a thundering sound and a scattering of birds.

'That noise would have woken the dead!' cried Sean.

Below the overhang, the valley spread out. A river twisted through the cleared country of settlers where crops and grazing cattle made a pretty patchwork. Beyond it all lay distant hills.

'Well, it's not a fish until it's on the bank,' said Sean sagely. 'Now can we go back to camp?'

Apart from the bush where the cedar had landed, the country fanning out from the base of the hill had been clear-felled. It would be an easy enough spot to access. Brandon turned to Sean.

'No,' said Sean, as if he were privy to his cousin's thoughts. 'It will take us days to get to that damn tree. I say we head downhill the way we came, back to our camp and the bullocks. It'll be pitch-black by the time we reach it tonight. Tomorrow we'll start making our way to the village and see if we can't find a bit of timber to cut so we don't return empty-handed.'

Brandon scratched at the slight stubble on his chin.

'That's settler's country,' Sean continued. 'They'll run us off the place if we're caught. Our four-pound licence fee doesn't mean we can plunder Crown land, land leased to the likes of them.'

'But we're not thieving anything,' said Brandon. 'It wasn't cut on their property. And do you really want to have nothing to show for a week's work?'

Sean shook his head. 'It's probably splintered. Ruined. Yes, it'll be ruined.'

Brandon studied the drop to the ground below. 'Yes.' He smiled. 'And what if it's not?'

≪ Chapter 12 ≫

After they left their camp, it took a whole week to journey out of the forest. The woodlands were dark until 7 am and already becoming gloomy again by four in the afternoon. They followed a rutted track that led back to the waterway, the heat and mugginess and the short travelling days proving arduous for man and bullock alike. Brandon watched for the first sign of the creamy-flowered white booyong tree, an avenue of their bolstering roots marking the direction to the waterway. From there, a small grove of white beech told them they were a quarter-mile from the river and their waiting pile of axe-branded logs. He'd be pleased to be on a better road. The bullocks were slow and the slide they were hitched to, a low platform with deep sides and skids, moved steadily. It was a poorly built contraption, won by Sean during a night of gambling, although, as they spent a portion of every week repairing it, Brandon knew the loser had come out far better off. It was pulled by four mangy paired and yoked bullocks, who were well past their prime but still managed to haul a reasonable load when required.

They reached the hoard of timber they'd cut during the season and re-counted their haul. They hoped that the buyer, Malcolm

Jack, was honest in his dealings with them. Brandon and Sean couldn't afford to sit idly waiting for rain and a summer flood to float their haul downstream. They were relying on Jack to do that. He knew where their timber was located and their logs would be rolled into the river with others when the time came to be carried on the freshening waters to the village of Wirra.

They saw no other camps or people as they continued their journey, but they knew that tucked within the trees were isolated sites where whole families resided year after year while the menfolk felled trees and stockpiled logs. It was strange to think of these small societies, sprung up amidst bracken ferns and fibrous creepers. Hidden from the world. Places where babies were born in canvas tents and children spent their early years rarely seeing the sun.

In time, they reached the worn tracks of previous cedar-getters' wagons and followed the well-defined route that hugged the river. It was an old-man river, its age evident from the stretch of floodplains that eased from its eroded banks. The width of the watercourse dazzled their eyes. It appeared motionless. Only a length of driftwood betrayed the current, which moved steadily out to sea. The river projected a magnetic beauty. River gums nestled close to the water's edge, within which the small azure body of a bird captured their attention. With its black bill and orange throat and belly it was a pretty sight flitting among the trees.

Their proposed destination – the cedar tree that had crashed to the base of the hill – soon led them away from the calm waters and the laughter of kookaburras. Skirting reedy swamps they reached countryside that had been heavily cleared, where tree stumps stuck out from the ground like ragged tombstones. Any valuable timber had undoubtedly been sold; the remainder used to build dwellings or yards or left to rot where it had been axed to the ground so that crops and grasses could grow. The land seemed desolate, empty, as if the heart had been cut out of it. There were cattle of course, for any settler of means was supplementing their income with the returns from the sale of meat, tallow and hides, however it was money from the sale of cedar that had made the area rich.

'Not a pretty sight,' said Sean, taking in the countryside.

His cousin rarely shared any depth of thought. Brandon knew they'd been away from company for too long. It could make a man melancholy, the killing of things. Chopping down trees, week after week, month after month. Yet knowing their worth made it impossible to stop. It was like a fever. The search. The exhilaration of finding a stand of cedar intact and ready for the taking.

Sean walked on the lead bullock's near side, a plaited whip resting over a muscled shoulder. 'Do you think they're dead? Our fathers?'

How was he to reply? 'Do you?'

'I wonder what's happened. I wonder who else left. If they came here or to America.'

They'd learnt last year that Brandon's half-brothers Marcus and Michael had emigrated to America using the money Brandon had sent home. It was likely that other members of their families had emigrated as well, however their frequent letter-writing from Australia had never been responded to with the same commitment. Only their fathers stayed in contact. Sean and Brandon left forwarding addresses at each town near to where they worked and it was not unusual for ten months to pass before mail found them. However neither father had replied to their scribblings for over a year. The silence that drifted from the other side of the world was now more terrible than the distance that separated them.

'If something's happened, wouldn't we be told?' asked Sean.

'Maybe. It depends who's left over there. Maybe they've all gone.'

'Well I'm not sending any more money until we know what's what,' said Sean.

Brandon hoped that desperation for their funds would lead to someone making contact, but perhaps there were now others living abroad that could be depended on. Honest family members whose goodness was reliable and preferable. Cousins and half-siblings who'd not caused the O'Riain families to be evicted from their small tenant farms, forcing them to live in squalor on the edge of the village.

Sean ran a hand along the closest bullock's hide, the animal's steady progress marked by sprays of dust that shot out from beneath its hoofs. 'It's never seeing them again. That's the cut. We should have gone to America,' he continued.

'The day we arrived at the docks there wasn't much choice,' replied Brandon.

'In America they've formed a Fenian Brotherhood. They're issuing bonds to raise money for arms. Irish immigrants are buying them in their hundreds and thousands. I've told you that before.'

Damn Hackett and his team of cedar-getters. That's where Sean's knowledge came from. They were adept at rousing Fenian sentiment after a vat of rum had been consumed.

Brandon kept pace with the rhythmic gait of the bullocks, the axes, saws, hoes and hammers clanging against each other in the slide. It was hard to begin again when Sean was continually dredging up the bitterness that should have stayed buried in Ireland.

'There's a fight to be had and maybe it can only be won in a new land,' said Sean.

Brandon hesitated. 'You're not talking about America now, are you?'

'No. I'm not.'

Brandon was overcome by a fierce desire to tell Sean to stop talking nonsense, however as his cousin never uttered a word that he did not believe in with all his heart, he knew he had to counter his fervour with a quieter approach. It was a method that he'd adopted over time, one that gradually allowed him to take the lead on many issues, when based on age alone that right should have been Sean's.

'I don't want to carry the troubles of the past into the present.'

Sean raised an eyebrow. 'It's too late for that. The troubles came with us.'

❖

The two riders appeared from the trees that marked the course of the river. It was the movement in the still of the late afternoon that attracted Brandon's attention; the undulation of nuggety brown against faded green as the riders disappeared into the tangled bush and then reappeared to weave in and out of the timber. The action noiseless. The land a canvas to their travels.

'Look.' Sean pointed.

'I see them.'

As they observed the riders, one of them suddenly moved and the crack of a whip carried through the air. A flock of parrots rose skywards from the river timber, startled by the sound. The wave of crimson and blue skirted the river and then flew towards the bullock team. The riders galloped into open country in their direction, following the birds.

'They're in our path,' said Sean.

'They'll question us. Best to keep moving,' advised Brandon.

The riders came to a halt and dismounted.

'It's women,' said Sean after a moment. 'We're in luck.'

It was true. Their slender frames and long, full skirts were visible now. One of the women held a large bird on her extended hand. She considered the approaching men and then started walking through the grasses. When she stopped again, she removed a hood from the bird's head. It lifted into the air, soaring towards the flock of parrots. Brandon tipped his head to follow the raptor's progress. The parrots winged northwards as the hunter gained height, its span of wings dark compared to the pale sky. On reaching the upper air currents, it appeared more intent on freedom than the feast that fled below. Then, without warning, the raptor changed direction. A single parrot tailed the fleeing mass. The hunter took a curved path towards its prey. Quickly closing the distance, it folded its wings, dived, and struck the smaller bird with its claws. With its catch secured, it flew back towards the women on the ground.

The bird landed as Sean yelled out, 'Woo!' to halt the team. The bullocks slowly came to a stop, not far from where the women stood.

The taller of the two wore a hunting suit of deep purple. It was a pared-down version of the full crinoline skirts favoured by the wealthy in Sydney, a necessity, Brandon supposed, if a woman was to ride a horse. She held up a heavily gloved hand but barely took notice of them, so engrossed was she by the slate-blue falcon. Having landed in the grass, it was beginning to dismember the crimson parrot.

Brandon ignored the young woman's arrogant gesture and walked forwards. It was a long time since he'd witnessed falconry. Mr Macklin had been partial to the sport, using his birds to supplement his larder. But hunting for no good reason other than for the sake of a kill made it a sport Brandon could never comprehend. Next to him, the woman's companion gripped the reins of their horses. She glanced at Brandon and then back to her mistress, avoiding the bloody scene at her feet.

He tried to hide his disgust at the killing. There were scratches on the gloved woman's cheek, fresh enough to be glossy with blood. It appeared the bird needed more taming. Its owner was unperturbed by her injury. She was tall, similar to him in age, with eyes too widely spaced and a thin nose, but she was unusual-looking enough to be more than attractive. As the falcon began pecking out the parrot's entrails, she finally acknowledged him.

'They rarely survive Glanville's claws but this little one needed a bite through the spine on landing. Tenacious, don't you think?' Her servant passed her a lace-edged handkerchief, and she dabbed at the scratches on her cheek. 'Who are you?' The woman spoke in a clipped English accent.

'We were cutting cedar. Up there.' Brandon pointed to the hill.

'Did I ask your profession? I know you live in the forests. You're white as ghosts. Who are you?' she said.

'Brandon and Sean O'Riain,' explained Brandon.

'And we *work* in the Big Scrub,' said Sean. 'We don't live there.' There was an edge to his voice.

She squinted at Sean as if not quite believing he'd spoken. 'Irish. I wonder that we needed more.'

Brandon was impressed by her confidence. Two women alone in the bush were a target if they met the wrong company.

'I could say the same of the English,' replied Sean.

A look of deep indignation crossed the woman's features. 'You're on private land.'

'We're aware of that, miss,' said Brandon, desperation feeding his politeness. 'But our timber speared off the top of that hill and landed just over there. We were hoping to retrieve it.'

'*Retrieve* it,' she repeated. 'Hetty, we have educated Irishmen.' She watched the falcon, who was partway through his meal.

Her companion was short and slight with bulbous lips, but that was all Brandon gleaned of her appearance, fixed as she was on her feet unless her mistress addressed her.

'You can fetch your wood, but when you have done that you will come directly to me.' She waved a hand vaguely towards the east. 'It's seven miles. I'll expect you in a day or so. And if you find yourself lost, ask for the residence of Mr John Truby.'

'But why?' asked Brandon.

'Because nothing comes free. And as I've done you a favour, I'm expecting you to do me one. Do we have an agreement?'

Sean shrugged and Brandon inclined his head. The woman reverted to studying the falcon and the now-mangled parrot. Only the girl showed interest in their departure, watching as Sean commanded the bullocks to walk on.

'We don't have to do as she says,' said Sean, when there was space enough between their two parties to ensure the women couldn't hear. 'In fact, I'd rather not.'

'I think it's probably best if we do,' said Brandon.

'And so it starts again. Us jumping to the wants of the English.'

'What harm can come of repaying a favour?' said Brandon.

Sean regarded him steadily. 'It depends what kind of repayment they want.'

⪻ Chapter 13 ⪼

Brandon and Sean gripped either end of the saw. Its teeth bit into the bark, layers of chocolate brown falling away until they reached the pinkish-red tissue. As the sawyers settled into the task before them, the rhythmic singsong brought forth the scent of the cut wood. Red dust smeared their faces, mingling with their sweat. Still they kept working, drawing the saw through the thick timber, until they were past the halfway mark and then three-quarters deep in the tree's red heart. They kept working until the final strokes struck a fragile hinge of wood. They sawed through it and then stepped back, smiling at their efforts.

The trunk had splintered in the fall. A single fracture ran nearly the length of the wood. Nonetheless the damage was skewed to one side, leaving plenty of useable planks that could be sawn free. It was a good load. One that could be taken straight to the lumberyard on the river for sale. Although more money could be made from the whole cedar trunks that were favoured by furniture-makers and shipbuilders, there was a steady market for cedar boards.

It was five days since their arrival at the base of the hill. They'd lived on fish from the river and a mixture of flour and water formed into little cakes and cooked in a skillet over the fire. That morning, Brandon had lain on his back, chewing on the tough bread, his body enclosed by tall, flowering grasses that waved about him like a golden sea. The birds had woken him at dawn with their loud calls as if amazed at surviving another night.

Their long hours of labouring had been rewarded. The slide was now stacked with sawn timber. The rest of the cut cedar was piled a few feet away and, beyond that, the bullocks grazed.

'We should get going with this lot,' said Sean. 'My feet are itching. A sure sign it's going to rain up in the mountains. I want to be in the village when Malcolm Jack floats our logs in. They say he's an honest man, but the chance of coin can make the best of us unreliable.'

'You know we have to go to her house,' said Brandon.

'Why? Why do we have to go? She's nothing to us but an Englishwoman intent on cheap Irish labour. You know that,' argued Sean.

'And what if she causes trouble for us, being on her land and all. Especially when we have to come back and fetch the rest of the timber. Anyway, we agreed on it.'

'Actually you giving a bit of a nod is hardly a binding contract,' challenged Sean. 'All right. Go then. I'll take this to the lumber-yard and wait for you in town. And see if I'm not right about the rain.' Sean lifted a finger, like a father warning his child.

'You'll see Maggie?' asked Brandon.

'Yes, but I hope the lass is friendlier. Last time she kicked me in the shin,' said Sean.

'You've always had a way with women.' Brandon smiled.

His cousin made a noise that sounded much like a growl. 'First you can help me finish up the last of the timber then we'll pack up camp and harness the bullocks.'

They worked steadily, laughing and joking as they carried the last of the planks to the pile. Then they stamped out the campfire, gathered their few belongings and walked the bullocks from their quiet grazing to the slide. When the animals were finally hitched it was past midday. Sean threw Brandon his axe. He caught it one-handed.

'You'll be needing that. I'm betting you'll be chopping firewood and carting water.' He spat on his fingers and tried to smooth Brandon's hair.

'Get away from me, you big oaf, and don't get into any trouble while I'm away,' said Brandon, ducking out of his way.

'Me? Of course not,' said Sean with a grin.

⋘ Chapter 14 ⋙

Brandon stopped on sighting the homestead. His destination was framed by cedar trees, which stood tall and prominent behind the house. Fanning out from the building, small paddocks of wheat were in various stages of harvest. In one, a team of bullocks were pulling a large box-shaped machine on wheels. The row of spiked prongs at the front of it appeared to pluck the heads of the grain as it travelled across the paddock. In another field, labourers were slashing the tough stalks of maize, while men raced through the crop trying to scare away the flock of cockatoos eating the grain. Nearby were cottages and stables, while in the distance another outbuilding sat long and low among swaying grass. Washing fluttered near one of the smaller dwellings and smoke hung above chimneys. Brandon was sure he smelt freshly baked bread. Not the teeth-grinding variety he'd eaten that morning, but the kind that warranted churned butter and perhaps a drizzle of honey. He thought of what it must mean to own such a holding. A property of green and brown and gold. Ripe with opportunity. The kind of potential that only came with rich soil. It was a place of wild beauty civilised by man.

At the front gate to the homestead, Brandon paused. Not since his arrival in Sydney had he seen such a home. Had the sprawling, single-storey building been capable of movement, he imagined it would have flounced as it walked, lifting its cast-iron lacework to avoid brushing the dirt as it circled the picket fence that enclosed it. He was no architect, but he saw in the timber panelling and the stained-glass windows abutting either side of the front door the highest quality of workmanship.

'You should go around the back.' The girl Hetty was walking towards him. She stopped at the gate where he stood. Now that he could see her face properly, he guessed her to be aged in her early twenties.

'You're Irish,' said Brandon.

'And?' she asked, flicking her blonde hair. She was no longer the meek servant of the other day. 'Around the back,' she repeated.

'I'm not one of their domestics,' replied Brandon stiffly. Opening the gate, he walked up the dirt path to the entrance, pleased to see that the girl hadn't persisted with her advice but instead was returning to one of the cottages.

The front door opened before he had a chance to knock. A young woman stood before him in a powder-blue gown, the skirt puffed out by a fashionable crinoline. He recognised her instantly. The scratch on her cheek was scabbed and swelling slightly about the edges.

'Good morning,' he said politely, removing his hat.

She tilted her head and widened already expressive eyes, her gaze falling on the axe he held. Brandon noticed her wariness and rested it against the wall. The woman instantly appeared more at ease. 'The Irishman returns,' she said.

Unsure how to respond, he spoke quickly. 'I'm here to see—'

'Fancy, an Irishman keeping his word.'

'What?' asked Brandon.

'To agree to an undertaking and actually do it,' she replied.

'Lizzy, who are you talking to?' A man's voice sounded from within the house.

'An Irishman,' she replied, 'although of what make I'm not sure. What are you? Gambler, highwayman, educated, rich or poor?'

A grey-eyed, full-bearded man joined the woman in the doorway and met Brandon's gaze with equal interest. Brandon presumed him to be Mr Truby. 'Can I help you?'

'In return for allowing him to collect a tree that had fallen onto our land, I asked that he come here,' said the young woman.

The man's shoulders relaxed. The cloth of his dark suit was scattered with wood shavings. 'Of course. The Irish boys. I'm sorry, we've had some thieving going on and only yesterday ten head of our cattle were driven off. There's talk of bushrangers. Have you heard?'

'No. We've been in the forest,' said Brandon.

'Can't you see how pale he is?' said the woman.

'I thought you might know something. Most of them that take up robbery under arms are Irish,' said the man, quite unapologetically.

'I can't help you,' said Brandon, choosing to ignore the insinuation.

'Of course you can't. I thought there were two of you.'

'My cousin's taking the timber to the mill.'

'Oh. I was rather hoping there would be two of you so that you could start straight away.' The man walked down the front steps, and behind him the woman closed the front door.

Although a little startled by the informality of their meeting, Brandon kept pace with the property owner as they walked the width of the house. A long veranda sat empty, apart from a wire cage. It was installed on legs and raised to table height, and inside separate enclosures two falcons were perched, their heads covered by leather hoods. The largest flapped its wings as they passed. Brandon watched the raptors until they reached the corner of the homestead.

The rear of the garden was unfenced and kangaroos hopped lazily from their path to graze in the shade of the trees. The centrepiece of the garden was a collection of large earthenware pots placed in concentric circles, filled with red and white roses and clumps of lavender. In the middle of this carefully laid-out arrangement stood a life-size statue of a woman. It appeared as if the flowers were planets and the woman the sun around which they revolved.

'My niece's addition. Quite fetching, isn't she?'

His niece. He'd thought her to be Mr Truby's wife. Flimsy clothing had been carved over the statue's figure, which did nothing to hide her womanly features. Brandon was unsure how to respond. It was such a thing of beauty that he felt unworthy of the statue's presence. He rubbed at the growth on his unshaven chin and concentrated instead on the fifty or so cedar trees clustered around the house. This was the timber that had surrounded the homestead on his approach, and he saw now that they formed part of a much larger stand. A portion of it had already been felled, the timber lying on the ground.

'I'd like them cut down,' said the older man. 'All of them. Once the second storey is built, they'll block the view.'

Brandon glanced at the house and then back to the man who he was now certain was Mr Truby, though he was yet to introduce himself. 'You'd build a house out of cedar?'

'We already have,' said the man.

'But it's worth—'

'A lot of money? Yes, it is. But it's a ready-made supply and I own it.' He gave a little smile at this important fact. 'And all of the cutting can be done here. Which is why my niece, Miss Schaefer, was quick to take advantage of your presence on my land.'

Brandon considered what it would mean to stay in one place for a time, then he thought of Sean. 'I'm sorry but my cousin and I work for ourselves. Besides, why would you be wanting to cut down these trees? They must be a good windbreak and offer fair shade in the hotter months. A man is always angling for a cool place to sit once the heat arrives.' He was aware of Mr Truby's scrutiny as he walked a short distance away and surveyed the area. The silent cedars, the marble woman, the roses and low shrubs and, at the far side of the garden, a half-dozen trees whose branches littered the ground. 'You'll only have a few straggly gums left. And a big house like this – well, it's like a painting. It needs framing.'

The man studied the stand of eucalypts at the opposite corner of the garden. 'You know, I've lived here for nearly thirty years and during that time I doubt anyone has spoken so plainly to me. I'm John Truby.'

'Brandon O'Riain.'

'You've had some learning regarding these things?' asked Mr Truby.

Brandon wanted to say yes, wanted Mr Truby to know that he was more than what he appeared. 'No, but I've travelled some, worked odd jobs and I've spent a few years out in the Big Scrub. You see things after a while.'

'Like what?' asked Mr Truby, with interest. 'Don't hold back, lad. Speak.'

'Colours, for a start. When I first arrived in the bush, the only thing I saw was a tangle of brown. A scrubland seared by the sun. Now I see silver and white, blues and reds, grey and brown. It's as if everything's been tinted in a particular way. And the sounds. A soft wind in the cedars is like a lullaby.'

Mr Truby gave an indulgent laugh. 'I'd take you for a lover of nature, Brandon, except for one significant flaw. While you're obviously not inclined to cut my trees, you'll happily fell others.'

He was right. Brandon appreciated nature, but this man's trees were another matter. If he was going to be felling timber he wanted all of the money from the task, not a small pittance. Besides, he doubted very much that he could convince Sean to work for an Englishman.

'I understand that cedar-getters make a lot of money,' Mr Truby said. 'I've also heard that it's gambled away or spent on rum.'

'Some do that,' agreed Brandon.

'But not you?'

'I have a young stepsister to care for.'

'Ah. And does she travel with you, this stepsister of yours?'

'No, she's in the village,' said Brandon.

The Englishman assessed the cedars and then Brandon. 'It must be trying for her with you boys spending most of your time away cutting. If you took this job, you'd be closer to her. You'd have a place to live. I have a mill and men ready to saw the trunks into planks. We only need cedar-cutters to begin.' When he noted Brandon's hesitation, he held up a finger for emphasis. 'And we'd only cut down half the cedars to start with. We'll leave the ones that are most beneficial in terms of shade and test your theory before we proceed further. How would that be?'

'I'm hoping for something more permanent,' replied Brandon, although the offer of housing was appealing.

'Are you?' asked Mr Truby thoughtfully. 'What else can you do? Can you ride a horse?'

'No.'

'Have you worked with cattle?'

Brandon shook his head.

'Can you repair a wagon wheel? Mend a harness? Winnow grain?'

'No,' said Brandon, his hopes of permanent employment fading with every passing second.

'Well, what can you do apart from cutting trees?'

'I was a shepherd in Ireland. I know a lot about sheep.'

'Pity,' Mr Truby sniffed, 'I don't have any.'

The opportunity was slipping through his fingers.

'I'm willing to learn.'

'Cut my trees and I'll have one of the men teach you how to ride.'

'And then?' asked Brandon.

'Then we'll see if you're worth employing,' said Mr Truby.

Three years earlier, Brandon had watched as Sean hid Mr Macklin's mare in a ruined cottage. That was the first and last time he'd had anything to do with horses. But to learn to ride one, to own one, well, here that meant something. It was the dividing line between the rich and the poor, between a man of ability and a drifter still seeking reward. In this country, the average man went through more leather soles than backsides of trousers.

'I'll have to speak to my cousin first.'

'You do that. And then come back with him,' said Mr Truby.

'And my sister?' asked Brandon hopefully.

'Let's see how the felling goes first. No point moving the whole family if things don't work out.'

They walked back past the roses and statue. Brandon spun on his heel, catching a final glimpse of the semi-naked beauty, before following Mr Truby around the side of the house. As they passed the birdcage, one of the falcons made a clicking noise.

'My niece's pets.' Mr Truby stopped in front of the enclosures. 'Magnificent specimens, aren't they? But I see that you don't care for them. You should make a study of birds, as you have with the colours of our bush, Brandon. They imitate our human lives almost exactly with their courtship and nesting, and the flashing of plumage to ward off competition. And yes, some also kill to survive.'

'It's the killing for sport, I don't agree with. That and allowing things to die through indifference,' replied Brandon.

'Indifference. A great many things in this world suffer because of indifference. I would hazard that many an Irishman would be quick to blame the English for the difficulties that have beset your people.'

'I wasn't referring to Ireland,' said Brandon, concerned at having caused offence. Working the previous season with Hackett's men had by necessity boosted his confidence, but he was aware that it had also made him outspoken at times.

'Don't worry, lad. I have become argumentative in my older years, which undoubtedly comes from having a young person draining my finances. But it's important to gauge an Irishman's sentiments before he's welcomed into an Englishman's domain. The times are ripe for disagreement, which makes us more wary than usual.' He continued moving along the side of the homestead, Brandon following. 'You've had some schooling?' he asked with interest.

'I went to school in Tipperary for a time and there was a teacher on the ship we came over on. We talked of many things, from ancient lands to the oceans and currents. What New South Wales might be like. And she was kind to my stepsister,' explained Brandon.

'An educated Irishman. Excellent. You and I will have plenty to discuss then when you're not cutting down my fine stand of trees. It's too late to be walking to the village now, Brandon. If you go over to that cottage, Hetty will feed you. You can leave in the morning.' He indicated the small house Brandon had seen Hetty walking towards earlier, and then went indoors.

Brandon retrieved his axe from the veranda, and made his way to the cottage Mr Truby had pointed out. He knew Sean wouldn't be pleased with this new arrangement, but the Englishman's offer was an opportunity for both of them to learn something new beyond felling, sheep and the growing of cabbages and potatoes. And there was the added benefit of longer-term employment and a roof over their heads. And perhaps a home for Maggie at last.

❧ Chapter 15 ❧

The cottage was tiny, with a sloping veranda and two small square windows on either side of the door. Some fault in construction had caused one end of the building to drop into the ground so that the other end slanted slightly upwards, giving the illusion that the lone chair by the front door could slide off the end of the veranda at any time. Brandon was about to take a single step up onto the veranda when Hetty appeared at the front door, a child tugging at her skirt and a baby in her arms.

'Yes?' she asked briskly. 'What do you want?'

Brandon removed his hat. 'Mr Truby said I should see you about staying the night.'

'What, with me?' said Hetty, affronted. She jiggled the baby impatiently, its small head bobbing with the movement. Next to her the small boy placed a hand in the pocket of his short pants and stared at Brandon.

Brandon's cheeks instantly grew warm. 'No. That's not what I meant.' What was he to tell her, that he was hungry and hopeful of a bed? 'I'm sorry I bothered you.' He stepped clear of her withering gaze and was ten feet away before she called out.

'Wait. Don't leave.' She took a step towards him. 'Please. If he sent you to me, then I'm to feed you. Come in.' She waited until he was on the porch again and then said, 'Boots.'

Brandon scraped his shoes off on the edge of the veranda and placed them close to the door, resting his hat on top. He placed the axe to one side and then took up a position in the doorway, not quite inside and not quite out. The fire in the hearth was smoking miserably, turning the air grey. Hetty settled the baby in a basket under the table, while the boy clambered up onto a chair. She opened the windows a little wider. The still evening did nothing to alleviate the smoke.

'You can come in,' she finally said.

'Shall I leave the door open?' suggested Brandon.

'Come dark I'm not meant to have the door open. Or the windows. It's rules, you see,' she said.

Brandon considered this strange but decided not to ask for further explanation. He lingered near the door, unused to being in such proximity to a woman. Hetty took a three-legged pot from the coals and sat it on the table. They stared at each other across the scrubbed surface, both sufficiently uncomfortable that they dropped their mutual scrutiny almost immediately and concentrated on the unimportant – in Brandon's case, the gappy timber under his bare feet, while Hetty became enamoured with the battered vessel and the wooden spoon that she used to swirl its contents.

Now that Brandon had time to consider her entire face, he saw that Hetty's lips weren't bulbous but in proportion. They were offset against a broad forehead, green eyes and blonde hair that appeared to have been plucked back a good inch or so on the left side of her face. Each element suggested a trademark beauty but combined, her features were mismatched. Her eyes too big, her mouth too wide, her elongated brow resembling the portrait of an English queen and her hair long and stringy. A thick scar reached down across the contour of her temple on the left side of her face, skirting the delicate eye area, to end in the middle of her cheek.

Hetty angled her head, hiding the deep redness from view. The little loveliness she'd been born with suddenly became more vivid with the temporary absence of her scar.

'He's asked you to cut the trees, I suppose.' She polished a spoon on her apron. 'The previous men lasted four days. One of them was a bird fanatic. Fed the pigeons with the bread I baked. The little things gathered in like they were starved. There were droppings all over the statue. You did see the statue. It's a beautiful thing. I couldn't blame Miss Schaefer for letting Glanville out. Not really, although it was a terrible sight the way he went at them birds.' She shrugged her shoulders. 'Are you a bird lover?'

'I like all animals,' said Brandon.

'Miss Schaefer says a person can't possibly like all animals. There's absolutely no prettiness in some. Take cats, for instance. They whine and screech and pee in any freshly ploughed soil, as if it was theirs to do with as they like. And dogs. A good dog will follow you about, happy to do your bidding. Chase a cow into the pen. Bark at the night's shadows. But turn your back and they're hunting the fowls, biting the postal rider and snapping at heels. Miss Schaefer says a person has to be quite selective about the company one keeps. And it's the same with animals. They have to be trainable, amenable and serve a purpose. And most importantly, they have to be the best of their breed. Where are you from then?'

Brandon gathered his wits, understanding that he'd be needing them with this girl. 'County Tipperary. And you?'

'I'm not rightly sure. Clare, I think, although my papers say Limerick. As one borders the other, it matters little. I came out as an orphan and was emptying bedpans for a time until Miss Schaefer hired me. Interviewed me in person, she did. It's just as I said, she's selective about the company she keeps.'

What a motley twosome we are, Brandon thought. He a runaway. She a foundling. Thousands of miles from their island home.

The baby under the table gave a squeal and Hetty nudged the basket with her foot.

'There's parrot soup. I wasn't expecting company.' She ladled out the broth, apportioning it between two bowls and sat the dishes on the table. Then she tore a small loaf of bread in half and shared it with him as well. She lifted the boy from the chair, placing him on the floor and sitting down, gestured to the remaining seat.

Brandon sat and drank from the bowl. The soup was hot and tasty. As he ate, he took the opportunity to look about the cramped interior of the house, and then through the window where the fading light emphasised Truby's garden fence and a low hedge. 'Do you like working for Mr Truby and his niece?'

'It's not really about liking them, is it? I mean, I need a job and a roof over my head. A woman wants to be safe. And it's not all bad. I help clean their house and dress Miss Schaefer. Do you have a wife?' she asked. 'You don't look that old.'

'I'm old enough,' said Brandon. 'And no, I don't.'

'I had a husband. And he left me with these two. I thought Mr Truby would let me go, for squatters don't like single women on their runs. Causes problems with the menfolk. That's why I have to keep my door and windows shut. It's either I bolt myself in, or he does it for me. 'Course, he says it's because one of the men will break in and have their way with me, but I wonder. It's something, isn't it, to be Irish and to be trusted,' she concluded, with a roll of her eyes. She drained the bowl and then, as if realising she had company, dabbed at the corners of her mouth with the hem of her apron. 'But they do trust me.'

'I believe you,' said Brandon.

'There's few other women here, you see. Only Miss Schaefer, Polly the cook and me. The men's wives, those that have them, live in the village. Mr Truby has one of the men help clean house and cut wood. He was a domestic in England before he was sent out here for stealing. It was Glanville that saved me. You see, he doesn't mind me about. He's happy for me to feed him. Think on it. I can thank a falcon I've still got my job.'

Silence fell between them. Brandon slurped down the rest of the soup.

'Where's your husband?' asked Brandon, his mind shifting through the menagerie they'd just covered – cats and dogs and birds.

'Who knows?' She wiped out her bowl with a towel and, filling it again, gave it to the child, who was playing on the floor with a clothes peg. 'He went up into the hills and never came back. It's been a year. Miss Schaefer said that if he was alive she'd send Glanville to find him and peck his eyes out for leaving me, but of course he's dead. He must be. Don't you think so?'

'I really couldn't say.' He placed the empty bowl on the table. 'Thank you.'

'You don't have to go. You can stay and talk awhile. It's the children, isn't it? Puts a man off, having young ones about.'

'No, it's not that. It's nearly dark,' said Brandon. He stood, went outside and pulled on his boots and hat.

'Wait.' She fetched a blanket of stitched pelts. 'Here.' She gave him the cover and then stepped onto the grass, keeping by his side as he searched for a place to bed down. 'That's made from those little furry creatures that climb trees. That's one thing my husband could do. He was a fine hunter,' she said, as if they were old friends strolling in the twilight. 'Do you miss the sea? I do. I'd like to smell it again.'

'It's not far, you know,' Brandon replied, not wanting to be drawn into talk that would remind him of a voyage across immeasurable water, and yet feeling her need for conversation. 'You can take one of the ships from Wirra to the mouth of the river.'

She followed him a little further until he found a stand of trees. Brandon scraped away the branches and leaves on the ground with his boot and then dropped the hide blanket on the cleared area.

'Well then,' he said, feeling uncertain at her continued presence.

'Well then,' Hetty repeated, a little more solemnly. Her reluctance to leave made Brandon nervous. He was aware of the inappropriateness of her presence, particularly as there was still enough light for any inquisitive soul to notice them. Worse, Brandon was growing more conscious by the minute of the soft femininity of her voice. The way her breath rose and fell as she spoke. It was a lulling, beguiling sound.

He sat the axe down and then spread the blanket, unable to formulate any conversation that didn't involve the felling of woody plants, while she shifted her weight from one foot to the other.

'Will you cut his trees?' she asked.

'I have to speak to my cousin first,' said Brandon. 'I'm not really interested in being a hired hand, unless there's the possibility of advancement in the future. There's no money in it.'

'You speak like a man who knows what he wants,' said Hetty encouragingly.

Brandon felt heartened by the genuineness of her interest. 'I want a better life. That's what my parents hoped for. Yours too, I expect.'

Hetty's face was concealed by the gathering darkness, but he heard her sigh. 'We all want a better life,' she agreed.

'It's something to aspire to.'

'And what does that mean, "aspire"?' asked Hetty.

'I guess it means to rise up from where we've come; to try to achieve something great with our lives.'

She gave a gentle laugh. Perhaps she thought his ideas folly. And perhaps they were. However, without hope of success then there was little else to cling to except the prospect of failure and Brandon refused to bow to that end. He wanted what his grandparents in the old country once had. A decent home, food and money, and the pride that came with such circumstances. Not a defeated, round-shouldered father who was prepared to barter his own stepdaughter for the continued right to exist.

'Don't you think that the betterment of one's circumstances is a right every man is entitled to?' asked Brandon.

'My, aren't we one for big words,' said Hetty.

'At least I'm not trying to speak with an English accent,' said Brandon.

Hetty pursed her lips. 'It just happens. I don't do it on purpose. Anyway, in my world the only way a person is entitled to something is if they take it.'

The cries of a child finally forced Hetty to say goodbye, and Brandon was left alone. He sat on the stitched hides, watching as the silhouette of her slight body reappeared several times to stand in the doorway of the lopsided cottage. He was not sufficiently enticed to risk the displeasure of Mr Truby, though his urges made a compelling argument. Instead, he contented himself with the sight of crisp white stars through the treetops. The air was dense with the sweet, powdery scent of freshly harvested grain. Eventually he lay back on the blanket and thought of his old home and wondered what those of his blood that came after him would eventually say about his life.

❧ Chapter 16 ❧

Kirooma Station, 1942

Life, Stella decided, had a strange way of morphing into the fiercely unexpected. Joe carried her up onto the veranda, over the threshold and into the homestead. He twirled her around in circles and then finally told her to open her eyes. Stella did so, doing her best to feign excitement, feeling the pounding in her husband's chest, his enthusiasm undiminished by the miles driven and the land that unfurled about them, warped by heat. Joe hugged her firmly but she saw that his attention was consumed by the view beyond her, out the back door towards his new existence. He set her down on the floor.

'I've waited all my life for this.' Joe took her by the wrists, his grip hard, as if by sheer action he could transfer his excitement into her.

Stella arranged her face into a pleased expression and said nothing. She still felt as if she were moving, like she'd recently disembarked from a ship and had yet to find her land legs. Their journey had encompassed mountains, plains, woodlands, creeks, lakes and rivers. Islands unto themselves. Strange places that were quite unfamiliar to her with names like Nevertire and Wilcannia.

For hours at a time they saw no one, nothing. Not a person or animal, domesticated or wild. It was only them and the country. And the sheepdog, who was slobbering on the back seat. Once they left the hills, the land composed itself into a combination of folds and flatness, its vastness suggestive of eternity. On leaving Broken Hill Joe had detoured, turning north towards Silverton and then driven on to the Mundi Mundi plains. Here they'd stopped where the curve of the earth was visible and while Joe marvelled at the sight, she considered the very real possibility of falling off the edge of the world.

It had not left, that feeling of instability. Her body ached from the long drive, from the bumps and ruts in the road. The searing heat and the stretch of flatness that first greeted them as they set out from the mining town faded into the gentle rise and fall of the land and the hills scattered with quartz skeletons, mounds of crystals shining in the sulphur light of the sun.

It was beautiful, this new scenery, but also frightening. She was no sightseer, able to admire and then drive on. This was her country now. She would have to learn how to belong, when her entire being willed Joe to turn the station wagon around and go home. Even the kangaroos, which were such a novelty after they crossed the mountains, made her feel unwelcome. Now she was the exhibit and they, in their growing numbers, bemused spectators.

'Here we are,' Joe had exclaimed when they'd reached a gate partially twisted at one end. KIROOMA was stencilled on a battered wooden letterbox with a metal latch. He leapt out of the station wagon, opened the gate and then drove through, before getting out again to close it. 'There's only eight gates to go,' he told Stella, hopping back into the car.

'Eight?' repeated Stella.

'Yep. We'll take it in turns. It will do you good to stretch your legs and start building up those typewriter arms of yours.' He pinched her bicep and she brushed him away.

'Are you telling me that every time we want to leave we have to open nine of these?' said Stella.

'It's not like we'll be driving in and out every day. Why do you think we stopped to pick up six weeks of groceries at Broken Hill? You'll have to plan our meals so we don't run out of anything. It's not like we'll be able to run to the corner store. Well, let's get going.'

Gates. Endless gates that had to be dragged across a land that grew redder the further they travelled, as if the earth had suffered a mortal wound. It was too much for her. There was simply too much space. Too much air. Too much sky. And then the homestead, with its peaked iron roof and huge proportions. Large enough to accommodate all of the tenants in her old apartment block. There was a double garage, with a work truck parked inside, machinery sheds, a woolshed and yards, men's sleeping quarters and old bough sheds from another age. It was deserted, a town without a populace.

When Joe left her to walk further into the homestead, Stella felt the loss of him immediately. It was like being cut adrift from the world; he too was moving imperceptibly away from her. She would have laughed at these foolish thoughts had she not felt so uncertain. Instead she followed him into the darkened space. She reached for his hand, but Joe was opening a door that led to a massive walk-in pantry.

'Let the explorations begin,' he announced.

They were in the kitchen, a space lined with cupboards, two stoves and an ancient fridge that needed kerosene to run.

Joe ran his palm over the red-brick walls. 'Sand mixed with cement and dried in the sun. Made right here on the property.' Some of the mortar had crumbled away. He picked at the soft lump of sand. 'They rebuilt the original pine kitchen with these after a fire that nearly destroyed the whole house.'

'How do you know that?' said Stella.

He appeared to be considering how to reply, for he spent more time than necessary studying the bricks.

'Is there a history on the property?' she asked.

'No. It must have been the bank manager who told me about that,' he said.

Orange curtains covered the casement window, which was situated above a wide sink. Stella leaned across the low timber benchtop and tugged at the material. The curtain rail clattered onto the sink in a flurry of dust and unused air. She stepped back in fright. Bright, harsh light filled the room and she blinked at the sudden contrast. Through the window was a narrow veranda looking out towards a paling fence. Beyond it, the shining corrugated roof of the distant woolshed was visible in the reddish landscape.

'Joe, can you help me with this?' She turned back to the room with its solid table and chairs. 'Joe?' There was no reply.

Stella entered the next room and the next, each dark musty space more cavernous than the one before. Instinctively she hugged her arms to her chest, her steps small, almost timid, as she examined the furniture left behind. Brocade sofas and armchairs, small round tables with carved feet, their tops buckled by heat. The statue of a fawn modelled in black and encased in a glass dome. She'd expected an empty house and it was disconcerting to find other people's belongings there, as if the occupants were on a holiday and were due back at any time.

A dim passage led to another room with book-laden shelves. Stella drew the curtains and partial light shone through slatted louvres. The window-space was bow-fronted with an inbuilt seat and before it was a table covered with a dustsheet. Stella lifted the material and discovered a large globe sitting on a three-legged stand, a compass dish at the base of the slender legs. She spun the earth on its mahogany axis, watching as yellow, green and brown – a whole world – showed itself in a single rotation. She ran a finger across the tracks of celebrated circumnavigators, past mighty cities and great nations and rested on a mountain range.

'Terrestrial globe noting all the latest discoveries and geographical improvements. Dedicated by permission of His Most Gracious Majesty George IV, 1825,' Stella read aloud from the decorative medallion. Antarctica was missing. Yet to be discovered, she supposed.

The bookcase covered two walls, the contents facing each other like warring tribes across a field of burgundy carpet. She read some of the names on the leather spines. Tolstoy and Dickens, Keats and Wordsworth. Novelists and poets from another time. She wondered if the previous owners had used the books to transport themselves back into a gilded age while about them the wilderness circled.

There was something about the room that made her feel as if she were once again on that imagined ship, for she grew unbalanced and believed that she could almost hear the splash of waves. She leant on a row of books, blaming the drive for her disorientation until eventually Joe's echoing footsteps drew her further on through a labyrinth of rooms. These fed from wide hallways and narrower passageways, each space containing furniture discarded by the previous owners. Stella found her husband in what she suspected was the middle of the homestead. Joe was looking up at twin chandeliers that, although layered in dust, still gave a lustre to the room that no amount of polishing could produce.

'It's a ballroom,' he said in awe, turning on his heel. 'An actual ballroom.' He pulled on a sheet, uncovering a gilt-edged mirror.

'How do you know?' asked Stella. Chairs lined the walls. She brushed one of the seats and scarlet shone through the cloud of dirt.

'Well, we know it's not the dining room, there's a great bloody table in there.' He grinned. 'Even Mr Wells's homestead wasn't graced with one of these.'

'Why did they leave so much behind?' asked Stella, drawing sage-coloured curtains that concealed no outside view, only tongue-and-groove boards. 'I mean, some of these things are antiques.'

'Three generations of the same family lived here. Apparently the owners had a spread of properties that stretched from Queensland into Victoria. I suppose they made so much money that they couldn't see the point of carting all this furniture back to Melbourne. What normal-sized house would it fit into anyway?'

He was right. Their new home was far from conventional. A single chandelier would have blinded her in her Sydney apartment.

'It's a bit big for us. We'll never use all this space.' She thought of the furniture they'd brought in the trailer from Sydney. There wasn't enough to fill one room.

'You're not really going to complain about the size of the house, are you?' asked Joe. 'Not after that butter-box you lived in.'

'No, of course not,' said Stella, although her tone was defensive.

'People in the city would give their eyeteeth for a place like this. It's a mansion,' said Joe, as he sat on one of the chairs, bouncing a little on the seat as if testing its workmanship. He lifted it, examining the carved legs, and nodded approvingly. 'It's probably a bit of a shock for you, coming from Sydney, but you'll get used to it. That's the thing about having nothing and then falling on your feet. It takes a while to appreciate the change in circumstances.'

'I hardly came from nothing, Joe,' said Stella tightly. Her husband's words reminded her of Miss Vincent from the typing pool. 'It's not like I couldn't afford my own flat,' she argued.

'Hey, sweetie, don't be so uptight. I'm just saying it as it is. This is a massive change. For both of us.'

Stella was beginning to learn how good her husband was at diverting a conversation before it became an argument. She'd hoped he'd seen her as more than a city girl whose days were limited to a nine-to-five office job, a one-bedroom unit and the romantic hope of a boyfriend visiting from the north coast hinterland, but, sadly, she realised that she was wrong. Maybe he believed he'd saved her.

'Your parents' attitude would soon change if they saw this place,' said Joe. He'd scarcely mentioned them since he'd learnt of their refusal to attend the wedding.

'It's difficult for them, Joe. They expected me to marry an Italian. It's nothing against you personally.'

'Really? They've probably got relatives fighting against us overseas,' said Joe.

'Don't say that,' replied Stella.

'Anyway, you can't put everyone into a neat hole and expect them to conform. You taught them that,' said Joe, giving her the briefest of hugs. He circled the room, running a hand across the pine walls, feeling the notches in the timber.

Stella regarded her husband steadily. Joe's shoulders appeared straighter, his posture more upright, as if a fizz of energy had concentrated itself in his body. In comparison, she felt like a wet towel wrung out to dry.

❖

They ate their first meal in the dining room, surrounded by peeling wallpaper, at a table warped by heat. Joe sat at one end of the table and Stella at the opposite. Lord and lady of the manor, he'd said, pulling out her chair. There was enough space for fourteen people between them. Silver placemats, mismatched cutlery and wobbly candelabra completed the setting. The silverware was tarnished black, however Joe insisted on using the items after discovering them in a cabinet. They ate cold baked beans on bread, having accidentally fumigated part of the homestead with smoke from the old-fashioned wood-burning oven they attempted to light.

'I'll give the flue a good bash in the morning. That should loosen things up,' said Joe, patting his stomach as if he'd consumed a feast. He fiddled with the kerosene lantern next to his elbow, throwing light onto the vacant spaces on the walls where paintings had hung, the once-protected wallpaper a vibrant, patterned green.

'And the generator,' said Stella, as mildly as she could. Not only was there no gas but there wasn't even normal electricity, at least not the kind that worked without an engine running in a specified outbuilding known as a powerhouse.

'I'll get it going. It's like the old days, Stella, before the world got all modern with fancy contraptions. Out here in the bush you get up with the birds and go to bed early.'

'But what are we going to do in the evenings?' she asked.

'I can think of a few things,' he said with a wink.

Stella's cheeks grew warm. 'Seriously, Joe.'

'We'll sit in that library of ours. In his and hers chairs like an old married couple and read by the light of kerosene.'

Despite her unease, Stella relaxed a little. 'And when will the overseer be arriving?' There were few things that she knew about this life, but she was keen to show Joe that she was not totally ignorant.

The water Joe was drinking spluttered from his lips. He wiped his mouth dry. 'Overseer? Wherever did you get the idea that we'd employ one of those?'

'I thought all sheep properties employed an overseer and a cook,' said Stella, recalling her conversation with Miss Vincent.

'We can't afford one.'

'Oh.'

'As for a cook, we'd hardly need one of those when there's only two of us,' he continued, his forehead furrowed as if perplexed by her line of thinking.

'Yes. You're right, of course,' Stella replied.

'It's different out here compared to closer-settled areas,' said Joe, more patiently. 'And there's a war on. It will probably be hard to find staff at times. We're in the Strzelecki Desert, you know.'

Stella took a sip of water. No, she hadn't known. But she did now.

⫷ Chapter 17 ⫸

According to some ancient bush tradition that Stella speculated was of Joe's making rather than lore, they were to take sherry in the library before dinner on Friday nights. It was only their second day on the property and she was still to properly unpack, consumed as she was by cleaning the mouse-invaded kitchen and the bedroom, chosen because of its position on the eastern side of the homestead, which, Joe informed her, was vital during the summer months. The room was large and high-ceilinged with tall, louvred doors that opened out onto a veranda layered with red dirt.

She was due to meet Joe in the library soon, however she walked gingerly outside into the evening heat, the grit crunching beneath her feet. A brush fence, made dense with grasses and slim branches, skirted that section of the veranda. Joe advised her to throw buckets of water on the fence at night. If a breeze rose, the bedroom would be cooled as the air blew through it. That's what it was built for, he'd said with authority. The top of the fence was irregular, handmade and old. There were gaps in some sections. Stella pinched the bridge of her nose and wrapped her arm about her body. Earlier, she'd walked the perimeter of the oblong-shaped garden. It was mainly dirt, tufted sporadically with grass. A grouping of shrubby trees grew at the far end, which rather lifted her spirits until she noticed that the branches had spikes for leaves. The orchard was even less enticing – the majority of the fruiting plants were dead.

Not one element of their new home was easy to grasp or accept. Not the dirt or dust, the smelly mice or the aching space, the lack of greenery or the basic requirements of life, water, electricity and gas. Everything was foreign and Stella felt her ignorance acutely. All she had was love. The deep love she felt for her husband. Stella hoped it was enough, for in comparison, Joe was supremely content.

Every time he set foot outdoors, he would let out a gentle sigh and gaze wistfully at the land beyond. Stella loved him for that. For his obvious delight, the pleasure every task gave him. No matter if he walked into the kitchen smelling of sewage after making a new seat for the outhouse or covered in dust from one of his yahooing motorbike rides, his face had the simple look of a man in his element. Her Joe almost appeared to have grown in size. As if the distance travelled marked the beginning of a metamorphosis from which a new man was emerging.

Stella knew that she too would have to find her place if she was ever to transition from city typist to country woman. Getting the house in order would help, but as she stood in the barren bedroom, the space only made habitable by a thin-mattressed iron-framed bed, she knew that letting go of her previous life would be difficult. She was already homesick for the conveniences of Sydney – the clean sanctity of her apartment, the corner shop and her church, which she attended faithfully every Sunday. She'd exchanged the knowable for the unknowable and far from seeing it as an adventure, she was scared.

Outside the sky grew blue-grey. There was a distant rumble and the generator came on, suffusing the room in a wan yellow light. Stella stared at the darkening horizon and then closed the doors, snaking rolled towels on the floor up against them to keep out the gathered soil. She lifted the lid of her suitcase and shook out the full-length teal chiffon halter-neck dress, purchased on a whim with the help of Angelina's coupons the day before leaving Sydney. Other items spilt out onto the rumpled bed. Silk stockings and lacy garter belts, a draped and ruched knee-length dress – the kind Rita Hayworth might wear – and a number of scarves in vibrant colours. She shimmied into the chiffon gown, pulling the material up over her sweaty hips, wiggled the side zipper closed and slipped her feet into kitten-heeled shoes with an ankle strap. Overhead the light grew dim and brightened again. She held up a powder compact, dabbing at the perspiration on her nose, and applied a rose tint to her mouth, rolling her lips over so the colour would take.

Ready, she decided. Stella ran down the long hallway, passing the closed doors of rooms barely investigated, willing herself not to look back. Her shoes reverberated on the floorboards as the power fluctuated. Next time she would leave a lantern in the bedroom, she decided. The dark unnerved her. This was a very recent understanding, thrust as she now was into a place where streetlights no longer shined comfortably through curtains and electricity wasn't controlled by the simple flick of a switch. Stella headed in one direction and then another. Finally she stopped near the library and walked on at a steadier pace.

'There you are.' Joe pulled a record from its paper sleeve. 'How about "Crazy Blues" by Mamie Smith. 1920.' He held up the recording for inspection.

'Where on earth did you find that?' asked Stella.

Joe blew dust from the gramophone and inspected the stylus. 'It was sitting next to the piano in the music room, but I figured we could use it here instead.'

A photograph had been placed next to the globe on the table. Stella picked it up.

'That's my father, Sean, when he was a young man. I made the frame at school the year before he died.'

Joe's father was barrel-chested with wavy hair and a short scruffy beard that ringed a square jaw.

'What was he like?'

'He grunted a lot instead of saying yes or no. Never spoke much, really. It was like he had a knot inside him that couldn't be undone. But every Sunday he'd sit in the shade and watch us play cricket. Keep the score. I think he added a few runs to my tally because I always came out better than what I should have. Made Harry furious.' Delight shone in Joe's eyes. 'Of course, Dad was pretty old by then. He was already in his late sixties by the time Harry went to war.'

'Was it difficult having an older father?'

'I didn't know any different, although I suppose Dad's age combined with the gap between me and Harry meant I was a bit of a loner,' admitted Joe. 'When I turned ten, Harry was twenty-six.' He took the image from her, placing it back on the table.

'Why did your parents wait so long to have you?'

'There were other babies, but they didn't survive,' Joe said matter-of-factly.

Stella thought of her parents and her Italian heritage that had shaped her life. Difficult though they were, she couldn't imagine losing them, as Joe had lost his over twenty years ago. First his mother from cancer, followed by the death of his father in a cane fire.

'I wonder who the other person was that's been cut out of the picture. You can just see a coat sleeve,' said Stella.

'It could be anyone, I guess, but Harry said the photo was taken here in Australia so it's possible it was his cousin, Brandon. They came over from Ireland together. Were as thick as thieves for a long time. They went into business as cedar-cutters. I had a conversation with Brandon once. Years ago now. He asked me what the one thing was that a man could never hope to regain once he'd lost it.'

'What did you say?'

'Honour. I couldn't think of any other answer. I figured that once a man lost his honour it could never be restored. But Brandon told me I was wrong. That honour could be salvaged through regret and a good deed,' he replied.

'So what is the one thing that can never be restored to a man?'

'Time. Time is the greatest loss of all,' said Joe.

Stella recalled a day a few months ago when they'd sat side by side on a beach in Sydney. Joe was unsettled on the towel, his brown face, neck and arms contrasting against his white torso and legs. He concentrated on the clouds bubbling on the horizon as the sea moved towards them in foaming curls. She'd thought it a glorious day however after only an hour Joe complained that they were wasting time. They'd departed soon after. Brandon appeared to have left an indelible mark on her husband.

Joe placed the disc on the record player, positioned the needle and then wound the handle on the side. Immediately the library was filled with the sounds of jazz. He approached Stella and bowed, then, placing an arm around her waist, whirled her about the room, flurries of dust rising as they danced. The tune was scratchy and occasionally the record skipped a beat as they pounded across the floor, however she couldn't help smiling. When the tune finished, she flopped into one of the chairs. Joe handed her a glass of sherry.

'To us,' he said, raising his glass.

'To us,' said Stella. 'Heavens, that's strong.' She licked her lips.

'Happy?' he asked.

'Yes.' And she was, as long as Joe was with her.

They sat in threadbare armchairs sipping their sherry, staring at the rows of books that would take a lifetime to read.

'A person could get a full university education in this room,' said Joe. 'New dress? I like it.'

She patted the material across her hips, grateful for the girdle that held her waist in tightly, although she could feel herself spilling out from the top and bottom, as if she were overripe. 'I bought it for our honeymoon,' said Stella, giving him a suggestive smile. She lifted the folds of the full skirt and waved them sideways as if she were a can-can dancer, grateful for the cooling air.

Joe sat his glass on a round table inset with tooled leather. 'About that,' he said leaning forwards. 'We might have to wait a little longer before we go.'

'But, Joe, we agreed on January. Everything's booked.'

'There's a war on,' he reminded her again.

'That means we won't be spending Christmas in Sydney either, or New Year's Eve,' Stella complained, her disappointment obvious. Joe had promised her a week by the seaside at Manly, allowing her time to visit her family. She'd hoped that by then their attitude towards her marriage might have thawed.

'I doubt anyone will be moving anywhere for a while. Besides, this place is extraordinary, Stella, and we've only just arrived. I couldn't possibly leave in six months. It's too soon. There's so much for me to learn. And you need time to get this mammoth old house sorted.'

Stella rotated the stem of the sherry glass on the arm of the chair. She wasn't immune to the implications of war, but their all-consuming three-month romance had rather obliterated the austerity of wartime Sydney.

'Stella, darling. We will go. But not yet. I'll send a telegram next time we're in Broken Hill. Let the hotel know that we'll have to postpone, for just a little while,' he added.

'For how long?' she asked.

'I don't know. This is our business now. We have to be on top of things.'

He was right, she supposed, and the house did need a lot of attention. 'Okay,' she relented, trying to be mindful of the precarious state of world affairs.

'I know you're disappointed.'

'I was looking forward to it. I've never really been anywhere,' said Stella.

'Well, you're somewhere now. And isn't this better than Sydney? There's nothing there for a person. It's soulless.'

The wind rattled the windows. Something hit the glass, almost like a scatter of small stones, as if someone were trying to catch their attention. Stella rose from her chair and, moving quickly, shut the windows.

'A dust storm,' said Joe, twisting in his seat and peering into the night. 'Buckets of the stuff, how amazing!'

They watched as the earth's layers pounded the house, the grit sliding down the windows. Stella couldn't quite share her husband's enthusiasm.

'I'll be heading out to have a drive around tomorrow,' said Joe, as the storm rose in intensity.

'I'll come too,' said Stella.

He went to her side and cupped her chin. 'Not this trip. I need to get my bearings and there's no point both of us getting lost. Besides, I'm taking the motorbike and I'll be away for a few nights, camping out. Roughing it. I think it's too much of an assumption this early in the relationship to be expecting that of you.'

'But I wouldn't mind, really,' said Stella. It seemed too much of an assumption on Joe's part to believe that she would be comfortable staying in the house alone at this initial stage.

As if foreseeing an argument, he rested his hands on her shoulders. 'I've shown you how to start the generator and the stove's working well now. There's plenty of firewood. One thing we're not short of is mulga to burn. You'll be fine,' he emphasised.

'But I don't really want to stay here by myself,' said Stella.

Joe frowned teasingly. 'My Stella, afraid of the dark?'

'It's not that. It's just a lot to get used to. And this place is so isolated,' she explained.

'Makes the off-chance of a visitor even more exciting, eh?'

'I'm serious,' said Stella. 'You never said I'd be by myself out here.'

'Stella, honey, this is our property, for as far as the eye can see. There's nothing to be worried about.'

Stella shrugged off his grasp. 'Fine. Go.'

Joe backed away, his palms lifted in a gesture of surrender. 'Everything will be fine, Stella. You'll see, sweetheart.'

'How long will you be away?' she asked stiffly.

'I'm heading out to find the main bore. Three days. Four at the most. Will you miss me?'

She thought of the long hours ahead. 'Yes,' she answered honestly. 'I already do.'

'Then come here,' he said quietly. 'I've a mind to start working on an heir.'

≪ Chapter 18 ≫

There was a line of perspiration along her upper lip. Her neck was stiff with tension. Three days, he'd told her. Four at the most.

The shock-induced composure Stella had experienced since their arrival was dulling under the strain of concern. It was impossible to believe that they'd only been on the property for seven days and Joe had been absent for most of that time. It felt like a month. A year. An eternity. The silence amplified even the slightest groan or rasp from the homestead. The sounds of traffic and typewriter keys were now ghosts from another age.

The rooms angled out from the ballroom like an empty cobweb. The ceilings were twenty feet high. The floorboards misshapen through age and weather. She walked down one passage and into another, still trying to find her bearings in the barn-like structure, turning to glance behind her as the wind rushed around the corners of the house, causing things that she was yet to locate and batten down to swing and bang. She thought of Hansel and Gretel and their trail of crumbs and knuckled at the moisture gathering in her eyes. Something slithered across the floor and she gave a shriek and ran in the opposite direction, turning left and then right.

Stella pushed at a door and it creaked on opening. The room contained a narrow four-poster bed. The remains of mosquito netting hung from a wire frame. She walked into the room and sat at a dressing table with an oval mirror. Just sat there, staring at her reflection in the half-light. The mirror was pitted. The timber surrounds cracked. The woman staring back at her wore a multi-coloured scarf on her head, tied at the top so that the ends stuck out like rabbit ears. She could drive out in search of Joe. Follow his tracks in the station wagon. Perhaps he was broken down on the side of the road and even now trudging home, the dog by his side. Perspiration coated her body. The idea of going out there alone made her bite at her nails. She was a child of bitumen and corner shops, pushbikes and park swings, of smart dresses and pretty gardens. This new place was beyond her. She pressed a palm to her forehead, recalling Miss Vincent's cruel words. The woman would laugh in her face if she saw her now.

Stella wiped away a tear and opened a drawer. The timber stuck a little and she pulled on the knob, the dressing table shaking with the effort. The drawer held an assortment of forgotten items: a silver-backed hairbrush; rubber bands; a pot of dried ink and a number of steel nibs, the type that were used for old-fashioned writing pens. She pushed her hand to the back of the drawer and her fingers closed around a book. It was a clothbound Bible, the brown hand-stitched covering worn by use.

On the first page the name *Hetty* was written in an ill-formed hand, and beneath it was what she assumed to be a location, or perhaps a property: *Mr Truby's Run*. The book was illustrated. Adam and Eve stood in a wooded glen at the tree of the knowledge of good and evil and on another page Judas betrayed Jesus. Stella flipped back to the title page and a folded letter slipped to the floor. She opened it carefully. The paper was thin and the ink faded, and the writer's hand, although readable, was poor.

I know you had to leave. I understand. But try as I may I can't help thinking that if things had been different, had we not been

who we are, that we might have been together. I look back
now and see how strong you were, to leave of your own accord,
when I should have been the stronger one and sent you away
sooner. But you were right. There never would have been any
peace for either of us if you'd stayed.
B

Stella stared at the scratchy writing and searched the drawer for
the rest of the letter. Surely there was a first page, with a name
and date and perhaps an address. But the drawer held no more
secrets and she again caught her reflection in the mirror, feeling
a shiver down her spine. She understood very little of the history
of Kirooma Station. Joe spoke knowledgeably about the property
when he chose to impart information, and she wondered what
other secrets were locked in her husband's brain. Only one family
had laid claim to the property they now inhabited, each term of
possession decreasing in years as if the resolve that was required
to live out here had lessened with each new generation. That she
could understand.

Replacing the note in the Bible, Stella picked up the hairbrush,
pressing her palm against the bristles. Caught within the soft
spokes was a long hair. She thought briefly of the woman it had
once belonged to and the unknown difficulties the letter hinted at,
and returned the brush to the drawer.

'Stella, where are you?' Joe called.

'Joe!' She picked up the Bible and ran from the room.

He stood at the end of the hall, his face dusty and his clothes
filthy.

She rushed to him, hugging him tight. 'Where have you been?
You're a whole day late. A whole day. I've been beside myself with
worry.' She started crying and then bashed at his chest. 'There's
a snake in one of the rooms and the generator stopped working.
I had no power last night.'

'Hey, everything's all right.' He wiped a tear from her cheek. 'I'm
sorry. I lost track of the time. There's so much to see.' He linked

her arm through his and together they walked down the hallway and through the house, Stella dragging her feet, Joe whistling.

In the kitchen Joe gulped down cloudy water from a tap that fed from the outside tank, smacking his lips as if it were nectar.

'I'll have a look for the snake later. I found the main bore and camped there last night.'

She had no interest in their damn bores. 'That water is bad,' she said, infuriated by how casual he was being.

'It's bore water, love. There's water three hundred feet down. We'll never run out. Boil it if you like. It won't get the taste out of it but it'll kill any bugs that might upset that city stomach of yours.' He gave a wink and heaved himself up on the benchtop. It groaned under his weight. 'What's that you've got?' he asked, staring at the Bible in her hand.

'Just a book.' Stella placed it to one side.

'Have you worked out a plan for the garden yet? I was thinking of replacing those dead fruit trees in the orchard. There's an orange tree that I reckon would come good with a bit of pruning. And the eastern side would be best for a vegetable garden. The hoe's in the shed next to the laundry block.'

Stella thought of the boxes of dry groceries that still had to be unpacked, and their own belongings that they had piled at one end of the dining room until the rooms that they'd decided on placing them in were clean of dust. Walls had to be brushed, cobwebs removed, floors swept, washed and swept again such was the dirt in the homestead.

'I haven't been able to do any laundry. There's no hot water,' said Stella miserably.

'Sure there is. You just have to load the wood box under the boiler and light it up. I cut plenty. The pile's out the side of the meat-house,' he said helpfully, as if she'd forgotten.

His expectation was so great Stella thought she might scream. 'Can you at least help me with the garden?'

'When?' He slipped from his seat and checked the calendar, which he'd nailed to a cupboard. He hitched his trousers up and turned back to face her. 'The sheep are due to arrive tomorrow. I'm not sure how many of the drivers will be staying with us but you best have a half-dozen beds made up for them just in case. I can't put them up in the men's quarters. The building isn't habitable.' He was still smiling, as if they had lived this way all their lives.

'You never said all these people were coming, Joe! Apart from a couple of the rooms, the rest of the house isn't liveable yet. And what about bedding? I don't have linen for all those men.'

'Don't worry about that. Most of them will have their own swags.'

'And food?' said Stella. 'What am I meant to feed them?'

'Potatoes, carrots, pumpkin and a couple of good-size legs of mutton. That'll hit the spot. Meat and vegetables. A hearty Irish–Australian meal.'

'And you expect me to cook all that? By myself?' she asked, stunned.

Pasta, that was Stella's specialty. She'd prepared it on Saturday nights in Sydney when Joe had visited. The rest of the time eggs, mince and baked beans formed the basis of her evening meals.

Joe came to her and lifted her onto the bench. 'Stella. I know this is new for you. It is for me as well. You must understand that I'm going to have my hands full on the property. The house and garden, that's your domain. I can't be expected to do your share as well. And it won't be so difficult, once you get the hang of things. Make a list of all your jobs and then do as much as you can each day. Before you know it, you'll have everything under control.'

Stella wanted to complain, however she felt physically flattened by his calm, rational approach. There was no argument that she could mount that wouldn't reinforce how she was feeling – like an incapable female, alone and out of her depth.

'Tell you what, I'll make the old orange tree my special project,' Joe said. He reached for the Bible and read the name written there before unfolding the letter. He looked at her questioningly and then read it.

'I found it in one of the bedrooms,' Stella explained flatly.

'That's it?' asked Joe, turning the page over. 'Nothing else?'

'Were you expecting something else?' she asked.

'Of course not.'

'It's like a letter of apology,' said Stella. 'It's important, don't you think, to apologise when you do something wrong. Like being late coming home.'

Joe reread the letter. The lines between his eyes creased. He wasn't listening to her.

'Do you know much about the previous owners?' asked Stella. 'Did any of them have a name like Hetty? That could be short for Henrietta.'

Joe placed the Bible on the sink. She thought for a minute that he was avoiding an answer, but then he patted the book thoughtfully. 'It could be anyone.' He pulled the scarf from her hair and then rested his hands on her thighs, firm and possessive.

'I feel sorry for her, and whoever B is,' she said. 'The person who wrote it.'

'Hmm.' Joe edged his fingers under her skirt.

'Aren't you intrigued?' persisted Stella.

'Not really,' said Joe, probing an ear with his tongue.

She was intrigued. The letter and Bible presented her with something else to think about other than wood or water or lonely nights.

. . . if things had been different, had we not been who we are, that we might have been together.

Those were not the words of a parent to a child. Or of one sibling to another. They were lines of love, filled with regret. Stella couldn't help wondering who the parted couple were. She assumed the letter was addressed to Hetty, the owner of the Bible. Perhaps one of them had been rich, the other poor, or the union simply not deemed suitable by their respective families. She could relate to that.

Joe cupped her chin. 'Where are you?'

'I'm not sure,' she answered truthfully. 'I feel like my whole life has been turned upside-down.'

Joe wasn't interested in talking anymore. His mouth was on hers and although Stella hated him for leaving her alone, she was aware of a hollowness within her that needed to be filled, and she hated herself more for that. She lifted her skirts and tilted her hips, wondering if this time a child would come of it.

⋘ Chapter 19 ⋙

Kirooma Station, 1943

Stella followed the dry creek bed, a braided channel of fine sand and silt-sized particles that slipped beneath the wheels of the car like rusted silk. All around her, a palette of red and coppery hues spread their rippling folds, the variation broken only by mulish trees and shrubs, and animals smart enough to take cover from the heat. She drove onwards, one hour merging into another, her view blighted by the ruddy sand, which bounced towards her like a playful child. The remains of rocks corroded by air and water buffeted the vehicle before eventually falling to earth. Deep-rooted mulga trees, their needle-like leaves standing erect to avoid as much of the midday sun as possible, clung to the wide, weather-scoured passage. She imagined water rushing along the hollow, which, to the uneducated mind, may have simply been another depression among the sandplains. But the creek did run. Roughly once every twenty years.

The work truck stalled climbing the side of the hummocky waterway and Stella swore softly. She hit the steering wheel in frustration and then reversed the vehicle back onto the familiar track. An eight-mile walk home was hardly an enticing thought yet nor could her nerves stand another minute of not knowing whether Joe was all right. Why did he keep doing this to her? She complained and worried and begged him not to go bush for long periods and still he kept up his wanderings as if her objections were unimportant. As if *she* were unimportant. But two days ago it had been her birthday and Joe had promised to return in time. They'd planned a celebration and she'd made him swear on Hetty's Bible to keep his word. How could he have forgotten about it, when the occasion was a single bright spot in a calendar of blank squares?

The red sand began to lift the further west she drove, the wind blurring the dunes so that the earth's surface appeared as low, rolling waves. The track cut north-west and Stella kept to the narrow trail until a smudge of brown began to grow on the horizon; a bulky accumulation of dirt swirling towards her. Stella stopped the truck near a scatter of trees and, using them as a windbreak, pulled the flipper windows closed. The storm hit side-on, buffeting the vehicle with wind and dust. She held tight to the steering wheel as sweat traced her spine and the country grew dark and blurred. The smell of dirt, solid and musty, filled the cabin. It was as if the earth were sweeping clean its surface, ridding itself of the old and the decaying. She shuddered at the force of the place she now called home.

When the worst of the storm had moved eastwards, Stella wound down the window, grateful to escape the airless compartment, and studied the map annotated with her own landmarks. Joe had finally given her a basic tour of the property a few weeks after their arrival last year, and had presented the chart with a flourish, as if it were a priceless diagram that might well lead to treasure.

Stella could now drive safely about a small portion of their land by following four defined tracks marked out in compass directions. The partial roadmap of their territory resembled a Latin cross. The homestead was located where the long and short beams intersected, with the vertical length pointing north-west to the salt pans across the border. Each length of road had been calculated by Joe. The three shorter arms measured a distance of fifteen miles, the longest over thirty. The roads converged into tracks that eventually merged into the hoof prints of sheep at the very ends. These were Stella's predetermined limits, and she was quite happy with this arrangement. She knew roughly where the main bores were. How long it took to get from the front paddock to the middle one. The number of gates along each route and the importance of carrying water should she become stranded. Not that she ventured from the homestead too often.

After Joe's initial delay in coming home during the first week of their arrival on the station, which he jokingly referred to in military terms as going AWOL – absent from where one should be but without intent to desert – an agreement was reached: Joe was to always inform her to which part of their holding he was headed. A week ago he'd unfolded the map and placed a greasy thumb on a paddock that bordered South Australia, the boundary of which formed part of the dingo fence. That's where he was going. And that's where he would return from in time for her birthday. He'd promised with a kiss.

His pledge had brought her out to the end of the known roads and now she sat in the truck at a point where the track narrowed to noth-ingness, sweeping the countryside for any sign of her husband. Stella wasn't sure how many miles it was to the border, but by aligning a finger along the length of the road on the map, she guessed the distance to be reasonably far. Joe's description of the area ahead was one of linear dunes that swept east–west, intersected by hard channels, which was why the motorbike had become his favoured mode of transport. She suspected that the two-wheeler had broken down or run out of petrol. It had been prone to blockages in the fuel line and although Joe maintained the engine meticulously, assuring her that there were no mechanical issues, twice before she'd found her husband pushing the broken-down bike, the dog padding faith-fully along at his side.

Stella drove through lightly timbered areas of rosewood and headed in the direction of a bore that was marked on the map as being located near the corner of the paddock. The road soon became non-existent and she slowed, steering around dead timber and angled tree stumps. Sheep grazed among tufts of grass, running off as she approached. She caught sight of Joe's bike track, which was only just visible in the soil and, with a sigh of relief, followed the tyre impressions for a half mile until the trough came into view.

Not far from the watering spot, sheep camped out in the open. Stella expected the normally quick-to-startle animals to run off, however on approach they remained motionless. She stopped the vehicle alongside one of the sheep. It lay on its side with its throat torn out. Another had been attacked in the flanks. Blood had pooled on the ground, pitted by plundering black flies. She covered her mouth, fearing that her dry retching might produce something fruitful. Once recovered, she continued driving past other animals, all dead from horrific wounds. These were Joe's prized young ewes. Four hundred of them had been carefully selected and then joined with rams purchased at an exorbitant cost. And that money was now bleeding into the soil. It was a disaster. No wonder Joe hadn't come home.

Dingoes. Stella had read about them in more detail once she'd discovered that Kirooma bordered the dingo fence. They were lean, leggy dogs, with a wide jaw, pricked ears and a bushy tail. The animal was a cousin of the wolf, the coyote and the jackal. A killer. A beast more suited to fairytales and horror stories than roaming their land. Stella accelerated, and the truck edged along a slight ridge. Some distance away, sheep huddled beneath trees. The motorbike was parked nearby. Joe's dog next to it. She shook her head impatiently and then something made her look towards the trough. A water leak had turned the area into a small lake with the trough at its centre. It sat like a canoe on an inland sea, awaiting an oarsman to dip his paddle and bring the small vessel to safety.

Her first thought was for the loss of water and then she noticed Joe. He was waist high in the muddy red spillage. Stella beeped the horn and waved. There was no response from him. She cupped her hands and called out to him, her attention briefly diverted by the screech of a white cockatoo sitting in a cage near the motorbike. She frowned at this and then got out of the car and walked down the ridge towards the pooling water.

The dread hit her suddenly.

Joe wasn't standing, he was sitting. Slumped over. Naked.

Stella screamed.

⋘ Chapter 20 ⋙

'What's all the racket about?' yelled Joe.

He stood up, a spanner in one hand, his sodden shirt in another. He wrung the material out in the trough, threw it over a shoulder and began to stride through the soupy bog towards her. He was ungainly in his movements, like a sheep dragging its body in full fleece through the water.

Stella fell backwards onto the soft earth, her tears of concern becoming ones of relief as she laughed at her stupidity. 'I thought—'

'What?' said Joe, when he reached the bank. 'Hell's bells, woman, I thought something was seriously wrong. Or that you had news for me.' A hopeful expression shone through the rivulets of red water trickling down his face.

Stella got to her feet. She knew very well that he wanted to be told there was a child on the way. But how could she tell him that she'd lost the desire to become pregnant, at least until he reverted to the man that she'd married? A man she once believed would come home to her every night. So she'd been asking any hovering small souls to stay away from her belly until a better time. Knowing it was a sin to even think in such a manner, she prayed nightly for forgiveness, however she placated herself with a strengthening argument. Wasn't her husband committing a sin by abandoning her? And what of this place they'd come to? What if there was no God or Virgin out here? What if this land proved unproductive? Then none of it mattered. None of it at all.

'I had to fix that leak, and I was smothered in dirt after the storm. I couldn't see a thing,' said Joe.

She noticed his boots and rifle lying on the ground close by. 'I thought something had happened.'

'It has.' He thumbed in the direction of the carcasses. 'The dingoes killed fourteen of them. I've shot one dog, but with this amount of damage I'd say there's at least two of them.' He removed his hat and wiped at the perspiration on his brow, then replaced it. Sweat had made the grey felt a dark brown where the hatband should have been. He sat on the ground and tugged on his shoes and socks. 'I had to put a few ewes out of their misery. That's what I hate about wild dogs. The damage they do. They only ever want the kidneys. You can bet they came through the dog fence in South Australia. Not through our portion – along the state border. Davis reckons he's seen the dingoes trying to get back through our boundary to the other side.'

'And who's Davis?' asked Stella.

'He maintains the fence. Works for the Wild Dog Destruction Board,' said Joe, as if the mention of another person on their isolated property wasn't surprising. 'Anyway, what are you doing here? Is there a problem?' Standing, he brushed his palms on his wet trousers.

'No. Well, yes. You're two days late, I was worried,' she told him.

He gave a wry smile. 'This is what, the third or the fourth time you've come out in search of me? Give it a rest, Stella. If something happens, the dog will eventually make his way home. I don't want you driving out alone. What if you get a flat tyre or become bogged in the sand and then try to walk back and get lost? It doesn't sit easily with me. Especially now we have a wild dog problem.'

She swallowed the words in her throat and instead said, 'When did you discover the problem with the dingoes?'

'Yesterday afternoon.'

'I see.' So Joe had spent her birthday out in the scrub before the dingoes had even been discovered. He had forgotten her again. Her eyes filled with tears, but it was her body that wept. She concentrated on the wasted pool of water, and envisioned herself wading out into its muddy depths and sinking beneath the silty surface.

'Are you going to bring this Davis to the house? I'd like to meet him too,' she said.

'He won't come to the homestead, love. There's no need.'

'Maybe I'd like to talk to him as well.'

'About what?'

'Anything and everything. I spend some long days by myself,' said Stella.

'He's not one for four walls and a ceiling. He reckons he only heads back to his own place to make sure nothing's been stolen and to fill up his tucker bag,' Joe explained.

'Do you see him often?'

'Every month or so. We often drop our swags near the same spot. He's been out here for years, and the stories he tells. Men going mad, women poisoning their husbands with arsenic. There's even a fence inspector up around Cooper's Corner that rides a horse without his pants on. Can you believe that?'

'No,' she answered blandly. 'You've spent a lot of time with him then.'

'A fair bit, yes. I nearly forgot. I trapped myself a cockatoo. Thought we'd take him home. Keep him as a pet. You can teach him to talk. He'll be a bit of a playmate for you. What do you think, eh? I named him Watson.'

He smiled, shaking out the shirt draped over his shoulder. He put it on, paying no attention to matching buttons with holes. 'And I found this.' He dug in his trouser pocket, then displayed a dark rock in his palm. 'It's an axe-head. See that sharp edge?' He ran a finger along it. 'Not from here, I don't reckon. They would have bent wood around it to make a handle and then probably tied it together with twine.'

131

Stella felt the last fragments of her patience beginning to disintegrate. Yesterday she'd dreamt of lying next to Joe in bed, of feeling the solid security of his body, then her concern began to mount with his continuing absence. Her distress had manifested into action.

'I've been worried sick, and you've been snaring parrots and fossicking for bits of stone.'

Joe's face deflated like a balloon. 'This is important. A museum would be interested in this. And it's not the only piece I've found.'

Stella pictured him on his hands and knees, digging in the dirt for relics while she battled to keep the vegetable plot alive, fought to stop the sand from entering the homestead and spent her evenings alone in the library, hoping there was enough fuel to keep the generator running so there was no need for her to go outside, alone, at night. 'You're a sheep farmer not an archaeologist.'

'That doesn't mean I can't be interested. This is an extraordinary place. There's so much history here. To think, another people roamed this land before us,' said Joe.

'To think,' repeated Stella. The Indigenous Australians never had to adapt. They were here first. 'So you won't be home for a few days?' she said, trying to keep the anger from her voice.

Joe spat on the stone and rubbed the surface before holding it up to the light. 'What? No, not for a few days.' He kissed her distractedly on the cheek. 'Can you take Watson back with you? Set him up somewhere cool with water?'

'Watson,' she repeated, but Joe wasn't listening. He'd already left to fetch the cage, a contraption he'd furnished out of branches and twine. His walk was almost a jog, as if he was keen for her to be gone.

Joe slid the cockatoo along the truck's bench seat, as the bird screeched and flapped. 'Be good now,' he said to the bird.

Stella looked at the pure white plumage and haughty sulphur crest on the top of the bird's head. She felt as if Joe's feathered friend had already evaluated her ability to care for him and was distinctly unimpressed.

'I'm not happy about this either,' she said, getting into the vehicle next to the cockatoo and slamming the door. Beside her, the bird turned his head to the bars of his cage. She thought of Joe's office back at the homestead, with its withered plants resting in jam tins, and the glass jars that held the variegated soils of their land. 'Don't blame me if he stuffs you.'

❦ Chapter 21 ❧

Richmond Valley, 1867

The next morning Brandon woke at first light. Men's voices were breaking through the birdcall. A flicker of movement attracted his attention and he watched a black-and-white bird fluttering overhead before shaking himself fully awake. Folding the hide blanket, he left it on Hetty's veranda and then, axe in hand, pursued the voices past the stables and a field of pale stubble to where men headed towards a paddock of grain. A burly worker swore as a second man threw a number of sacks atop the pile in a dray and then jumped up front. With a wave of his hat as if in farewell the driver climbed up into the cart and struck off along the track in the direction of Wirra. Brandon increased his pace. If he could get a lift in the dray it would save him the walk to the village.

'And where are you running to at this hour with an axe?' Miss Schaefer was dressed in her hunting garb, a falcon perched on her gloved hand. She had come from the direction of the homestead and was heading due west across the paddock.

'Miss,' said Brandon.

'You'll walk with me,' she announced. 'I hear you're to be employed, and as I'm supposed to be chaperoned at dawn and dusk, I'll take advantage of your presence.' She removed the hood from the falcon perched on her glove and the bird swivelled his head towards his mistress. 'Athena, Glanville. Get Athena.' The bird stretched its wings and flew skywards.

Brandon glanced at the departing dray.

Miss Schaefer followed his interest. 'You're heading to the village? Thriving metropolis that it is,' she said.

'Yes,' said Brandon, falling into step beside her.

'To fetch your cousin. Is he once or twice removed? You'll forgive me, but I doubt that my uncle will take to him in the manner that he has you,' she said bluntly.

'He's a good worker,' said Brandon, in Sean's defence.

'But is he a good person? One to be trusted? My uncle is canny when it comes to interpreting the varied aspects of personality. He has made a particular study of it. That and the differences between those saved and lost. Protestants and Catholics. The Orange and the Green. You do understand what I'm talking about?'

'Of course,' said Brandon. He was now wondering at the propriety of a worker escorting a lady.

Miss Schaefer's attention moved to the sky where the falcon circled overhead. Brandon was distracted from the bird's progress by the sight of bloated grey cloud hanging across the range, until Miss Schaefer clapped her hands in excitement. The bird suddenly swooped low towards the timberline behind the men's quarters and disappeared.

'He was struck by your forthright and rational nature. That is quite an irregularity out here for someone in your position. Be ready for his discussions. He is one for vigorous debate, an inclination more suited to parliament than this societal outpost, but it must be expected, for he has read more than any living soul I've ever met. A great friend of his, Mr Handalay, is embarking on an adventure out in the western portions of the colony and my uncle has taken it upon himself to begin compiling a list of all the great works that must be included in their library. You can read?'

'Yes, Miss Schaefer.' He looked again at the wagon. There was still time to catch it.

'Good. Now that we have addressed each other by name, the next time we meet you won't need to be so ill at ease,' she said.

The falcon reappeared in the sky with its quarry, a large bird clutched in its claws. The victim was struggling, causing Glanville's speed and height to alter repeatedly. It appeared to be taking a direct path towards them, eventually landing nearby.

'Is that another falcon?' asked Brandon.

Miss Schaefer clucked her tongue. 'I always doubted Athena would ever be trainable. The first hood I placed on her was ill-fitting and ever since she has been loath to wear one. If you can't keep the animal calm, they are useless. Temperament is everything,' she said, moving towards the grounded falcon and its wounded prey.

'You must excuse me.' Brandon ran after the wagon, his boots skidding in the loose gravel, hat in one hand and the axe gripped firmly in the other. Eventually he caught up with the dray and called out to the two men up front, begging a ride to the village if that's where they were headed.

'Fine day for it,' the driver called, as Brandon drew level with the travelling dray.

'Fine, to be sure,' replied Brandon, trying not to pant.

'You're a strange sort. Running with that there axe as if you were a madman,' said the driver's companion, his lilt revealing Irish heritage. He wore a peaked cap and a dirty necktie, his red nose proof of his hours spent beneath the sun.

'Mr Truby offered me a job,' explained Brandon.

'Did he now?' the man asked, sharing a grin with the driver, who barely took his watchful gaze from the road. 'You cutting down them trees of his so he can build another palace on top of the one he's already got?'

'Probably,' admitted Brandon. He was beginning to wonder if the breadth of the man's curiosity would eventually match the distance to town.

'Don't feed the pigeons,' the man said. 'It took me the better part of the day to rub the shit off that statue and clean up the mess Glanville made. Agreed?'

'Agreed,' said Brandon.

'Well then, lad. No point wearing out more leather on them boots of yours. Get up.'

Relieved, Brandon tossed the axe into the moving cart and then leapt up to sit among the bags of grain.

'I'm Peter and this is Pat. Where are you from?' The man tipped his cap back to reveal a shining bald pate.

'Tipperary,' replied Brandon.

'You'll be wanting to come tonight, then,' Peter continued. 'There's a meeting down at the river, behind the sawmill.'

'A meeting?'

'The Brotherhood. There's news that needs to be shared. You *are* with us?' asked Peter more pointedly.

'Of course,' said Brandon, not wanting to lose his ride but also conscious of falling in or out with the wrong people. He settled back into the lumpy sacks. He wasn't much interested in attending any gatherings. But he'd said the right words and Peter and Pat exchanged complicit nods, assured of their passenger's allegiance.

'What's Mr Truby like to work for?' asked Brandon to change the subject.

'He came out here near thirty years ago,' said Peter over his shoulder. 'Just rode in like the squatters do and selected his run. Been here ever since. Overlanded his cattle from down south and then set about clearing country and planting his crops. He was already rich but he added to his fortune with cedar. 'Course, if he runs out of money he can cut up his house and sell it. Be worth a fortune.' He gave a deep chuckle, impressed by his humour.

'You worked for him long?'

'Long enough. He's good for an Englishman. His wife died with not a child to show for the union. The girl is his niece. Haughty to some, friendly to others. He took her on near ten years ago after her parents died. No fortune, but she'll be wealthy when they carry

137

Mr Truby out of his house in a cedar box. How long you been here for, then?'

'We arrived nearly three years ago,' said Brandon.

'Half of Ireland must be deserted by now. Have you folk left over there?' asked Peter.

'I don't know. We haven't heard anything for nearly a year.'

'Best you make the most of things then, lad. Nothing worse than pondering on what's become of them, not when there's a living needed to be made. So when are you starting with Truby?'

'I'm not sure. I'm yet to discuss it with my cousin and we've logs to be floated downriver and sold,' said Brandon.

'Then we better get you to town. It's been raining up in the hills since yesterday.'

Brandon thought of Sean's itchy feet and smiled.

❧ Chapter 22 ❧

The dray turned into the main street of the village at midday. On Brandon's left were the cool, clear depths where the waters of the Richmond and Wilson Rivers met. An iron paddle-steamer was docked at the wharf, its red funnel emitting a wisp of dark smoke, and towards it travelled a flat-bottomed tug towing a raft of pine logs. Fishing boats and smaller passenger craft ferrying people to opposite sides of the river manoeuvred quickly out of the tug's way, a man cooeeing to another as they passed. Upstream was the shipyard and the provisions store Brandon and Sean sometimes frequented while ahead, a scatter of indiscriminately built timber structures fronted the wide road, which breasted the riverbank with its grassy soil and scattered trees.

Brandon thanked Peter and Pat and, axe in hand, jumped clear of the cart. Moving out of the path of a man on horseback, he stopped outside a supplies store. It was a new addition since his last visit and he briefly admired the window display of gleaming axes with the favoured hickory handles, before wondering where to begin searching for his stepsister. He was more than looking forward to seeing Maggie again. It had been eight months since they'd last seen each other, on the day he and Sean departed for the Big Scrub. He'd felt desolate deserting her and she'd been unable to hide her tears. He looked to the left and then right and started walking towards the far end of the street to the house where Maggie boarded, intent on enquiring where she might be.

The road was busy with riders and walkers. A Chinese man displaying vegetables in a barrow on the riverside called to Brandon as he passed, offering beans and potatoes at a very good price. Brandon crossed the road.

'I know you,' he said to the seller. 'You sold my cousin and me rotten potatoes. A whole bag. Rotten. What do you think a man is meant to live on when he's in the forest?'

'Not me. I sell very good vegetables. Very good. You see?' The man held out a potato. Brandon knocked it from his hand.

'Managed to drag yourself away from your blessed cedar, have you?'

Brandon turned and stared at the young woman who'd called out to him. She was carrying two baskets and crossing the street away from him.

'Maggie!' Brandon exclaimed. His memory of the girl he'd last seen was obliterated by this woman, who might well skin a rabbit merely by the sharpness of her expression. She'd taken on the proportions of her mother, Cait. Everything was average about her. Height and weight. Appearance. Except for her chestnut hair, and those eyes. They were the deepest brown. The colour of the Sargasso Sea. He held up a warning finger at the vegetable seller and was then forced to run at a fair clip to reach her side.

'Maggie?'

'Don't talk to me all friendly like,' she replied without even a glance in his direction, the baskets swinging violently as she moved. 'It's eight months since I last saw you and Sean. *Eight months*. "Don't worry," you said to me when we were running for our very lives in Tipperary. "Don't fret none," you told me when we were on the ship. "I promise I'll get us a home when we arrive," you said.' She looked about them, drawing in the small village.

'Plenty of Irish girls have emigrated to New South Wales but few have been silly enough to go to the bush. I should have listened to them girls I met in Sydney. I should have sure-footed it straight to the Immigration Depot. Got my own employment. Found a nice job with a kind family. Instead, I'm here. Still waiting. Deigning to be graced with a visit from you and Sean.' She dropped the food-laden baskets, bread and carrots spilling in the dirt, and held out her palms. 'I've more calluses and blisters than when I was digging potatoes at home.' There were tears in her eyes.

'Maggie, what's the matter?'

She was sobbing now. Brandon tried to take her in his arms, as he had during her frightened nights in the hull of the groaning ship, however she was quick to use the heel of her palm to push him away.

'I hate you! I want to go home,' she yelled.

'We can't go home,' said Brandon.

She struck out at his chest. 'That's because of you. You and Sean.'

There was hurt on her face, but also intense anger. He wasn't prepared for that. For her unhappiness. He was doing his best. Had been doing his best since their arrival in New South Wales. Within days of coming ashore he'd heard of the money that could be made from felling cedars. So he and Sean joined the rush north-wards to where trees were said to still be plentiful, signing up with Brian Hackett, who needed more men to help fill his contracts. The Richmond Valley was now home. And to Brandon it was as good a place as any to stop.

'At some stage we would have been forced to leave Ireland, Maggie. You know that. Most of the people we knew have probably emigrated by now.'

'I don't know nothing. I only know what happened to me and now I'm here. In this place.' The creases around the corners of her mouth were pulling downwards.

'And if you'd stayed in Ireland,' he asked her, 'what then? Father couldn't afford to keep feeding us all. You would have eventually

141

become a labourer or perhaps have been forced to go to one of the bigger cities to find work. It was either that or the church, for most of the younger men were sure to emigrate if they hadn't already.'

They were standing next to a low-slung timber building that offered bed and board for travellers. There was talk that the owners sold sly grog and, with no permanent police stationed in the village, it was highly likely. A sign promised entertainments on Sunday afternoon following the running of a regatta.

'We should go somewhere else to talk,' suggested Brandon.

Maggie gave a huff and leant down to gather up the spilt food.

Brandon watched her quick, deft movements. The sun drew out the red-gold highlights of her dark hair, her plait swinging across her shoulder. There was a patch of perspiration clinging to the material of her brown dress and on one arm the stitching was beginning to loosen. His stepsister was nearly sixteen. All her growing up had been done in his absence. Among strangers. While he'd been scaling trees, trying to provide a future for them, Maggie had gone from scared child to angry young woman and he'd only seen glimpses of the transformation. He was sorry for that. For not being there for her, however everything he'd undertaken had been done with Maggie in mind.

'Have you heard from Father?' he asked.

'No.' She stopped arranging the vegetables in the basket and looked up at him. 'Have you?'

'Not a word.' He hardened his tone when he saw the shine in her eyes. 'There's no point thinking about them.' Their family had splintered like wood chips.

'He's dead then.' She looked like she was going to cry again.

Brandon took one of the baskets from her and, draping an arm about her shoulders, led her towards the river. 'We don't know that. He could have emigrated to America with the others,' he told her, although he wondered if he was trying to appease not only Maggie's concerns but his own as well. 'Come on.'

He escorted her across the street through a throng of raggedly dressed axemen who were making their way to the travellers' stop, and then began walking along the river in the direction of the wharf. He picked up a pebble and tossed it across the water, the stone skipping three times before sinking. They stopped and stood at the canal's edge, where the lap of liquid against earth drew their gaze, the patterning of the sand changing with each gentle wash that eased along the bank. The mottled dark-green and gold of a large cod swam past, oblivious to their presence, while on the far bank two women strolled, their bobbing parasols like great white birds spreading their wings in flight. They walked a little further in silence and then Maggie sat down with a habitual sigh to stare at the vessel moored at the end of the wharf.

'Another fine captain,' muttered Brandon.

'There's plenty that come unstuck on the sandbars at the mouth of the river,' replied Maggie, sounding like a wizened seaman.

Timber was being winched onboard by a crane from the wharf; long, thick lengths swinging across men and water to be stacked on the deck. Brandon drew his gaze from the action and poked at one of the baskets. 'Who's this for?'

'The Minchins raised the cost of their lodgings so now I run errands to make up the difference, as well as doing the washing for three families.' Maggie spread her hands, examining the reddened knuckles. 'I was cleaning two houses, but I lost them jobs. Nothing I did was good enough for the people that lived there. They said I couldn't clean. That I wasn't c-capable. But I know,' she jabbed at her own chest, 'that it's because I'm Irish Catholic.' She pointed down the road. 'People say things weren't so bad before they built that church. That they worshipped under an old fig tree then. But now there's more of them than us.'

'What are you talking about?' said Brandon.

'Them Presbyterians,' said Maggie. 'That's who I was cleaning for.'

'Sometimes people prefer to stick with their own kind.'

'But you told me it wouldn't be like this. That our life here was sure to be better and we'd be accepted,' complained Maggie, jiggling one of the baskets in her lap. 'Some of them Presbyterians are real nice but others, especially the ones close to my own age, why they cross the street rather than walk on the same side as me.'

'I'm sorry you've had it so hard, Maggie,' said Brandon.

Her chin lifted. 'And what about you? Still living in that ferny glen of yours? Making your fortune with your red-gold wood?'

'You should see it, Maggie. The trees are the tallest you can imagine and when you're high up among the branches it's like you're on top of the world.'

She leant back on her hands. 'And what do you get for being on the top of the world, Brandon? A fine view or a lungful of cool air. Either way it's of no benefit to me, when I make fourteen pound a year and have but a handful of shillings to show at the end of it.'

'Listen, Maggie, I've money now. You know I've been saving.'

Her brown eyes were mistrustful. 'I've seen no proof of it.'

Brandon untied the leather strips holding the pieces of rawhide to his boots and then removed them. Both shoes had holes in the bottoms, and the hide coverings prevented further wear, and hopefully the loss of the pound notes, which he pulled free, fanning for his stepsister's benefit.

Maggie reached for the money but Brandon drew it free of her grasp. She sulked a little and then laughed.

'How much?' she asked, her voice adopting the hushed tones employed in confession.

'Close to fifty pounds since we stepped ashore, Maggie. I've spent nothing except what's needed to survive. Axe-heads, flour, sugar and tea,' he told her. 'And the money I sent home.'

'Where is the rest of it?' she asked.

'Sewn into the waistband of my trousers.' He patted the moleskin trousers he wore and then replaced the pound notes and then his boots, finally securing the rawhide with the leather thonging. 'I want to buy a few acres.' He waited for a response, the hope of a positive answer from his stepsister taking on an importance he'd not anticipated.

Maggie sorted through the basket and absently began chewing on a carrot. 'So you're not going to be a cedar-getter forever.'

'No. There's a man called Mr Truby fifteen mile from here who needs cedar cut. There could be a job there afterwards. Something permanent. You might be able to live there too if it all works out.' He reached for her hand and squeezed it.

'Really?' said Maggie, the beginnings of happiness playing across her mouth.

'You know that's what I want. For us to be together.'

'Do you know what I'd like? A new dress, nut brown. Like the colour of the Sargasso Sea. You remember that, don't you, Brandon? When we got caught in that mighty storm and we were blown far off course. We stayed put for weeks and talked about better times coming. Days of wine and roses.'

'And they will come.' The sun was suddenly brighter with her smiles. Brandon walked to the water's edge, his boots sinking into the soft sand, then he pivoted on his heel to face her. 'Mr Truby agreed to teach me how to ride. You can't get anywhere in this country without a horse.'

'A horse!' screeched Maggie. As usual, she was quick to lose her happy mood. 'I'm rubbing the flesh off my knuckles and you want a bloody horse?' She tossed the partially eaten carrot into the river.

'I'm not walking everywhere the rest of my life,' said Brandon evenly, 'and in the future I don't expect you to either. Anyway, if I can ride a horse Mr Truby might offer me a proper job. I might be a stockman or a boundary rider. And, as I said, when the time's right, I'll buy a few acres.' He squatted in front of her. 'Don't you want that, Maggie? We'd have a home to come back to at the end of the day. You and me. And Sean. Just like I promised.' He wanted her to be happy, and hadn't realised how important that was to him, but Maggie was staring at him as if he were mad.

'A horse. Our problems started with Mr Macklin and his horse,' she challenged.

'Stop it,' said Brandon.

'Fine,' she replied, positioning each basket in the crook of an elbow as she stood. 'I won't talk about it, but don't expect me to forget.'

'Where are you going?' he called after her.

'I don't have no money sewn into my trousers, Brandon. Some of us have to work.'

Brandon watched her go, the baskets swaying in tandem with her hips. She carried the gift of resentment, his Maggie. Waved it about her like a standard-bearer, employing it when least expected so that, although she remained unaware of how he and Sean had saved her from Mr Macklin, she still managed to make him feel responsible for everything that had happened to them, and anything that might confront them in the future.

❧ Chapter 23 ❧

Brandon swung the axe across his shoulder and headed towards the sawmill. He might not speak of the past, however he often thought of that fateful day. The way Macklin had thrown their religion at him and Sean as if it were a piece of rotten cabbage. He thought of the man falling from his horse. Of the dull thump as his body hit the ground. And Sean's anger. And now there was Maggie to contend with. Always Maggie. The fine mood he'd arrived in town with was gone. He swore when he trod in a pile of sticky horse dung.

Ahead, the road was blocked with bullock teams waiting in line to offload at the sawmill or to join the queue headed for the wharf; the jangle of leather and the creak of wheels an undercurrent to talking men and the bellowing of an impatient bullock. Although the road was wide enough for a bullock team of twenty to make a steady U-turn, the street was currently impassable. Men on horseback and those with drays were drawing hard on reins and backing up in an effort to escape the congestion. Brandon skirted the choked thoroughfare by keeping to the edge of the road and headed towards the peaked roof of the sawmill. The lumberyard adjoined the mill and was the place to find news of Sean and the price received for the load of cedar his cousin had delivered. The men working there could also be relied upon to provide reports of where new cedar stands had been opened up or if another navigable waterway had been discovered. History had shown that where there was inland water stemming towards the coast there were also thick belts of red gold.

Sean was standing at the entrance to the sawmill, talking to Brian Hackett. The stringy form of the man they'd once worked for towered almost a foot above his cousin. Brandon was inclined to head directly to the merchant, Mrs McKenzie, and negotiate a price for their waiting timber upstream, before the buyer she employed, Malcolm Jack, gave his opinion on its worth, however Sean noticed him almost immediately. He lifted a hand in greeting, beckoning him over.

Hackett may have given them a start in the cedar business but nonetheless Brandon was in no rush to see the man again. Hackett worked hard but he also drove his men hard and spent any free time standing about a vat of rum, drinking himself into oblivion. Some could handle the heavy workload he gave them, others couldn't. There were two unmarked graves Brandon knew of, where exhaustion and alcohol had fuelled pathetic endings. He crossed the road unwillingly, managing an acknowledgment as Sean greeted him with a typically jovial pat on the shoulder. Hackett gave a surly nod.

'Cousin. You're here. I wondered when you'd arrive. There's a meeting tonight behind the sawmill,' said Sean.

'So I've heard,' he replied.

'See, I told you,' said Sean to Hackett.

The older man stuck a wooden pipe between his lips and chewed on it. 'Thought you'd be too pearly white for the cause.'

His skin was beyond pale, almost transparent – the result of living a life in murky forests and too much grog. But he was fast and strong enough to do his share of cutting. A feat, considering he must have been close to sixty years of age.

'And I thought you'd still be drinking and gambling up in the hills,' said Brandon in response.

Sean gave Brandon a warning frown.

Hackett ignored the comment. 'You shouldn't have left the team, Brandon. We made a killing this year. Hundreds of thousands of super feet of timber. Made our fortunes, we have.' He took the pipe from his mouth and pocketed it.

'And how many of your men were injured this year?' replied Brandon. 'How many maimed?'

Hackett drew in his cheeks until his face hollowed.

'Brandon, steady on,' said Sean. 'You know what it's like when you've just come out of the forest, Mr Hackett. A man gets a bit edgy, what with all the bright light and the people.'

Hackett drew up threateningly close to Brandon. 'You know nothing about anything, lad. Which is why I don't take offence when that mouth of yours starts talking foolish and dangerous.' Hackett's spittle was hot on Brandon's face. 'I gave you a chance, greenhides though you both were. You've got yourself your shiny axes and your saws, and a woeful team of bullocks that would be better off running hot and juicy over a fire, but you're still walking deep into the forest wearing the leather off your shoes. Felling trees in stupid places. You don't like me because I treat my men hard. But I don't treat them any different than I do myself. And most of them have been with me for over twenty-five years. In '41 there were two hundred sawyers working in the great black forests along the Macleay River. And a quarter of them were with me. The land fairly hummed with the song of the blades. That's what it was like this year for the team. As I said, you made the wrong decision leaving.'

'Well, it was my decision to make. Besides, we've done all right,' said Brandon.

'Sure. Chasing a tree that fell off the edge of a cliff.' Hackett smirked. 'Only good enough for coffins and houses I hear.' The man tipped his hat and left.

Brandon turned to his cousin.

Sean was leaning against a stack of timber. 'What? He asked where we were working so I told him.'

'He's not our friend,' said Brandon.

'And he's not my enemy. So don't make him one. He's on our side. Hackett's one of us,' said Sean. 'He's head of the Brotherhood and—'

'Did you sell the timber you carted into the village?' Brandon asked.

'Yes, and I got a good price for the logs that'll be floated down as well. I had no idea how long you'd be gallivanting around with the bird lady.' Sean's hand formed a beak and made a pecking motion. 'So I went direct to Mrs McKenzie. She's a tough one, but I figured it was best to tell her the number of logs in case Malcolm Jack decided to rebrand a few of them and make himself a profit.'

'Good. I was concerned about Jack. You never can tell. There's a job at Mr Truby's if we want it. Cutting cedars next to the homestead. He seems like a fair man,' Brandon told him.

Sean lifted an eyebrow. 'They always are in the beginning. And what about Maggie? I only saw her briefly yesterday. Have you seen her?'

'Yes. And she's seen me,' said Brandon, the image of a furious Maggie tossing a perfectly good carrot into the river not easy to forget.

'Went that well, did it? What is it with you two? One minute you're the best of friends, the next you're ready to strangle each other,' said Sean.

'It's just the way we are. You know that.' Brandon sat the axe-head on the ground and twirled the handle, a circle of dirt forming around it.

'What else can you do with that axe?' said a deep voice.

Brandon grabbed the handle as it slowed. Arthur Henderson, the lumberyard foreman, was heavyset with a permanently furrowed brow and shoulder-length grey hair, making it difficult to decipher his age.

'Good to see you again, Brandon O'Riain. Your cousin gave me a time with his haggling for that last load. I can't promise you the same amount for the next. There's a few cracks in the wood.'

'I know. We'll be pleased with whatever you can give us,' replied Brandon.

'Market price. It's always market price for the quality. Come on,' said Arthur.

They followed him through the mill, which was twice the length of the longest pieces of timber handled there. Logs were stored along one wall near a gently sloping ramp, down which each length could be rolled onto a carriage running on tramway rails. The tracks led to the large steam-engine-driven saw in an adjoining shed, which puffed and spun its leather belts, driving the circular metal with its sharp teeth. Two boys were sweeping up the sawdust and shovelling it into a barrow to be wheeled to a pit outdoors. They cheekily scrunched up their noses on passing and Sean ruffled one of the children's hair in return.

Once outside they continued to the rear of the yard, which ran down towards the river. Three men were throwing axes into a log some distance away. The target was marked with a splash of red paint and each man was trying to hit it. The last thrower struck just wide of the spot, and he pulled the blade free of the wood with an irritated groan.

'I told them it was too far a distance. But there's a five-pound wager and a bottle of rum on this, and of course the acknowledgement of a good throwing arm and a fine eye,' said Arthur. 'And as you've brought your axe with you . . .'

One of the men redrew the line in the dirt. 'Thirty feet, lad,' he said to Brandon. 'You must keep one foot behind the line at all times.'

Sean had started exchanging money with Arthur.

'Hey. That belongs to both of us,' Brandon reminded his cousin.

'You've a vested interest in the competition then,' replied Sean with a grin.

Brandon wasn't interested in the rum or the money, but proving his ability was something else. The three axe-throwers were a grizzled lot. Older than him. More experienced. With meaty forearms and a hankering for free grog. He could tell they doubted his chances to even hit wood, let alone the target. Thirty feet was a length of empty air to tempt any axeman and Brandon was no exception. Far greater distances had been covered by better axemen but today there was only a yard stacked with lumber, some uninterested men and a few feet of air to bridge. Brandon contemplated the size and length of the axe shaft he held and took a step back behind the line. He reckoned on five rotations, six at the most, however there was a slight wind to account for and, with the target on its side, the natural drop of the axe as it fell to earth also had to be considered.

'Come on,' urged one of the men.

Brandon gripped the handle with both hands, lined up the dull end of the blade with the target, lifted his arms and dropped his hands back over his head between his shoulders. He leant back, feeling the weight of the axe tugging at his muscles and locked his wrists and elbows. His mind drew itself inwards until there was only the axe and the distant target, then he stepped one foot forward and released the handle. He felt it slip from his grasp, his fingers stroking empty space, his eye never leaving the log as his body moved forwards. The axe spun, end over end, slicing through air, and landed with a thwack in the middle of the target.

Brandon's heartbeat slowly eased. Around him, the gravelly voiced bystanders broke his concentration as sunlight flashed on the river. He retrieved his axe.

'There's real art in that,' said Arthur, reluctantly handing over money to Sean, who counted the winnings three times before pocketing it. 'If you can cut as well as you can throw, lad, you should be back on Hackett's team.' He held out his hand to Brandon, who shook it.

'You're coming tonight,' Arthur said, his grip tightening. It wasn't a question.

'Of course he is,' said Sean, almost too quickly.

'You *are* coming,' Sean continued, once they were back on the street and alone. 'I said you would.'

'Tell me the point of it, Sean. Really, tell me the reason a man would squat in the dark like a thief with men we don't know, talking about a country we all left years ago.'

Sean stopped abruptly. 'Do I have to spell it out for you? After everything we've been through and lost – family, friends, our livelihoods?'

'I just wonder at the sense of it,' said Brandon, wary of stirring his cousin's zeal even more.

'The Fenians in America have been issuing bonds in the name of the Irish Republic. With the money they've raised, they're buying arms, Brandon. Hundreds of thousands of people have subscribed. This is not some small movement. This is a people who want their country back. We have to be in it. We can't let others do all the work.' Spittle had collected in the corners of Sean's mouth. 'We talked about such things when we were with Hackett. Had you stayed with the men on those nights instead of keeping to yourself, Hackett and the others might not be so unsure of your loyalty. This is a small place, Brandon. It's best to make an effort.'

'Fine. I'll come tonight,' Brandon said, although it was against his better judgement.

'Good,' said Sean. He led them beyond the limits of the village and across the river flats, where their hobbled bullocks grazed. The grass was flushed a vibrant green, the trees bracing the riverbank, enticing with their outstretched limbs and dappled shade.

'I have to tell you something, Brandon,' began Sean, his halting speech at odds with his earlier enthusiasm for the Fenian cause. 'The word is that Maggie's seeing someone.'

'Seeing someone? Who? Did she tell you that?' asked Brandon, his voice rising.

'No. I haven't spoken to her. Some of the men hinted at it,' admitted Sean.

'She said nothing to me this morning.'

'And why would she? She's been left to make a life for herself in our absence. You can't blame the girl if she wants to marry. They all do eventually,' said Sean.

'Marry? But this is *Maggie*. We've made plans.' Brandon walked ahead of his cousin, trying to fathom how his stepsister had grown old enough in the short time they'd been away to become involved with a boy. For that's what he'd be. A pimply, useless, shallow-brained youth. He waited for Sean to reach his side. 'This family lost everything with Macklin's death.'

Sean drew close to him, his expression darkening all too quickly. 'Say it. Say what you really mean. That I was the one who killed Macklin. That I was the one who ruined our lives and made us flee our home.'

This wasn't the first time his cousin had spoken of his actions that day.

'That's not what I meant.' Brandon backed away in a gesture of surrender. It had taken him months to forgive Sean for throwing that rock, a process that might have been easier if his cousin had showed a thread of remorse.

'Sure,' said Sean bitterly.

'Listen to me. Don't you ever consider that maybe it was all for a reason? That somehow, somewhere, there are better things ahead for Maggie. For all of us. Otherwise, why would our lives have been destroyed? It can't have been for nothing.'

Sean appeared bewildered. 'I can't answer you, Brandon. Maybe what happened simply happened and there's no reason to it.'

'I don't believe that.'

'Well, you've seen Maggie. She's grown. Become a woman. And there's not many of them about here. I only hope that she's choosy, for I'm betting there's any number of men willing to take her on.'

Brandon had never given thought to the possibility of Maggie wanting to live a separate life away from him. The very idea was unimaginable.

They set up camp next to the slide. There was salted meat, flour and fresh river water and these few ingredients became tack-hard bread and something brown and lumpy in the cast-iron pot. They ate with the crock between them, taking turns to dig into the food with pieces of bread, sucking at the spilt portions until the meal was finished and all that was left to swallow was a few mouthfuls of water. Sean talked throughout their eating, regaling Brandon with the expressions of disbelief that had showed on the men who witnessed the axe-throwing. One minute his eyes were as round as organ-stops, the next his nose wrinkled with indignation. Were Sean an artist, rendering through a charcoal sketch, the men's features would have been shamefully exaggerated. Brandon couldn't help but laugh at his cousin's mimicries and fell onto his back, clutching at his stomach until their mirth eventually eased and once again, Maggie took hold in his mind.

❦ Chapter 24 ❧

Late that night Brandon reluctantly followed Sean along the sloping embankment. They stopped for a moment to orientate themselves. It was blacker than black on the riverbank. Land and water merged together so that only the splash of a river creature or the clink of chain on rafted logs offered direction. A distant glow drew them on, the tangy scent of the waterway a quiet presence as muted voices gradually formed into the accents and tones of the strangers they were due to meet. Twenty or so men were gathered around a campfire right at the water's edge, concealed by a steep slope. It was a canny place to meet.

'Who's there?' someone called.

'Sean and Brandon O'Riain,' answered Sean.

Brandon stole a glance at his cousin.

Sean walked to the edge of the circle and claimed a space for them on the ground amongst the men. A bottle of rum was passed across to them. Sean took a swig and then handed the bottle to his cousin.

'Go on,' he urged Brandon.

'Are you sure he's Irish?' said one of group. There was a snicker of laughter.

Brandon drank and passed the bottle along. A branch was thrown onto the fire and with the catch of flames came recognition. Hackett was there with some of his felling team, and the two men who'd given Brandon a ride in the cart from Truby's holding. The foreman of the lumberyard, Arthur Henderson, was also present with those men who'd bet against Brandon's axe throw. The rest were unrecognisable to him, while Sean acknowledged most of these unfamiliar persons and in return they addressed him by name.

'We're all here for the same reason,' began Hackett. 'Most of us know each other. And I know you. But we've a newcomer tonight. This is Sean O'Riain's cousin Brandon.' Hackett nodded across the fire to where Brandon sat. 'I can't vouch for him. You men must decide if he should stay or not.'

'He was in your team,' one of men declared. 'We worked with him.'

'Never spoke much,' said another.

'Or drank much,' replied a third.

'Are you *sure* he's Irish?' said the first speaker again.

'I'm Irish,' said Brandon angrily.

'He can throw an axe.' The man who'd drawn the line in the dirt at the yard spoke up.

'Enough,' said Hackett. 'He was a good worker when he wasn't snarling. But the boy and I don't see things the same way, and I can't say for sure that he's one of us. A believer of the cause.'

'I can vouch for Brandon. I grew up with him,' said Sean.

'You know what this is about, don't you, lad?' asked Hackett.

'The Irish Brotherhood,' Brandon replied.

'Free Ireland,' someone muttered. Every man present echoed the sentiment.

'He's the same as us,' said Sean. 'Just because he doesn't speak up doesn't mean his heart's not with ours. I'll tell you the story of his birth. Then you decide.'

'Don't, Sean,' said Brandon.

'What say you, boy?' said Hackett. 'You don't want your story told or you don't want your story told to the likes of us?'

'It's not that.'

'Well then, what is it? And speak up. Us old men don't have the hearing of you young ones. It comes from the sound of money crashing to the ground.'

The men laughed at this.

Brandon's voice rose. 'The past should be kept in the past.'

'The past never goes, boy. It's with us forever. You'd do well to keep that in mind,' said Hackett.

'Let me tell them, Brandon. About how it was. When you were born. He was born in '50, three years after me,' began Sean.

Brandon was unsure where Sean first learnt of his dismal beginning. Most likely he'd overheard a conversation in Uncle Fergal's cottage. For his own father often crossed the fields to visit his brother, particularly on those occasions when his new wife, Cait, was in a rage. Brandon recalled nothing about his mother. She remained a mystery until he was eight, when his father came to him and they walked to the crumbling stone wall. There, in the shadow of the ruins of Carraig Phadraig, he shared the story of her final hours.

Brandon cupped his head and thought of his father, to whom the story really belonged. Somehow, this tale – his father's story – had also become Sean's. But he supposed it belonged to every one of the men grouped about the fire and that worried him, for the telling of it would bond them, as Sean knew it would, and there was no escaping the strength of shared pain.

'Brandon's mother and grandparents lay chilled and white on the dirt floor of their cottage for five days, in a netherworld where life and death fought for their souls. His father, Liam, knew who would win. The diabhal. He felt him stalking. Lapping the cottage like a wild dog. Waiting. Had the fiend been one of us he would have fought the beast. Strangled him senseless with his bare hands. But what was a man to do, when the sickness came?

He had no choice.' Sean paused. There was a growing murmur from the listening men.

'Liam left them in that final, fatal hour, and climbed the rise to the ruins of Carraig Phadraig with Brandon in his arms. He expected the boy to die as well. That's when he began fretting about the burials. For who back then could afford a coffin?

'But there was one that was being reused to bury the dead. It was the best he could do. Something proper and dignified. Except, except—'

Sean broke off, the emotion raw in his voice. 'He laid them out with my own father as helper and then one at a time placed each of his family members in that coffin and carried them to the grave-yard. The coffin was set above a hole and the hinged bottom fell open as intended. It's a terrible thing for a person to be dropped like that. To land with an inglorious thud, to hear the crack of one skull hitting another. He didn't want that for Brandon. It was difficult enough for my uncle having his wife and parents buried that way.'

The fire sputtered and an ember fizzed, shooting a spray of red into the blackness above the heads of the listeners. The man beside Brandon clapped him on the shoulder. The rum was passed directly to him, and this time Brandon gladly accepted.

'The English,' said Hackett. 'The damn English. It was the sending of our food to England during the bad times that made things so terrible. There would have been plenty enough to feed all of Ireland if they'd kept it there. But no. They had to take what we grew with our own hands and send it away. And who among us could have afforded the little that was left to buy? They tried to kill us all. They killed your mother, you know, as sure as if they'd shot her, Brandon.'

'She died of the sickness,' he said.

'The Almighty sent the potato blight but the English created the famine. My father taught me that,' said Hackett.

The men shouted in agreement.

'Quiet! I have news,' Hackett continued. 'I've been in contact with our Fenian brothers in America. The raids into Canada were unsuccessful. The British were too strong.'

'No!' said Arthur Henderson.

The circle tightened in shared anger.

'Had the uprising in Ireland happened at the same time, as planned, Britain would have had two wars to fight, in the home country and Canada. We may even have bartered with Britain to exchange Ireland's freedom for possession of their province of Canada,' said Hackett, his voice laced with disappointment.

Brandon was intrigued with the thought of Irishmen coming up with such a plan. Although he'd grown up hearing tales of his fellow countrymen opposing the English, some of them paying harshly for their beliefs, he'd never considered the possibility of a well-organised large-scale uprising. He was both surprised and worried by this knowledge, for he only wanted peace.

'The Americans interrupted our supply lines. It seems for all their dislike of Britain for not supporting the Union during the Civil War, the Americans are more concerned with keeping the peace. For the moment, the movement is stalled, but rest assured, they'll take up the fight again and so must we,' concluded Hackett.

'When did all this happen?' Brandon whispered to Sean.

'Last year,' said his cousin.

'So what now?' asked Arthur Henderson, his grey hair shining silver in the firelight.

'We make our point in the old way. We take our justice as best we can. For those of you whose families suffered. For those who were forced to pay tithes for the upkeep of the Church of Ireland, those damnable William of Orange men, I say now is the time to remind people that we have not forgotten. Who's with me?' cried Hackett, rising to his feet.

The circle of men grunted and stood. Sean tugged at Brandon, forcing him to stand.

Flares were lit. Hackett held a torch aloft, the light playing across his features. 'We do this tonight, and then we go our separate ways. Two months from today we meet again.'

The group moved away, following the course of the river, with Hackett in front.

'Come on,' urged Sean.

Brandon was dragging his feet, ensuring they remained at the rear of the group. 'What's this about?'

'Revenge,' said Sean.

Brandon grasped his cousin's arm. 'You best tell me what troubles you're leading us into.'

Sean pulled away impatiently. 'Hackett's father was killed by a Protestant working for the Constabulary back in the '30s. They were trying to take his cattle because he'd refused to pay tithes to the church. This happened in County Wexford and it just so happens there are two Protestant families from the same county about five miles from here.'

Brandon felt a sourness grip him. It was as if he were back in the old country, a young boy running scared and hungry from a father he adored. He mumbled Saint Patrick's name and pulled hard at Sean's arm.

'You're talking about something that happened over thirty years ago. And those people are innocent. What are they planning to do to them? You can't tell me you want to be a part of this.'

Sean shrugged him off and began to move faster. 'And you can't tell me that you're prepared to sit on your arse and do nothing, Brandon. We're downtrodden because we've allowed ourselves to be downtrodden. Well, not here. Not in this country.'

'Why would you want to risk all that we've worked for? Take revenge on innocent people for Hackett's misplaced retribution, for the sake of religion,' said Brandon.

'The sake of religion?' repeated Sean. He stopped and pushed Brandon in the chest so that he stepped back, unbalanced. It was the first time since their childhood that Brandon had felt any real threat behind one of his cousin's physical strikes.

'There is a devil in you,' hissed Sean.

'Perhaps there is a devil and angel in all of us,' said Brandon. 'Which are you tonight?'

Sean hesitated and then, throwing Brandon a look of disgust, he disappeared into the darkness.

Brandon felt as if he were suffocating. Every bit of progress that they'd made over the previous years was at risk of being destroyed in the next hours, and all for the sake of the bitterness that oozed from men who used patriotism as an excuse for retaliation. He watched the dipping torchlights until they faded and then he turned in the opposite direction, heading back to the slide and the bullocks. The moon had risen. It hung whole and new. He tried not to think of what might be happening further along the river. All he could do was wait. He sat in the dark, tense and watchful, thinking of his family, of the life he hoped for in New South Wales, while apprehension at Sean's involvement gnawed at him. Eventually he fell asleep.

❖

'Brandon! Brandon!'

Brandon woke slowly and pushed himself up into a sitting position by the slide. In the east, the horizon was not yet visible. 'Sean? What's the matter?'

'I have to get out of here.' Sean's breathing was ragged and the words caught in his throat.

Brandon, still groggy with sleep, reached for the waterbag and squirted his face, and then shook his head to wakefulness. 'What's happened?'

As he asked the question, he immediately recalled the previous night's events. Fearful of what might have occurred, he tugged on his boots and got to his feet, pulling his shirt over his head so that he was dressed in an instant.

'Things got out of hand.'

The shortness of the sentence carried with it a deadly implication. Brandon could feel disaster in his bones.

'How? Tell me?'

'We don't have time for explanations.' Sean strode to where the hobbled bullocks grazed and led them towards the slide.

'Tell me what happened,' Brandon said again, following him.

'First things first. Help me.'

Moved to action by his cousin's anxiousness, Brandon helped Sean rest the wooden yoke across the necks of the first pair of bullocks and then fastened it to the U-shaped oxbow underneath. He grew more uneasy as each moment passed. Hackett was a strong leader for those who believed in the cause and Sean was a patriot, eager to follow.

'What happened?' he repeated, his patience gone.

Sean moved to the next pair of bullocks. 'Trust me, cousin. I'll explain later. It's best that we leave. We should go back and pick up the rest of the cut timber.'

'So the coppers will be after you? Is that what you're telling me?' Brandon reached for his cousin's shoulder and held tight.

Sean ran a hand across his mouth. 'Probably.' He looked Brandon in the eye, defiant.

'Damn it, Sean!' Brandon released his grasp.

'It's done now, so don't be giving me one of your speeches on our shiny new life. If you'd been there to help, things might have turned out differently,' Sean said bitterly.

'How? We're cousins. I went to that meeting with you. I'll be tarred with the same brush, you can be sure of that.'

Sean grumbled in reply and attached the pole to the swivel beneath the centre of each yoke. The bullocks lifted legs, shifting their positions. One of them bellowed.

'What about Maggie?' asked Brandon.

'What about her?' Sean drank from the waterbag lying near the cold embers of the campfire and then placed the stew pot in a bag and threw it into the slide.

'We have to tell her we're leaving.'

'You tell her. Then catch up,' replied Sean.

'No. This is your doing. You'll be the one to tell her, Sean. Not me. If the coppers are after you, then it's likely we'll be hiding out for a time. I made promises. If they can't be kept then Maggie should know the truth.'

'You're worried about what she thinks of you,' said Sean, scratching at something on his cheek. 'Considering she's only your stepsister, you're mighty considerate.'

'Don't be ridiculous. Anyway, she's your cousin.'

Sean splashed water on his face and stood quite still as if weighing up their options. 'Come on then. But let's make it *quick*.'

⋘ Chapter 25 ⋙

Half an hour later Brandon and Sean stood in the open doorway of Maggie's room at the Minchins' lodging house. They were trying to comprehend the sight in front of them.

Maggie called out, startled, and the boy in bed with her pushed back the covers and quickly stood, indifferent to his nakedness. He was around Brandon's age, with strong arms and beady black eyes. He moved protectively in front of Maggie, who sat up, clutching a blanket to her body.

'What the hell do you think you're doing?' Brandon yelled at the boy.

'Stop it, please!' said Maggie.

'Who do you think you are?' the boy queried. 'Barging in here.'

Brandon elected to answer with his fist. The blow struck the boy in the nose and he fell back onto the edge of the bed, before immediately standing again. Maggie screamed. Sean placed a restraining hand on the young man's chest and the boy glared in return.

'Be quiet,' said Brandon. 'Maggie, get your things. We're leaving!'

But Maggie was staring at Sean, who stank of smoke. The growing daylight revealed smears of ash and something red that could only be blood on his clothes. She shrank back against the wall, clearly unsure.

The boy was furious. 'Who the hell are you? You pasty-faced—'

'Don't be calling us names, you turnip-nosed cretin,' shouted Sean.

'It's a sin, what you two have done. A sin! Do you hear me?' cried Brandon.

'Yes,' agreed Sean, giving the boy a shove. 'Clear off, before I tell your father.'

'Father? Whose boy is he?' asked Brandon.

'I'll tell you later,' replied Sean.

The boy gathered his clothes and boots from the floor and pushed his way past Sean and Brandon. 'I'll be seeing you, Maggie,' he called out loudly.

'Come on, Maggie,' Brandon said sternly, wishing he could run the boy down and throttle him black and blue.

'No!'

He took her by the wrist, his anger almost at boiling point. 'I swear I'll drag you out in nothing but God's glory if you don't do as I say!'

She shook him off and looked to Sean for assistance.

'You know what he's like once he decides on something, Maggie. Gather your things and come outside and speak with us, and then you can decide whether to come with us or not.'

Sean's solemn tone made the difference. Maggie shook Brandon off and snatched her dress from a peg on the wall.

'Wait outside, by the horse stall around the side of the house,' she told them, glaring at Brandon.

People could now be heard in another room, so the two quickly retreated from the house and ran the short distance to the narrow horse stall.

'That boy is Niall Hackett,' Sean finally revealed, breathing heavily.

'Not—' Brandon could hardly believe what he was being told.

'Yes,' confirmed Sean. 'I met him yesterday with his father.'

'Damn it!' Brandon began to pace back and forth. 'I can't believe she would do such a thing. I can't believe it. It's our fault. We left her alone for too long.'

'Brandon, listen to me. It's wrong what's she's done, I'm not disagreeing, but think on it this way. Maggie has someone to care for her.'

'*Care* for her? Th-that b-boy?' asked Brandon furiously.

'We can't have her with us on the road. You know that. It wouldn't be fair to her,' said Sean.

'I'm not leaving her here,' he argued.

'She'd be better off staying. She has a job and a place to live and if Niall marries her—'

'*Marries* her? Maggie marry a Hackett? Over my dead body. Anyway, if it hasn't happened yet and he's already bedding her I don't think he has a wife in mind. He's just a boy.'

'He's *your* age, Brandon. And Maggie's fully grown. She can look after herself.'

Brandon pointed a finger in Sean's face. 'No she can't. She's *my* responsibility. I promised my father. I won't hear another word about it.' He dropped his hand and glanced back towards the cottage. 'Tell me now, before she gets here. What happened last night? How much trouble are you in?'

Sean leant against the horse stall, his head set back at an angle. 'We were meant to burn their houses. That was all. But one of the women rushed us and she was cut. She'll live, but she was cut bad.' He rubbed at his forehead. 'It was me. I was the one who did it. I know. I know. To hurt a woman. But I tell you, Brandon, she flew at me like a banshee. And the others, well they were busy trying to burn the house and she ran out screaming ungodly things and flung herself at me. The rest of her family followed. Her man wasn't there. They said after that he was a cedar-getter made good and had come to the Valley to start anew with his family. Why wasn't she seeing to her children? Why did she do it?'

'Why did *you* do it?' countered Brandon angrily. 'They're here for the same reasons we are. A new life.'

'Are you worried about my soul, cousin? If you are, I can find a priest and confe—'

Brandon spoke over the top of him. 'They'll know it was done by Catholics. Who else would attack Protestant Irish? You're all fools and you're being led by a fool.'

Sean struck his head once against the boards and then straightened. 'Then it's a fool I am, Brandon, but at least I'm a Republican fool.'

Maggie ran across to where they waited, her face flushed. Brandon expected her to be sharp with rage, however she waited expectantly for one of them to speak, a fancy shawl about her shoulders that he doubted she had the money to afford.

'What's going on?' she asked. 'Is it because of the escaped nun?'

'What nun?' said Sean.

'She spoke in Lismore about the dreadful times she had while in a convent in America. They say the horrors she put up with were something dreadful. They made her eat worms and a priest tried to rape her, so she ran away and now she's writing a book about it. She converted to Protestantism. She's travelling all over, giving lectures about how bad Catholics are. A fight broke out in the streets of Lismore afterwards. She's caused a dreadful brawl between the Green and the Orange men.'

Brandon gasped. 'When did this happen?'

'A few weeks ago. I think. I'm not sure,' said Maggie.

Brandon looked at Sean. 'You can bet that bastard Hackett had more on his mind than what he told us last night, then. A little extra revenge for an outspoken woman.'

Around them, the village was stirring. The clip-clop of a horse and the scream of a child reminded Brandon that very soon word would spread of last night's disaster. 'Come on. Let's just get away from here and out of sight so we can talk.'

He'd not expected his stepsister to comply so readily, however the three of them walked quickly from the village, cutting through an area pegged out for a dwelling, where lengths of piled bark waited for use on the yet-to-be-built roof. To their right lay the river. Behind them, in the distance, two distinct lines of smoke stretched into the sky.

They arrived at the slide with its yoked and waiting bullocks.

'You best tell me what all the fuss is about.' Maggie's tone was cautious. 'It isn't the mad nun, is it?'

'Sean was caught up in some trouble last night. The village will be out searching for the culprits. I just thought it best we all leave,' explained Brandon.

'*Some trouble?*' Maggie stamped her foot. 'You come into my room uninvited, punch my Niall and then expect me to leave because Sean's been in *some trouble?*'

'This is serious, Maggie,' said Brandon.

'How serious? Serious enough for me to lose my job? For it will be hard going to find another here. Or do you expect me to go cutting trees with you? If so, then you're stupider than I thought you were, Brandon O'Riain. And I'm no better for listening to you. I'm going back.'

'To Hackett's son? You're not getting entangled with him, Maggie,' said Brandon firmly.

'We'll be married. He promised me.'

Brandon moved closer, squeezing her arm. 'Promised you? How long ago? If there's no ring now then why would a boy his age bother with one when he's already got what's on offer so cheaply?'

Maggie slapped him hard across the face. 'I *hate* you.'

He dragged her towards the slide. 'I know.'

Sean shook his head at Brandon and then, moving to stand next to the bullocks, cracked his whip, pressing the team to action.

Brandon lifted a struggling Maggie into the rear of the moving slide. She clasped its wooden side, her knuckles white with fury. 'I don't have all my belongings.'

'Then you should have gathered them when I told you to,' said Brandon. 'That boy's father is the leader of the Brotherhood, Maggie. And Sean's got caught up in a scrape of their doing. I can't believe that you'd honestly want to be entangled with people like that, in a fight we can't win.'

Sean's whip cracked again, flicking the back of the lead bullock.

'And how do you know we can't win?' said Maggie. She jumped from the slide and ran around to walk beside her cousin who had positioned himself next to the bullocks.

Brandon's mouth dried at her words. He'd thought Wirra a good place for Maggie to stay while he and Sean worked in the forest. Wirra was increasing in size and importance due to growing demand for cedar and pine, but it was still a tiny village. And he'd believed it safe. Safe because of its smallness. Its isolation. Not once had he considered the possibility of Maggie being caught up by Irish Brotherhood sentiment, and certainly not with Brian Hackett's son. What he'd seen in that cramped room made him ill.

Brandon walked around the rear of the slide and then to the front where Maggie and Sean kept pace with the bullocks. They stopped speaking when Brandon joined them, his stepsister's features growing stiff and controlled. He felt his separateness distinctly. In trying to do what was right, he'd suddenly become the outsider.

'We best not collect the rest of the timber from the base of the hill. We'll leave it there for a few weeks until things quieten down,' Brandon said to Sean.

'So what do we do? Go cedar-cutting and take Maggie with us? It's a rough life for a girl.'

'I don't know,' admitted Brandon.

'What about the English squatter's offer of work? An honest job with a Protestant might help us in the long run,' said Sean.

'It's said that he won't have single women on the run.'

'Don't be daft. Of course he will,' argued Sean.

'Truby won't. Except the cook and the girl, Hetty, who is his niece's companion.'

'Well, Maggie can stay with her, then,' said Sean.

'And who are you to say what can and can't be done on another man's property?' said Brandon.

Maggie let out a loud snort. 'You've become boringly righteous, Brandon O'Riain. If this man needs labourers, then he'll hardly turn you away for fear of a young girl. After all, haven't you just proven that I can barely look after myself, nor be trusted to choose a husband? Surely, then, you can convince this Truby that I need caring for and that I'm of no harm.'

Maggie could never have been thought meek, but Brandon was still astounded by the sharp way she pronounced the word 'righteous', as if it were something to be ashamed of.

'This isn't just about harm being done to you. It's a mighty enticement to men knowing there's a single woman about. Mr Truby will be more concerned about you causing trouble, disrupting things. He doesn't give a damn about your precious wellbeing.' He'd not meant to mock her, and he saw now that he'd cut deep. But she rallied quickly, offering a sickly smile.

'Then you'll have to do your best to protect me. Anyway, I'll only be staying for a little while. I'll not be packed away like a child. I intend on sending word to Niall once we're settled and he'll come for me. You'll see.'

❧ Chapter 26 ❧

Kirooma Station, 1944

The homestead, with its empty rooms and structural groans during the long, pitch-tar nights, was not the only hurdle Stella encountered in her third year of marriage. Joe's periods of camping out on the property became more frequent and the intervals Stella spent alone grew until time began to slip away and the days merged silently into the next.

She lived for the six-weekly shopping trips to Broken Hill, where the bustle of the country town with its shops and milk bars were like a salve to her spirit. Shopkeepers knew her now, although there was little opportunity for conversation when Joe was always by her side. She envied the ease with which other shoppers stopped and chatted, and she looked forward to the exchange of a friendly smile and a few brief words with the local grocer, Mrs Andrews. There was little other contact with the outside world. Her mother wrote once a month, managing to ignore Joe's existence, but the satisfyingly gossipy letters from Carmela and Angelina were dwindling in frequency now that they were both involved in the strict courting regime of their marriages.

The isolation was made harder by the ongoing war. Joe continually advertised for staff, but rarely received any responses. However if the search for willing hands was difficult, keeping them for more than two or three months proved an impossibility. There was a huge demand for labour and Kirooma was very remote; the men's quarters were rundown and Joe's expectations of his stockmen were extreme. Men worked from dawn until dusk and ate their meals in the mess room attached to their quarters. Stella rarely saw them. At least at shearing time the government could be relied upon to send a team of contractors. For six weeks of the year, Stella was assured of Joe's presence, and of the politeness of men who tipped their hats or nodded when she entered the shed simply to sit on a freshly packed wool bale and soak up the hum of life.

She had argued with Joe about his prolonged absences, wanting to make him understand how unwanted and neglected they made her feel, but this made no difference. Stella came to recognise the holding for what it was: a woman, fresh and new, with cloistered valleys and unexplored paths, enticing in her unpredictability and harsh beauty. Here was a different love challenging her for Joe's affections, and in the heady months of this all-consuming attachment, she couldn't compete with the wind-shunted land that drew her husband like a siren's call. So she conceded defeat. Temporarily. Instead, she hoped that the novelty of their surrounds would eventually lose some of its sparkle and in time, Joe would come back to her.

Stella served herself a few slivers of cold mutton at the sink before placing a domed meat-keeper over the joint to keep the flies away. Joe had returned from ten days out on the property and she noted his arrival in the diary kept in the kitchen.

'What are you doing?' he asked, from where he sat at the table eating.

'Writing down the date you came home,' said Stella, placing parentheses around the words 'four days overdue'. She underlined the fact not once but three times, each stroke becoming deeper and darker until the lead tip of the pencil broke. She rested the pencil on the page and retied the apron at her waist. 'Did you see Mr Davis this trip?'

'Nope.'

'No news, then?'

'Nothing,' replied Joe.

Her husband's journal sat next to hers. Placed on the bench the moment of his arrival home, it was a leather-bound volume purchased at great expense. No shoddy pocket notebook for Joe. This was a work unto itself, noting planting and harvesting times, phases of the moon, along with animal husbandry notes and first-aid advice. Stella flicked back through the pages, reading the entries; the time of the year a mob of sheep were moved to another paddock, the date shearing was to commence, the particular day a fence was repaired, the number of hours a hollow-eyed orphan lamb was fed before it died. She read one passage:

May 1944

Ram KR10. Found today on the western edge of the Pope's paddock after three days' search. I am so disheartened by his loss and by the length of time it took to find him. Perhaps he could have been saved. I should have known he would be here, wanderer that he was. He is on the leeward side of a tree, slanted sideways by the wind, within sight of a narrow channel that might carry water were it to rain. The sand has massed about his body shrouding his thick fleece in a mantle of red. I thought to move him and then decided that he should stay where he lay. He chose the spot of his dying, after all.

Stella carefully turned back to the present day's page, wondering at the man that could express his thoughts so eloquently and yet was unable to be depended upon in the most basic of ways.

'Why don't you sit down?' he said.

Stella carried her meagre plate of food to the kitchen table and braced herself with a steady, pleased smile, a response practised in the mirror.

'Aren't you hungry?' he said.

'Not really.' She'd grown used to eating on the move, picking at pieces as she worked, enjoying the lightness of her body. The change had happened gradually, borne out of the dissatisfaction of continually eating alone, but she was beginning to feel a benefit. It was as if her body needed to purge the heaviness she felt. It seemed right to her, for hadn't the church from its earliest days taught the need for self-denial? It was a test, she decided. God was testing her. In this empty place.

'The orange tree's pretty healthy. I hoed around the edge of it and gave it another water,' Joe told her.

Across from her, Joe ate mutton and pickle sandwiches. Six slices of bread. Orange cordial. Three large glasses. There was a sketchbook on the table and in a row beside it a collection of shrivelled weeds, a broken bird's nest and three stones of varying colours. Once they were noted in the book, Joe would spend a half hour or more arranging the motley assortment into the groupings of discoveries that cluttered every available surface in the station office. Stella chewed on the meat, watching as he examined one of the limp plants with a yellow flower and then began to draw it. Beneath the forming picture was a neat handwritten description of the subject.

'I saw it out near the dingo fence in the dunes,' he said, adding feathery strokes to the stem. 'No idea what it is, but it's good to have a record of things. Dealing with the absence of water makes for some interesting specimens. Some of the plants I've seen have surface roots that spread out over large areas, or deep tap roots to suck up every bit of available water. I've even watched a plant roll up its leaves to protect itself from the sun.'

Deep creases marked happy lines around Joe's mouth, and she envied him his uncomplicated joy.

'I could watch our country every day. Watch it change and change again and still remain the same,' said Joe. 'The light is so clear and bright. I'm sure it makes our patch of sky seem bigger than it really is.'

175

'Yes, there's certainly a sameness about it.' Stella selected another stringy piece of mutton and ate it.

'Watson seems well,' said Joe.

'He is.' The cockatoo had the run of the meat-house. The gauze was now patched and the carcass hooks replaced with perches that Watson was currently doing his best to chew through.

'Good. And that rain we received last month really helped the grass,' said Joe.

'Did it go far west?' asked Stella.

'Nope.' He pushed the chair out from the table, stretching his legs. 'Pity about that. With a few showers we could get a bit of rough feed further out.'

Stella willed herself to be happier. Joe was home, for a while, at least. There were preserved tomatoes and mutton. They could have a feast and, later, dance in the library. She needed to spin and twirl. To know happiness. To feel Joe's arms about her. Feel him totally, obliviously. She went to the pantry and began gathering ingredients: the canister of flour and a scoopful of salt from the sack leaning against the back wall. She would wait for the dough to prove, and then roll and roll and roll it until her arms ached and it was a hair's breadth in thickness. She tripped on the way back to the kitchen and spilt the salt on the floor.

'Throw some over your left shoulder,' said Joe, with a smile.

Stella was quick to obey, although she didn't need to be reminded. As a child she'd been shown a picture of Leonardo da Vinci's painting *The Last Supper*. There was Judas Iscariot, the betrayer, and the scattered salt he'd knocked with his elbow. She tossed the grains.

'There. You've blinded the devil,' said Joe, biting into his sandwich.

Some days she considered it might be worthwhile dragging the bag of salt outside and methodically throwing the whole lot behind her. It was a month since they'd made love. Joe had come down with a dry cough on his last visit home and had slept in one of the spare rooms, concerned he might make her ill. Stella couldn't have cared less if she'd been on her deathbed afterwards.

'You seem different,' said Joe.

'I just miss you,' she replied, sweeping up the salt.

'The bush woman's lament.' Joe stuffed more food into his mouth. 'I'm going to have to head out again this afternoon. There's a ewe I've been keeping my eye on. Picked up some sort of sickness. I'd like to save her if I can. She's carrying a fine fleece.'

But you've only just come home, she thought. 'Can't you bring her back here to the yards?' She was trying hard not to seem needy.

'You know what sheep are like – finicky. They lie down and give up the ghost at the earliest opportunity,' said Joe.

She turned her bottom lip, feeling the pressure of her teeth in the soft skin. 'And what are you going to do? Camp beside her?'

'Maybe.'

Stella couldn't tell if his reply was meant to intentionally rile her. 'You won't even stay the night? Don't you ever miss me?'

Joe walked to her side, kissing her lightly on the top of the head. 'A couple of days. I promise.'

She grabbed at his arm, pulling him downwards until their lips met and they kissed properly. Joe pulled away first with a silly grin on his face.

'Lucky one of us has some self-control,' he said. 'Have we got any of that meat left from the last lot I cured? It was a good salty brine, that one.'

'No, we don't.' She pushed back the chair and stood. 'I've learnt to do quite a few things in the time I've spent by myself. However killing and cutting up a ration sheep isn't one of them.' At the sink, she stared out at the sun-blasted land. She opened the canister of flour and began spooning it into a bowl, her fingers shaking.

'Have you enough meat for while I'm away?' asked Joe.

'I'll manage.'

'Goodo.' Joe left the kitchen whistling a tune.

Stella looked down and noticed weevils crawling across the mounded surface of the flour.

'Damn it,' she cursed, swiping the bowl of flour from the sink so that it smashed on the floor.

That night after Joe left, Stella stripped off her clothes. There was a bucket of water on the floor and she dunked a sheet in it and then lay on the bed, draping the wet material over her body. She counted the length of their summer nights by this ritual. Sixty minutes of cool relief before the fabric dried and the heat stirred her from sleep, and then the procedure of dunking and draping resumed all over again.

She kissed the cross on the silver chain about her neck. The night sky was moonless and starry. She slipped from the bed to her knees.

'Mother Mary, I have been your most devoted child. I've prayed and attended church all my life until I came to this barren place. Please, don't desert me now. Don't leave me alone. I know I've wished away a child in the past in order to spite my husband. But I swear to you that I've not done the things that a woman can to stop a child's life. I understand that would be a mortal sin. Instead, I have prayed to you, and in my devotion I've not fallen pregnant. So I know that you hear me.

'I prayed not to have a child to protect the baby. I didn't want to bring a child into this world. But now I understand that I was wrong. That a child is the one thing that will bring us together and keep Joe at my side. So, I ask for your forgiveness and blessing, Mother Mary. And I pray that now is the right time for a baby, for what man can turn away from his own child?'

Stella crossed herself and then lay prone on the floor, her arms outstretched, a supplicant to the wooden cross on the dressing table opposite.

'Come, little one,' she whispered into the night. 'Come and find me.'

❧ Chapter 27 ❧

Richmond Valley, 1949

Stella turned on the car's ignition and let the motor idle. It was three weeks since her arrival on the cane farm and she worried that the battery in the station wagon might well go flat if it sat for too long unused. The vehicle was parked next to Ann's sedan in the carport, which was a flimsy structure with a corrugated roof, thin metal posts and no sides that had the potential to blow away in a storm. She rested her head against the seat and closed her eyelids.

The proportions of the old Kirooma homestead came clear and fresh into her mind. And beyond it, the land stretching out through scrub and weed, trees and swelling dunes until the cracking surfaces of ancient lakes crawled towards her. Salt was precious. Valuable. A compound favoured by kings. Wars had been fought over salt. She'd only needed to head north-west from the homestead and sooner or later, if she survived the trek, the white glimmer of a salt lake would appear. For those of faith, these crusty deposits could be scraped free, exorcised and blessed for the faithful to use in their homes. Instead, good Christian that she was, Stella only ever thought of the meat that could be preserved if the generator ceased functioning.

That is, until her baby died.

A pair of birds swooped from one of the boughs of a gum tree to land on the ground. They strutted across the grass, pecking unenthusiastically, and then flew away again. Stella searched through the glovebox for the pack of cigarettes, lit one and drew heavily. She never had managed to give up smoking, much to Joe's annoyance. A triangle of trees to the right of the carport marked the end of the garden. The plants were thick, bushy and olive green. Beyond them, the land extended outwards to the fields. She'd not ventured further than the house and immediate surrounds. It suited her, this limited space. She'd grown used to walking the garden perimeter every day. Lapping it like a long-distance runner, single-minded in approach to her task. Ten laps of the garden took less than forty minutes. Each trip took her past the boundary fence and the mighty cedar tree. Each circuit brought her close to the grand house at the bottom of the hill, and the now-familiar suspicion that she was being spied upon.

She said a prayer aloud as she sat in the car, reminding herself not to set her expectations too high nor to castigate herself for an execrable past. There was nothing that could be done about it now. A small voice trembled within her. It wasn't her fault. She'd had no experience with real love before Joe and even less understanding when it came to a person being able to adjust to such changed conditions. Yet at times the anger within her was so great Stella feared she might implode. At others, a sadness of such depth came upon her that she was barely capable of cooking meals. It was terrifying, the way her emotions overtook her.

She held the cigarette between her thumb and forefinger, twirling it back and forth. Then glanced again at the trees. Through the branches she could see a cream-coloured wedge of something. Stella squinted, trying to make sense of what she was looking at. She switched off the car's engine, slid from the seat and, once outside, dropped the cigarette and ground it out with the heel of her shoe.

The path through the trees was barely visible. Stella pushed branches aside, stepped over clumped grass and then slid through fence wires into an adjoining paddock. The area opened to reveal a large work shed, adjacent to one of the harvested cane fields. An engine was running and she caught a whiff of petrol along with a familiar sweetness, which she now knew came from the harvesting of the cane. Stella had known of the shed's existence, having previously seen it when exploring the garden, however the patch of cream sighted from within the car led to a new discovery.

Now she was clear of the garden Stella saw that the cream colour belonged to an aged cottage that sat just outside the house paddock. An electricity line ran from Harry and Ann's place to a pole at the dwelling. The cottage stood apart from everything else and its positioning hid it from Harry and Ann's house. She walked towards it, feeling inexplicably nervous. Close by, a yellow cat meowed and ran off.

The cottage was derelict. A screen door swung open and shut in the breeze, pacing out her approach with the rhythmic clipping of a latch that wouldn't hold. The two small windows on either side of the door were shuttered. The garden non-existent. Stella walked across the oblong slab of cement that lay at the front of the hut. Withered weeds and burrs were stretched across its surface. Marks on the wall suggested a veranda had once extended out from the front. Someone had attached aluminium swimming-pool steps as a means of accessing the door. She balanced on the rickety rung that was wired to the side of the house and swung open the screen door. The wooden second door opened with a twist and a shove and Stella tentatively peeked inside.

She entered the building, noticing the sunlight that pierced through cracks and gaps in the walls and floor, but the interior of the cottage was in semi-darkness. The kitchen was fitted out with a wood-burning stove, an old kerosene engine fridge, two chairs and a simple timber table. A plate and a cup still sat in the sink. The corners of the room were cobwebbed and a large spider had taken up residence, undoubtedly keen to partake of the numerous daddy-long-legs which, like squatters, had infested the area.

Stella opened the only other door in the room. It was a tiny room, with a handbasin in one corner and a narrow bed in another. A timber frame held empty coathangers. In one corner, the wall had pulled away from the floor and a piece of timber had been hammered into place, probably to keep out inquisitive rodents. She stared at these few objects and then drew the curtain, dressing the lone window. The metal rings attached to the material scraped along the rod and she flinched at the harsh noise and then stepped forward to inspect what the flush of light revealed. The tongue-and-groove boards were covered with paper and plastered with photographs and news clippings of people, motorbikes and sheep. Stella felt the saliva increase in her mouth as she moved closer. In the centre of the wall was a page torn from a rural newspaper. The article featured the rural property of the month, a station located in the far west, on the South Australian border. Stella raised fingers to her mouth in amazement.

It was Kirooma.

'Are you there, Stella?' called Harry.

A door slammed behind her. Jolted by the sudden noise she swung around to greet her brother-in-law. He stood in the doorway and flicked the light switch on. 'I was on my way back to the house for a cup of tea when I saw you.' He surveyed the small room. 'It wasn't much but Joe liked this place.'

Stella thought that perhaps she'd misheard.

'Joe was a bit of a loner,' he continued.

She turned from Harry back to the wall collage. The pictures were a faded yellow. Fly-spotted. Forgotten. Her immediate guess was that she'd stumbled upon a childhood hideout, a special place where the brothers used to come, away from the prying of adults. However Harry's comment stunned her. How could he have let his younger brother sleep in such ordinary surrounds? It was a miserly space for a man to occupy. 'How long did he live here for?'

Harry gave a cough and cleared his throat. 'He moved in when he came back from the Wells's run over the range. Joe would have

182

been twenty-one, or thereabouts. He had a bit of a mouth on him back then. Knew everything. Was impossible to give orders to.'

'Why didn't he live with you in the main house?'

'Ann and I had four kids. It wouldn't have bothered us if he'd stayed on, but he was pretty adamant about having his own space.'

The photographs were all from Joe's childhood. Two brothers by the river fishing. Playing cricket on the lawn. Joe was tiny beside his big brother, Harry. Stella noticed that none of the pictures went beyond Joe's childhood. It was as if his life stopped before his teenage years. And now out of the two boys tacked to the wall, only one survived.

'Are you telling me Joe lived here until he and I were married?' she asked. 'For ten years or more?'

'On and off,' said Harry. 'Sometimes he stayed at the hotel in the village. And he was partial to a swag in the back of an old utility we owned.' Harry leant close to the wall examining the images. 'Our dad had the cottage relocated here from just down the hill. It used to be one of the staff cottages. One of the women who worked in the main house lived there. Dad used it for harvest workers for quite a few years and then later, Joe played here as a kid. He liked the old building. The history of it.' Harry rolled his eyes. 'Yeah, he was a funny one. He'd take off every day and go roaming and I wouldn't see him for hours. And when he did appear he'd be yabbering about a bend in the river where the cod gathered, or a tree with a section of bark prised off its trunk that he was convinced was used by the local Aboriginal people to make a canoe. As if he knew such stuff – he was only a boy.'

Stella recalled Joe's intricate sketches of a yellow daisy and the detailed account of the two weeks it took for him to track and kill a wild dog. To her knowledge, her husband had not received training in either of these arts. 'Perhaps he did know. Perhaps he knew more than all of us.'

'Sure,' said her brother-in-law with obvious disbelief. 'He received the same schooling as the rest of us.'

'You mentioned Mr Wells. Joe always spoke very highly of him.'

'And I was pleased when he wrote to tell us he was jackerooing on that run. I figured that it would settle him down, teach him a bit of discipline. But when he finally came home Joe had all these peculiar notions about how a man should live his life. High-falutin ideas about sheep and owning his own land, that a man's destiny had to be followed. As if what we had, what our father built, wasn't good enough. That's when he started working at the rural merchandise store. A year after that he bought a ram and five ewes. The start of his breeding program,' Harry said sarcastically. 'That was Joe. Always wanting more.'

'Can you blame him?' The words came out hastily. Stella knew how she must sound to Harry, bitter with recrimination.

'It was Joe's idea to live here, Stella. No one shoved him out the door,' insisted Harry.

No, she thought, but he obviously had nowhere else to go.

'Anyway, if you'd stayed here on the farm, we would have fixed the place up. Bought one of those pre-fab houses and added it on,' said Harry.

Stella couldn't envisage the run-down cottage renovated. It needed a bulldozer through it. 'Did you ever tell Joe that?'

'What was the point? He was never going to hang around here. Maybe if he hadn't gone away for those couple of years, things might have been different. But then again, he was one of those kids who always wanted everything at once.'

Harry drew the curtain and turned off the light, waiting in the doorway for her to leave.

Stella took a last glance at the collection of memories on the wall. At the young boy jauntily leaning on a cricket bat and the property that stole his heart and nearly destroyed hers. She followed her brother-in-law through the kitchen and outside into the raw sunlight, the whitish straw of the grass and olive-green trees vivid after the darkness of the cottage. The randomness of birth hit her forcefully. Harry was the eldest. On this farm, like so many others, to be the eldest was to be handed the God-given right of inheritance. Joe once told her that. Now she truly understood.

'Harry, you can tell me to mind my own business, but I was wondering, did your father leave the farm equally to you two boys?' said Stella.

His attention had been diverted by the engine in the shed, which was beginning to sputter.

'Yes, to both of us.' He hesitated. 'Joe didn't tell you?'

Stella gave a single shake of her head. By now it came as no surprise to learn that Joe had been keeping other secrets; parts of his life that were taped tightly shut so that a knife was needed to prise open what remained.

'Joe wanted to be paid out his portion so he could pursue his own interests, but I couldn't afford to do it.' His gaze roamed the sparse paddock. 'Our father always said that if we stayed together, worked the farm together, then neither of us would ever starve. Joe must have known how grim it was going to be for us to pay him out, but he wasn't interested in the mechanics of the situation. It was tough. We had some bad seasons. I had kids at school. Anyway, eventually Joe and I came to an understanding, about the same time you two were engaged. Ann and I had no choice. Joe kept at me like a debt-collector for his share of the money until finally we worked out a payment plan. I kept things amicable, however the bank wasn't happy about increasing the overdraft, and we knew we were really going to struggle with the interest payable. Then out of the blue, Joe's situation changed. After your wedding he informed us that he'd purchased Kirooma. So I figured he wasn't desperate for the rest of the funds.'

'The bank was pretty willing to lend us money back then, what with the boom in sheep prices,' said Stella.

Harry ignored this. 'You asked the other night what we fell out over. Money. That was one of the reasons.' He toed the edge of the cement slab with his boot, kicking at a tuft of grass until it was uprooted. 'I suppose you'll be wanting his share now. Well, it won't happen overnight. I'll have to get a loan from the bank.'

Stella looked at her husband's brother, wondering at how to reply when she'd just been told that she basically owned a half-share in a cane farm, even if it was only on paper. She took a breath, understanding only that she was dependent on the generosity of the man before her.

'Money isn't the reason for my being here,' she finally said.

'And this job wasn't offered out of guilt,' said Harry, 'if that's what you're thinking.'

Harry was far older than Joe. The age difference showed itself in a heaviness, as if his soul weighed him down at times. He was the only brother left. The last man standing. If he thought the choice to retain the cane farm at the expense of his relationship with Joe was a righteous one, then surely it was a win marred by loss.

'Then why did you offer me the position?' she asked.

'Because Joe's dead, you're his wife and I needed help. Frankly, I thought it was pretty unlikely that you'd come. It's not like you don't have your own family. Anyway, I figured that no matter what occurred in the past, a woman shouldn't have to pay for someone else's sins.'

The motor gave a final sputter and then stopped.

'I have to go.' Harry walked away, crossing the paddock and bending over to clamber through the fence. He walked with a lopsided gait, one shoulder slightly higher than the other, just as her Joe had done, burdened by the tasks at hand, by the implements they used, the livestock they tended and by the business they were desperate to retain, no matter the cost.

⋙ Chapter 28 ⋘

S tella prepared Ann's nightly cup of cocoa and carried it down the hall to her room. She found the patient out of bed and awkwardly shuffling to the wardrobe, her legs flung wide as if a foot-length of wood was wedged between her knees.

'Can I help you?' asked Stella.

'No thanks.' Ann took a shawl from the shelf. 'I'm stiff but it doesn't hurt quite as much.'

'That's good news.'

'Small steps, I suppose.' Ann was puffed, as if she'd been running. She returned to the bed and, with the steady movements of one guarded against pain, slowly lowered herself onto the edge of it.

Stella set the hot drink on the table and drew the curtains. Ann carefully manipulated her body along the mattress, lifting her hips to the left and right in a crawling movement until she'd resumed her normal pillow-bolstered position. Stella pulled the sheet up as Ann arranged the shawl about her shoulders and then she walked about the room, pushing the rubbish bin further into a corner, straightening the rug and gathering up a newspaper that had slipped to the floor. With these small tasks complete, she returned to stand in the doorway as she did every night.

Ann peered over the top of the book she was reading and held up a finger to signify she had almost finished a passage.

Stella dutifully waited until the book was put aside. 'Can I get you anything else?'

Her sister-in-law reached for the warm drink and cupped it between her hands. 'No thanks. How was your day?'

'Busy, as always,' said Stella.

'Are my boys behaving themselves?'

'I rarely see them.' Occasionally Stella would wait up for the men to return, glad of their company and their tang of sweat and earth and honest work. It reminded her of happier times.

'Harvest is always busy. And you? How are you enjoying being here? We're not working you too hard?'

'No,' said Stella.

'I wondered if it was going to be a little too quiet for you, but then considering where you lived, I imagine that isn't an issue.' Ann waited for a response and when one wasn't immediate, she picked up the book she'd been reading, sliding the bookmark up and down so that the tasselled cord attached to the card flipped over the top of the spine.

With each day Stella was beginning to recognise that she craved the familiar confidence of a woman to talk to. She missed the girlfriends of her youth and specifically her cousins Angelina and Carmela, with their unbridled loyalty and fierce criticisms. The closeness that she and her mother had once enjoyed. That level of understanding that only women shared. In her time out at Kirooma, all that had been lost.

'The tomatoes are nearly ready to be picked,' said Stella, lingering in the doorway.

'You'll be able to make us a famous Italian dish for dinner then.' Ann gave one of her signature smiles. Pleasant, but slightly dismissive. Or perhaps she was simply tired. 'You might have to use some salt for once, though. Harry loves his salt.'

'I never use it. You look much better this evening,' Stella said, keen to change the subject.

Ann lay back against the pillows. 'I've been trying to wean myself off the anti-inflammatories. If I stay in bed much longer my muscles will shrink.' She placed the book down on the bed. 'Well then, what have you been up to?' she asked as if recognising Stella's need to talk.

'I saw the cottage. Joe's place.'

'Ah,' said Ann. She shifted slightly on the bed.

'Harry was with me,' she clarified, feeling the need to justify her exploration.

'He took you there?'

'Not exactly. I saw it through the trees,' admitted Stella.

'It was Joe's decision to move in there,' replied Ann, her tone defensive.

'I know. Harry told me.'

'I was wondering when you were going to be ready to talk a little. You've been so quiet.'

'Have I?'

'Yes. You're in and out of this room as quick as can be, usually with barely two words to say. The rest of the time you're either working or lapping the garden on one of your walks. Harry says you don't speak much at breakfast either.'

Overhead, small insects were buzzing about the light. They dashed at the bulb, some flying away, others straying too close and, like Icarus and his fated journey to the sun, succumbing to the heat. Stella briefly pressed her fingertips to her lips in thought. She'd recognised that there was a wall between herself and Harry's family since the day of her arrival but given no thought to the possibility of her having placed it there herself.

'Grief is different for everyone,' Ann went on. 'When my sister died, I retreated into myself. The whole world changed for me. Friends told me that things would get better eventually, that it would become easier to live with the pain. Initially I doubted them.

189

However, they were right. The loss never leaves you, but somehow each day becomes a little easier.'

On impulse, Stella drew a chair next to Ann's bed and sat down. 'I feel so guilty.'

'Because you weren't there for him,' said Ann softly.

'No. No, it's not because of that.' Stella touched her bare wedding-ring finger, wondering how much she dared share. 'I didn't want to go out there. Joe told me about the property the day after our engagement. If I'd been more aware, if he'd told me—'

'You may not have gone,' said Ann.

'Yes,' said Stella.

'You can't blame yourself for feeling that way. It was a very remote place to live. I may have felt the same way. But wives follow their husbands, we follow our hearts.'

'Fools that we are,' replied Stella.

They shared soft, almost conspiratorial, smiles.

'What was it like out there?' asked Ann.

'Lonely,' said Stella. 'I thought there would be more staff.'

Ann hugged the novel to her chest. 'You're telling me that you had over one hundred thousand acres and not enough stockmen to help run the place? Even after the war ended?'

'We had good years, but between the stock losses during the dry times, the mortgage and the operating costs, we struggled. And the wool-clip was always discounted because of the sand in it.' She dropped her head into her hands. 'The money we spent. One ram alone cost a fortune. Joe found him under a tree about twelve months later. The flies circling. That's the thing about animals. The more expensive they are, the quicker they die.'

'We never knew. We thought you were doing well,' said Ann.

'How could you have known the truth? As far as I'm aware Harry and Joe had no contact with each other once we moved to the property. Was their argument really about money? They were happy at our wedding,' said Stella.

'The occasion demanded it. Harry and Joe were never close. The age difference between them certainly compounded things, but when Joe turned his back on the farm, well, it devastated Harry. He'd done his best to raise his little brother,' Ann told her.

'I never thought about that. You and Harry being left to care for him.'

'It was a big responsibility. Joe was only a teenager when Sean died, so Harry had to take over the property and look after his brother. Harry always believed that the two of them would run the business. That Joe would support him, as he'd stood by Joe when he was a kid. That sure didn't happen,' said Ann flatly. There had been a sudden shift in the air. She picked up the novel and opened it, adjusting the bookmark.

Stella was staggered by Ann's attitude – and Harry's, for that matter. She knew she should leave, however she resented the insinuation that all fault lay with Joe and that Harry was the wounded party.

'So apart from Harry's expectations, and the money owed to Joe, were there any other major disagreements between them?'

Ann's face became drawn. She snapped the book shut. 'You really don't know, do you?'

'Know what?' asked Stella tentatively.

'When Joe left you in Sydney to finish packing after the wedding, he returned here to see Harry.' Ann was no longer the cordial sister-in-law of earlier. There was a bite to her words.

'He told me he wanted to say goodbye to everyone,' said Stella carefully.

'He just used that as an excuse to hide the true reason for his visit.' Ann leant forward, the movement showing itself in the flicker of pain on her face. 'When he purchased Kirooma Station, Joe crossed a boundary. In more ways than one.'

'What do you mean?' Stella asked.

'The fence. The garden fence. The one where the cedar tree stands at the bottom of the garden.'

'I don't really understand what that has to do with the argument between Joe and Harry,' said Stella.

'It has everything to do with it. No member of this family has deliberately crossed that border for years. At least that's what we all thought.'

'I see.' Stella was beginning to wonder if her sister-in-law's medication wasn't making her a little confused. 'We are talking about a garden fence,' she clarified. The kelpie came to mind. Harmless and friendly.

Ann's expression was steely. 'None of us were aware that Joe had gone straight over to that house the last afternoon he was here until the next day. We were standing near the garage, ready to wave Joe off when he announced to us what he'd done. Harry was stunned. I have never seen my husband look so devastated, and I hope I never do again. Of course, Joe tried to justify the visit, and he went on and on about it being time to put the past behind us, as if we were the ones that required a lecture on forgiveness.'

These were muddy waters that she was being dragged into. Stella wanted to ask who the neighbour was and what argument had led to the animosity towards the two households. Crossing a dividing fence, talking with people when it wasn't allowed – surely these weren't the issues that caused irreconcilable disagreements.

'A person remembers someone as they behaved in life. Joe was never like my Harry. In the end, he placed his own desires above everyone else, and that included you. He abandoned his family and dragged you with him, and what have you got to show for the last seven years? You lost your child. You've got no house. No money. Nothing.' Ann punched each word out.

Tears came to her eyes, for all that she had lost, but also because Ann was right. 'He was my husband,' replied Stella.

'Yes he was. And I'm sorry to say it because obviously you loved him, however Joe was also a troublemaker and, in the end, a coward. But I think you realise that.'

⤜ Chapter 29 ⤛

Kirooma Station, 1946

If it weren't for the tin pannikin in the sink, she'd never have realised that Joe was home. He was usually so careful to tidy after himself, almost as if the slightest remnant of his existence might leave a trail, exposing him to the demands of everyday life that he was at such pains to avoid. She rinsed out the mug and sat it in the drying rack, her palm tapping the stainless steel, the wedding band clinking. She rotated the ring, once, twice, and then went in search of her husband. She moved through the homestead, opening and closing doors with more force than necessary, and then pulled on a pair of boots, tied back her hair and donned a wide-brimmed hat and went out in pursuit of him.

'*Gone again, gone again,*' screeched Watson from his cage.

'Actually he's back,' said Stella.

The bird ceased scrambling along the perch at this news.

It was early. A coolness ruffled the breeze. The sky was yet to turn bright and, in its absence, the red of the land seemed harder, darker, pressing in on her like a stranger trying to catch her attention. She skirted the homestead. Trickling water ran from a hose onto the original orange tree. She noticed a boot print in the freshly tilled earth at its base. Stella went out through the back gate to the work shed. The wooden benches were piled with old farm equipment that Joe was refurbishing: spring-loaded rabbit and wild dog traps, a piece of corroded copper pipe and a length of rubber belting used to drive the overhead gear in the woolshed. Countless other unrecognisable items lay in the dirt.

The motorbike was halfway between the house and the woolshed. A pool of oil stained the ground and a carelessly flung spanner suggested the owner had grown impatient with repairs. The crate tied to the rear of the bike held two jerry cans of fuel and a water bottle. Nothing unusual. A mile away, sheep called to each other from the yards. She may not have heard them were it not for the wind blowing steadily in her face. She supposed Joe would be nice to her. The dust hanging above the pens suggested it was a fair mob, which meant he would need her help today.

En route to the woolshed Stella stopped to pick up a stone that lay on the red soil. It was small enough to fit in her cupped palm and its jagged edge was sharp against her flesh. She made a fist and continued on, her boots scuffing up the soil. She walked up the ramp used for rolling newly pressed bales out of the shed and into the dark space, becoming instantly overwhelmed by the sweet scent of lanolin mixed with manure. Her eyes adjusted to the dim light and she moved past the slatted tables and timber bins to where the dog slept in a wicker basket of wool. Joe sat on an upturned drum at the far end of the board, hunched over a letter.

She moved towards him, squeezing the stone in her palm. 'Hello. You're back.'

'Stella,' said Joe, as if she were the last person he expected to see.

'When did you get home?'

'Last night,' he replied.

'Is there mail?' She stopped in front of him.

'The usual,' said Joe. He folded a letter.

'What's the usual?'

'The bank's given us a serve about the late payment of interest,' he told her, although he couldn't meet her gaze.

'Why was it late?'

Joe stuffed the letter into his top pocket.

'Is it because you were out driving around instead of attending to the office work?'

Stella noticed the compactness of his body. Like her, he'd grown lean over the four years since their wedding. There was not an inch of fat to live off. They had become like desert creatures, scrawny and furtive. Hiding. Surviving. Tolerating. He rose and took her in his arms. She knew this for what it was: an attempt at atonement. He wanted her understanding, but she felt stifled. Trapped. She pushed against his chest and he freed her.

Stella walked across the board and rested her arms on the frame of the window. The sheep were bulging against one of the gates that had not been closed properly, and it swung open. She watched as the animals began streaming away from the shed, following a hoof-trodden track to the north. 'If you let me go through the mail and occasionally manage the accounts, this wouldn't have happened.'

'I can handle it,' said Joe.

'I suppose they penalised us because of non-payment,' she said. 'More expense.'

'I said I'll handle it.'

'Can you?' She faced him, hearing the bite in what she said. 'Because it seems ludicrous to me that over the time that we've been here, you've always collected the mail. Always made a point of reading everything first. I rarely even see a bank statement.'

'Every time we go to Broken Hill you complain about the gates. So, what? Now you want to collect the mail? Anyway, you have access to the station ledgers. I'm not hiding anything.'

'Then when you go back to the house, leave the mail on the kitchen table, including the letter from the bank. I don't need you to vet our correspondence. And nor can we afford to miss a bank payment through mismanagement.'

'Me getting the mail hasn't bothered you before. And it wasn't mismanagement, it was a timing problem,' answered Joe. She could sense his anger was building.

Stella gave a short harsh laugh. 'A timing problem. You wandering around in the desert isn't a timing problem. It's childish.'

'And how would you understand anything about children?' he yelled at her.

Stella gave a rueful shake of her head. She clutched at the stone. 'What child would want to be born in this vacuous place,' she said sadly. 'To a father who doesn't care enough for his own wife to stay at home. The Handalays must have thought they'd been born under a lucky star the day you agreed to buy this property. And I wondered why it was on the market for so long.'

'It was an opportunity,' argued Joe through gritted teeth.

'Not a very good one. At least, not for us.'

'You haven't helped.' Joe shoved his hands in his pockets.

'Look what you expected me to adapt to,' replied Stella.

'Plenty of women do.'

'They probably have a husband that comes home every night. The only thing I ever wanted was for you to come home to me. *To me*. The woman you married.'

'I'm sorry I'm such a disappointment,' he said finally.

Stella decided to leave before either of them said anything else. How Joe treated her was intolerable, but still he managed to make her feel guilty, as if he were the injured party and she the sterile, ungrateful wife.

'By the way,' she called over her shoulder. 'You left one of the gates open. The sheep are getting out.'

Joe swore and ran past her, whistling to the dog who pricked his ears and bolted down the ramp, closely followed by his master.

Left alone in the woolshed, Stella opened her hand. A thin line of blood spread across her callus-thickened skin. She held the rock to her chest and squeezed harder.

❈ Chapter 30 ❈

Richmond Valley, 1867

By chance it was Hetty who saw them first. She was sitting with her children beneath the same tree that Brandon had camped under when he was last there and she rose on their approach, brushing her skirts and shading her face from the sun. Sean steadied the team, bringing the bullocks close to the rear of her cottage and Brandon went to greet her, expecting a response that was unlikely to be warm with Maggie in their company.

'You're back,' said Hetty. She clasped her hands together and then let them fall by her side, before checking on the child, who was plucking at the dry grass, and the baby, who lay asleep. Her gaze took in the four bullocks and slide, Sean, and then Maggie. 'Who's that?'

'My stepsister.'

Hetty drew her eyebrows together. 'She can't stay. I told you the rules about women.'

Brandon removed his hat. 'I couldn't leave her alone in the village. There's been trouble there. Some Protestant farmers have been attacked, their homes burnt.'

She considered this. 'Well, you're here now. I suppose you best bring her to me then, while you see Mr Truby. You'll have to tell him about her.'

'I will.' He waved to Sean and Maggie and soon the four of them were grouped awkwardly together by the tree, the sun spearing down through its leaves.

Hetty gave Sean a half-hearted hello before beginning at the hem of Maggie's skirt and working her gaze thoughtfully past her waist to the freckled skin and unbrushed hair.

'You've been told how things stand here? About women?'

'I thought—' Maggie's friendly disposition disappeared. 'Brandon dragged me here. I didn't want to come.'

'The reasoning doesn't make any difference to the fact of how things work,' concluded Hetty. She gathered the baby in her arms and then took the little boy's hand. 'Still, you better come with me while they do their business with Mr Truby. No point standing out here getting faded by the sun.'

Maggie looked to Sean and Brandon for guidance.

'Go with her, Maggie,' Brandon told her, and then he and Sean headed towards the homestead.

'Not particularly friendly, that Hetty,' said Sean.

'I did warn you.' Brandon opened the garden gate. 'Both of you.'

Sean gave his standard response when an answer didn't suit him: a single grunt.

They walked up the dirt path and knocked on the front door, Sean running a thumb across the deep-red portion of the stained-glass window as they waited.

'Could we hide Maggie here while we do the job?' said Sean.

'What? And you think someone wouldn't see her?' said Brandon.

Miss Schaefer came to the door. She was dressed in slate blue, the colour of her falcon. Brandon took in the slight waist, bounded by whalebone, and the way the silk bodice slid across the curve of her chest up to her narrow neck. He realised that his interest was cause for amusement, for her mouth formed a pretty bow.

'You've returned sooner than expected.' She spoke only to Brandon, as if Sean were not even present.

'Is that a problem?' asked Sean.

She continued to focus on Brandon. 'Mr Truby is in the garden. You've been there before so I won't bother with directions. You'll find him playing patience.'

'Thank you, Miss Schaefer,' said Brandon.

She hesitated a brief moment, then closed the door in their faces.

'Another friendly one,' said Sean, as they walked around the corner of the house.

Glanville cocked his head on their passing. The adjoining cage was empty. It seemed that Athena had not survived her companion's attack.

The statue was as beguiling as when Brandon first sighted it. He observed Sean standing wonderingly before the semi-naked woman, staring openly at her curves and indentations, before lifting a tentative hand and reaching for a gauze-covered breast.

'Don't,' said Brandon.

Sean retracted his hand, but took a step closer to the statue.

A cough sounded. Mr Truby was sitting at a table covered with green felt, a black-and-white collie at his feet. Brandon led the way to the older man until they could clearly see the playing cards spread out before him: seven columns of cards alternating in red and black, the lengths of each column varying. The Englishman placed a card at the end of one of the columns and then sat back, clearly satisfied. 'Good. You've returned. And this is?'

'My cousin Sean,' said Brandon.

Truby crossed his arms in front of his chest. His examination of Sean was slow, filled with the curiosity of a man delivered of an unexpected parcel. Brandon worried at how his cousin appeared, his clothes dirtied, blood-stained and smelling of smoke from the night's events and his tiredness evident in the deep half-moons beneath his eyes. Eventually the dog yawned and whined simultaneously, the sunlight highlighting long whiskery hairs sprouting from a wet nose.

'And what do you think about the animosity that exists between the Orange and the Green?' said Mr Truby.

Next to him, Sean grew tense. There was the slightest movement of his fingers as he curled them into a ball.

'We stay clear of all that,' said Brandon.

Mr Truby selected three cards from the deck and, after studying the evenly spaced columns on the felt, placed the first card, a four of hearts, on top of a neat column ending with a five of clubs.

'I was asking your cousin.' He looked directly at Sean and it seemed to Brandon that there was a gleam in the squatter's eyes, as if he'd gauged his cousin's predisposition and was now trying to provoke him.

'I think a person should stick by his beliefs,' said Sean with little hesitation.

Brandon felt all hope of employment slip away. 'We have four bullocks, can we hobble them and let them graze, Mr Truby?'

'And what are your beliefs, Sean?' said Mr Truby, ignoring Brandon's question. 'Are they the kind that can ruin a man's prospects through ignorance?'

'Are you saying I'm ignorant?' countered Sean.

Brandon placed a restraining hand on his cousin's shoulder.

'I am simply asking a question.' Mr Truby sat the playing cards on the table and leant back in the chair. His coat fell open, revealing a holstered pistol. 'Some men wear their ill-discipline on their faces and carry their grudges like a tramp hauling his possessions on his back. So, let me tell you plainly, Sean. I have seen you and you have seen me. We have the cut of each other. I'll have no trouble on my run.'

'You asked us here,' stated Sean.

'And you might not be staying,' said Mr Truby, adopting a milder tone. 'Now, why don't you go and tend your bullocks, while Brandon and I have a talk.'

Sean opened his mouth to protest but Brandon drew his cousin aside. 'Go. Go,' he entreated.

The Englishman returned his attention to the game and refused to draw his gaze from the table until Sean had departed with a muttering of indecipherable words. He placed a card on the table. 'Sit, Brandon.'

There was no other chair available, so Brandon sat on the ground to Mr Truby's right. With little food in his stomach since yesterday and a morning's travelling behind him, he was happy to rest, although he felt like he was at school again, with an eccentric but well-meaning teacher by his side. The Englishman was rubbing a fingernail on the green felt and then flicking something free of it. The dog got up and lay back down next to Brandon.

'Your cousin. What's he like?' asked Mr Truby.

'Like me, I guess. But he means no disrespect and he'll cause no trouble,' Brandon was quick to reply.

'No. No, he's not like you.' Mr Truby dealt out another three cards and considered them. 'And I doubt even your good intentions could control him if it was required. I don't want anyone here that might cause a problem. I wouldn't like to think that I was employing someone who couldn't be trusted.'

'He can be trusted.'

'Really? I saw it. The set of his mouth. The way he spoke and refused to meet my gaze. He's very Irish,' he concluded.

Brandon frowned at this. It seemed a strange thing to say. 'So am I.'

'Maybe.' Mr Truby appeared unconvinced. 'But do you hate the English?'

'N-no,' replied Brandon. He held a grudge against the English. How could he not? However this was Australia, where life might well deal out different hands to different people, but where there was every possibility for a man to rise up and better his place in society. A new world was no place for old hatreds. What was the point otherwise of hoping for a fresh beginning?

'So you don't hold us accountable for what happened to your people?' said Mr Truby.

'I—'

'Perhaps that's unfair. You see, some men like your cousin *do* hold us accountable. I've seen his type before. At heart, he is a dissenter. A person who refuses to submit to authority or to comply with any regulation. They argue for the sake of it and fight for the pleasure, which is rather a pity when there is so much to enjoy in Australia.'

'I like it here, Mr Truby. I'm trying to build a new life.'

'Good, because my niece agrees that you are a welcome addition. Apparently I was less stultifying after your initial visit.'

Brandon supposed that was a good thing.

'You'll cut my trees and learn to ride and maybe in time there will be a longer-term job for you here.'

It was what he wanted, he decided. To be on a large holding, to have the opportunity to learn something new, but he also had a difficulty, which, given Sean's behaviour, he was reluctant to share with Mr Truby. But he knew he had to. 'I have a problem.'

Mr Truby lifted his gaze from the cards.

'My stepsister, Maggie. I had to bring her with us. She's with Hetty.'

Mr Truby stared at the playing cards. His nostrils were flared. 'She will have to return to the village. It's not good for the men to have single women about. It makes them fractious.'

Brandon looked at Mr Truby and then at the ground. 'Oh,' he said quietly.

'I see you are close to her,' said Mr Truby.

'She's my stepsister, sir, younger than me, and I promised my father that—'

'A deathbed promise? For they are the worst. It poses an ethical dilemma, for in the majority I would say it's quite unlikely that many a promise can be fulfilled. The giver must live with deceit, and the dying loved one is sent to their maker under false pretences.'

'It wasn't like that, sir. Although the promise is just as binding,' admitted Brandon.

'And your earnestness suggests it would be painful not to fulfil the obligation.' He locked his fingers together. 'I'll not have a girl walk to the village alone. You and your cousin will do a fortnight's work. Cut as many trees as possible. Let's call it a temporary reprieve.

At the end of that time, your cousin can return the girl to the village.'

'Yes, Mr Truby.' Brandon thought about what he could say in Maggie's defence, how she was young and entangled with Hackett's son, but he had known of Mr Truby's rules and telling him of her situation would only prove that the Englishman was right, that women did cause problems. And Maggie had history enough to confirm that.

'Your stepsister can stay with Hetty. And tell her not to go walking about or to be over-friendly with anyone.'

'Yes, Mr Truby,' Brandon repeated, as he was dismissed with the wave of a hand. He felt as if he were once again in his father's presence, waiting for instructions on how to proceed with living.

Brandon left the garden, anxious and perplexed by the situation he now found himself in. He'd finally gotten what he wanted – a permanent job – but not protection for Maggie or Sean. It was not the first time that a person had sized up Sean and formed an immediate dislike of him. That was a problem in itself. However, Sean aside, it seemed that at some point he would have to choose between Maggie and employment at Truby's run. He knew the choice should be obvious, but it was not a decision that he could easily make.

❧ Chapter 31 ❧

Brandon found Hetty and Maggie sitting on the edge of the sloping veranda. His stepsister had been coerced into helping Hetty wind wool, for she sat with her elbows on her knees, one corner of her mouth twitching in irritation as Hetty looped the yarn around Maggie's outstretched hands. Next to them, the baby in the basket cried softly and Hetty paused to pat the child's stomach before resuming her task. Sean lay sprawled across the floorboards, an amused expression on his face as he watched Hetty's little boy run up and down the length of the veranda. The child scrambled in front of Maggie and his mother before jumping over Sean's spread-out legs, squealing when Sean growled in response.

In another place, at a far better time, the peaceful scene he approached might well have caused him to count his blessings.

'What a picture you all make,' said Brandon, standing before them.

'Well?' asked Sean, sitting up.

Brandon explained Mr Truby's verdict. A slight tug of annoyance appeared on one of Hetty's eyebrows when she learnt of her employer's decision to briefly permit Maggie's presence. In comparison, Maggie lost the surly turn to her lip and let out a little cry of delight when she heard she'd return to Wirra soon. She freed herself of the wool and passed it to Hetty, making a little curtsy.

'Things won't be the same as before,' Brandon warned her. 'You probably won't have a job or anywhere to live, so don't look so pleased with yourself.'

Maggie approached him, hands on her hips, and leant forward just a little. 'You caused all this, Brandon, dragging me away in the first place, so if I don't then you can use some of your precious savings to set me right until I can find lodgings and work or marry,' she announced airily. 'Whichever comes first. Because I *will* be marrying Niall.'

'You will *not*,' said Brandon, his annoyance rising at her defiance.

'And who are you to be telling me what to do?' Maggie moved closer to him.

His anger and frustration finally broke through. '*I'm* the person with the money you'll be needing. And I *forbid* you to marry him!' he yelled.

She pushed her lips tightly together, her face compressing. He stared hard at her, feeling the rage coursing through his blood, afraid of what was in him at that moment and what he might not be able to contain. He strode away from the cottage, hard and fast.

Sean caught up with him and put a hand on his shoulder to slow him. 'Brandon, this place isn't for me. We don't have to stay here.'

Ahead, one of the stockmen was leading a horse to the stables, the outlines stark against the mid-afternoon sun. Brandon dropped his gaze to the ground, trying to restore his composure. The last part of what Sean said was true enough. They could leave Mr Truby's run at any time and take their chances making a living in the forest or go on the road again, until they finally discovered a place where they could settle. But Brandon didn't want that.

'I like it here,' he said simply.

'Why, because he talks to you nicely?'

'You don't like him because he's English and Protestant,' said Brandon sharply. 'How hard is it for you to keep quiet and be polite?'

'He started the argument,' said Sean.

'You sound like a child,' Brandon chided.

'If I am, then it's a child who recognises when he's being played. You saw the way he looked at me. As if he saw straight through me.'

'Maybe he did,' said Brandon.

'Meaning?' A shadow crept across Sean's face.

Brandon thought of his father's words, that it was far better to have fifty enemies outside your home than one within. He loved Sean like a brother and, as with Maggie, their closeness had started at an early age, however his cousin's behaviour was becoming dangerous. 'We can't risk anymore trouble, Sean. You understand that, don't you? Things have been tough enough for us already.'

'Which is why I don't like the Englishman. I have a feeling about him. About us staying here,' countered Sean.

'And where do you suggest we go? Especially after your involvement in the attacks last night. This was your idea and it's the safest place for us at the moment. And that's why we're here. Because of last night. Damn Maggie for getting mixed up with Hackett's son and ruining everything. I told you Truby wouldn't have her here, but I'd hoped that in time, once we'd proved ourselves, he'd allow her to stay on. There's no chance of that now.'

'There are other jobs. A man could cut palings or earn a shilling or more per hundred length of shingles. And there are more than a few landholders who think themselves above splitting logs and sheets of bark for a roof,' said Sean.

'Haven't you listened to anything I've been saying? Besides, I like what Mr Truby is offering. A chance to stop moving and living in the woods. And I refuse to run anymore,' he finished pointedly.

'Fine. It's a safe place here for the time being, I agree with that,' Sean relented, 'but what's the point of trying to stop Maggie from being with Niall? Even if we decided to move on, she'd find a way to be with him. She's stubborn. It runs in the family,' he said, with a lift of his eyebrow.

'It's a sin what she did,' said Brandon. 'Having that boy in her bed.' The image was seared into his brain.

'But if he marries her?' suggested Sean.

'Marry that cretin?'

'She'll have a home and somebody to care for her, Brandon. And isn't that what you promised your father?' argued Sean.

Not like this, he thought sullenly. Not with the deed done before the wedding, to the son of a man he hated. On the veranda, Maggie waited. She couldn't remain beyond a fortnight and Brandon didn't want her to leave. During their months of separation, he'd thought of her constantly. There were still times when he resented her for the spark she'd lit in Macklin. For the burden of having made a promise to his father, Liam. He thought of them running from their home in Tipperary. He was sorry Mr Macklin was dead. For all he knew, Macklin may well have been the better man, for the one who might possibly replace him was not the sort he wanted for Maggie either.

Brandon wished he were in the forest smelling fresh-cut wood, not trying to decide what was best for his family. If he'd felled more trees, saved more money. If he'd been wealthy. However, he might just as well have been in Ireland, for the decision had been made for him. Maggie couldn't stay. She had to go back. And no matter what he said or did, her heart was set on the Hackett boy. But if she married him . . .

He pushed in at his eyes, as if the pressure might help him think. 'We have two weeks to try to come up with something so that we can all be together. Until then, we need to do what we're told. And you need to lie low,' he told Sean.

'Why does he?' asked Hetty. She had walked quietly towards them, and stood only a few feet away, Maggie close behind. 'Were you involved in that trouble with the farmers?' she asked Sean, grabbing her son's collar as he rushed past.

Sean shrugged, as if the part he'd played was small and not of any significance.

'We're here now.' Brandon changed the subject. 'Let's try to make the best of it.'

'So you were involved. Pity I don't get to pick and choose my company.' Hetty sniffed.

'What about me?' said Maggie. 'Have you weighed up my life yet, Brandon? Cut it into little pieces with your axe and reassembled it to your liking?'

Brandon took in his stepsister's pout. 'I'm trying to stop you from making a terrible mistake.'

Maggie burst out laughing and then just as quickly stopped. 'I don't need another father, Brandon.'

'Really? You've just whored yourself with that boy,' he countered.

'Niall is more of a man than you'll ever be,' Maggie hissed.

He took her by the shoulders and shook. Hard enough for her teeth to clash and for him to immediately regret it. Maggie raised her head slowly, her gaze no longer unbreakable but teeming with hurt, as if the damage he'd done went far deeper than either of them had expected. A single large tear fell down her cheek. Brandon's rage changed quickly to regret. He wrapped her in his arms, feeling the looseness of her body and the rhythmic thud of their shared anger. She continued to weep and he stroked her hair, conscious only of their closeness.

'Maggie,' he said reassuringly. 'I'd never hurt you.'

'You just did,' she replied, breaking free of his embrace.

Hetty studied him with renewed interest, as if she wasn't quite convinced of what she'd just witnessed. 'Nice to see such brotherly love,' she announced. 'What a pair you make. A tall handsome man and a middling girl. Pity you're related.'

Brandon chose to ignore the pithy remark, but he noticed Sean had grown suddenly quiet, and that he too was concentrating on him.

'The men's quarters is a mile's walk to the south.' Hetty pointed to a long, low building situated against a backdrop of bushy, crowned trees. 'Maggie, you'll stay with me.'

'Thank you, Hetty,' said Brandon.

'Don't thank me. I'm reckoning you lot will cause more worry than you're worth. But what would I know?' Hetty picked up her squirming son, and left their family group without another word.

Brandon thought he was equipped with a fair brain. He knew his figures and could add up long columns of numbers if required and he was no stranger to reading, but search as he might he could find no answers that might mend the rift that currently existed between himself and Maggie. All he could do was try to make her understand.

'Maggie,' he called as she made to leave. 'If you marry Hackett's son you'll end up living in the Big Scrub with a team of men who work all day and drink all night. I suspect you want something better than that. Don't you? If you do, please don't rush into anything.'

Maggie inclined her head to one side, like a suddenly attentive bird. 'One day, you might ask yourself if *I* have a right to decide what's good for me.' She gave Sean a sympathetic look and then followed Hetty.

'Brandon?' said Sean. There was a warning tone in his voice.

'What?'

'You have to let Maggie go.'

'She's my stepsister.' Brandon frowned, surprised by Sean's comment.

His cousin started trudging through the grass towards the men's quarters.

'*Exactly*,' he replied. 'And she wants someone else.'

❧ Chapter 32 ❧

Brandon poured water into his hat and the old dog slopped it up, his front legs splayed wide as he drank. He ruffled the animal's fur, tipped out the remaining liquid and pushed the hat firmly back on his head. Maggie had barely spoken to him over the last seven days. Her shunning was made worse by the time she spent with Sean. He knew he had to accept that one day she'd marry and have children of her own, and he should have been relieved by that thought. However every time he tried to justify Maggie's leaving he pictured sweat along her hairline and young Hackett – naked, angry, possessive.

Overhead, brief snatches of the sky could be seen through the treetops, swirls of blue and white that appeared to fly from nature's masts. He ran a palm across the bark of a cedar, feeling the ribbing of its outer shell and decided that he would leave this one until last. It was the grandest of all the trees growing in that area and it had taken hold on a ridge, which looked slightly downhill to where the homestead could be seen through the trees. Its ungainly roots had become a place of rest at noon and he'd grown used to its quiet refuge. Were it allowed, he would have camped there, preferring it to the low-slung cots and snoring workers in the men's quarters.

'I see you have a favourite.'

Miss Schaefer stood before him in a gown of buttercup yellow, a parasol held aloft as if she were taking a stroll on an English estate. She held a small dog on a lead. The animal strained at the collar about its neck, pushing on its front legs so that its chest protruded like a figurehead on a ship, its paws gripping at the earth.

'It is a pretty tree. I wouldn't cut it either. That's what you were thinking, wasn't it?' she asked.

'It would be a pity,' Brandon admitted.

'Then don't,' she told him frankly. 'You're alone?'

'Sean will be back soon. We're about to start on another tree.'

'Come,' she invited. She waited until he was by her side and together they walked through the timber. 'You didn't like me the day we met. Is it women you're averse to or falconry?'

He thought of Glanville shredding the innards of his prey and Miss Schaefer in her hunting suit, blood oozing from the scratch on her cheek, which was now nearly healed.

'Hmm, the former you're hesitant of, the latter you dislike,' she answered.

Brandon kept his counsel. He was unsure how to behave in the presence of a lady, especially this young woman in front of him. He had witnessed Miss Schaefer's haughty disposition and her liking for blood sports, which were at odds with today's small talk.

They stopped in a clearing on the ridge's crest. The rhythmic pounding of Mr Truby's steam engine down at the mill carried on the breeze. The dog snapped at the grass.

Miss Schaefer gestured at the homestead. 'It's quite deceptive. From down there, this slope seems more like an undulation. I always thought it was an illusion. A combination of light and the angle and height of the trees. What do you think?'

'I couldn't be sure,' said Brandon.

'Come. You must have an opinion,' she persisted.

'It's all those things, as well as the fact that your house sits in a slight depression.'

'You see, it's not so difficult to make conversation.' She walked about the rise, stopping to peer through the trees again at the homestead below. The dog did its utmost to move in the opposite direction and Miss Schaefer jerked the lead impatiently. 'That tree you favour. What do you like so much about it?'

Brandon considered the question. 'Its height and grandeur. It's simply a beautiful specimen.'

'And what is beauty?' she asked, twirling the parasol so that its fringing fluttered prettily. 'It's a straightforward question. There are no right or wrong answers.'

Brandon wiped his hands nervously on his trousers. 'In nature, beauty is about harmony, balance.'

She moved towards a tree and, closing the sunshade, rested against the trunk. 'My uncle said you were observant and considered in your speech. He admires those qualities. But perhaps I shouldn't be telling you that in case you use that knowledge to wheedle your way into his confidence.'

'I would never do such a thing,' said Brandon.

She gave a girlish giggle. 'I'm only teasing. Really, you must learn the art of banter. It is quite an amusing means of passing the time.'

'I'm sorry. I'm tired from cutting,' he replied.

'The chopping down of such beauty must be hard at times.' She looked him straight in the eyes. 'Am I beautiful?' she asked.

He thought of what he might say, that some of the most attractive women he'd ever seen were those in rough calico dresses, with a small child in hand. Miss Schaefer's prettiness had harsh edges, and there was a shrewdness about her that was accentuated by the scent of lavender water and the rustling of silk.

'Brandon! Brandon!' Maggie's voice echoed through the trees.

'I'm sorry, I have to go,' he said, pleased at the interruption.

Miss Schaefer shrugged. 'Another young woman seeking your attention.'

He ran downhill through the cedars, hearing the urgency in Maggie's voice, weaving through the growing area of decapitated trunks to where a bullock team waited to drag another tree to Mr Truby's mill.

Maggie waved as he approached and then resumed twisting her skirt between her fingers.

'What's happened?' he asked.

'It's Sean,' she explained, clearly upset. 'He's fighting, down at the mill!'

Brandon ran across open ground, through the mill where the steam-driven engine throbbed and out the back to where men crowded around two fighters, one of whom was red-haired. Without hesitation he thrust his way through the bunched spectators and blocked the fighters by placing himself directly in the middle of their argument. Sean's punch collected him mid-swing and Brandon fell to the ground. His cousin dropped his fist, and gave Brandon a vacant stare, before realising what he'd done.

'What in Saint Patrick's name . . .' stuttered Sean.

The circle of men fell back as Brandon got to his feet. Mr Truby had arrived on horseback with a curled whip in one hand and fury etched onto his face.

'Who instigated this fight?' he barked.

Sean's opponent, a sickle-backed man of fifty years or more, gave a cough. 'It was me, Mr Truby. I do my share of work and I don't need to be putting up with the likes of this one calling me maimed and useless.'

'And you, Sean O'Riain, what do you say to Duffy's charge against you?'

'If a man can't do his share, then he shouldn't be here,' said Sean.

'And Brandon?' said Mr Truby.

'He only tried to stop us. I've no argument with him,' said Duffy.

Truby turned back to Sean. 'As you are so keen to thrash the life out of something, we might put you to use elsewhere,' he said.

'I was employed to cut trees,' Sean answered gruffly.

Mr Truby crossed his wrists one over the other and leant forward in the saddle. 'For the next week, you're employed to do *whatever I damn well say you are*. Come with me,' he ordered Sean, before turning to Brandon. 'You as well.'

'What is the matter with you, Sean? It's almost as if you intentionally go out of your way to complicate our lives,' said Brandon, as they followed Mr Truby and his horse out of the mill

Sean smiled. 'I didn't start it. So don't go blaming me.'

Brandon knew he was lying.

≪ Chapter 33 ≫

They arrived at a bend in the river. It was a pretty spot populated by scraggly-boughed gums grown massive due to their proximity to the water, and a sweep of low grass coloured a vibrant green as if the soil here was somehow richer. The river was clear, tinged slightly brown. The sandy bottom edged out towards the deep, where fish jumped and dashed across the surface before diving away from long-legged waterbirds that stalked the far bank. The scene brought back images of Ireland to Brandon. Its bubbling streams and countless shades of green. A land so evergreen it was hard at times to notice the changing seasons. Not like this northern part of New South Wales, where blustery winds marked the change from chill winters to heated summers, with spring lasting a few unremarkable weeks.

Brandon and Sean followed Mr Truby on foot. Their legs pained from the cracking pace their employer set and their lungs begged for air, so they were more than pleased when a hut came into view and Mr Truby drew the reins and slowed. They passed the rough dwelling. A set of yards lay ahead.

The steady bellow of cattle grew louder as they approached, as did a putrid stench of decay that thickened with their every step.

The yards were built close to the waterway, which proved to be the source of the bawling cattle, who were enclosed within.

Brandon covered his nose to stop himself from dry retching. 'What have you got us into now?' he said to Sean.

His cousin ignored this, as he had all Brandon's questioning for the duration of the five-mile walk, and instead bowed his head and finally whispered, 'He converts folk, your Englishman. He takes a simple-minded Irishman and steals away the one thing freely given. Religion.'

'Is that what the fight was over with Duffy? Religion?' Brandon asked in disbelief.

Sean ignored him.

Mr Truby waited, swishing at the black flies that rose and fell in the air like breath, coating his back like an extra garment. Brandon and Sean kept their distance from the Englishman, whose interest was fixed on the single man at work in the enclosure. The stranger ran into the mob, scattering the animals, and with a large hammer hit one of the cows over the head. The beast staggered but remained upright. A further blow was needed to bring the animal down.

'Not terribly scientific,' said Mr Truby, from the vantage point of his horse. 'However the method works.'

They watched as the man swung an axe into the skull of the freshly killed animal. Bone and brains splattered everywhere.

'This way,' said Mr Truby.

On the far side of the yards, four large cast-iron boilers, each big enough to hold a person, were positioned above fires that cracked and popped with the ferocity of the blaze. Each vat drained a glutinous yellow fluid from a tap into nearby barrels, releasing a stench that was hard to tolerate. Not far from the bubbling meat, land had been levelled flat and it was here that already filled casks awaited collection.

'One man can do about one hundred and thirty sheep a day, but cattle take longer. It's the size of the beast. They must be hacked into pieces small enough to fit into the boilers. It's a job that needs a man with a ready arm and a keen eye,' said Mr Truby.

'And as I said earlier, you seem to have a taste for thrashing, Sean O'Riain.'

Brandon and Sean traded brief glances and then concentrated on their feet.

'There's a drogher due here in a few days to collect the tallow and transport it back to Wirra and then on to Ballina. From there, it will be loaded onto a ship bound for Sydney. I want the rest of these old cows boiled down by then.' He flicked the reins and the horse moved closer to the yards. 'McCauley!' he yelled.

The yard worker looked up vaguely. Upon seeing Mr Truby, he left his task and climbed through the split rails. He wore only trousers, tied at the waist with a strip of rawhide leather, and his entire body was soaked in blood, his hairy face and arms red. He stopped to kick at a pile of offal that was massed with flies and ants and then dunked his head in a barrel of water, bobbing up and down numerous times before drawing himself free and shaking his entire body like a dog. Scars laced his torso. The markings of a lashing.

'Yes, Mr Truby.'

'I've brought two men to help you.'

'I usually work alone, Mr Truby. That was our agreement.' He drew his fingers through long shaggy hair. The water revealed a greying beard and small eyes in a large face, as if he'd seen too much and was gradually withdrawing from the world.

'And I'd never take a job from a determined man, McCauley. I appreciate your enthusiasm, however these two require education. Brandon will only stay for the afternoon while Sean will see the task through.'

'I'm not a slaughterer,' muttered Sean.

McCauley walked towards them, a meaty smell growing in intensity until he was close enough for Brandon to see that the left side of his nose was missing.

'Slaughter or be slaughtered, that's what I say,' said McCauley.

'McCauley here is the best at his job,' said Mr Truby. 'He's used to cutting up whales.'

'And other things,' interrupted McCauley, his tone menacing.

'I don't have to do this,' said Sean.

For the first time in his life, Brandon sensed Sean's fear.

'We agreed on two weeks' work, lad. So if you refuse to do as I say, I'll be taking your four feeble bullocks and boiling them down for candles and lighting oil as well.'

'You have no right,' shouted Sean.

'Nor do you have the right to cause trouble on my land. Think about that, boy, while you're up to your armpits in gore. McCauley, Brandon is to chop wood for the vats and then stir them and Sean is to help you quarter the meat and carry it to the boilers. And if the red-head doesn't do as I say, you have my permission to boil him down as well.'

'Love-er-ly,' replied McCauley, scratching at the hollow where a nostril should have been. 'Different smell, a human has. A bit like pork or chicken.'

'I'm not staying here,' whispered Sean.

'Be quiet,' said Brandon.

'Brandon, be back at the men's quarters by dark.' Mr Truby tapped the rump of the mare with the heels of his boots and rode away.

'It's a long time since I've had company,' said McCauley to Sean. 'You can share me hut. My home is yours.'

Sean considered the land about them. It occurred to Brandon he might well run.

'Get yourself a knife and I'll show you the quickest way to cut a beast down for the vat.' McCauley moved back to the yards where he leveraged himself through the railings.

'Share his hut?' muttered Sean. 'Not in this lifetime.'

Brandon left his brooding cousin and chose an axe that lay on the ground along with a selection of knives. There was a grinding stone next to the implements and he wound the handle, angling the axe-head against the stone so that the metal sparked as the grinder rotated. He was tempted to tell Sean to shut up and do what was expected, instead he concentrated his annoyance on the dull blade, which had seen far better days. Once the jagged edge was smooth, he began filing the blade into a fan-shaped curve.

'What are you doing?' asked Sean brusquely.

'What I was told,' Brandon replied, inspecting his handiwork.

'You don't really expect me to do that.' He grimaced at McCauley, who was kneeling in blood and dirt while he hacked into the cow.

'I don't really care what you do,' Brandon replied tersely.

'Meaning what?'

'Meaning,' said Brandon more strongly, 'that I'm *tired* of getting caught up in *your* wrongs.'

'You wanted to come here in the first place!' said Sean.

Brandon lowered the axe so that the head rested on the ground. 'I turn my back and you're cosying up to the Brotherhood and burning houses. Now you're fighting men far less able than you? And all because of this small question of religion?'

'"Small question"? Even though it killed your mother?' said Sean, his voice rising.

'The famine claimed her.'

'I've always wondered about your leanings. I figured you kept your mouth shut when it came to the Catholic faith simply because you're not the fighting kind. I admired that about you, Brandon. That steadiness you have. And I was happy for you to make decisions because you always appeared to have your family in mind. But it seems to me that your head's become muddled when it comes to the importance of the old country and our religion and I'm beginning to wonder if you're willing to forget your birthright simply to satisfy your own ambitions.' They stared at each other. Anger showed in the beating pulse at the base of Sean's neck.

'That's ridiculous,' Brandon replied, trying to ignore the niggling nub of truth Sean's words stirred. 'We have the opportunity to have more than our fathers ever dreamt possible, but we don't seem to want the same things.'

Sean selected a knife from the assortment laid out on the ground and ran a thumb along the blade before spearing it into the dirt so that it quivered on impact. 'I want what every Irishman wants who came out here to start a new life. Respect.'

'You don't want respect, all you want is to pick a fight.'

'And all you really want, Brandon O'Riain, is a brown-eyed girl. Your stepsister.'

Brandon dropped the axe and punched Sean square in the nose. His cousin staggered under the force.

'Take that back!' yelled Brandon, his arm still raised.

'You think I'm an idiot'—Sean wiped at his nose and stared briefly at the blood on his hand—'but I've seen the way you look at her.'

'You're a fool,' said Brandon, horrified by the accusation.

'Maybe I am, but I know what I've seen and I'm telling you, Brandon, it's wrong. The two of you were raised as brother and sister.'

They faced off against each other, neither of them relenting. The space between them grew heavy with rage.

'You lads gonna glower at each other all day?' McCauley balanced hunks of meat on his shoulders en route to the boiling-down vats, blood and juices dribbling down his back.

'I'm not,' said Sean. He considered the bush that ringed them and then set off along the river, away from the dying cattle.

Brandon picked up the axe, feeling the familiarity of the tool. It was made of inferior timber, the handle already splintering. He stared at the blade, turning Sean's words over and over in his mind. God help him, it was true. He no longer thought of Maggie as his stepsister, and Sean knew it too.

'Not one for a bit of blood and guts?' McCauley came to his side and together they caught sight of Sean as he disappeared into the fringe of scrub that bordered the watercourse.

'He's never taken to being told what to do.'

'A poor man can't afford the luxury of being uppity. Unless he knows something more than the rest of us,' said McCauley, sitting on a stump. He unfolded a chunk of damper from a filthy cloth, broke the bread in half with blood-wet fingers and offered a piece to Brandon.

'Do you like it out here?' asked Brandon. 'And this work?' He glanced at the blood-smeared bread and tried not to grimace as he took a bite, reluctant to offend the older man.

'It's what I'm good at. Taking life and making it into something else. I spent many years on whaling ships. Liked it, too. The profits were always split between the crew and every man was equal no matter where he came from. Dark-skinned or light. 'Course, I wasn't always at my best.' He straightened his spine, displaying the scars that lined his withered torso and back. 'I wanted what others had. A knife with a carved ivory handle, a nice plate of beaten silver. You could say I'm a collector of objects. But it's a small world on a ship. Eventually you have to pay for your takings.'

'And now you're here,' said Brandon.

'No one tells me what to do. Every day is mine. Except when the squatter shows up with a straggler,' said McCauley, chewing on the bread. 'I'm figuring it's your mate that caused the trouble, you're only here to be reminded of who's in command of the ship.' He finished the bread and, after drinking down water from a leather bag, gave a belch. 'The squatter doesn't take to any type of shenanigans. I saw him shoot a man dead once. He went down like one of them cows over there and never got up. Worth remembering.'

McCauley got up and shuffled back to the yards, leaving Brandon to ponder the man who he was so keen to be employed by.

≈ Chapter 34 ≈

Brandon left his clothes on the grass and plunged into the water. He kicked out and then dunked his head, immersing himself in a sphere of yellow-brown light that dimmed in the further reaches. He recalled when Sean had pushed him into a stream near Sydney and he'd quickly discovered the difference between sink or swim. He was not a strong swimmer, but while working for Hackett he'd been forced to help chain logs after they were pushed into the river, and he'd grown used to water. Fish skimmed by, quickening at his presence – dark whiskered catfish and beak-headed silver perch. Spiny crayfish crawled in the shallows. He surfaced, blowing water from his mouth and rubbed at his skin with handfuls of sand, trying to rid his body of the stench of the tallow works. The site was downriver, the smell of decay gone from the air. Yet the odour remained entrenched in his pores, like the sight of those cows being bloodied with a hammer.

He clung to the riverbank, staring up into the interlaced branches of stooping trees as the afternoon shadows lengthened. The ache in his muscles eased with the coolness of the water and gradually his mood brightened, although he was still reeling from his conversation with Sean. There was a pile of firewood stacked near the vats and he'd left McCauley on good terms, even accepting a pouch of crushed tea-tree leaves that the slaughterer swore treated any number of ailments from scabby blisters to sore throats. He'd done what was expected and had not complained, which was more than could be said for his missing cousin.

Brandon ducked his head under the water again and when he resurfaced he was no longer alone. Miss Schaefer and Hetty were standing on the riverbank. Hetty had a stick, which she was using to poke at his belongings until his shirt was fixed to the end of it. She waved it in the air like a flag. As the women laughed he slowly sank further into the water and paddled across to where a large limb had fallen across the river, partially bridging it. He moved along the length of it, scuttling sideways like a crab, conscious of creating the slightest splash before lifting his head, his nose only just above the water.

'There you are.' Hetty was behind him, his clothes gathered in her arms. 'You don't need to worry. Miss Schaefer's gone to find Glanville. He flew off after his supper and we've been searching for him.'

Brandon retreated from her. When standing, the water came up to his waist. 'And she left you alone, having found my clothes. I could be anyone.'

'But you're not anyone,' said Hetty, quite unashamedly staring at his body. 'I've seen naked men before.'

'Really,' said Brandon warily.

She moved closer to the water's edge. 'It's your boots. You've got leather wrapped around them. That's how I knew they were yours. Aren't you getting cold?'

'No.'

'It doesn't take long for the water to chill a person, especially when the sun starts to set.' She looked to the hills, where sunlight already bathed the crowns. Then she sat down on the fallen tree limb with his clothes in her lap, rippling the surface of the water with the sole of her shoe.

'Who gave you the tea-tree leaves?' She held the leather pouch aloft.

'Can you leave my clothes there?' said Brandon.

'Come and get them.' Hetty clasped the garments to her chest.

'Hetty . . .' said Brandon, more forcefully.

'You were with McCauley at the yards, weren't you? I can tell by the stink of your clothes. Mr Truby doesn't send many out there. It's a dreadful business and for a man to spend his days—'

'Hetty!' yelled Brandon. 'Could you please leave my clothes so I can get dressed.'

She ignored him and began dipping the tail of his shirt in the river. 'I heard about the fight. You'd do better without your cousin. We all would,' she told him, sinking the material a little deeper.

'And you'd do better to leave me alone.'

'Come now. I told you, I've seen a man in all his glory. Don't be shy,' said Hetty teasingly. She leant back on the log, her palms supporting her, as if she were enjoying a spectacle at a fair.

Brandon felt his patience give way. It was getting late and being accused of tardiness wasn't a complaint he needed after Sean's earlier actions. He measured his options and, lacking any other choice, waded towards Hetty, aware of the water level lowering along with her wandering gaze. He reached the bank and stood before her, his skin sheeny with water. Unexpectedly, he found himself meeting her stare. It was as if a line had been cast, connecting them in an inexplicable way. She was right in front of him now and Brandon saw the consuming interest she took in his body, felt her fingers tracing the flatness of his stomach until she was cupping his privates in her small cool hand.

He'd never actually lain with a woman. When he was young he'd taken to spraying the side of a ruined crofter's house, marking the abandoned walls with his pleasuring. After a time he'd grown sore and sorry and decided to stop before he was caught or grew hardened skin from the friction. But this was different.

Brandon's tongue touched hers. He heard her swallow. Knew his cheeks burnt red. He fixed on her ragged hair parting, where flecks of copper flared amid the blonde. His mind grew foggy with desire.

'Stop,' he said, when Hetty's exploitations became insistent. He pushed away from her, disentangling their bodies and gathered his clothes, which had fallen to the ground. He had felt her need as strongly as his own. That was the trouble.

He waded back into the chill of the river, where he sloshed the garments up and down in the water to rinse them. Once his clothes were reasonably clean and he'd regained his composure, he draped the wet shirt over a shoulder, stepped out of the water and pulled his trousers on, conscious of his savings sewn within.

Hetty had returned to the bough. Already, the space between them had grown beyond the few feet that kept them apart.

'I'm not one for taking advantage of a man,' she said lightly.

Brandon knew she was trying to dispel the awkwardness.

She made a fuss of picking leaves and other debris from the hem of her dress. 'I'm not some ignorant girl,' she continued, offhandedly. 'I don't want another baby. Miss Schaefer told me that a woman can use a sponge and—'

'Can we not talk of it?' Brandon pulled the shirt over his head and collected the pouch of tea-tree leaves from beside Hetty, the woman watching his every movement. He sat on the bank to tighten the leather thonging around his shoes, ensuring that none of the money stashed there was missing.

Hetty stood up. 'All I was trying to say—'

'I understand your meaning, Hetty,' said Brandon, wishing she'd leave and save them further discomfort.

'Is there someone else?' Hetty asked. 'This isn't about your sister, is it?'

'There you are.' Miss Schaefer's appearance was briefly foreshadowed by the snapping of branches and twigs. Glanville was perched on her gloved hand, hooded and peaceful, a far cry from a predator capable of tearing another bird to shreds. 'And was the water refreshing?'

Brandon tightened the leather about his shoe and got to his feet, hurriedly tucking in his shirt.

'Hetty, will you fetch the horses,' said Miss Schaefer.

'Yes, miss,' said the girl obediently. She gave Brandon a soft, confused look, and left.

Miss Schaefer waited until they were alone before she next spoke. 'Did Hetty help dress you as well?'

Brandon stuffed the small bag of tea-tree leaves in a pocket. He had no idea how long Mr Truby's niece had been present. Perhaps she'd watched from the safety of the trees and witnessed Hetty's wantonness and his own brief pleasure. It would be his undoing if Mr Truby discovered the liaison. 'I should be going.'

'You'll do no such thing,' said Miss Schaefer. 'It is too late in the day for Hetty and me to be out here alone. You must escort us home. That *is* where you're headed?'

'Yes, of course,' said Brandon.

'Good. There are boundary riders and other workmen as well as the natives to keep clear of and I would be loath for Hetty to fall foul of some torrid individual. I, of course, have Glanville for protection. And this.' From a small bag secured at her waist she showed him a pistol.

Brandon should have been taken aback by the sight of a lady with a firearm, but the bush was no place for unpreparedness, although he rather thought that Mr Truby's niece would be capable of handling any situation, with or without a pistol. They walked from the river through the timber, Glanville's head pivoting left and right as they disturbed blue-tongue lizards and mottled ground-dwelling birds that scattered across the grass. On the edge of a cleared paddock they stopped to wait for Hetty, who led two horses towards them.

Miss Schaefer appeared to be consumed by the scenery ahead. 'Did you know that the peregrine falcon mates for life? The court-ship is quite exciting to watch. There is much anticipation and a degree of uncertainty but there is also the most marvellous display of precise spirals and steep dives. Aside from this mix of aerial acrobatics, I always imagined that there must be something else that leads to such bonding. An affinity that can't be explained. Something that makes one bird catch another's eye.' She gave him a crooked smile. 'Perhaps it is the falcon's fine plumage that attracts the female. Once displayed, it is not so easily forgotten.'

Brandon nearly tripped on a log at this remark.

⫷ Chapter 35 ⫸

Kirooma Station, 1948

Stella walked around the side of the homestead to where she'd planted the orange and lemon trees the year of their arrival. They were reasonably healthy this season, thanks to the sheep manure she'd carted over in the wheelbarrow from the woolshed and shovelled onto their roots, and the water she'd bucketed onto them during the sweltering summer months. There were twelve trees in Joe's orchard, some of them already bearing fruit. The grove had been planned with the original orange tree at its centre and had benefited greatly from Joe's pruning. Stella ran her hand through the soft leaves of the plant and then walked to the garden shed. She selected a tool from the mass of old implements stored there and returned to the copse. Had she tried swinging the axe five years previously, she would have failed miserably. But her arms were now toned from working in the garden, chopping firewood and struggling with unruly sheep when she was called upon to do a man's work in the yards. She stared at the orange tree and then swung the blade.

⬦

In the library Stella consumed the histories of the world. The same unbalancing sensation she experienced on her entry into the room years earlier struck her every time she sought refuge within its walls. She would walk about the room holding a book in one hand, the other absently brushing the volumes as she circled. It was while reading a history of Egypt that she realised her Joe was like the Great Sphinx of Giza. A pharaoh surveying his domain. The statue had been standing for over 4000 years. Her husband would be the same. Unbending. Defiant. It would take a storm of great proportions, the force of wind and sand, to wear him down.

Stella waited patiently for Joe to say something about the mangled orange tree, but months had passed without a comment. She hoped for an argument. A quarrel rank with bitterness that might finally dredge up the issues that were close to breaking them and provide an opportunity for them both to explain how they felt. About each other. And about the all-consuming business of grazing, which once again was losing money, causing them to clash with the god who fed, clothed and housed them: the bank.

The orange tree struggled on, though she refused to tend it. Its amputated limbs shot, but it never quite managed to thrive. Eventually, a section of it became gnarled and the wood split from the main trunk and died. Stella considered trimming the lifeless portion, but she knew tidying the plant wouldn't change anything.

One evening she went to water the orchard and found the battered remains of the original tree missing. The only evidence of its existence was a roundish hole, where the ball of roots once sought moisture and life. She felt a presence and turned around to find Joe standing behind her.

'I'm assuming you don't want to replace it,' he said dryly.

Finally, he was acknowledging her vandalism. It had only taken months. She felt a sense of superiority and readied herself for the argument she'd long waited for.

'It's a pity you took your anger out on it. It was a very old plant. The things it would have seen. Horse-drawn carts and carriages. Men in top hats,' said Joe.

He moved about the grove, toeing at the freshly watered soil, pinching off yellowing leaves with quick movements as if he were the head gardener in a botanical park, when for the past few years it had been her dedication that ensured the plants survived.

'Sweet orange – *Citrus sinensis*,' said Stella, as if to prove her cleverness, gleaned from a gardening book in the library.

Joe came to stand quite close to her. Clearing his throat, he removed his hat and twiddled the brim in his hands. The expression on his face suggested that he too practised looking contrite in the mirror. 'I can stay home this week, if you like.'

That was it. After all that time and now with one brief conversation he held out a meagre excuse of an olive branch and expected her to take hold. It was a pathetic offering. Stella began to laugh. Slowly at first and then louder, until she gasped.

'I *am* trying, Stella,' said Joe.

'It's a bit late,' she replied.

He took her hand but Stella shook him off and began to walk away. He reached for her again. This time his grasp on her wrist was painful, but she said nothing, surrendering herself to yet another iteration of the hurt that she already suffered. She turned and kicked him in the knee. He buckled slightly, his mouth drawing together and then he began to drag her away from the garden towards the house.

Stella fought back. Pounding at his arm, kicking his legs.

'Let go. Let go!' she yelled, repeating the words. 'I *hate* you.'

Stella matched each of their steps with a kick or punch, but Joe's progress only became more determined. His pace never varied, nor the strength of his grip. Eventually she began to grow weary of the struggle. They were unmatched opponents and Joe's resolve unnerved her. This wasn't her husband. This was not the man she knew.

In the bedroom Joe led her to the bed and pushed her down onto it by her shoulders. He squatted on the ground and calmly took off her shoes. Then he looked at her, as if expecting an invitation. Stella pushed her lips together and scrutinised the man before her.

His face was crinkled. Deep lines fanned out from the corners of his eyes. Dirt-filled contours were etched in his neck. His hair was thinning. She calculated his age and with a sense of shock realised that Joe was now in his early forties. He was heading towards middle age. His youth was gone, and so was the man she once knew.

He removed his shirt and then undid the buttons on hers. He slid the sweat-crusted material from her shoulders and nestled his face in the side of her neck, as if her scent meant something to him. Stella stayed quite still. They'd not slept in the same bed for over two years. Not made love for so long that when their skin met, she shivered. She'd forgotten what it was like to want a man and to be wanted in return. There had only ever been Joe, fool that she was.

When Stella tried to recall how it had once been between them, her traitorous mind could only replay images of them in the library that first Friday night, dancing to the scratchy record on the gramophone. The bottle of sherry consumed after the disappointment of the honeymoon that never eventuated. The chiffon folds of her dress pushed up to her waist. Her buttocks pressed hard against the library shelves and Joe so intent that at the end when he drew away from her, he'd been dark-eyed and panting.

But that wasn't all Stella recalled. During their lovemaking she had fixed her gaze over her new husband's shoulder on the sepia globe and it wasn't her love for Joe that she'd thought of, but rather what she'd considered in her apartment months earlier. That Joe's aspirations had indeed led her somewhere and she'd ignorantly followed.

Stella lay back on the bed under Joe's rushed insistence and allowed her underclothes to be removed. He kissed her only once. His lips were gentle on hers, and then he pushed himself hard inside her. The iron bed rattled and she concentrated on the pressed metal ceiling, counting the intricate scrolls and the recurring pattern in the design. He hurt her with his urgency, and she let him, realising it was needed, this final coupling, if only for her husband to finally comprehend that what they'd once had was now gone.

'You've lost a lot of weight,' he murmured, rolling onto his back. 'You're not as squelchy as you used to be.' He squeezed her fingers, as he had in their younger years.

Stella sat up on the edge of the bed.

'Seriously. I liked those pudgy bits.'

'When are you going again?' she asked.

'You're okay with it?' he replied, propping his head in a hand. His naked body sprawled across the mattress.

'I'm leaving you.' She stood up and wrapped a discarded sheet about her body.

Joe sat up in the bed. 'Stella—'

She lifted a hand. 'I've tried to tell you how I've felt and you've chosen not to listen. Six years, Joe. Six. I've had enough.'

Joe pulled on his trousers, hopping from one leg to the next, and then buckled his belt. 'You can't divorce me. We're Catholic. Anyway, there's no money. If you think you can walk out of here and take a pile with you . . .' he challenged.

'I'm well aware there's hardly any money. I read what you write in the ledgers.'

'Wool prices aren't what they used to be,' argued Joe.

'Nothing is like it used to be,' countered Stella.

They squared off like fighters, the bed the only barrier between them.

'Maybe if you'd been more interested,' yelled Joe, picking up his shirt from the floor.

'And maybe if you'd actually loved me,' Stella flung back at him.

He said nothing to this. Stella couldn't have received a clearer answer.

'What does any of this matter now? I've made up my mind.' She waited, wondering how she would feel if he apologised to her after all this time, what she might say if Joe told her that he still loved her.

'I have no idea why this hasn't worked out for us,' said Joe, buttoning his shirt.

That was it. He was willing to relinquish her that easily. He'd merely been waiting for her to instigate the discussion.

232

'I know you don't. That's what makes this whole thing so pathetic.'

'Right.' Joe tucked in his shirt and gathered up shoes and socks. 'Can you wait until after shearing? I'd appreciate it.'

Stella calculated the weeks until mid-July and the time it would take for the wool to be loaded and sent to market.

'Four months,' she said. 'Then I'm leaving.'

Relief rushed through her body, making her slightly giddy. She would return to Sydney. Apply for a typist position, perhaps even a secretarial role. She'd been exposed to business, understood ledgers, and was so used to keeping a record of station life in her diary that she considered herself to be as qualified as the next person when it came to keeping tabs on the running of a small office. And Angelina and Carmela. What a joy it would be to see them again.

'Four months,' he agreed with a single nod, lingering in the doorway. 'I'll ask for an advance on the wool proceeds. Organise some money for you that way. It won't be much,' he warned. 'Are you sure you want to do this?'

'Is this life really what you expected, Joe?' replied Stella. 'The risk and the hardship? You came out here with dreams of being a great pastoralist but you beg your living from nature and the banks, and now you've little money and no marriage.'

'I don't regret my decision, if that's what you're asking.'

He would never understand how much he had hurt her. 'You're very fortunate. Because I do.'

'It was always too big a world out here for you.'

'Actually it was too small. And you made it smaller.'

When Joe left, Stella sat down at the dresser. The generator was yet to be started so she lit the kerosene lamp, watching as the flame flared and then settled. She opened the drawer and took out the silver-backed hairbrush that lay within, feeling the aged bristles against her palm. Her body had failed her. There was no child. And now, after the endless loneliness, very soon she would be husbandless and homeless as well. But she would have her freedom, and that was worth everything to her.

⚔ Chapter 36 ⚔

Richmond Valley, 1949

From the earliest weeks on the Kirooma property, Stella had
pointedly allocated Sunday mornings as a sacred time for
prayer and devotion. She'd tried to address Joe's tendency to treat
the day as any other by telling him how important this weekly
observance was to her. He'd argued that the land was his church,
that the bush allowed him a closer relationship to the divine than
any other form of religion or manmade structure. How could she
dispute this line of reasoning? Joe was in love with his new life.
He was a self-made man. And he had accomplished what many
dreamt of but lacked the dogged persistence to achieve. Land of
his own. For the grandson of an Irish tenant farmer, the purchase
of Kirooma, unaided by family, was a mighty feat.

She thought of him now, as she left the house at midnight and
with little thought headed directly to the boundary fence. Overhead,
the sky was clear and bursting with the glow of the stars. She hesitated only briefly and then shimmied through the wires beside the
cedar tree. She did it because she could and because it was forbidden, even reasoning that she was doing it for Joe. Or perhaps it was
for herself. A penance of sorts. For what she had done.

She took two steps into the forbidden world, her fingers never quite leaving the tautness of the metal fence, her feet toying with grass that belonged to another. She was like a dingo, prowling in the dark. Not for prey but for answers.

She stood motionless, wondering what her excuse would be if she were caught by Harry or his sons, but at midnight, she hazarded, the only people who were still awake were old souls and those like her. People who were misplaced in the world.

The neighbouring houses backed onto each other in the gloom like soldiers napping while on patrol. Stella completed her initial reconnaissance, guessing the time it took to walk the length of the border, calculating the minutes required to negotiate the lawn to the large house, as if she were an illegal trying to cross into a new country. She'd never set eyes on her neighbours, never seen them tending their own backyard. She'd always felt pried upon, but perhaps they felt that the O'Riains were doing the same to them. She walked towards the house, her eyes growing more accustomed to the dark. Another ten steps she told herself. No more. To her right, a statue gleamed. A woman, cold and immortal in the star-light. Stella moved onwards, though she knew it was time to turn back, that her defiance of Harry's rules had gone far enough. She had arrived as a helper, now she was a trespasser. It was time to leave.

The dog's bark was loud. Stella froze.

'I can see you,' a man announced. The voice was scratchy with age. A veranda light came on. Stella shielded her eyes as a barking animal hurtled through the grass towards her.

'He won't bite,' said the man. 'Sit down, boy.'

Nonetheless, Stella remained perfectly still, berating herself for not running. Every criminal ran, it was a fact, instinct. Clearly, she had much to learn. The dog halted at her side and licked at her bare leg. She began to back away, hopeful that the dog was the same obedient kelpie that had walked the boundary a few weeks ago, shadowing her from the other side.

'You're Stella. Stella Moretti. The girl who married Joseph.'

She stopped at the sound of her maiden name and searched the veranda for the speaker. The light was still shining in her eyes. He was sitting a little off to one side but with the distance that lay between them, he was a mere silhouette, yet to be filled in with shape and colour.

'Yes,' she replied. 'I should go.'

'Why? You've crossed the boundary. That's a small thing, I imagine, for a woman like you. Although there will be a hornet's nest waiting if word gets out.'

'And will it get out?' asked Stella cautiously.

'I'm not one to kiss and tell, lass.' She heard him chuckle. 'You've gone further than most in one lifetime already,' he continued. 'I'd be interested to hear about it, this place you've come from. I heard once that it's the outer limits that the kangaroos leave first in a dry time. They head eastwards when things get tough, in search of better pasture. I figure you've done the same. I'm not calling through the night, lass. If it's conversation you're wanting I'm happy to oblige, but you'll have to grace an old man with your presence up close in one of my fine cane chairs.'

A wobbly light patched the lawn and Stella realised that this stranger was lighting a path for her to follow. The dog rushed back towards the house. She heard the man's breathing, slightly laboured, and the dryness of a cough.

'I've whiskey, if you're a drinker. If you're not by now, you should be.'

Stella crept across the grass, her nerves frayed. She worried who might be awake and observing her, but was anxious about this stranger more, this old man who she was warned to stay clear of, who, she knew now, was the person who watched her by day and now sat waiting for her in the dead of night. Perhaps he might be able to explain the discord within Joe's family. Yet it was more than that. She hoped he might be able to tell her more about Joe himself, and provide some reasoning for her own terrible actions.

'Come now. I won't bite.'

Stella stepped up on the veranda and sat in the chair next to the man, the powdery scent of old linen reminding her of the musty smells of the Kirooma homestead.

He held a kerosene lamp up to her face and in the shared flame she saw white hair that fell almost to his shoulders and mottled skin that hung from a skeletal face. The man seated next to her was ancient.

'Stella Moretti O'Riain. You know, I've never been interested in how things were but rather how they could be. Which is why I sit out here staring through the binoculars at a family that refuses to learn from the past.' He set the lamp down. 'So, you're Joseph's widow. He chose well.' He moistened his lips, his fingers resting on the field glasses sitting on the table between them. 'And you're a grower of things. Of beans and carrots and plush red tomatoes. A scant three weeks since your arrival and already you're putting dreary Ann to shame in the vegetable stakes.' He leant a little closer. 'And you're a strong young woman. You married into the O'Riain family and followed young Joe out into the scrub.'

'He came to see you after we were married.' She was aware her tone carried the pitch of interrogation.

The old man nodded. 'I see we're straight to business. Yes, he did.'

'What did you talk about?'

'The birds and the bees.'

'I'm serious,' said Stella.

The cane chair squeaked as he readjusted his position. 'So am I. A young buck needs some tutelage when he's embarking into the murky depths of matrimony, especially your Joe. He was a late bloomer. Not that I've had much experience.'

'Ann said that there was an argument between Joe and Harry after Joe visited you. Why? Can you tell me?' asked Stella.

He looked away from her. 'It's complex,' he said curtly, 'and the quarrel began long before Joe sat in that same chair as you.'

Stella ran her hands across the arms of the chair, feeling the crosshatch of the rattan, trying to visualise Joe sitting in the very same spot. 'I don't even know your name.'

'You can call me Irish. Just plain Irish. Australians love their nicknames.'

They shook hands, a single clasp of callused and papery skin.

From beneath the table Irish took a glass and a half-bottle of whiskey. He poured two nips into a tumbler, his hands shaky, and passed it to her, then he filled a pannikin for himself. 'Drink.'

Stella did as she was told, grateful for the calming effects of the alcohol.

'You don't mind that I stare at you through a pair of age-battered eyes that couldn't see half the distance if it wasn't for these army-issue binoculars?' he said.

'It did bother me,' said Stella. 'Not so much now.'

Irish chuckled. 'Ah, yes. Now that you've met me, I'm the harmless old man across the fence. You remind me of my youth, of a time when women threw me admiring gazes and men treated me as an equal and a thousand possibilities teased me to action.' He leant slightly towards her. 'I have to wonder at you coming back here, to Harry's place. Have your family all died?'

'No. They disapproved of my choice of husband,' Stella told him, cradling the whiskey glass in her lap.

'Rules and regulations, eh? Well, most families have them. I liked young Joe but he was a loner, and solitary men don't make good husbands. And yet you chose him regardless, which makes me suspect that some kind of fault runs through you as well. The line's not visible to everyone, but it's certainly there. Deep beneath the surface. I see it sometimes when you stare at the mountains, your face creased with despair. The way you lift your palms to your face and press them close and then glance skywards as if the saints of your blessed religion were listening and could actually offer help.'

'You don't believe in God?' asked Stella.

'Religion ruins a people.'

238

'What people?'

'Any people who have a tendency towards fanaticism. That's why I don't believe anymore. Joe was the same. He understood the cost of blind devotion. That it can become an excuse for unwarranted actions and lead rash men down dangerous paths. But I told him he'd have to allow you your foibles. The Sunday prayers in the music room. The ash you marked your forehead with at Lent. Especially out there,' he said.

Stella drew back in shock. 'How do you know that?'

'He never told you? I assumed that was one of the reasons why you'd come to stay with Harry and Ann. To speak to me about Joe. Interesting. He was a cagey one,' said Irish.

'But who told you that? Joe?' asked Stella.

'Who else?' said Irish. 'He wrote to me quite often.'

'To you? Why? I don't understand.'

'We were friends.'

Stella rubbed her temples as if the action might clear her mind. 'But he never mentioned you.'

Irish shrugged and took a slurp of whiskey. 'The opinion of those in the village is that you're tough. That a woman would have to be, enduring as you did for so many years far beyond the range. But I don't think you are. As I said, I've watched you. Crying. Praying. Walking. You're brittle. Wounded. You carry your pain quite clearly – to me, at least. And there's more to your story than you're letting on.' He had grown animated during his speaking, his whole body moving slightly in the chair so that by the time he finished, he sat back, clearly tired from his exertions.

'Tell me about Joe,' said Stella, feeling invaded by this man who'd clearly noticed more than most while observing her through his binoculars.

'Don't you like stories that start at the beginning and finish at the end?'

'That depends if the story is relevant,' she said.

Irish gave a laugh. 'You are a feisty one.' He skolled his drink, his throat making a small series of clicks. 'Do you like our cedar tree, Stella? I guess it to be about one hundred and forty feet high. It survived the initial onslaught of the cutter's saws nearly one hundred years ago only to watch as the grove that once sheltered it shrunk until only it remained, saved by being on the border of no-man's-land. To my knowledge, only a couple of people have crossed the boundary since 1867.'

'Including Joe,' said Stella.

'Yes,' he confirmed. 'Quite intriguing, really, when you think of the men involved. Sean and Brandon O'Riain were the best of friends. They should have ridden through this country laying the boundaries of their new land by blazing trees with an axe. Each swing of their wiry arms should have marked out territory like dogs peeing.' His voice lowered. 'That's how they became in the end, territorial. Defensive. First towards those who sought to denigrate them and then towards each other.'

'You knew Brandon and Sean,' said Stella.

'Oh, yes. I knew them. In another time. That's the worst of longevity, you remember everything and everyone.' He dipped his head in the direction of the garden. 'Examine the trunk of that cedar in daylight and you'll see there are matching initials carved in the bark on opposite sides. The marks of warring cousins, once the very best of friends. In the end, even the tree formed a part of the quarrel. But I suppose that's what saved it. And still saves it. Possession. Life has always been about who owned what. In the old country and the new.'

❊ Chapter 37 ❊

Richmond Valley, 1867

Mr Truby was outdoors, sitting at his green-felt table. Brandon hoped to avoid him after the hours spent at the tallow works two days previously, however it was not to be. The Englishman called out to him, so he approached, noting the deck of cards was still in its case.

'I'm sorry about Sean, sir,' said Brandon. 'The fight and all.' He knew there would be a reckoning of some form. McCauley's description of his employer killing a man had made for two sleepless nights.

'I hope you've learnt that actions lead to consequences.'

'Yes,' agreed Brandon.

Mr Truby drank from a glass of water as a hot northerly wind gusted through the garden. He fished a leaf from the surface of the liquid and studied the foliage, so absorbed it might have been a sliver of gold. 'Good. Come with me.'

He stood and walked up onto the veranda. At the rear of the homestead he opened the door, gesturing for Brandon to follow. Brandon hesitated, but removed his hat and entered a long hallway and then a large parlour. The room was constructed completely of cedar. The panelled walls, floor and ceiling glowed with the polished wood so that the interior shamed the ornate gilt-framed paintings and the crystal decanters sitting atop silver salvers.

'Come in, Brandon.'

He moved from the door to the oval table where Mr Truby had sat.

'Come now, sit down, lad.'

Brandon positioned himself carefully on a cushioned seat opposite the Englishman and set his hands on his thighs, conscious of his river-washed clothes among such finery. A decanter and two cut-crystal glasses were at his left elbow; on the right, a large terrestrial globe on a finely turned mahogany stand, with a compass resting beneath.

'Ah, yes. It's quite something to see the world laid out. It's my favourite piece, I must admit. My father knew the globemaker, John Smith. He had a shop on the Strand in London and my father purchased this fine example from there in the year of its manufacture, 1825,' said Mr Truby.

'It's very fine,' said Brandon. He was wary of why he'd been summoned indoors.

Mr Truby folded his hands one over the other and rested them on the tabletop. 'The summer doesn't lend itself to great action in this country. When I was young, my friends and I yearned for the warmer months. Cricket. Wonderful game. Have you ever played?'

'No.'

'Pity. It's a sport that's worth pursuing. I once took four wickets while at Cambridge. It wasn't a top-drawer game. Still, it's something to talk of in those circles where a hint of importance is the key to acceptance. Great emphasis is placed on sportsmanship in cricket. I rather think that's why it's proved so popular. The idea of fair play towards one's opponent. Rather a benchmark for life, don't you agree?'

'I suppose so.'

'Don't you measure yourself against others? You must, for how else do you judge if your life is better or worse, whether *you* are better or worse, than others,' said the Englishman.

Brandon found the globe to be extraordinarily interesting at that point. He fixed his gaze on the southern parts beneath Australia where the words *unknown lands* were scrawled. He was hesitant to say anything lest he appear ignorant, but at the same time he found himself thinking of Sean and the differences that set them apart.

Mr Truby coughed, and Brandon was drawn back into the conversation that he was doing his best to ignore.

'You're beginning to lose that ghostly pallor, Brandon. Tell me, what is it like in the forest?'

He thought of what the woodlands meant to him. 'The air is thick. Sometimes almost too heavy to breathe. In the winter, when it's cold, that changes. It's as if there is too much oxygen. It's sharp, like fresh water when you crack the ice from the top.'

His employer oriented the globe so that Australia was replaced by ocean. 'I've ridden around the edges of it. Cut down whatever was left on my land, probably taken what was outside my boundary as well, but I couldn't live there, day after day. I'd feel surrounded. Claustrophobic. A person needs to be able to see where they're going. There must be a clear path. Do you understand what I'm saying?'

'I think so.' But he didn't, not really.

'Do you have any idea how I made my money, Brandon?'

'No, sir.'

'By being able to see ahead. The day I arrived in the Valley I rode as far as I could in every direction. Where this house stands is the point I left from. A clump of trees back then. Not an auspicious beginning, however I had a sense of what could be achieved. A man needs money, of course. Money gives us possibilities. Nothing can replace the coin you make from your own endeavours. You recognise that, I think.'

'I understand that a person has to work to succeed in life,' said Brandon.

'Exactly. And one needs to be aware of opportunities as well.' Mr Truby removed the stopper from the decanter and poured the liquid into two glasses. 'A drink?'

'I don't drink rum, sir.'

'Ah, but this is sherry. Christopher Columbus took sherry on his voyage to the New World. And after Francis Drake sacked Cadiz in 1587, he brought back nearly three thousand barrels of sherry from Spain. If one's going to drink, it should be something with history.'

He raised a glass and Brandon did the same, unable to formulate any argument that could warrant refusing the man opposite. He took a sip. The taste was dry, but pleasant.

'Four generations ago my ancestor married a woman who, by the end of their unfortunate alliance, left him almost penniless. It took the next three generations to regain only a portion of what was lost. Which is why I have certain rules. Women being one of them. You do understand?' He licked his lips. 'I have always found women quite difficult to manage. They are flighty, undependable characters, prone to emotional outbursts and often prove difficult to control.'

Brandon moved forward on the seat. 'Maggie is like that.'

'Then we must find a better situation for her. One that will benefit everyone. I will think on it.' Mr Truby set the glass down. 'Now to business. I want the new storey above us to have a room like this. Exactly the same. In every way. I thought perhaps you could sort out the best planks from those already cut at the mill.'

'Of course,' said Brandon.

'It's important for the room to be perfect. In England, one prefers a grand view. And, as you said on the day of your arrival here, framing is of importance.'

'You'll need bigger windows than this room has. I mean, wouldn't you want bigger windows for that very reason?' said Brandon meekly, nervous of speaking his mind.

'You're right.' Mr Truby went to a desk in the far corner of the room and returned with papers. 'Move those, will you.'

Brandon lifted the decanter and glasses and placed them on a side table as Mr Truby unrolled the plans for the house. He ran a spotlessly clean fingernail, which was slightly long and pointed, across the parchment and tapped an oblong box that was drawn on one edge of what Brandon supposed was the outer wall. 'There. You're right. They could be twice the size, couldn't they?'

Brandon studied the windows of the parlour and then the drawing on the table. Then, after asking permission, he walked to the end of the room and paced out the distance between the corner and the first window. He returned to the desk to reread the measurements noted within the diagram.

'Here. You'll need this.' Mr Truby passed him a magnifying glass. 'The architect has the absolute worst handwriting – cramped, tiny. A sign of small-mindedness.'

Brandon read the measurements. 'Both windows could be two feet longer, I think. But I only cut timber. I'm not a builder, Mr Truby.'

The older man viewed him with renewed interest. 'It seems to me that the successful completion of nearly every task has more to do with common sense and discipline than previously acquired knowledge. There are plenty of educated men who understand very little.' He sat back at the table and pointed at Brandon to do the same. 'Tomorrow you'll measure this room and I'll show your estimates to the builder.' He leant back in the chair. 'Now, as we have discussed the merits of industriousness, the importance of sherry and the melancholic attachments of a son to his dear father's globe, let us debate a subject considered unparalleled by many. Religion. Are you a churchgoer?'

Brandon felt his anxiety return. A week had passed since the Protestant attack. Time enough for the postal rider to deliver news from the village. 'I don't have much opportunity,' said Brandon, trying to sound as detached as he could.

'So you're not a religious man. The religious ensure they never miss a service for fear of being refused a seat at the Lord's table when the reckoning comes.' Mr Truby stopped abruptly, as if willing a response. When none was given, he continued. 'But, for those of us unable to sit beneath his roof there is Sunday and the Bible at home. Come now. It's just us here. There is no priest nearby wielding incense. Are you one of the faithful?'

'My stepmother believed in the old gods.' Brandon was eager to change the subject.

Mr Truby got up from his seat and walked to the window, where a magpie had begun to bash against a pane of glass. 'She was a pagan?'

'I suppose so. But my father was a believer. He read to us when we were little about the seven deadly sins until we were too scared to do anything other than what we were told.'

Hands clasped behind his back, Mr Truby observed the bird as it continued its useless plight. 'Rules. A guidebook for living. I can appreciate those learnings of the Catholic faith, for Protestants are not much different when it comes to good and evil. It's the confession I abhor. The false belief that the slate can be wiped clean when evil has been done. Chanting prayers does not atone for one's sins.'

Brandon had never heard such a thing. 'What does?'

'Punishment. Discipline. I am yet to understand how a pope can make his priests judge and jury, who then in turn send away a member of their flock with a few Hail Marys. It is insubstantial.'

'But it's faith,' replied Brandon.

Mr Truby moved away from the window and back to the table. 'And what is faith? Confidence in a religious belief. Do you think a man can truly receive atonement through the vehicle of confession? What if he murders and only his priest knows? Do you think prayers and reflection can undo the deed?'

The Englishman's conviction made Brandon uncertain. He'd not had the opportunity to seek out a priest after Mr Macklin's death, but it was true, he doubted it would have made him feel absolved of his part in the crime.

'Doesn't your faith demand absolutism? It would seem a Catholic has no room for argument when it comes to a discussion of your beliefs. So tell me. What do you truly think?' Mr Truby asked.

'That if a man does a very bad thing, eventually the law will make him pay. It has nothing at all to do with religion,' said Brandon slowly.

Mr Truby leant on the table with his knuckles. 'Exactly.'

Were they speaking of religion or Sean?

'I don't believe you're the type to place religion above your well-being. Not now. Not here in this valley. Consider the opportunity awaiting you if you chose to put your future above all else.' Mr Truby moved to his desk and sorted through the documents stacked in piles of varying sizes. He pulled out a newspaper and then held it up for Brandon to see as he returned to the table. He drank down the sherry and then poured again for both of them, waiting until Brandon had drained his glass before continuing.

'This is the *Protestant Standard*. Last month, a Miss Edith O'Gorman gave a lecture in Lismore. She spoke of her time as a nun, which was clearly quite traumatic. Her account certainly did not endear her to those of her discarded faith, who broke up the gathering in a riotous fashion. Can you not see that a religion that requires such brutal defence, one that sets itself against a truthful woman, can only be false?' He folded the newspaper. 'This chapter has brought scandal on your church. Isn't it difficult enough being Irish? Why overcomplicate your life?'

Brandon rubbed his brow in confusion. His employer made a compelling argument for the Protestant faith, one that made Sean's Fenian leanings seem doubly wrong. He needed time to think and the sherry wasn't helping. He asked permission to leave, the chair falling backwards in his eagerness to stand. He picked it up and pushed it towards the table, straightening it carefully.

Mr Truby sipped his sherry. 'Thank you, Brandon. I enjoyed our conversation. A bit of stiff debate energises the mind.'

Once outside, Brandon went straight to the middle of the cedar trees. He felt confused, and he knew the sensation could not be blamed on the sherry alone. He stared up into the close-knit branches and thought of the Tuatha Dé Danann, the kings, queens and heroes of long ago, who were banished from heaven because of their knowledge. They'd come to Ireland among dark misty clouds and landed in the mountains to rule as immortals. Not one true God or religion, but many gods. Why did he think of these gods of the underworld, the ones his stepmother burnt offerings to, now?

The conflict between the Orange and the Green was age-old and battle-worn, formed by centuries of grievances. And, Brandon realised bleakly, Mr Truby had just stoked a fire that possibly had always been within him. It was, quite simply, the struggle for the possession of his soul. For the Englishman was right; he'd never quite been a true believer.

He thought of his father. If he were dead, he'd be turning in his grave.

⧽ Chapter 38 ⧼

The scents of the evening were already gathering, steeping the summer air with lavender and the tang of native trees. Hetty was on the side veranda, near the caged falcon. She had a wooden box under one arm and was bashing something on the bannister with the other. As Brandon neared, he saw the patch of blood on the wood, and the victim. She was holding a dead mouse by the tail, assessing her handiwork. He considered sneaking away before she caught sight of him, for she was also on his list of people to evade, however, like with his employer, there was little possibility of that occurring as Hetty glanced in his direction. Committed to speaking with her, he waited for a witty remark or pithy retort, an unsubtle reference to what had transpired at the river. Work kept him occupied but he had to admit, the thought of her woke him during the night.

'Miss Schaefer's away at the moment visiting a friend. She likes him fed twice a day, but I don't like killing them in the morning. It doesn't seem right when the sun's shining and everything is fresh and new. So I kill them and store them overnight.' She poked the battered mouse through the cage wire and Glanville pecked the carcass from her fingers. 'That's all,' she told the bird. 'Feeding time is finished.'

She reached for another mouse. It wiggled free, jumping from her grasp and running across the grass. Hetty shook her head at this loss and then tied twine around the box of dead mice to secure the lid and placed it on a table with a lump of wood on top of it.

'I shouldn't like him. Not when I have to do the killing for him. But he is very beautiful.' She made a series of clucking noises that caused Glanville to give a lofty stretch of his wings. 'But he's not one to be trusted. He killed Athena, the other falcon. Well you were there the morning it happened. I saw you walking with Miss Schaefer. She must have let him do it, but still, it makes you wonder. Glanville and Athena were caged next to each other for over a year.'

'He has a killer's instinct,' said Brandon.

'Perhaps. Or maybe he was just hungry. When I was at the orphanage, I saw children scrabbling on the floor, fighting over bits of bread. Hunger can make a person mean. It's probably the same for falcons. I have some food if you want to join me. There's a hunk of meat and potatoes ready and I swear it'll be better than what McCauley has concocted over at the men's quarters.'

'McCauley's here?' asked Brandon.

'Haven't you heard? Your cousin never came back. Took off into the scrub. McCauley arrived this afternoon to tell Mr Truby. He's to walk those bullocks of yours to the tallow works when he leaves in a few days. I'm sorry,' said Hetty. 'Not about your cousin, but the bullocks. It's a hard thing to work for something and then lose it.'

The blood began to pound in Brandon's chest. 'Is Maggie at your cottage?'

'I'm not sure. Cook had her washing the floors in the big house and she wasn't doing a particularly good job of it. It's a privilege to work in a house like that. She should be more grateful. Maggie told me she was used to work, but every time I see her, she's dawdling about, or she can't be found at all. I warned her I wasn't going to watch out for her anymore.'

'The last few years have been hard on her,' replied Brandon defensively.

She gave a huff as if what he said was ridiculous and he chastised himself inwardly. Hetty had no one, after all.

Brandon considered walking overnight to Wirra to search for Sean and returning to the property before daylight. But the moon was on the wane. It was the waiting that gnawed at him, for who knew what his cousin might do next.

'You'll eat with me,' said Hetty.

'No,' answered Brandon distractedly.

'Why? Am I not good enough?' said Hetty, lifting her skirt as she stepped through long grass.

'I'm tired, Hetty. That's all. Anyway, what about Mr Truby and his rules? I doubt he'd care for us to be seen together.'

'He enjoys your company. I've seen him wandering around the garden while you're cutting trees, stopping to talk to you. You're lucky. He doesn't take to most. Like your cousin. He's a slippery one. Your sister's not much different. She can barely be in the same room with me, though she's happy to have a blanket and the use of my fire and food. We'd never be friends, she and I. Your sister doesn't want any. I think you're the same.'

'Maggie's my stepsister,' he corrected.

'My apologies. Stepsister,' replied Hetty.

'And she's not one for people.'

'Sure she is. It's just that I'm not her sort,' said Hetty.

'What do you mean?'

'I'm Protestant. And you lot being Catholic, well, I suppose you would have sniffed that out quick smart. Mr Truby converted me to the faith within a month of my coming here. I don't think the mistress bothers with such things, not where staff are concerned, but Mr Truby is one for education and emancipation,' said Hetty.

'We're not slaves, Hetty,' said Brandon.

'Silly.' She widened her eyes and gave a little grin. 'I've been liberated. I was a sheep blindly following others, when the one true faith was waiting to welcome me.'

'And you were happy to become a Protestant?'

Hetty shrugged. 'Makes little difference to me. I get to keep my job. Anyway, I hardly ever went to church and now I only have to sit through an hour of Mr Truby's readings on a Sunday. You *will* eat with me?' she asked hopefully.

Brandon found himself being led to the little cottage. After what had occurred by the river he was unsure if he cared for her or not, but he'd liked her body pressed against his and that was a complication he'd not anticipated. The girl drew him in. She was strong and outspoken without being plagued by the hysterics that beset Maggie on occasion. And Hetty made him forget. He'd not thought about Maggie since the river and as he stepped through the cottage door, he put thoughts of Sean aside too.

The children were in their usual places – the baby under the table and the little boy playing on the floor. The child reached for Brandon's trouser leg as he passed, and he leant down and patted the boy's head before sitting at the table. As Hetty served up the food, he listened to the scrape of her spoon against the wall of the cooking pot. A horse nickered in the distance. He was still unused to the woodless breadth of land around him. All he knew of Australia were waterways and belts of trees. Of cutting and rushing to the next dense stand. Following the men who would make their fortune, hoping to make his own. But perhaps he'd not seen clearly enough. A man could work all his life and still not be accepted or succeed if he was a square peg in a round hole.

'You leave your children alone during the day?' said Brandon, when they were partway through the meal.

Hetty gave a giggle and pointed to his mouth. Embarrassed, he wiped at the meat juice dribbling down his chin. It was the best possum curry he'd tasted since arriving in Australia.

'I have to. Tommy is used to it now. 'Course, if he climbs on a chair or the table or pokes at the fire . . .' Her lips twisted in concern. 'He's had more than his fair share of spills, but with age he'll learn.' She spooned up some meat from her bowl and fed Tommy the morsel. Then she lifted the boy's clothing to display a burn mark across his back. 'I came back to feed the baby and Tommy had knocked the pot from the fire.'

The boy escaped his mother's grasp and began running around the table.

'It must be hard at times,' said Brandon.

'What good can come of worrying?' She leant across the table for his empty bowl, the material on her neckline falling open to reveal the rise of her breasts. Hetty noticed where his attention drifted, and her face coloured slightly. She carried their plates across to a bucket of water.

'What's it like being a Protestant?' asked Brandon.

'It's boring, really.' She dipped the bowls in the water and then sat them near the fire to dry. 'There's no praying to the saints, no worship of Mary, no popery. That's what Mr Truby calls it. The first time he ever said the word, his lip turned up at the corner like a cat's snarl. He also said that most of us poor Irish are uneducated and that's the way the Catholic Church likes it. He's right. Most of what's said is in Latin.' Hetty walked to her cot, the alcove concealed by a curtain of hessian.

He observed the way she moved. The neatness of her walk. The way the cloth of her skirt draped either side of her rounded bottom as she leant across the bed. Hetty was not one for the petticoats and cheap crinolines that other women of her class wore and he realised that he admired that about her. Brandon followed her across the room so that when she turned, clutching a clothbound Bible, she almost fell into his arms.

'What is popery?' he asked, resting his hands on her waist.

'Candles. Incense,' replied Hetty, reaching back to drop the Bible on the bed.

'And what about the old gods?' Brandon drew her closer. 'Do you know them?' He rubbed a thumb along her scarred skin.

'Yes.' She fitted her hips against his thighs. 'The shapeshifting

Morrígan, a queen of war and fate. Sometimes I pray to her. Is that so very wrong?'

She ran her palms across his chest. Brandon reached down and began to lift her skirts. He hoped she had no expectations. That, like him, she only cared for this moment.

The door flew open. Maggie stood on the threshold.

Brandon moved quickly to the far side of the room. The guilt that flooded through him was beyond anything he'd experienced, the sensation confusing him to the extent that he was incapable of speech.

Hetty in comparison was far more assured in her reaction, as she folded her arms across her chest. 'You took your time today. Haven't you washed floors before this?'

Maggie placed a hand against the doorframe, as if without the support she might fall. 'How *could* you, Brandon!'

'Oh my girl, you have a lot to learn,' said Hetty. 'One day your petty attitude will be your undoing.'

'She's not one of us,' said Maggie.

'Maybe I'm not either, Maggie. Maybe I'm sick to death of the Green versus the Orange, and the narrow-mindedness that goes along with it. Maybe I don't want any type of religion at all,' said Brandon.

'Except for the old gods,' said Hetty, moving closer to Brandon and taking his arm.

Maggie pointed a finger at Hetty. 'She's hexed you. Between her and the Englishman they've taken your soul. How dare you lecture me on how to live my life?'

He loosened Hetty's grip and walked towards his stepsister. 'Let me explain.'

'I thought there was something between us that bonded us, like a real brother and sister, so that although we might have our disagreements, we understood what the other thought. But now I see I don't know you at all,' said Maggie angrily.

'Maggie, you know what you mean to me.' Brandon tried to reach for her but she stepped away.

'If I did, I don't anymore,' said Maggie, turning to leave.

'Wait. Sean's gone. He ran away two days ago.'

'Of course he did. When the postal rider came the day of the mill fight, he had the news. About those farmers being burnt out. Sean's name was mentioned. It's all anyone is talking about here. It's just as well he's run away.'

'You knew? And you said nothing?' asked Brandon.

'And how is a person meant to gauge what side you're on?' she spat. 'I see that I was right.' She hurried from the cottage.

Brandon tried to follow, but Hetty caught his sleeve.

'It will do no good, Brandon. Wait until the morning. Once she's settled down a little it will be easier to speak to her. Find her now and there will be no reason to what she says. You might even make things worse.' She led him to the table, and made him sit. Hetty sat opposite, covering his clenched hands with her own.

'You don't understand. This is *Maggie*,' said Brandon, slowly pulling away from her grasp.

Hetty gave him a hard stare. 'I hoped I was wrong about you. But now I see I was right all along. I think you'd better leave.'

≪ Chapter 39 ≫

A few evenings later, Brandon came across McCauley sitting in a broken-backed chair out the front of the men's quarters. He was plaiting a whip, the wattle of his chin quavering as he pulled long strips of rawhide back and forth. The ten-foot-long strips of leather lay curled in a pile at his feet. He glanced at Brandon as he approached and then drew his concentration back to his task.

'I've been looking for you,' said Brandon.

'What? No hello for a friend?'

'I'm sorry.'

'You've come about that cousin of yours, but I've not seen hide nor hair of him since he ran off,' McCauley told him.

Brandon sat on a stump next to the slaughterer as the evening sky changed from mauve to navy. He'd been hopeful, but he was not surprised that the man knew nothing of his cousin's whereabouts. Sean obviously knew his name had been mentioned in connection with the Fenian attacks and he'd gone into hiding. 'It's quiet tonight. Where are the rest of the men?'

McCauley broadened his one good nostril, the vacant hole on the other side increasing in size. 'Reckon the men don't like my company. That and the stench. It's hard to get the smell of meat out of a person.' He trimmed a length of leather with a pocket-knife. 'Anyway, it seems to me you've got a woman problem. There was enough of a din going on the night afore last to wake the dead.'

'You heard that,' said Brandon.

'A man hears many a thing out here. So much silence makes us good listeners, and a woman's voice, well, it has an incantation of its own. My mother's voice was so soft it sounded like the warble of a small bird. But the other night, well, it was more like a nest of geese. The men took bets on what the barney was about. The word is, Hetty has a hankering for you. A man could do worse.'

'I suppose, but I'm not looking for a wife.'

'That won't stop a woman. And you've got the confidence of the squatter. The boys smelt grog on you the other day. It's a dry camp here, lad. Any of them would swap places for a chance of a snifter at the end of the day. Some'll trudge twelve mile to the shanty down-stream. 'Course, after a while, they don't come back,' said McCauley.

'It was only sherry and it's not like I drank it all.'

McCauley threw the partially completed whip into the air. It landed with a thump and a scattering of leather strips. 'Well aren't you a father's favourite. Depending on your father, of course. Mine would have whipped me for leaving a drop in a glass.'

'It's only because I'm working over there and Miss Schaefer's away. He's lonely,' said Brandon.

McCauley lifted a finger bent in three places. 'He'd be lonely even with his young niece stopping at home. Miss Schaefer prefers Sydney Town. She'll have a plan, that one. Probably thinks after he's gone that she'll sell it all up and take her coin south.' He gave a chuckle and, reaching for the whip, began twisting the hide together with knobby thumbs. 'The girl will be on the receiving end of a bit of comeuppance when the time comes. The boss rode in here like many a squatter and took what he wanted, but the land he uses and what he's paying for are quite a few thousand acres in difference.'

'I don't understand,' said Brandon.

'It's simple. He leases Crown land but he uses a whole lot more than what he pays for. Since '61, when the Land Acts came into being, he's been fighting his cause down in Sydney. He's trying to keep his holding intact. He doesn't want any selector coming in and buying up land he's been working for over two decades.'

'What will happen?' Brandon picked up a leather strip sliced from the cow hide and twirled it.

'If I knew such things, boy, I'd be hobnobbing with the best of them down south. What I do know is that the squatters have too much of a hold on the land and that it'd be fairer if it was split up a bit. Don't get me wrong, I'm no supporter of the government, but it'd be a pity to see New South Wales end up like England.' He rested the partly plaited leather on a trouser leg and eased his fingers into straightness.

In the dwindling light, Brandon noticed that McCauley had a prime view of the homestead and outbuildings. A soft glow was beginning to show in one of Hetty's windows.

'You could do worse than that girl.' McCauley pursed his mouth and stretched his lips back and forth as if testing the fit across what remained of his teeth.

'She and I don't exactly—'

'What?' said McCauley. 'You expecting it to be all dripping and bread? I've heard she bites, but a man needs a bit of spirit. Slap your spurs on and go for a ride, eh?' He chuckled.

'What happened to her husband?'

'Never laid eyes on him. Not once. The story I heard was that he was sent out as a boundary rider and kept on going. He had a horse and a rifle. Probably more than what he'd ever owned in his life. But there was also a whisper that he tried to buy a few acres of the land Truby's sitting on. Went to an agent and tried to broker the deal under the new rules. Never came home, did he?'

'Does Hetty know?' said Brandon.

McCauley's lumbering jaws moved, as if he was chewing something. 'She'd have her thoughts as to what went on. It always seemed strange to me that Mr Truby let her stay.'

'Hetty told me it was because she was good with the falcons.'

'Someone has to bash in the brains of those mice, I suppose.' The leather flapped between his fingers as he resumed his plaiting. 'Always good to have a spare whip, although there's nothing worse than breaking in a new one. It's not like I can rope the old whip to it and train it up, like I do with a new bullock. Which reminds me, I'll be taking those four head of yours when I leave. Ain't no grudge on my part. I'm just doing my job,' said McCauley.

The loss of the bullock team, shabby though they were, was a blow, but it meant little after Sean's disappearance, and even less compared to the fact that in a few days, the agreed fortnight would be up and then Brandon would have to decide what to do with Maggie. Should he take her into the village and place her with a family, trusting strangers to keep an eye on a girl whom he himself hadn't seen since the argument in Hetty's cottage? Or should he desert Mr Truby with Maggie in tow, try to find Sean and leave the district?

'Go on, then. Get yourself out back. There's a bit of cow meat left if you want it,' said McCauley.

The men's quarters was an oblong building lined with rows of cots, a couple of tables and two chairs carved out of tree stumps. Brandon walked through it, sidestepping his bunk with its sagging canvas stretched across the frame. The smell of perspiration seemed to have seeped into the walls so that the room was heavy and airless with the exhausted sleep of men who spent all day working the fields and riding after cattle. Outside was a small shack that served as the cookhouse, however McCauley had prepared his food near the campfire. Brandon squatted by the fire and lifted the lid. A chunk of bread sat atop overcooked meat. He used the bread as a shovel, eating what was left and then ran the bread around the inside of the container.

'So, you're the one that's caught the squatter's fancy.'

A man appeared from behind the cookhouse. A saddlebag was strung across one shoulder and he was lean and pasty-white.

Brandon knew him for a cedar-cutter, one of Hackett's men. He rose warily, chewing the last of the bread.

'What do you want? Is this about Sean?'

'Not exactly.' The man lifted the lid of the pot, traced the inside of it and licked his finger. 'Young Maggie's being cared for.'

'What are you talking about? She's here,' said Brandon.

'Is she? Have you seen her lately?'

Brandon blinked. He hadn't seen Maggie. Or even asked after her, as Hetty wasn't speaking to him.

'Mere slip of a girl, she is. Walked all the way into the village by herself.' He knelt on his haunches and poked at the smouldering timber. 'You know she's going to have a child? It's true. Young Niall has been doing the job for a while now.'

For a moment, the land surrounding Brandon seemed to constrict in size.

'What did you say?' Brandon wanted to tell the man he was wrong, but he'd seen Maggie in bed with Hackett's son and if it had happened once then there was bound to have been other occasions.

The stranger appeared amused. 'The thing is, though, the lad can't be sure the child is his. It's a fair quandary,' he said.

'What are you insinuating?' said Brandon angrily.

'Only that if the girl is so willing to open her legs then it begs asking if she's done the same for another.'

Brandon remained still for a moment, staggered by the bluntness of the man's words. Then he rushed forwards in a fury, knocking the man over, and punching him. The stranger rolled away and got to his feet, fighting back, impassively at first, then, as if wearied by the onslaught, he delivered a single blow to Brandon's stomach. He doubled over in pain.

The man retrieved his hat and saddlebag, which had been lost during their struggle. 'If you want your sister back, Mr Hackett expects a show of good faith.'

'You're holding her against her will?'

'Let's just say she's having a little visit with the Brotherhood.'

'Whatever Hackett wants of me, it has nothing to do with Maggie,' said Brandon tersely.

'Doesn't it? You came to the meeting by the river. It makes a person uneasy, knowing that there's certain happenings you're aware of and that you walked away from.'

'Those farmers were innocent.'

'There's twenty men who'll say you were there. Twenty men who'll lay blame on you for the fires. Men who'll name *you* as the leader of the Fenians in this district.'

Brandon shook his head. 'This isn't Ireland. I want no part of this.'

'And Maggie?' The man glared at him from under the bent brim of his hat.

'Is Sean involved?' asked Brandon reluctantly.

'This is between you and Mr Hackett,' said the man.

'What does Hackett want?'

'Information in exchange for the girl. He wants a map of Truby's run.'

'And how am I supposed to get that?'

'You'll find a way.'

'You want me to break into his house? To steal?' Brandon was astounded. 'I can't do that. If I get caught, I'll be jailed for sure.'

'And then where would your poor sister be? With child and no one to care for her.' The man stared at him, as if wondering what all the fuss was about. 'I'll be back here in two nights.' He took the saddlebag from his shoulder and threw it to the ground. 'Put the map in this and hide it behind the cookhouse. I don't expect to leave empty-handed.'

The man walked into the dwindling light and re-emerged a few moments later on horseback. He tipped his hat, as if they were friendly acquaintances, and then rode out into the warm evening, although to Brandon it had taken on an unshakeable chill.

Before him, the fire smoked dismally as the last of the wood turned to ash. His body grew slack and he stared at the fire before returning inside the men's hut.

'What did he want?' McCauley stood in the middle of the quarters.

'Nothing,' Brandon replied, lying down on his cot.

'Sure, no one ever wants anything. That's why a person would ride out here, for nothing.'

'It's best you don't get involved.'

Brandon turned on his side, away from McCauley. He'd ruined Maggie. He'd dumped her in the village so that he could pursue his fortune and in doing so had become no better than any other cedar-cutter. He had become a destroyer of things – of trees and people's lives and of friendship – leaving only broken forests and sawdust in his wake. And now he was being forced to destroy his chance for a new beginning.

❧ Chapter 40 ❧

Kirooma Station, 1948

Stella found Joe in the library, his socked feet on a footstool, a glass of sherry at his elbow. A grazier enjoying the simple pleasures of success. He was reading; the pages turned towards the light. He lifted a leg, scratching absently at his thigh, and yawned. She watched him from behind one of the bi-fold doors, her arms wrapped about her body to ward off the chill air, feeling the heat of the fire he'd lit in the hearth. The scene was so comforting that it took her a moment to remind herself that the picture was at odds with the life she knew.

She'd expected that his agreeing to her leaving at the conclusion of shearing would put a stop to any further attempts at civility, however over the subsequent months the opposite occurred. Joe ceased staying away for weeks on end and took to camping out only a couple of nights every seven days. He left early and returned late, as he had in their early years of marriage, his warmed meals consumed alone, but Stella knew that he was there at night. In another room. On the opposite side of the homestead. Sometimes she believed she could hear his breathing, along with the soft snore he made when he rolled from his left side onto the right. She would reach across the bed to the spot that remained cold.

And now he was in the library. Behaving as if they were just like any married couple, leading a normal life. Only weeks ago she would have worried that Joe's behaviour suggested that he was in denial about her intentions, that he still thought reconciliation possible and that when the time eventually came for her to leave, there would be a terrible scene.

But now she carried a secret, one that would change everything.

'What are you reading?' she asked, selecting a book from the shelves and sitting in one of the twin armchairs, the table with its globe straddling their separate worlds.

'Dickens. He goes on with some interminable descriptions.' Joe closed the novel. 'Would you rather listen to some music?'

'No thanks. I'm used to the quiet.' It was true. The frightening void of the years spent alone in the house had seeped into her. Sometimes she woke at night and moved through the old building, talking aloud to the memories of people who'd been there before. To the young woman, Hetty, whose letter Stella had found in the Bible. She had memorised the paragraph, for the words carried a poignancy that spoke to her own situation.

I know you had to leave. I understand. But try as I may I can't help thinking that if things had been different, had we not been who we are, that we might have been together. I look back now and see how strong you were, to leave of your own accord, when I should have been the stronger one and sent you away sooner. But you were right. There never would have been any peace for either of us if you'd stayed.

Stella thought again of that last line. She wished she were tougher, more like the woman described in the letter. She'd been ready to escape, but now she wasn't so sure.

Joe buttoned an old tweed jacket tightly across his jumper.

'Where did you get that from?' Stella asked.

'In one of the wardrobes. Too good not to make use of. Keeps the wind out when I'm on the bike. Quite the part, eh? All I need is a coolabah tree and it'd be just like in the books. Me boiling my billy, camped out under the stars.'

'Joe?'

He'd risen to throw a piece of mulga on the fire. He adjusted the burning log, replaced the poker in the brass stand, and turned to face her. 'What?'

She couldn't put it off any longer. He needed to be told.

'I'm pregnant.'

Joe blinked. He wet his lips, as if buying time, clearly trying to decide how he should respond. 'Really?'

They spent a long time regarding each other across the room, trying to bridge a void that was almost impossible to cross. 'It happened—'

'I have a fair idea when it occurred,' he interrupted, not unkindly. The corners of his mouth bent slightly upwards and he offered what in the past may have eventually become a smile.

Stella refrained from saying anything else. Joe always fidgeted when he was bored by conversation, but she saw now that he was quite still. For the first time in years, her husband's attention was centred on her and only her. It was as if Joe had been spun back to earth with a resounding thud.

'Are you pleased?' he asked tentatively.

'I'm not sure. Considering,' she said. The discovery of the child had scared Stella. Still scared her. Not because of the baby, which lay safe inside her like a bird in a nest, but because of what it meant. She wanted the child, but not the situation: the hollow house, the hermit-like existence, the husband who was indifferent to her suffering.

Joe moved from the fireplace, poured a glass of sherry and set it on the table beside her. Then, with his glass in hand, he walked about the room as if he were a gentleman taking a turn in his parlour. He swallowed the remains of the drink then poured another and returned to the fire, where he draped one arm along the mantelpiece and stared out the window into the night. The flames cast his features in partial shadow and she saw him washed by the undulations of the gibber plains, a mere silhouette of the man she once knew.

'You'll stay?' he said finally. His free hand patted the mantelpiece, the fingers drumming a beat known only to him.

Stella touched the mound growing in her body. A life within a life. It had taken time for her to accept the magnitude of her pregnancy. She wanted to shield her child from the anguish that filled her, and for some weeks after her bloods ceased she'd contemplated ways of emptying her womb. But how could she do it? Strangely, it was not because she was Catholic and opposed to abortion. Her faith was vital, but what stopped her was the thought of ending something that was already so very dear to her. Each precious movement made Stella whole again, optimistic, willing to withstand the unbearable. She might have considered leaving her husband, but she would never divorce him. And the child came first. It must come first.

'Things will get better. Things *are* better. Maybe we both needed to blow off a little steam. Make each of us realise what the other needed,' said Joe.

Stella sipped at the sherry, wishing for a waspish retort that would wipe the growing satisfaction from Joe's face.

'We'll have to get a girl to help in the house,' he said.

'I suppose,' Stella responded cautiously. 'Could we afford that?'

'Of course,' he said dismissively. 'How long before . . .'

'I drop?' She used the terminology Joe employed when he was talking about a female animal ready to give birth. 'About five months.'

'Didn't you write it in your diary? You put everything else in there,' he said.

Stella thought of that afternoon. 'No.'

'We can expect it around December, then,' he concluded.

'Probably.'

'Christmas. Maybe once you have the baby you'll feel more settled. More at home.'

'Maybe,' she replied.

'I do care about you, Stella. I always have. Just not in the way that you expected. I'm sorry for that, for not being the person you wanted me to be, but you have to understand that I'm no different now from the person you met and fell in love with. That's not anyone's fault. It's just the way it is.'

'You don't see it, Joe. You don't understand,' said Stella.

Joe's tufted eyebrow lifted slightly. 'What don't I understand?'

'How much you love the land. That you'll always love the land more than me. More than our child. It's your life. Your grand obsession,' said Stella. 'It's incredibly compelling, your devotion to the property—'

'But—'

'It's also extraordinarily selfish.'

Joe readjusted his position, rubbing his back along the edge of the mantelpiece like a beast of the field scratching an itch. It appeared a confident action, but it also spoke of an unsureness, as if by feigning disinterest he might conceal his concern of an uncertain outcome. 'But you'll stay here with my baby?'

'*Our* baby,' Stella corrected, meeting his gaze with her own.

'Our baby,' he repeated, though with a flicker of annoyance.

'I'll never forgive you for bringing me out to this godforsaken place and abandoning me,' said Stella.

This time Joe's half smile became full. 'Everything will be better. You'll see.'

And for Joe, it was. He left the very next morning and stayed away for two weeks.

❋ Chapter 41 ❋

The man Stella was supposed to marry was green-eyed, with honey-coloured hair. He came from a good, solid family and was the son of one of her father's friends. There was talk of Tony Cosimo eventually taking over his father's business, a restaurant in George Street. Their first meeting had been organised by both sets of parents, with the Cosimo family business selected as the chosen venue. Tony was to stand outside the restaurant clutching a rolled-up newspaper and Stella was to wear something red.

It was a preposterous old-fashioned arrangement that Stella baulked at from the very beginning. Normal young people met their prospective partners at dinners or dances, not through parental vetting. But she was twenty-eight years of age and her parents were concerned that she'd never marry, so in the end she agreed to the introduction purely to appease them. On the designated day, at the appointed hour, twelve noon, she waited for Tony to appear. She stood on the opposite side of the street, not wanting to appear eager, especially because her decision was already made. Stella wasn't going to allow her parents to dictate her life. However refusing them outright was not worth the continuing arguments and so she waited near a fruit kiosk, the red scarf still in her handbag.

Eventually, a young man appeared from within the restaurant, dropping the newspaper he carried on the ground. He quickly retrieved it and then slouched against the window, lighting a cigarette. It was him. Tony. Stella observed him through the gaps in the passing traffic, this man that her parents thought was right for her. He smoked quickly, flicking the ash frequently. He was tall and well built like a swimmer, with wide shoulders and narrow hips. Through a break in the traffic he caught sight of her, his lingering interest plainly obvious. Stella's cheeks reddened. The man was rolling the newspaper into a cone and staring directly at her, expectantly.

Two men entered the restaurant, briefly greeting him as they passed. He laughed at what they said, his smile so wide it could have cracked the sky. Stella kept watching from across the street, unable to move. He was beautiful. Instinct screamed at her to dodge the cars and trucks and walk calmly towards him. She suddenly became aware of how long she'd been standing across the street, and fumbled in her handbag for the red scarf. Her wristwatch showed the time as ten minutes past the hour. The silk scarf was between her fingers.

But it was too late. Tony threw the newspaper into a rubbish bin and moved to the kerb, lifting his hands as if to say, *What's wrong with you?* Then he walked back into the restaurant.

Stella spent the remainder of her lunch hour sitting on a bench, trying to convince herself that she'd made the right decision. After all, Tony hadn't crossed the street either.

Her parents were furious. Tony's parents were astonished. His father insinuated that Stella thought herself too good for his eldest son and eventually arranged for a nice girl to come from Italy to marry his boy. There was much talk in Stella's home about Australian culture, that life here had made her wayward and a disrespectful daughter. The incident played on Stella's mind for many months. Almost two years to the day after that fateful lunch hour, she met Joe.

◈

The Kirooma house was pleasantly dark. Stella sat in the music room at the piano, a finger on middle C. Every time the baby kicked, she would strike the key, the noise of the out-of-tune piano echoing through the rooms, until the child finally stilled after a day of sudden moves. It was many years since she'd thought of Tony. So it was strange that after the passing of so much time that she found herself trying to justify her inaction that day. A moment of indecision led her away from Tony Cosimo and a split second of certainty drew her into Joe's arms. It had been eating at her, how a person's life could be so totally altered by one simple choice. There should be a handbook for living, she had concluded. Some instructive tome for leading a model life. For a long time she'd thought all she needed was the Bible, but now she wasn't so sure. It was extraordinary for a whole species to be wandering the earth with no reliable markers to follow.

Stella closed the piano lid. The later stages of the pregnancy had made her tired, the heat of summer adding to her irritability. The doctor in Broken Hill predicted a mid-to-late December delivery and the remaining days strung out before her. She waddled stiffly along the hall, moving through rooms grown familiar by her unwavering presence. She had become like the previous inhabitants, so ingrained in the timber dwelling that she was now part of the foundations. Her whispers merging with those that came before.

She laid her hands on her belly. The baby was quiet. Stella felt the swell of love that had centred and guided her over the last few months. The child had banished the ache that once held fast and even softened the resentment that had stewed within her. She was now rapturously, gloriously in love with life, her renewed happiness so great that Joe's presence mattered little anymore. Where once he had been her sole desire, his attraction so great she could

270.

imagine no other man's arms about her, she now only wanted one thing. To be left alone with her baby.

It was a little cooler in the garden and Stella walked around the house to the orchard, zigzagging through the trees, marvelling at the pale green of the sun-withered leaves as the night drew its cloak around her small world. When her heart beat a little faster she slowed, reaching for a nearby branch to steady herself. She smiled at the worry that inched its way into her mind, berating herself for being concerned about what was probably nothing. Then a queasiness came over her and pain struck, harsh and unrelenting.

Stella fell to her knees, the branch snapping on the way down.

She clawed at the soil and yelled out for Joe, willing her voice to carry across the dunes, devastated by the impossibility of ever being heard. She conjured up the pages in the kitchen diary, the day of his leaving and the long-past date of his expected return, the bitterness of his unreliability striking her cold. He'd promised he would only be gone for two weeks, but they were already entering the middle of the third. She couldn't believe she'd trusted him.

When the next contraction came, Stella knew she had to push. The child wanted to be born. She felt a gradual yielding from within. Her body was letting go, willing the little soul onwards and she massaged her stomach, cooing to her little dove to fly free, relishing the discomfort that announced the arrival of her baby. The contractions came and went, petering out and then returning to encircle her body, increasing with renewed pain. The ache grew unrelenting and with each surge, her exhaustion grew until her strength gave way.

Stella opened her eyes to the stars as another contraction came from deep within her. She screamed in opposition to the tightening spasm, feeling the hard ground beneath her, and then the ache eased and she lay back to stare at the night sky. She had hoped for a sprint, but the birthing of her child was turning into a marathon. She concentrated on the sky as her rapid pulse slowed. Of all the books in the library, not one had concerned the matter of birthing. Not a single page on what a woman should do or expect.

The collection was vast, however it occurred to her that not one of the hardbacks was written by a woman. Even in childbirth, she was at the whim of men.

❖

When the faintest light marked the start of another day, the child came into the world. Stella drew the baby up from between her thighs and held her close, cupping the fragile head. She stroked the fine hair and kissed the child's lips and whispered the word that would bond them for life.

'Daughter.'

Slowly the air was warmed by the sun and the wind became sultry with heat. It rose upwards, drawing in the waiting atmosphere and then rushed along the ground, showering her and the baby in dirt and yellowing leaves. It carried the accustomed scents of sheep and dung, of dry earth and the great spaces that lay in the interior. Stella clasped the baby to her chest, sensing change. She understood that she was forever transformed and that everything she did from this moment on would stem from the birth of her daughter.

Her mind blurred. About her, the orange and lemon trees began to recede from view. They faded gradually until the change was so marked and the surroundings so altered that she lost all sense of where she was. She was aware of the earth beneath her, of the gritty wind and a harsh blue sky and yet she was moving towards another time and place.

She crossed a glimmering salt lake, its vast alluvial layers laid down over millennia, her arms growing lighter, her body cooling, until she too bordered on evaporation.

≪ Chapter 42 ≫

Joe was at Stella's side in the bedroom, fanning her with a folded newspaper. 'If we leave now we'll be at the neighbours' in four hours. There's an airstrip there. I can call ahead and give the flying doctor the time we'll arrive. You should see a doctor.'

Stella glanced at the paper swishing back and forth and thought vaguely of Tony standing outside the Cosimos' restaurant.

'Why? There's nothing anyone can do now.'

She lay on the bed, barely registering the pain that striated her body like sedimentary deposits. In her mind, she was a desert wanderer, traversing dunes and gullies, shadeless plains and skies so dark that the chance of another breaking dawn seemed impossible. She had Joe's glass jars in a bag on her shoulder and she unscrewed each one, spilling the meticulously gathered contents. She was bending down, squatting on her haunches, scooping salt into one of the containers.

Joe wrung out a wet facecloth and rested it back on her forehead. 'Are you listening to me? Can you really not remember when it happened? Was it two days ago? Three?' he asked. He dabbed butter on the sun blisters covering her face. 'Stella, are you listening?'

Her husband was a fool. That was the worst part of being human; one's ears could never be turned off. Some primal instinct attuned them to every sound. To the danger of predators. To the awareness that there was silence within silence. In her dreams she screwed the lid on the jar and studied the salt within.

'When did it happen, Stella?' Joe pronounced each word distinctly. 'Stella?' He shook her gently.

All she could recall was a difficulty in standing and the heat of the sun on her shoulders as she'd clutched the baby to her chest. And then later, the bed, soft and loving like a mother's hug. That's where Joe had found her. If she attempted to unearth any more of her already buried memory Stella feared that the minis-cule threads binding her together might unravel. 'I couldn't sit in the station wagon all that way, Joe. Not in this heat.'

'All right. I'll run you a bath. You're covered in dirt and—'

Dirt and sweat and tears. Stella was drowning in it all. The cotton dress she wore was stiff with blood. 'I close my eyes and hear her crying. I'm sure I'll hear that sound for the rest of my life.'

'But you told me that she never made a sound.'

She clutched at his arm. 'I was strong enough to walk out there, Joe. I crossed the border to the west. Elizabeth saw it too.'

Joe switched his gaze from his wife to the child in her arms. 'What did you see, Stella?'

'The light. I saw the light on the salt. It was so crisp and clear I had to shade my eyes.'

He stroked her cheek as if he truly cared, and in that instant she saw that deep within the man was the greatest good. She realised that he did know the difference between love and hate and good and bad, but what he had not yet learnt was that his own satisfaction came at a cost. He might hold her hand and care for her after the death of her baby, but he'd left her, and she'd lost the baby alone.

'We have to bury her,' said Joe carefully.

Stella tightened her hold on the baby girl in her arms. She was wrapped in a towel, a sliver of hair poking up from the gap in the material. She touched the tiny forehead and granules of salt dropped to rest in the folds of the cloth.

Joe got up from the bed, his shirt dark with perspiration. 'We can't delay any longer. It's too hot.'

'I've never left her. Not once. I know what it's like to be deserted and I'll never do it to Elizabeth,' Stella told him.

He patted her arm and then left the bedroom. Stella listened to his footsteps growing indistinct as he walked from one end of the homestead to the other. He returned with a large container, the one he took with him as a lunchbox when he was out on the property. It was filthy from rolling around in the tray of the truck or being strapped to the motorbike. He sat it on the dressing table and removed the lid. 'We can put her in one of these, with some ice. I can let the sheep out of the yards and then tomorrow morning, when you're feeling more rested, we'll drive to town.'

'No,' Stella heard herself say. 'I'm not doing that.'

Joe sat on the bed next to her. 'You need to see a doctor and Elizabeth needs a proper burial. You do understand that, don't you?'

Stella picked up the glass of water on the table next to the bed and threw it against the wall. 'No!'

'Well you can't keep her in that,' said Joe, his voice a whisper. He gestured to the timber packing case that she'd carried in from one of the outbuildings. She'd lined it with a hessian bag and filled it with salt from the store in the pantry.

'What else could I do?' said Stella, her lips trembling. 'You never came back. Even for her.'

Joe regarded her steadily. 'You're going to have a bath.' He took Elizabeth from her weak arms and placed the child in the cocoon of salt, spooning the grains on top of her until the small bundle was partially covered.

Stella thought of the Sphinx and the mummified remains beneath the Egyptian desert. Perhaps the same sand and salt that had once crisscrossed great countries and now blasted across their lands had finally begun to chip away at her husband, for he knelt by the crate and started to cry.

'Bury her here,' said Stella. 'In the garden.'

'Without a priest? In unconsecrated ground?' Joe shook his head, swiping at the tears massing on his cheeks. 'That goes against our beliefs, Stella. I can't believe you'd want to do that.'

'After everything that's happened, do you really think I care about the church's blessing?'

Joe placed a palm on the floor, as if steadying himself. 'You will eventually. When your head's clearer and you're feeling better.'

'What good is it to Elizabeth to be dragged to another place? This is her country. This is the only place she's ever known. This is where she will stay.'

Joe sighed. 'If you're sure.'

'I'm sure.' Stella closed her eyes.

⫷ Chapter 43 ⫸

Richmond Valley, 1867

Cait used to summon the old gods in times of need. Brandon recalled his stepmother sitting outside their hut on a moon-bright evening when his young half-brother Michael was sickly. She'd thrown bits of herbage and moss into a fire, turning the air bitter, specks hovering in the white smoke before being borne away on the breeze. Cait sang while she did this, her body swaying gently, her arms extended, palms facing the sky. She moaned to the gods, begging for their assistance like a druid summoning help from the heavens. Brandon hid like a thief listening to her wailing, his eyes twitching left and right in anticipation of the gods, until his father discovered him and dragged him away. But it seemed to him that Cait's practice of calling in such powers was not without merit, for the boy survived.

Brandon wondered what his father would say if he saw him now. It was mid-morning. He'd lit a small fire in the centre of the cedar trees and was fanning it gently with his hat. There were no herbs, nor could he remember the words that his step-mother uttered those long years prior but he thought perhaps that some kindly unseen god might help him make the right decision regarding Hackett's demands. He threw a handful of McCauley's tea-tree leaves onto the flames. The slaughterer had told him that they would heal anything.

He looked up to see Mr Truby standing before him. He smelt of horse and sweat, and dust was smeared across his face. Brandon was used to seeing the gentleman in a black frockcoat strolling or sitting in his garden and had until this minute forgotten that his employer was a squatter who knew land and livestock and the value of both.

'Have we been working you too hard?' Mr Truby queried.

Brandon rose. 'I can't do much by myself. It takes two men to cut down a tree.'

Mr Truby stamped out the smouldering twigs with a boot. 'Can't have the place burning down,' he said quietly. 'Your family have left you?'

'Yes. I'm sorry for the trouble we've caused. I suppose you want me to go too.'

Mr Truby seemed not to hear these words for he turned his attention to his dog, who'd followed him through the trees. 'McCauley said you had a visitor last night,' he continued, as if they were discussing the weather. 'I don't like uninvited guests.'

'He was a stranger to me,' explained Brandon hurriedly.

'And tell me, what did this stranger want?'

Brandon took his hat off and rubbed at his scalp and then pulled it firmly back on his head. He walked a few paces one way and then the other, his stomach tightening as if he were having a fit of gripe. 'If I tell you, things will go terribly wrong and I'll lose this job and none of it's my fault.'

'If you don't tell me, you'll be leaving here anyway,' said his employer.

Brandon looked at the man with his dusty beard and sharp eyes and then at the trees which, although so straight and tall, seemed to be crowding down upon him. 'I've been asked to steal a map of your property,' he finally admitted, with a great exhalation of air.

Mr Truby had been leaning against a tree trunk, his boot resting on a twisting root, however he straightened at Brandon's revelation, his shoulders pulling back so that the buttons on his waistcoat strained where they met. 'For what reason?'

'I have no idea.'

The dog walked to Mr Truby's side and he absently patted the animal. Brandon thought him very calm considering what he'd just been told. 'A man does not appear out of the haze and demand an undertaking without having some power to do so. What hold does this person have on you?'

The story Brandon began to formulate was concise and plain, weighted in his favour with honesty, but scant enough in detail not to reveal anything specific. He would say he owed Hackett's man a large debt from gambling. But when he glanced again at Mr Truby, Brandon knew his employer was aware of his frantic attempts at concoction and so he decided on the truth.

And so he blurted, 'They've taken Maggie and she's with child, and if I don't do what they say they'll blame me for the farm burnings and I'll never see her again.' The words rushed out of him and when he finished he knew that once again his life was about to change.

'And were you involved in the Protestant attacks?' asked Mr Truby, his tone mild.

'No,' said Brandon, firmly. 'On my oath, no. I went to the meeting because everyone expected it of me and I didn't want Sean going alone. But I had nor wanted no part of the rest of it. I swear. My coming here was not to start another war.'

'Regardless, you've found yourself in one,' Mr Truby said distantly, mopping at the sweat on his forehead with a monogrammed handkerchief. 'I will give you the map and in return you will do something for me.'

'Why would you give me the map?' said Brandon cautiously.

'For the same reason you were considering stealing it. To protect my own interests.'

'Oh,' was all Brandon said. He could feel the makings of a bargain, as if he were fighting over the worth of his logs with one of the agents down at the wharf. Except that this time, he had nothing to exchange. And that made him uneasy.

'It would be in both our interests to come to an agreement, Brandon. After all, you have just admitted to considering theft while under my employ. Here is what I propose. I will use your name to buy land. To all intents it would be a sponsorship, if you like, as far as the world is concerned, but it would be a dummy agreement. You'd appear to be the landholder and then within a period of time, say three years, you'd sign the land back over to me. It's a simple transaction. On paper only. No money would ever change hands and of course, apart from your name on the contract the land would always be mine.'

'But why do you need my name?'

Mr Truby frowned. 'To ensure the land I currently control remains mine.'

'But what has that to do with a map?' asked Brandon.

'They want my map, lad, because it clearly shows the surveyed and unsurveyed land that runs along the western boundary of my property. Land developed and worked by me, but available for sale under the new land regulations. John Robertson's bloody 'free selection before survey' scheme essentially means that the whole leasehold area of the colony is up for sale. I imagine this Hackett person thinks it more expedient to steal my map than consult the Lands Department. That way he'll know in advance exactly which acreage gives him access to water and can apply accordingly. Well, we'll see about that. I haven't worked this holding to see a portion of it given away to new settlers. Let them go elsewhere. They can build their bark huts and run their miserable herds on someone else's hard-won dirt. Not mine.'

'Is it legal, what you're asking of me?' said Brandon, finding it difficult to reconcile the sherry-sipping gentleman of past days with this unfamiliar version before him.

Mr Truby laughed. 'This from the boy who has Catholic hooligans for friends and was considering theft.'

'I don't want to do anything wrong.' Brandon knew he sounded pitiful.

'If you do as I say, I will vouch that you were here the night of the Protestant attacks, and your sister may come and live here with you, until we find her a more suitable situation,' offered Mr Truby. The Englishman moved through the trees towards the house and Brandon could do nothing else but follow.

'Maggie can come here?'

'That's correct,' said Mr Truby.

'Even if she's with child?'

'Yes.'

'And Sean?' called Brandon.

Mr Truby spun towards him. 'Your cousin must never set foot on my land again.'

As his employer walked on, Brandon lingered in the shade. A willie wagtail dived low to land on the grass where other birds twittered.

'Brandon?' Mr Truby waited, and Brandon walked reluctantly towards him. 'When are you to hand over the map?'

'Tomorrow night. I was to leave it behind the cookhouse at the quarters.'

'Good. I shall fetch you a map and you shall put it there,' said Mr Truby.

Brandon didn't respond. He was still contemplating what had been asked of him.

'You're vacillating. What is there to think of, boy? Your options are narrow, the risk limited on your part and the rewards in your favour.'

'It's just that Sean and I—'

'There is one other condition. You will remain here on this property for the entire three-year term. You must be seen to be improving the land you've purchased and, of course, growing your crops. Or sheep, perhaps,' he suggested, with a smile. 'In the meantime, you will deposit the map and then meet me at the stables, for we will be riding to the village today. The sooner this business is settled, the better.'

'But I'm no horseman, Mr Truby.'

'Then a good long stretch in the saddle should rectify that problem. One hour and then we leave,' said the Englishman. With that, he strode off towards the house.

Brandon watched him go, still trying to decide between his limited choices. He would be able to save Maggie, but at the cost of Sean. A brutal choice. It was then that he recalled Hetty's words. If a person wanted something, it had to be taken. His choice was clear.

❊ Chapter 44 ❊

Brandon could barely sit upright for the pain in his lower back and thighs. Every step jolted his spine, each bone in his back compressing against the next in a series of shudders. He regretted ever wanting to learn how to ride. There was nothing wrong with a man's feet if he could afford to keep leather on the soles of his shoes. And the great advantage he once supposed could be gained from an increased height mattered little when his concentration was restricted to the narrow track between his mount's ears.

'Straighten your back. Hold fast with your thighs. Loosen the reins. You ride like a child.'

Brandon decided that if Mr Truby repeated the refrain one more time, he'd purposely fall from the horse just to rid himself of the man's impatient instructions. It wouldn't take much effort. He'd spent the first four miles on the way to the village trying to stay in the saddle as his backside slid continuously from left to right, and the remainder of the way trying to match his movements with the gait of the animal beneath him.

'Shoulders back. Sit up,' said Mr Truby.

Brandon ignored the command from the man who sat like a king with his back ramrod straight. He wished for the silence only the forest could bring, with its cool greenery and the music of a muffled breeze.

'You wanted to learn how to ride,' said Mr Truby.

'Not like this,' said Brandon.

'I don't have a sister that needs saving.'

'And I'm not desperate to retain land that isn't rightfully mine,' replied Brandon.

'Ah,' said Mr Truby, as if satisfied. 'You do have a backbone.'

'What's left of it,' he complained, easing out the muscles in his shoulders.

'I think we could be friends, if circumstances were different,' said Mr Truby.

'You mean if I was rich as well.'

The older man laughed. 'We are the products of the society we live in.'

'Then it is a messy place,' said Brandon.

They rode into the village at noon. In the short time since his leaving, the frames of two new houses were visible, the hammering and yelling of tradesmen competing with the steady hum of the sawmill. Brandon examined the busy street, searching for Sean, hopeful of catching a glimpse of his bluff cousin and discovering if he knew of Maggie's whereabouts. He hoped Sean had nothing to do with Hackett's blackmailing, however so much had transpired between them that he was wary of seeing him again. If all unfolded as Brandon hoped and Maggie and he were compelled to live on Truby's run for a time to fulfil his part of the bargain, then so be it. It would hardly matter to Sean and frankly Brandon knew they needed space between them. Time to sort out their differences. The dream of the three of them remaining together had lost its lustre. Sean would always be his cousin, but Maggie was his only care.

'Have you given thought to what we talked about the other day?' said Mr Truby.

Considering the breadth their conversations had taken, Brandon was unsure what his employer was referring to.

'The escaped nun has caused something of a commotion. And the uproar won't stop with one incident in Lismore. She is on the lecture circuit, sharing her complaints regarding your faith. Making your future even more difficult,' Mr Truby said pointedly.

'Perhaps I should return to the forest, then.'

'Have you not thought of at least anglicising your surname? Many have done it. I have it on good authority that Mick Cassidy, the head man at the loading dock, was Mick Ó Caiside before he arrived in the Valley.'

'Is that true?' Brandon knew of people who had done that, but never thought of doing it himself.

'As I live. He's been promoted quite quickly. An event unlikely to have happened had he kept his old name. Brandon O'Riain is very Irish. Brandon Ryan, R-Y-A-N, less so. Changing a few letters in your name so that it sounds more English, more acceptable, is hardly an issue. It's a sensible move, particularly in these volatile times.'

'R-Y-A-N,' said Brandon slowly, testing the fit of it.

'You're really only taking the "O" away,' said Mr Truby. 'The bulk of the name stays the same.'

'Why are you so keen to help me?' asked Brandon.

'I'll not lie and tell you a story of an aged bachelor not blessed by a son. It will be difficult for this transaction to be believed if I enter the Lands Department with a view to sponsoring an Irish Catholic. Think on it. There are benefits to be had, for both of us.'

Brandon's mount stepped clear of a boy wielding a cart of chopped wood as they attached themselves to the traffic – a single wagon, men on horseback and numerous people on foot, trudging as he had once trudged. He'd never seen so many people in the small settlement. A ramshackle group of hawkers had set up shop on the riverbank. Boxes and barrows held an assortment of goods: green-skinned melons and bright oranges, blood-red plums and cooked joints of beef. A boy with a crate slung about his neck on leather straps offered fresh river mussels, while another vendor displayed turkeys and black ducks, their bodies dangling from a pole. A passing rider tipped his hat in Brandon's direction and he reciprocated as he'd seen others do. It seemed a horse did far more than place you five feet off the ground.

The masts of a ship rose beyond the sailmakers' loft, the sails lowered, the system of exposed ropes, cables and chains dangling like a skeleton. Dairy cows were being walked along the wharf to dry land. Some of the boat's passengers were sitting on their baggage by the roadside, the women's calico dresses and saucer-shaped eyes suggesting that the ship they'd recently alighted from was not their first.

'This way, Brandon.' Mr Truby halted outside a building. He dismounted and, wrapping the reins around the hitching post, said, 'Listen carefully, for I'm only going to tell you this once. Lift your right boot clear of the stirrup, lean forward, swing your leg over the horse's back and put it on the ground. You're tall enough to leave your left foot in the stirrup as you dismount. And try not to make a spectacle of yourself. You've been sitting on that horse like a rag doll. Now. Do it.'

Brandon did as he was told, feeling the slight movement of the saddle as he swung a stiffened leg across and down. He was slow, painstakingly slow, but when his foot landed on earth and his second boot followed he felt a measure of achievement that almost overwhelmed the tiredness of his body.

'Now, tie her up. Two loops of the reins and then jab the end through,' said Mr Truby.

Brandon obeyed, tying the lead securely. He might not be taken with riding, however he wasn't keen on walking home.

'Follow me.' Mr Truby carried a roll of parchment under one arm. They stopped at a shop window where a notice outlined the building's varied uses and the particular days of the week upon which a representative from each business would be in residence. The Bank of New South Wales and the Lands Department topped the list, followed by a shipping desk and the postal service. Brandon also observed a strongly worded sign advising that the recipients of mail from recently arrived vessels would be posted in the window and that customers were not to wait inside on those days.

Inside the office, a man noted their arrival from behind a counter. Brandon took his hat from his head and massaged his lower back. The waiting area was crowded. He counted eighteen people as Mr Truby spoke to the clerk before a middle-aged man appeared from behind a closed door and, welcoming Mr Truby, led them both into his office.

'Sit, please.'

They all drew up chairs. The nameplate on the desk stated that Mr Jefferson Cruice was attending them. He was a middling sort of fellow, with sandy hair and a thin yellow beard, which did little to hide a pointed chin.

'Mr Truby, what can I do for you?'

The two men began discussing the recent gazetting of the town. A street plan had been drawn up the previous year and a hotel and dedicated post office were planned for construction. Brandon listened keenly, until their talk deviated to the upcoming visit of Prince Alfred Ernest Albert, the Duke of Edinburgh, the second son of Queen Victoria. He was on a world tour on the steam frigate HMS *Galatea*, and among his Australian ports of call was Sydney next year.

It was impossible to forget that the country that was now his home was shaped by English intent and power. Brandon considered his present difficulties and the troubles of the past. His conversation with Truby had made it clear that if his circumstances were to improve, it was he who would have to do the changing. Having lost most of his family and the place of his birth, it was no small thing to change his name as well, but if he did, life might be easier. His presence more acceptable. His Irish–Catholic heritage not such an obstruction to prosperity. With a new name, a man might hail from the Protestant north, not the famine- and poverty-stricken counties of the south, and with that change might come acceptance. Re-arranging letters in the alphabet was a relatively small thing. Like riding a horse. Painful at first, but eventually a person became used to it.

'Brandon has been working for me for many months and I believe he has great prospects in agriculture. He has an interest in trialling the growing of sugar cane, which as you may have heard has created some interest further north in the Tweed Valley. I would like to sponsor him. He has his own money, being a cedar-getter for some time now, however I would like to add to his savings so that he acquires a decent parcel of land,' Mr Truby explained.

'Well, sir, I can certainly assist. And you, young man, are very fortunate to receive Mr Truby's patronage. I have a roomful of selectors outside, all of them having recently stepped off the vessel you see moored in the river and all keen for a slice of the Valley.' Mr Cruice leant forward. 'We have some tidy blocks that are now open for selection and sale. So, you can choose forty to three hundred and twenty acres at one pound per acre. Ownership is conditional on the selector's residence, improvements to the land and the payment of monies owed. Now, I'll just show you a map and then we can—'

'Mr Cruice, I have a map.' Truby unfurled the parchment on the table, taking the liberty of using the objects located before him to weigh down the paper corners. Mr Cruice's nameplate, a sailing boat carved from a piece of polished cedar and a glass-domed paperweight were soon pinning down the curling edges of Mr Truby's property. Another map, of no use to Hackett, was already sitting at the cookhouse for collection. 'These are the portions I have in mind. This section along the river.'

Mr Cruice cleared his throat and made much of hooking a pair of reading glasses about each ear. He lowered his face to the map until he was mere inches from it and then scratched at the paper. 'All of this region that you've pointed out, Mr Truby, is part of the area of the colony that is open for selection. Although we both know that it has been unclaimable to date.' An ink-stained finger drummed his bottom lip. 'I am aware that it is land you've held for many years and have fought to retain since the new Lands Acts came into being. There are accounts of you running off selectors and blocking access to water, although it is all supposition, for not one person has been game enough to report you to the authorities.'

Mr Truby brushed lint from the lapel of his jacket. 'As one of the first pastoralists in this district I have seen more than most what can happen when the government lets any selector in. Why, the Valley has riffraff in its midst who should not be granted one square foot of land. Speculators and Fenians, need I go on? I have fought, Mr Cruice, but if I must concede to the government's short-sighted demands then it is *I* who will be choosing my neighbours.'

Cruice retrieved a ledger from a desk drawer, his movements considered, as if judging Mr Truby's explanation. 'The district has had its share of troubles recently. The trial starts today for those men accused of burning the Protestant farms.'

Brandon felt his grip tighten on the arms of the chair. He hoped Sean was not one of them, for there was nothing he could do to help.

Opening the ledger, Mr Cruice selected a steel nib from a ceramic bowl, affixed it to the pen and dipped the nib into an inkwell.

'Name?' He glanced at Brandon. 'Name?' he repeated, the pen hovering close to the page.

Brandon moved his chair ever so slightly, the squeak of timber causing Mr Truby to briefly glance in his direction.

'Can I have your name, sir?' said Mr Cruice again. 'Damn.' A blob of ink lay quivering on the neatly lined page.

'It's Brandon Ryan.' The name that came from his lips was new and shiny, like a freshly born lamb.

'You can read and write?' enquired Mr Cruice. 'The Lands Department doesn't take to crosses in the place of a signature.'

'I can write,' said Brandon, offended by the question.

Mr Cruice glanced over the top of his glasses at Brandon and then placed his attention on Mr Truby. 'And the portions?'

'Here, here and here,' he replied. 'In total, eight thousand acres.'

Eight thousand acres. Brandon thought he would faint.

Mr Cruice laid the dip pen down and removed his reading glasses. 'Eight *thousand*? I can't sell this young man eight thousand acres. Why what will the Lands Department say when they see such a transaction? Three hundred and twenty acres, that is the most I can grant to an individual.'

'Come now, Jefferson. It's a fact that you brokered Captain Aim's purchase last year. His son now owns a tidy parcel of three thousand acres. One could complain readily of that familial arrangement, whereas Brandon is of no relation to me.' Mr Truby crossed his legs at the knees, his foot swinging like an erratic pendulum. 'By the time the Sydney office works through the backlog of selectors' claims, and I believe they are a number of years behind, Brandon's boys will be grown and then you'll have more Ryans to use as holding names.'

'You have children?' asked Mr Cruice.

Brandon mumbled an indecipherable response. Not only was he now a horseman with a newly fashioned English name, he was also a seventeen-year-old father with a clutch of ready-made sons set to become Protestant landholders.

'Two boys. Both healthy,' Mr Truby said with enthusiasm. Only the Englishman's bobbing foot betrayed him. 'You can simply say it was a clerical blunder if anyone in Sydney sees fit to challenge ownership. Such things do happen. Shall we say eight thousand pounds for the land and one thousand for yourself to cover any hardship.'

It was a large area of land, but an even larger sum of money, enough to tempt the most honest of men. Brandon wondered if the government man sitting opposite might refuse.

Mr Cruice grew pale. 'And what about the country you own beyond that strip? It will have no access to water.'

'One of the difficulties of agriculture I'm afraid. But as I already work that parcel I'm sure Brandon will allow me access.' From his coat pocket, Mr Truby produced a chequebook and, making use of Mr Cruice's pen, filled in the two separate pages, signing them with a flourish. He then availed himself of the pounce pot on the desk, liberally sprinkled the cheques, blew the crushed cuttlefish bone free of the paper and placed the two cheques in front of the Lands Department employee.

Mr Cruice pulled out an official map and, after a moment's deliberation, used a pencil to crosshatch the portions under discussion. He then noted the portions in the ledger and began to draw up a bill of sale. Once completed, he slid the document towards Brandon. 'I need your signature here.'

Brandon accepted the offered pen and with only the slightest hesitation signed his name. Brandon Ryan.

'Well, it will be lodged today, Mr Truby, however all the processing takes place in Sydney and there are always delays.'

'The wheels of government.' Mr Truby shook hands with the man and as they left the office, Mr Cruice pocketed the cheques.

'A good day for business,' Mr Truby told Brandon as they exited the building.

Outside in the street, people were gathering around the recently posted mail list. Habit made Brandon push through the crowd and read the notice, disappointment striking him when he came to the end of the roll and saw nothing for the O'Riains. He turned away and came face to face with Sean. His cousin blanched white on seeing him and then, as if having eaten something sour, winced at Mr Truby. The three of them stood uneasily as people jostled past.

'We're leaving,' said Mr Truby.

'Can I have a minute, please?' replied Brandon. He waited until the Englishman was with their horses and then he pulled Sean aside.

'Was there anything for us?' asked Sean.

'No.'

'Shouldn't have expected it, I suppose. What are you doing here?' said Sean.

'You have some explaining to do,' said Brandon.

'I can't stay long. I've been cleared of involvement in the fires, thanks to the witnesses whose memories failed them, but five of the Brotherhood are being tried in Lismore, including Arthur from the lumberyard and Hackett's son. The boy might have been with Maggie that night but he's damned by association,' said Sean.

'So that's why Maggie's of no interest to the boy anymore. Hackett certainly wouldn't bother caring for her in Niall's absence.'

'I thought you'd be happy about that,' replied Sean.

'Not when she's being held by Hackett against her will and being used as bait. Fine cousin you turned out to be. Getting Maggie and me involved in all of this.'

Sean's brow wrinkled. 'Maggie prefers being in the village and anyway, none of this was my fault.'

'And running off from the tallow works? I suppose that wasn't your fault either?'

Sean shoved him against the wall and then, remembering they were in a public place, stepped away. 'Keep your voice down. You forget that if you'd been with us, Hackett would never have been able to blackmail you into taking the map. And it was Maggie's relationship that gave Hackett that opportunity.' He slung an arm around Brandon's shoulders, walking him away from the Englishman's watchful gaze.

'Where is she?' said Brandon.

'Safe. Listen to me, Brandon. Truby's squatting on country that doesn't belong to him. Country that's open for selection. There's enough land available for every Irishman in this valley to have his own holding the length of the river. We intend to mark up the portions on the map and assign a man to each one. Then we'll lodge our claims. There'll be no running us off, as he has others. There'll be too many of us. That's how we'll beat him. You did leave the map where you were told?'

'Yes,' Brandon answered slowly.

The opening and closing of the shopfront's door momentarily distracted Sean. 'What were you doing in there, anyway? You didn't come just to check if there was mail from home, did you?'

Brandon considered lying – the map at the cookhouse would buy him a few more days – but what was the point. He was now a landowner and it would only be a matter of time before Hackett discovered that there were no longer any blocks available for selection along that stretch of the river. 'I'm now the owner of eight thousand acres of Truby's run, Sean. It's legal. Well, as legal as it can be.'

Sean shoved him hard against the chest. 'You told him!' He swivelled abruptly on his heel towards the Englishman and then back to Brandon. 'You bastard! You told him our plans.'

'Hackett's man was seen by McCauley. There was no need for me to say anything,' replied Brandon, more calmly than he felt.

'I can't bloody believe it. You've bent the knee to him. Allowed yourself to be caught up in his machinations,' Sean hissed.

'I did it to save Maggie,' protested Brandon.

'You're a bloody fool,' replied Sean, his face red.

'No, Sean. You are. Following Hackett around, carrying the past on your shoulder like it's a load of wood. Walk away from those men. No good can come of being associated with the Brotherhood, or of waving the green banner. It's hard enough being Irish.'

Sean's punch hit Brandon squarely in the jaw and he buckled under the pain. But when he straightened, his cousin looked like he'd been the one who'd taken a blow. Brandon could sense his disappointment and the inevitability of the growing chasm between them.

'What's happened to you?' Sean looked defeated.

'We can't live the old way. Not here. Not now. Not if we want to make something of ourselves.'

'And Maggie?'

'Mr Truby has agreed that she can live on the property for three years. They were the terms. I'll be taking her back with me today.'

'You'd do anything for that girl, wouldn't you? It's gone past keeping a promise. You're obsessed with her, and she'll end up hating you for it,' said Sean.

'Where is she?' demanded Brandon.

'At the Minchins', where she was before. There's no one holding her. Never was. She's free to come and go as she pleases. I gave them coin for her board and keep. They won't give you any of it back,' warned Sean.

'This was never about the money.'

'Really? You with your English lord and those fine acres in your name? That's *all* it's about,' Sean argued. 'That and *Maggie*.'

'Brandon!' Mr Truby rode towards them and glared down from the saddle.

'Did you ride here?' asked Sean, the question thick with disbelief as he noticed the spare horse.

'Yes,' said Brandon.

'Well, aren't we the country gentleman.' Sean gave a mock bow.

'I have to get Maggie, Mr Truby,' Brandon explained.

'Be quick about it, then. I'll wait for you at the crossroads.' Truby nudged the horse into a walk.

'Was there ever any place for me in your fancy plans?' asked Sean. 'Or were you too caught up bettering yourself to worry about your blood relation.'

'You don't like him, and you never wanted to work there,' said Brandon, annoyance beginning to edge out his patience. 'It's a good opportunity and you threw it away simply because he's a Protestant and an Englishman.'

'You're a low Irish beast, turning your back on your people,' Sean sneered.

'And you're an ignorant savage who only knows how to live on potatoes,' retaliated Brandon.

About them, a small crowd began to form. The handful of men and women listened as they traded insults and then began calling out for a fight.

'You're not my kin anymore!' yelled Sean, the colour of his skin beginning to merge with the red of his hair. 'Go with your Englishman, ruin Maggie's life, and see if I care.'

Brandon watched as his cousin headed in the direction of the wharf, his arms pumping at his sides like pistons. When he was finally lost from view, Brandon pushed through the gathered spectators who booed at the lack of entertainment and untied his horse's reins, tugging the animal into movement. He knew he'd never be able to justify his own actions or make Sean take responsibility for his part in their undoing as cousins. Sean was only likely to sneer about his intolerance of the Fenians, his friendship with the Englishman and the fact that the newly minted Brandon Ryan was now the holder of eight thousand acres of land.

≪ Chapter 45 ≫

Richmond Valley, 1949

'Irish? Are you there?' Stella waited on the veranda. Although it was nearing midnight, she found herself scanning the garden for signs of life, but only the outline of the statue was perceptible, a marble woman standing guard against the night. Stella knocked a little harder at the back door. At the end of their initial meeting, they had agreed to reunite two days later. It was a clandestine arrangement, one more suited to the green of camouflage clothing than a neat house dress. It involved Stella tiptoeing from Harry and Ann's home in the dark, sliding through the boundary fence by the cedar tree and running across the grass, her whole body caught up in a fizz of nervous tension. She wasn't used to sneaking around after all the time she'd spent by herself during her marriage and it was a shock to feel so alive after the years at Kirooma.

'Come in,' called Irish, finally.

Stella opened the creaking door. A hallway stretched into blackness, the only light coming from a single candle that flickered weakly on a table.

'In here.'

She turned immediately to her left and entered a large, cedar-panelled room. The dog padded towards her, gave her a cursory sniff and then wandered back to sit on a threadbare rug. The dark timber glistened, infusing the area with a rosy-red glow. Kerosene lamps were scattered about the room, throwing light onto tables and chairs, gilt-edged paintings and crystal decanters that shone as sharply as the chandelier at the Kirooma homestead. Stella tried not to appear too inquisitive, however her gaze darted about a room filled with treasures more suited to a museum. It was a room from another era.

Irish was propped up on a bed that curved up at each end like a sleigh. There was a blanket across his lap and a large fringed pillow supporting him. Stella knew immediately that she'd woken him.

'I don't keep the generator running at night. The electricity is a bit hard on my eyes,' he said.

'Should I come back?' she asked.

'No. No. I sleep when I can, but mostly I stay awake. We're a long time dead.' He coughed and reached for a glass of water at his side. 'I hear my grandson commenting to others that I've had a good innings, but it doesn't matter what age you are, a person always wants more. Come sit.'

'You have a family?' asked Stella.

'Yes. A son and grandson.'

He sounded as if the air couldn't reach his lungs. Stella sat on a chair with leather strap arms and an upholstered seat cover, the decorative design reminiscent of the Far East. Behind Irish, mulberry-coloured brocade curtains patterned with clusters of grapes shut out the night.

'It's a campaign chair,' said Irish. 'It folds up quite neatly. I imagine it was carried by a donkey or elephant to a military head-quarters. Quite something, isn't it?'

Stella moved uncomfortably in the stretched seat. Next to her was a table covered in green felt. A deck of cards sat squarely in the middle as if waiting for the player to resume his game. 'Does your family live with you?'

'No. Geoff lives in another house on the property with his son, Clinton, who runs the business. He's a good boy. Clever. Keeps an eye on the sugar cane and the tea-tree plantation, and runs a few cattle. One day the land will be his and I'll be pleased to leave it to him. He's a few years off thirty and champing at the bit to get his hands on the reins of the property. He visits me twice a week. I joke that he only comes to check if I'm still alive. He hates that, but I'm aware his wife is eagerly waiting for my demise. Wants to live in the big house. Play the lady of the manor.' Irish's eyes lit up mischievously. 'I've already signed the building over to the National Trust. The entire contents as well. Carol will be peeved and she's the peevish sort. Don't tell anyone, will you?'

'Why don't you want to keep it in the family?' asked Stella, gazing about the room. 'It's so beautiful.'

'Did you ever read Coleridge's poem "The Rime of the Ancient Mariner"? One of the sailors shoots an albatross, which is regarded as bad luck, and the ship's crew hang the bird around the killer's neck. That's what this house has been to me, a burden to be carried as penance. It's time to let it go.'

'I don't understand,' said Stella.

'I don't expect you to.' Irish settled back a little further on the sleigh bed, pushing on the upholstery with his knuckles as he manoeuvred into a more comfortable position. She noticed how thin his legs were, the prominent shoulders, and the way his chest was hollowed in, as if his organs were shrinking along with his body.

'Can I ask you some more about Joe? You said that you'd spoken together before we moved out west. That you wrote to each other. Did he ever say why he married me?' She looked briefly at her hands. 'You see, we didn't have a good marriage and I've been looking for answers as to what went wrong.' An explanation would never excuse Joe's behaviour, or her own, but it might be enough for her to forgive herself for what she'd done.

'You know why he married you,' said Irish.

'Actually, I don't. Joe was obsessed with Kirooma. I justified his absences by comparing the property to another woman. That's what it was like. As if he was having an affair,' said Stella.

'He was away a lot?' asked Irish.

'Constantly,' said Stella. 'For weeks at a time. Camping out in the desert with his sheep.'

'That doesn't mean that he didn't love you.'

Stella gave a bitter laugh. 'Then why did he leave me alone?'

'I can't answer that. There is lightness and darkness in everyone. Each of us has our own desires, wants and needs, and, whether it's right or not, we also have certain expectations when it comes to the people in our lives. Especially the ones we're closest to. I'm not making excuses for Joe, but I do wonder if love can weather individual eccentricities, particularly when a marriage occurs after only three months.'

'You think we should have spent more time together first,' said Stella.

'I'm a believer in solid foundations. That's really all I'm equipped to say on the matter.'

'I see.' Stella didn't know what she'd expected but she'd hoped for more than Irish's defence of her husband. 'Could I have a drink, please?' she asked.

Irish waved in the direction of the drinks trolley. 'There's whiskey, rum, sherry, brandy and a rather tasty cognac. Let's have that. Pour me a glass as well.'

Stella went to the stash of decanters and lifted the stoppers on each, sniffing at the contents. Each scent was familiar except for the last and she poured the spirit into the balloon-shaped glasses her host directed her to use, carrying the drinks back to where they sat.

'Hold it in your hand, like so,' said Irish, cupping the glass so that the base of it rested in his palm. 'It should be drunk slightly warm.'

Stella took a sip of the intense floral flavour.

'Better,' he commented, swallowing a mouthful, his tongue sweeping his lips with pleasure.

'Yes,' said Stella. She clutched at the glass. Her fingers were shaking. Had she and Joe *both* been to blame for their complicated union? It seemed impossible to believe that she carried an equal portion of responsibility. Not when she was the one waiting at the homestead, trying to build a life with an absent husband. 'Joe's office was filled with odds and ends he'd found out on the property. Soil and plants, stones and bones. It went beyond being a hobby. I couldn't understand that. I suppose I never understood him.'

Irish inclined his head in thought. 'Joe was always a collector of things. There was a great need within him to understand the importance of every object, every plant and animal, and the connections between each. The bush spoke to him in ways that most of us could never comprehend. When he was a boy he'd stretch out on the ground and wait for the magpies to settle by his side.'

'You knew Joe when he was a child?'

'I did. It was a privilege.'

Stella moved closer to the edge of the chair. 'You said the other night that he wrote to you. I thought he might have said how he felt about me. Given some explanation as to why he ended up behaving the way he did.'

'I never heard where they found Joe,' said Irish bluntly.

Stella got up from the chair, directing her attention at the felt-topped table. There was a mark running from the right edge, as if it had worn down from the continual movement of a player positioning rows of cards. She took a sip of the cognac.

'You have a taste for silence I think.' Irish sat back and studied her.

'The quiet has been my home,' replied Stella. 'And everyone knows he was found in the desert.'

'Where exactly?'

'Beyond the dingo fence. He had no reason to be across the border in South Australia, but that was Joe. He'd tell a person one thing and do the opposite. Leave home for a week and stay away for a month.'

'I understand it took some time to find him,' said Irish.

'He'd been gone for six weeks. He ran out of fuel and water. I blame myself. I should have gone in search of him sooner, but he always got annoyed when I had in the past, and I wasn't at my best. I was still recovering from the loss of my baby. Davis found him. He was a friend of Joe's who maintains part of the dingo fence. Joe was curled up near a dead tree. I distinctly remember asking the constable that came to the homestead if his body had been on the leeward side. We'd owned this ram, you see. A prized animal. KR10. Joe found him dead on the leeward side of a tree. It's silly the things a person remembers.'

'Sit down, girl. My carpet is worn enough without your toing and froing.'

Stella did as the old man asked. 'The dog came home. Walked all the way. Joe always said he would if anything happened.'

'Animals are far smarter than people.'

'I gave him to Father Colin at Broken Hill,' said Stella. 'I'm sure he would have found him a good home.'

'It's not so very long since Joe's passing,' said Irish.

'No. Not long at all,' replied Stella. She swirled the contents of the glass.

'Joe used to sneak over here when he was little. Not often, but his visits became a lot more regular after cancer claimed his mother and then, of course, Sean died. Harry was busy running the property. It was a difficult time for them. I'd seen Joe poking about. Slipping into the work shed to clamber over the steam engine. Rummaging through our rubbish tip. I thought he was one of those children who'd take off for fear of getting into trouble, but he was confident enough to knock at the front door one day. A little runt of a boy, he was. Only about thirteen or fourteen at the time. He'd seen Tommy riding around on an old Triumph motorcycle we'd purchased after the Great War and asked if he could see it. That was the beginning of our friendship.'

'Who was Tommy?' said Stella.

'A friend's son. He and Joe were thick as thieves despite the forty-year age difference. I let Joe ride the bike. I've never seen a boy take to a thing the way he did. He'd polish it, grease and oil the engine, blacken the tyres. Tommy was happy for Joe to use it because that old Triumph was always immaculate. And the look on Joe's face when he came in from the paddock. Stopping that old motorcycle in a spray of dust, a grin so wide it hurt to see it.

'I began to realise that Joe was the grandson I believed I would never have. He was whip-smart. A little sponge willing to soak up everything. We'd study old maps together. Ride around the property on horseback. Talk about books and go exploring, head due west to the river, dip our lines in the water and roast our catch before coming home. They were grand days. That's when I began to make plans for the future, and I shared them with Joe. That was my mistake. A person never really has any inkling how life is going to unfold.' Irish sighed, his chest rising and falling in a series of ragged pants. 'Then Clinton was born. Geoff and his wife had given up on having children. They'd tried for years. The doctor said it was a change-of-life baby and he was right. Clinton's birth did change everything.' His gaze was direct, but watery. 'Joe wasn't impressed with Clinton's arrival, especially when I told him that with the child's birth the entire property had to be left to him.'

'You were going to leave your land to Joe?' said Stella.

'A half-share. Then on Geoff's death, Joe was to get the lot.'

She imagined what it would have meant to have lived in a closer-settled area; the difference such an inheritance may have made to their marriage and to Joe's relationship with Harry. Irish's gift would have changed everything.

Irish nodded. 'A few years later, Joe packed his swag and headed north-west to a sheep property. I knew he was disappointed but there was nothing I could do about it. Clinton was Hetty's grandson and I owed her.'

Stella closed her eyes as a familiar tightness began to stir within her. When she opened them the old man appeared to be asleep. 'And is that the reason behind Joe's disagreement with Harry? The fact that you promised Joe land and then reneged?'

Irish made a noise that was neither chuckle nor groan. 'If only. As far as I know, Harry never knew about that discussion. It was between Joe and me. If he had, I imagine he would have thrown Joe off the farm. He's a grudge-holder, Harry, just like his father. The man can't help himself. No, the dispute between our families goes back much further. My friendship with Joe, well, that only added to old resentments.'

Stella placed the now-empty glass on the table. It was late and the cognac had made her slightly muddle-headed. 'So you won't share what those old resentments were?'

He lifted the brandy balloon in a salute and, draining the contents, sat the glass to one side. His skin was as pale as parchment in the soft light. 'It was a petty disagreement.' He tugged at the blanket across his knees, fiddling with the fringed ends. 'Sean and I, well, we had more than our share of quarrels.'

Stella studied the old man before her. 'You knew Sean well?'

'Very well. Sean O'Riain and I were cousins.'

The skin between her eyes creased into two formidable lines. 'You're Brandon.'

'Brandon Ryan. I anglicised my surname and converted to the Protestant faith. One of my many failings, depending on who you speak to.' He gave her a gummy grin.

'But Harry never said . . . Joe never mentioned . . .'

Brandon yawned. 'You might fetch an old man another blanket from that chair.'

Stella's head was spinning, but she did as she was told, spreading the blanket across him. 'Brandon?'

He was asleep.

303

⊰ Chapter 46 ⊱

The dog followed her outdoors and, with her mind addled by all that she'd heard, Stella sat heavily on the grass. She stayed that way for several long minutes and then lay down on the lawn beneath a swollen moon, stroking the animal, who soon whimpered quietly by her side in sleep. The grass was spiky against her back and Stella rolled on her side, squeezing her knees close to her chest, her head cradled in her palms. Exhaustion leached through her and her eyes closed.

A young boy entered her dreams. She saw Joe riding a Triumph motorcycle, his hair wind-split and gritty as he traversed the verdant land that spread out towards the distant hills. He was shiny with joy at the wondrous world unfolding before him. Suspended in time. Untarnished by what was to come.

She saw him next on the edge of what was once a vast inland sea, holding one of his precious findings to the sky. Reading the indecipherable signs that meant something only to him. He was the land that shifted and shuddered. The vastness that dwarfed. The lonely child. The man that patched and repaired the country that had become his own. Who cared too much about some things, but not enough about others.

She woke at dawn. The dog was gone, as was the sweet coolness of the night. Birdsong floated through the air. She sat up, absorbing the new day, sorting through the dreams that had left her ragged with remorse, and then started walking back to Joe's childhood home. Inexplicably, she pictured Kirooma. Not the old homestead, which had become both her palace and her jail, but the timelessness of the land on which it sat.

She discovered that she'd stopped at the cedar tree. She located Brandon Ryan's mark of ownership almost immediately, a definitive *BR* sliced into the wood. She supposed that all of them were branded, in some way. By parents and lovers, siblings and friends, even husbands and wives. And some cuts went far deeper than others.

She scrambled through the fence and negotiated her way through the decaying trunks, her mind saturated with too many facts but not enough answers.

'*Coming back, coming back,*' screeched Watson from his new cage, an A-frame contraption erected halfway down the garden.

'Be quiet,' whispered Stella, tapping at the gauze.

'*Pretty boy, pretty boy,*' the cockatoo replied, spreading his wings and flying from the ground to the uppermost perch.

'What did he tell you?'

Her nephew John was sitting on the back veranda, a mug in one hand, a cigarette in the other. She smiled quizzically at him as if she had no idea what he was talking about, and walked towards him.

'I saw you,' he told her, flicking the ash from the cigarette and then taking another long draw. 'So did Watson.'

'I was in the garden,' she lied. 'I couldn't sleep.'

John took a sip of his coffee and then emptied the remains on the lawn. 'And the other night? I came out here to have a smoke before I went to bed. I followed you. I saw you go through the fence. You were over there for at least an hour.'

Stella said nothing, and sat next to him on the step. Their legs stretched out side by side, as if they were sunning themselves at the beach.

John took a number of quick puffs of the cigarette. 'You shouldn't have gone over there, Aunty Stella.'

She could have argued. Reminded her nephew that at her age, she could do anything she wanted. 'I had a difficult marriage with your uncle and I thought Irish— I mean Brandon, might have been able to help me understand Joe a little better.'

'And did he?'

To her horror, tears started to well up. 'I'm sorry. I've not slept much.'

John stubbed the cigarette out and flicked the butt into some nearby bushes. 'Brandon Ryan is an old rogue. It's bad enough that he converted to Protestantism and distanced himself from my grandfather because it suited his ambitions, but he's also a criminal. I bet he forgot to tell you that.' He flicked the striker on the zippo lighter so that it flared in a series of short, sharp bursts.

'What are you talking about?'

'He's a thief. He stole that land of his, and he took Joe from us as well. And that doesn't include what he did to my grandfather or the rest of this family. Enough good reasons not to be speaking to him. My dad will be pretty angry if he finds out that you've been over there. Don't go back again. It's not worth it.'

She reached for the packet of cigarettes by John's side and took one. Wordlessly he lit it for her.

'Brandon Ryan isn't a good person, Aunty Stella.'

She drew hard on the cigarette. 'Well. Neither am I.'

306

≪ Chapter 47 ≫

Broken Hill, 1949

'You do seem much better this morning. All a body needs is rest and a chance for contemplation. God will forgive you, Stella, for the burial of your child. They were extenuating circumstances.' Father Colin sat by the hospital bed, his grey hair contrasting with the ruddy pallor of his skin.

Stella crossed her feet at the ankles and smoothed the new dress bought on her behalf by the grocer, Mrs Andrews. During the last weeks she couldn't recall having asked for God's forgiveness, nor of having expressed to Father Colin anything remotely similar. Not that he was the type of man who believed in the possibility of any of his faith thinking differently to him. He was steadfast in his beliefs and painfully consistent in his attentions towards her. The priest had appeared every morning since her admittance into the hospital. Stella felt rather over-tended, like one of the sheep running at Kirooma, forever under Joe's scrutiny.

'And is your husband collecting you this morning?' he asked.

'No, Mrs Andrews is. The hospital was going to billet me with someone in town but when she heard I was here, she offered to have me. I'm to stay with her for a few weeks,' said Stella, trying to sound bright. The doctor had noted her melancholy disposition and warned her that it would require further treatment if there wasn't an improvement. Shutting the door on her bleak thoughts was proving impossible. However, she was quick to note that a calm response to any questions asked of her seemed to keep the medical professionals happy, although they still ran through her chart every morning as if trying to pilot unfamiliar seas.

'Ah, Mrs Andrews, the grocer,' he said with a shake of his head, as if the poor woman's soul was already damned. 'She is not a churchgoer, of any denomination.'

'I'm not sure I will be in the future either,' said Stella, watching as a nurse moved along the corridor, hopeful her discharge papers would soon be signed so she could escape Father Colin, whose diligence was tiring.

'My dear, if you feel you need to repent, then say your Hail Marys. However I really do think that on this occasion you are being too hard on yourself. It is a sad but unfortunately very true fact that many a man and child have been buried in property graves without the presence of a man of the cloth, with only a Bible for guidance. Sometimes not even that.'

'And what of the women? What happens to them?' asked Stella.

The priest frowned. 'I'm afraid I don't understand.'

'What happens to the women who die out in the bush? You only mentioned men and children. Are we that unimportant?'

'It was only a phrase, Stella,' he said, patting her arm.

It was a significant omission to her. She folded her arms across her stomach and the emptiness within.

'Shall we pray one last time before you leave?' he suggested.

'No. Thank you.'

Her frank reply was greeted with consternation. 'Well, perhaps you have thoughts of home on your mind, but you *will* speak to your husband about coming to church here in Broken Hill, won't you? Even if you manage it once every six weeks, I think you'd find it beneficial. There is so much comfort to be found in silent meditation and in our church community.'

'Father, I have as much chance of getting Joe to church as I do of having him come home at night,' said Stella.

'I know, my child, I know. Such dedication should be commended. Men who embrace the land are embraced by it in return, and often it's hard to shake them free of that grasp, to make them understand the importance of companionship. But I will write to him and entreat him to make the effort. There is great strength to be found in the company of others.'

Not for Joe, Stella thought. He had no craving for human connection. He existed outside of it.

'And if he doesn't want that?' she asked.

Father Colin shrugged. 'I've seen and spoken to many a soul who's spent his life in the bush. A man can be anything he wants out here. Worker or grazier, happy wanderer or miserable nomad. There's a certain savagery to the outback. We're exposed to the basest elements of life and it takes a special type of man to reside in isolation, to have the hours marked out by the very birth and death of the animals that provide his livelihood. Some of us learn to live with the changes, although perhaps it's not quite what we envisioned for ourselves,' he finished pointedly.

'So, I must simply accept my situation,' said Stella. Outside the hospital window trees quivered in the breeze. A haze had taken root in the sky, dulling the customary blue. Father Colin muttered something about the cross that each of God's children was required to bear. It was then that she swung her legs over the side of the bed, ready to leave, with or without discharge papers.

'This is a very old Bible.' He reached for the book that stuck out of the top of the carryall on the floor. 'Does it belong to your family?'

'No. I found it at the homestead when we moved in,' said Stella. 'Do you know anything about the people who lived at Kirooma before us?'

He adjusted his starched collar, as if the fit were too tight. 'I met Mr Handalay once, at a function here in Broken Hill. It was his father that first settled Kirooma in the 1860s. They were extremely wealthy. Made their fortune on the goldfields and were quick to buy up land, but the third generation lost interest. All three sons took up professions in Melbourne, and that's when Mr Handalay placed the property on the market. I believe he left a lot of their furniture in the homestead when he and his wife left, and I also heard that the library was constructed from the hull of a wrecked ship. Can you hear the waves crashing at night?' he asked with a smile.

It made sense to Stella. In that room, she'd never quite had her land legs. The ocean, like the lives of the previous owners, was steeped into her home. 'And that's all you know?'

Father Colin tapped the side of his skull with a knuckle. 'I'm afraid my memory isn't as good as it used to be. Is there something you were particularly interested in?'

Stella thought of the letter in the Bible. 'No. Nothing.'

He bowed his head, as if duty truly was its own reward. 'You'll come and see me when you're next in town?'

'Yes.' The lie slid smoothly off her tongue.

Stella waited until the priest left and then moved to the window. Joe had visited a week earlier. He'd spent a whole hour telling her of the condition of the sheep, the bore that had broken down, and the orchard, which he'd diligently kept alive for her with buckets of water. The subject of her health and baby Elizabeth was skirted as neatly as a man on a motorbike avoiding a tree-stump, the exclusion so obvious that it only served to emphasise the disaster more. Stella had wanted to scream at Joe. Instead, she informed him of her intention to recuperate at Mrs Andrews's home.

He'd been aghast; told her he was surprised she had made such a decision without at least discussing it with him first. She had laughed at this, and kept on laughing until the nurses were called and Joe was asked to leave. Whether Mrs Andrews was the right choice Stella remained undecided, however an empty homestead held no allure.

'Stella.'

She turned to find Joe in the doorway holding a potted blood-red Sturt's desert pea. His hat dangled from his hand.

'I've come to take you home,' he said with a proprietary air.

'Joe? But I said Mrs Andrews was picking me up. It's all been arranged. I was to stay with her for a fortnight at least.' Stella's body began to stiffen. Perspiration seeped up through the pores of her skin.

Joe took a step into the room. 'I've spoken to Mrs Andrews and the doctor. Everyone feels it's better if you come home. Delaying things probably isn't in your best interests. It's better to be in your own environment.'

'You mean *your* best interests,' she replied sharply. She dug her nails into her palms, trying to stem the trembling that threatened to spread through her body.

He came further into the room as if inch by inch he intended to push his way back into her life. 'Stella, you have to come home. You can't run away from what's happened.'

'How could I run away from it?' she said loudly. 'Elizabeth's death will be with me forever.'

'Just come home and we'll talk. Okay?'

'You never want to talk,' she replied. Crying wasn't going to help. She was aware, at least, of that. Tears were for people who were capable of feeling. Since Elizabeth's death, a numbness had settled within her but now Joe was standing at the end of the hospital bed and all Stella wanted to do was open the window and jump.

The man before her meant nothing to her. Theirs was a poisonous marriage. She backed away and leant against the windowsill, clinging to the bricks-and-mortar security of the building.

'Stella, please. Don't make a scene.' Joe sat the plant down on the bed and held out a hand to her.

She stayed by the window, feeling the same haze that drifted outside on the horizon beginning to take hold of her. Just as the dust obscured the clarity of the sky, so her own thoughts grew unclear. She was curious enough to understand that she'd not been the same since Elizabeth's birth and death. That somehow, during the many hours she'd nursed her dead child, and placed her in the salt-preserving cot at night, she'd lost the ability to comprehend reason or reality. It left her with the unsettling sensation of being eggshell thin, as if a hairline fracture already ran through her and the slightest knock was capable of breaking her in two.

'Stella. This is ridiculous,' said Joe.

'I just—'

'You just what?' he said.

Joe was standing at her side. He slid his arm about her waist before placing his hand gently on the small of her back as if ready to guide her as he would one of his woolly ewes down the race.

'Come on,' he said, with a look of encouragement.

They skirted the bed and he shoved the hat on his head and collected the plant and her bag. 'I thought you'd like this for the kitchen. Give the place a bit of colour.' His arm snaked out about her, their bodies joined from shoulder to hip. He walked her along the corridor, nodding pleasantly at everyone they passed.

'Mrs O'Riain, it's nice to see you looking so much better,' said a nurse.

'Wonderful to have her up and about again. Thank you for your splendid care,' said Joe.

'You're very welcome, Mr O'Riain,' said the nurse.

'Well come on, my dear. We best get you home,' Joe said, for the benefit of anybody nearby. 'The doctor tells me that routine is important. Having a reason to get up in the morning. Tending to things. I've done my best with the orchard but you're the one with the green thumb.'

He led her outside to the parked station wagon. He opened the door, sat the plant in the middle of the bench seat and then waited until she was seated.

'There, all set?'

He closed the door and then walked around to the driver's side and took up his place behind the steering wheel, placing her carryall in the back on his way around. The man of the house, always in control.

Stella wound down the window. The engine turned over and the vehicle cruised onto the road. The air was hot and dry. It stung her eyes and made her face crease up protectively. The Sturt's pea shifted left and right with the road's corrugations. She lifted her hands to her throat, convinced that some invisible cord was strangling her, as surely as her own body had strangled her child. Joe began talking about the latest weather report. His hopes for the coming season. More rain was needed for the grass to grow. She nodded and made occasional sounds as if she were listening, then she fixed her gaze on the road ahead and waited for Joe to run out of words. Why couldn't he see it as clearly as she could? He and Kirooma had become her jailers and, ultimately, they were at the beginning of the end.

⋘ Chapter 48 ⋙

Richmond Valley, 1949

Hetty.

Stella stopped her morning patrol of the garden. She was opposite Watson's cage, surrounded by the green of rain-fed country. Tea-tree plantations and sugar cane were interspersed by arteries of channelling water that somewhere to the east mingled with the foamy sea.

The bird screeched at her. *'Gone again. Gone again.'*

Only recently she'd sat in a baggy military chair drinking aged cognac and listening to tales of the past. Stories of a young boy who'd grown to become the man she'd married and once loved. Her conversations with Brandon Ryan had been convoluted, and she'd been focusing only on what he knew of Joe. Perhaps that was why it had taken a couple of days to shake loose a single name. He'd mentioned someone called Hetty.

Stella returned to her bedroom and retrieved the old Bible. She might well be wrong, but she had a feeling she wasn't. And Hetty wasn't the only name of significance. There was also the letter. Signed with a single initial: B.

'Stella?' She heard Ann calling out for her, so she slipped the book into the pocket of her apron and hurried down the hall.

Ann was in the lounge room listening to music. Her breakfast tray was almost empty, apart from a piece of jam toast that lay upturned on the carpet at her feet. Stella cleaned the spill and then placed the wireless a little closer to her.

'Thank you.' Ann moved gingerly on the couch.

'Can I get you anything else?' Stella asked.

'No,' said Ann.

Her patient still wasn't speaking to her beyond what was necessary. Their recent argument had ruptured their delicate friendship and made Stella realise that it wasn't just Harry who resented Brandon and Joe, but the entire family. Perhaps they'd been expecting her to apologise for him. If that were the case, then Ann would be disappointed. Stella's peace branch was quite wilted. It had run out of water long ago.

'We might have to get rid of that cockatoo. He makes a dreadful noise,' said Ann.

'Don't you like birds?'

'That's not really the point,' replied Ann, brushing crumbs from her lap.

Despite the tensions, Ann was steadily improving. It was the second morning that her sister-in-law had taken breakfast out of bed. The colour had returned to her skin and she'd even managed to dress herself. Stella imagined that in a few days Ann would be much better, which was a relief. If John knew about her nocturnal visits to the big house, it was unlikely to stay a secret for long.

'As you're so much better, I'll be leaving in a couple of days,' said Stella.

Ann positioned a cushion a little lower behind her back. 'We haven't discussed your leaving. Anyway, I'm not quite back to my old self.'

'I think you'll manage.'

'This is because of our disagreement, isn't it.' She batted away a fly from her face. 'I was trying to explain things to you.'

'What, that you and Harry were against the way Joe lived his life, because it wasn't what Harry expected of him? That Joe had the audacity to speak to someone that you hold a grudge against? Joe was entitled to live his life the way he wanted. Right or wrong. Good or bad,' said Stella.

'Really?' replied Ann, her knuckles white where she clutched at the couch. 'What about you, Stella? During all your time out west, are you telling me that you didn't once complain to your husband or think ill of him? Can you truly tell me that *you're* not angry with him?' She lifted the teacup and took a sip.

Stella refused to be baited into another argument. She was beginning to recover from her time out west, and her visits with Brandon were helping to fill in the many holes that pitted her knowledge of her husband's life. So, why was she keeping her visits to the old man so closely guarded? She may have initially agreed to Harry's rules out of politeness, however genuflecting to her brother-in-law was no longer a priority. Stella gathered up the plate of spoiled toast. 'If you need me today, I'll be at Brandon Ryan's house.'

'W-what?' Tea dribbled down the front of Ann's navy dress.

'You're going to find out sooner or later so I might as well save you the bother and tell you straight. I've spoken to him on a number of occasions. If my seeing him offends you then I'm happy to leave earlier. I'm partially packed.'

For the very first time since her arrival on the farm, Stella felt as if she were in charge of her life again. She left her sister-in-law and walked straight from the house through the garden, and its maze of long-ago-cut trees. She paused at the trunk of the sole surviving cedar and then slipped through the fence. Within minutes, she was knocking on Brandon Ryan's door. She realised immediately that it was far too early to be disturbing an elderly man and she began to back away, however the dog greeted her with a series of barks and Brandon came to the door.

'Back so soon,' he said hoarsely. 'You're just in time for some tea. At this hour I need to wet my whistle to get things mechanising.'

'I'm so sorry. I didn't think about the time,' Stella apologised. 'I can come back later.'

'You're here now.' Brandon joined her on the veranda and they sat side by side, as they had the first night of their meeting. But they were no longer strangers. In the daylight he appeared almost too frail to withstand the slight morning breeze and she admired the concentration it must have taken when he lifted the pannikin of tea, his grip shaky.

'I imagine there's a reason you're here so early,' said Brandon.

'Yes. It was something you said the other night. A name you mentioned. With everything else I forgot until this morning.' She took the Bible from her apron and opened it, showing him the name Hetty scrawled at the front. Then she passed him the letter. 'B is for . . . ?'

'Brandon,' said the old man, reading the lines.

'It's you,' said Stella. 'You wrote this.'

'I did,' he admitted, carefully folding the letter. In the garden, the dog chased butterflies.

'I found the Bible and the letter within the first few weeks of moving to Kirooma,' said Stella.

'I always wondered if she'd received it. She couldn't write very well. Few of us could back then. Luckily I was keen to learn and I had a reasonable teacher,' said Brandon.

'You mean Hetty. That's who you were writing to,' persisted Stella.

'Hetty. She was a good woman with a solid character. Did you find anything else?'

'Nothing personal like that, although the Handalays left a lot of furniture. Some of it would be quite valuable now.'

'Was there a large terrestrial globe? It was about this high.' He raised his hand a couple of feet from the ground. 'There was a compass in the bottom of the stand. It's a very fine example. It would have been in the library.'

'Yes, there was. I have it with me. It's one of the few pieces that I took when I left. But how do you know about it?'

'I remember the last time I saw it,' replied Brandon.

'When? Where?'

'Right here,' he said. 'At the front of this house. The day my world fell apart.'

❧ Chapter 49 ❧

Richmond Valley, 1867

Maggie sat on a length of fallen timber, locks of chestnut hair whisking about her in the wind, each strand furling and unfurling until she reached for the unruly tendrils and twisted them into a thick knot at the base of her neck. She stared towards the hills, where a setting sun sent out biting rays of orange light. Little Tommy played at her side. The child rolled across the ground, smiling in delight, and then lay on his stomach, poking at the soil. He reached out to pull at her skirt but was ignored so thoroughly that he soon returned to his play.

Maggie's sadness was reflected in everything she did – in the untidy mending of sheets, in the butter that was over-churned, or the complaints from others of her surly behaviour. The air about her had taken on a brittleness that was difficult to bear. Every evening since they'd returned to Truby's run, she sat on the fallen timber, her body like a pool of still water. She'd wait until the gathering twilight became night, then she would return to Hetty's cottage to eat and sleep, before waking to go through the motions of living once again.

The notion of confronting Maggie to try to draw her free of self-pity entered Brandon's thoughts hourly. He knew she hurt, and he longed to break through the remoteness that separated them. And yet every time he saw her, words failed him. By trying to save her, in doing his best to give her a better life, he'd caused her to drift further away, and he feared losing her forever.

He too had his own place for watching and remembering as the light dwindled. A single grey-barked eucalypt with a tangle of leaves for shelter and, this afternoon, a laughing kookaburra, whose song appeared to be written especially for him.

The bird gave a final chortle and flew from the branch. Hetty arrived and he was pleased at her coming. Here was someone who was not past forgiving. She had accepted Maggie's return with little comment, knowing that Mr Truby played a part, and she'd been wise enough not to ask questions. At least not yet. What domestic would query Brandon, when he'd ridden in and out of the property with the squatter at his side?

Together they observed the changing colour staining the countryside gold. There was comfort in having Hetty at his side.

'She must sense me standing here, but she never turns. Not once. What is she gazing at?' said Brandon.

Hetty shaded herself from the glare. 'Everything. Nothing,' she replied, the two words conjuring up the mystery of women's business. 'Maggie told me last night that she wants to return to Ireland.'

'I don't believe you,' said Brandon, turning to face her.

'You can't save someone if they don't want to be saved,' replied Hetty, in her practical manner. She squeezed his arm as he guessed a mother might and took a series of small steps away from him to kick at a tangle of fallen twigs and leaves. 'She's unhappy. Maggie and I aren't friends, don't suppose we are, but her pining hasn't eased. You don't have to like a person to see they're hurting.'

'It's been a month,' Brandon reminded her. 'A whole month.'

'*Only* a month,' she corrected, 'during which she's lost the child she was carrying, and learnt that the man she hoped to marry is in a barred cell. And yet you sit here wondering why she's so distant. Why she's so sad. It's no small thing for a woman to lose a baby, Brandon, no small thing at all, and she blames you for everything.'

'Regardless of whether I'd brought her here in the first place or not, Niall Hackett still would have been arrested.'

'Let her go. Let Maggie make her own way in the world. Niall might take her back after he's released in a few years. If he did, it would be for the best.'

'It's not for the best, and anyway, I made a promise.'

'Not to her, I'm betting.' Hetty broke the slender branch she held so that the pieces fell in even lengths to the ground. 'Such an agreement means nothing, at least not to her.'

'It's for her benefit,' replied Brandon, growing angry.

'Is it?' queried Hetty. 'I wonder about that. I've seen the way you watch her.'

'She's *family*.' He'd forgotten what Hetty could be like. There was a quick-wittedness to the girl, which had helped her survive as a famine orphan, although that same cunning could be used as a weapon. He hadn't forgotten that she enjoyed the favour of Mr Truby and his niece. But now he did, too.

Hetty gave a little scowl. 'I wonder about you, Brandon. Haven't you ever wanted someone? Been in love so much that it feels as if your heart's twisting from the force of it.'

'No,' he replied.

'Yes you have,' continued Hetty. 'Please, Brandon. It's just us. I have fed you and housed Maggie, and I know what I've seen. I saw it clearly the night she came to our cottage. You were devastated when Maggie saw us together. Guilty. As if what *we* might have together was unnatural. You try to conceal it, probably even from yourself, but you're a man who loves and wants what he can't have.'

It was one thing for Sean to speculate on his feelings for Maggie, but Hetty's words stripped him bare. Brandon didn't know what to say.

'You only see me as a stupid, ugly girl, the little beauty I possessed ruined by Miss Schaefer's bird, but I see and feel just as you do and I'm telling you that if you care for Maggie, then you'll let her be with the man she loves, for there is no future for the two of you. You must understand that.'

His face flushed. 'She can't be with Hackett's son. They're Fenians. They'll ruin her life. I couldn't let her go to him, not after what happened in Ireland.'

'Tell me,' said Hetty as she grew close again and plied his arm.

'She's the reason we ran from Tipperary. My father promised her to our landlord. But I couldn't let Maggie be married to him. She was a child. If Sean hadn't done what he did, I probably would have killed him myself,' said Brandon. He listened to the tread of Hetty's feet in the dry grass.

'Sean killed your landlord?' Hetty said, with admiration. 'Still, I have to wonder at you two boys. A landlord for a husband, whether good or bad, has benefits that few right-thinking people would turn away from.'

'Maggie doesn't know what happened. It would be too much of a burden for her.' Brandon couldn't believe he'd told Hetty of their past, but there was nobody else he could talk to. Somehow, this outspoken woman with her practical manner had wormed her way into his confidence.

'Well, she isn't a child anymore. Maggie's a grown woman. And your dislike of Niall isn't a good enough reason to ruin her life for a second time.'

Brandon flinched at her accusation. 'You have no idea what you're talking about.'

'Don't I?'

Tommy left Maggie's side, ran to his mother and then continued towards the cottage. Hetty called after the boy, shrugging when he tripped and fell and began to cry.

'I hear you're to build your own cottage on the river and that new cutters are to take over the felling of the cedars at the back of the homestead. You're to learn about sugar cane and play the landlord of a fair holding,' said Hetty with a knowledgeable air.

'Who told you that?' asked Brandon.

'I heard Miss Schaefer discussing it with Mr Truby the day after her return from Ballina. She's not impressed with your foothold, as she called it.'

Brandon decided he might as well continue to confide in Hetty. The bitter disagreement with Sean had made him feel unbalanced, as if he were the rickety chair on Hetty's sloping veranda and one push might send him over the edge.

'It's only for three years and then it reverts to him. Don't say anything about it, will you, Hetty? There'll be trouble aplenty if word gets out.'

She gave a shrill laugh. 'You can't hide your doings in this district. Anyway, you did it for her, didn't you?' Hetty gestured to Maggie, still keeping vigil on the fallen timber. 'I hope she's worth it. For God is watching us all.'

After Hetty left, Brandon waited as the sky dimmed. The hilltops were smudged with yellow and then the colour gradually dissipated, replaced by a deep blue. He thought of leaving before Maggie saw him, however as the trees and outbuildings darkened in the fading light, he noticed her move. She was walking towards him, her skirts swishing through the grass.

He toyed with a fraying shirt cuff, and then stiffened his body, gathering in all the anger and sadness and frustration that hovered like a starving cat at a cook's door. She came to stand directly before him, her face solemn. Her eyes were puffy and wet.

'Why are you so cruel to me?' she asked.

The question winded him. 'I'm not cruel to you, Maggie.'

'I've done my best, Brandon. I never wanted to leave Ireland. I'm not like you and Sean. I would have been content there, even if I was starving. You'll probably think me silly for saying that, but it's true. Ireland is in my bones.'

'There's nothing there for us now,' he said gently, not wanting to upset her further.

'And there's nothing here for me either, so what should I do? Live my life as a spinster cooking your meals and keeping house, while you marry and have children, or is there something more of me that you're asking?' She took hold of his shoulders and he felt the weight of her as she tipped her face up towards his. 'You have to let me go.'

'I can't,' said Brandon softly.

She dropped her arms. 'You were always so good to me when I was little. You used to hold my hand. Help me with my chores. We've always argued, but it's been far worse since we arrived in Australia. You know why, don't you?'

'It's been difficult for everyone,' he said tentatively.

'That's not the reason. Over there, we were part of a family. We were bound by rules and common sense. But here, we've been forced to grow up without them and I think that's been the hardest for you. I know you feel responsible, that Father would have made you promise to keep me safe, but somehow that care has altered what was between us. I've been wondering why that is. Maybe it's because everything is upside down here. Like the fiery sun that was so weak and miserly at home, or maybe it's because the stars hang so heavy and unrecognisable. But what's different is also the same. The sun and the stars are unchangeable and so are we.' Maggie wrapped her arms about him. Her head resting against his chest. 'You love me,' she said quietly.

Brandon stayed quite still, scared that the slightest movement might cause her to let go. He could feel the gentle beat of her heart, recognised the hint of grain she'd been pounding for bread and from beneath the calico she wore, unfamiliar womanly scents made rich by the heat of her body. He drew her closer. Their bodies matched like two pieces of a puzzle and a rawness seared his chest, sending his mind soaring like a bird on the wing. He saw everything, the simple crofter's house of his youth, the sheep he once tended, the waters sailed and every tree he'd ever felled. All of it had led him here to this single moment under an ancient eucalypt tree. Sean and Hetty were right. He wanted Maggie for his very own.

Brandon took her face in his palms, feeling her skull beneath his fingers and kissed her cheeks, tasting the salt of her tears, tangy and warm. He could not tell what might be between them. But he felt something elusive. And fragile. He drew away, suddenly fearful of admitting to a desire that, far from lessening with age, had grown deeper and fuller over time. It couldn't be kept secret anymore. Maggie was staring at him with a beatific smile. It centred him and made him strong and he thought of where they might run to. Of the forest with its trailing vines, thick undergrowth and mountain streams. He leant towards her, conscious only of her lips.

Maggie quickly pulled free of his embrace.

He reached for her. 'Maggie—'

She placed a finger to his mouth, silencing him.

Words stuck in his throat. He was still in the place she'd taken him to. A lost room, an entire universe comprehensible only to them, filled with infinite possibilities.

'I love you as a brother, nothing more,' she said.

Brandon felt first the petulance of a schoolchild rise within him, and then mortification at being rejected. He stalked a few feet away to stand with his back to her. The hope that had lodged within him subsided. Everything had changed.

'We're not related by blood,' he said firmly.

'I'm sorry, but you'll always be my brother. Nothing more,' she replied. 'Brandon, don't be like this. It always was easier when you were angry with me.' Her attempt at playfulness changed to sadness. 'Mr Truby has agreed to find me another position.'

Brandon couldn't believe what he was hearing. He turned to face her, fearing her loss more than the refusal of his love. 'You don't have to leave, Maggie.'

'It's for the best.'

'But we're family. We promised Father that we'd stay together,' he argued.

'And we have, but at some stage we all have to grow up.'

'I won't let you go.'

'Yes you will, for I'm not yours to keep,' said Maggie.

She left him alone, her confident stride more telling than anything else she might have said. He thought of running after her, of putting an end to the plans she'd made. A scheme made in secret that would separate them forever. But the connection between them had been broken and he could see no way of recovering what was now lost.

❧ Chapter 50 ❧

Construction had begun on the second storey of Mr Truby's house. Men were erecting the frame; the sawing of wood and the striking of nails echoing through the garden. Brandon had expected to assist but was instead relegated to marking Xs on the tallest cedar tree stumps at the back of the property with a piece of chalk, so that the timbermen could cut the remains closer to the ground. Mr Truby had the entire stand of cedars felled except one, and deemed the truncated wood unsightly, an unwanted addition to what would eventually be a much larger garden.

Brandon completed the chalking of the trees and looked out from the rise across the now-cleared slope towards the outbuildings. The mill was throbbing due to the increased demand for wood. Men carted timber to the homestead and scaled ladders. The carpenters were concentrating their efforts on the far end of the homestead, where part of the roof had already been removed. Beyond the house, he could see the blacksmith shoeing a horse out the front of the stables and Miss Schaefer walking with her dog. His gaze took in the soft green of the landscape, the pale yellow fields of slashed grain and the line of cattle grazing into the wind.

He walked to the lone cedar tree left standing and noticed men carrying crates out from the back of the house. Then Mr Truby appeared, a blanket thrown over a shoulder and the terrestrial globe in his arms.

Intrigued, Brandon walked down the slope and was heading to the front of the property when he met Miss Schaefer on her walk.

'Good morning, Miss Schaefer,' said Brandon, passing her.

'Stop,' she commanded curtly. 'I want to speak with you.'

He turned to face her. The banging from the builders vibrated through the silence that hung between them.

'I have heard of the most remarkable occurrences. Of attempted thievery and land granted. And now I am to believe that you have changed your name, effectively converting to our religion.'

It was as if a list of charges were being read out against him. Brandon was puzzled by Miss Schaefer's attack, for it was none of her business.

'You have been an easy convert, Brandon *Ryan*, perhaps too easy,' she said.

'I've never been a very religious person.' Brandon spoke carefully.

'My uncle spoke of paganism.' She leant forward. 'I understand it is the religion of the peasantry, but still, I was quite staggered to hear of it. I'd heard you were reasonably schooled and above average in intellect.'

'Perhaps I don't hold to any religion now,' said Brandon.

Miss Schaefer flung her head back and laughed. 'You are as changeable as the wind.'

'Religion has not done me any favours,' said Brandon just as abruptly.

'You've grown outspoken. How things alter in a few days.'

He concentrated on the little dog, who was pulling determinedly at the lead in her hand.

'So now you are a non-believer,' Miss Schaefer continued.

'Yes.'

'Some of us wear masks to hide our true selves from the world,' she said. 'You're not a simpleton. If you were, you'd still be with your cousin, however I think you believe that you've found a nice little position here. Your name is now on eight thousand acres of land. Land that holds the key to the successful running of this property. Without it, we have no access to water and without water, the rest of my uncle's property loses substantial value.'

'It's a dummy contract,' Brandon reminded her.

'Don't speak to me in that tone. It is a contract that forms a very important part of my uncle's estate. My inheritance.'

'Then I'll break the contract and leave today.' He may have sounded confident, but immediately Brandon wondered what he would do if he were forced to leave Mr Truby's employment. He'd given up so much to be here. 'I didn't ask for this, it was your uncle's doing.'

'That's what he said.' The dog growled and Miss Schaefer wrapped the lead about her wrist so that the dog was forced to sit amongst the folds of her lavender skirt. 'It seems I underestimated you,' she said icily.

She left without another word and headed to the front of the property. Brandon followed her to where a covered bullock wagon waited. He arrived just as Mr Truby was adjusting the globe and blanket on the rear of the wagon and inspecting the loading of sacks of grain and other items. Hetty and Maggie stood close by; Miss Schaefer and her dog a little apart from them, a canvas bag at her feet beside an irate Glanville in a cage.

'Hello, Brandon,' said Maggie.

'Maggie,' he answered. It was difficult seeing her again so soon after their conversation the night before. Next to her, Hetty appeared engrossed in the movement about them, her attention firmly directed away from him. Brandon wondered why Mr Truby was letting the women loiter when there were the usual morning chores to be done.

Two men hoisted a trunk onto the wagon. One steadied the cumbersome chest while the other clambered up to disappear into the the wagon's rear. Together they pushed and pulled it under the canvas covering. Their efforts shook the globe. It started to slowly spin.

'Careful,' said Mr Truby, steadying the world with a hand.

Brandon wondered where his employer was going. There were five horsemen standing by, thumbing reins and smoking pipes.

'Eventually you'll get beyond the outer limits,' Mr Truby said to one of the riders. 'Keep your eyes sharp and your wits about you. The natives might appear friendly but it's not always the case. Your guide, Munroe, will meet you at Boulder Pass. After that you're in his hands. Hopefully he'll steer you in the right direction.'

He beckoned to his niece. Miss Schaefer allowed him to give her a very brief kiss on the cheek. Then, barely acknowledging Hetty, she was escorted wordlessly to the wagon and assisted up into the front where she sat on a trunk, her dog firmly clasped in her lap.

'Where is she going?' Brandon asked Hetty quietly, as the falcon and remaining bag were placed in the rear of the wagon.

'They're taking her to Wirra and then she'll catch a ship to Sydney. She and Mr Truby had a difference of opinion over some land,' Hetty explained knowingly. 'Apparently she needs further education on the niceties of being a lady.'

'She told you that?' asked Brandon, not sorry to learn of Miss Schaefer's leaving.

'The cook told me,' whispered Hetty.

'Maggie, be ready, girl,' Mr Truby called.

Brandon took Maggie's arm and led her away from the others. She was wearing her fancy shawl, last seen the day he'd found her in Niall Hackett's arms. 'What's going on?'

'I'm leaving for my new position,' said Maggie.

'What, now?'

'I wanted to tell you yesterday.' The mention of their last meeting caused her to gaze briefly at the ground. 'Don't make this difficult. There are people watching.'

'You were going to leave without saying goodbye,' continued Brandon.

Maggie gave a brave smile. 'I'm to work for a family to the west of here.'

'How far west?' he asked.

'It will take some travelling to reach. Mr Truby says that the Handalays are very wealthy. He's entrusted the globe to my care and I'm to see it takes pride of place in the library once it's built. It's a housewarming gift and I must say he was sad to part with it, but Mr Handalay is one of his closest friends.'

'You mean there is no house where you're going?'

'There will be.'

'Maggie, I've wrapped the globe in a blanket and wedged it between the crates,' instructed Mr Truby. 'And do pay attention if it rains, I don't want those books ruined. And the orange and lemon seeds for the orchard are packed with the provisions. Once they're planted, they must be watered every day.'

'I'll do my best, sir,' said Maggie, moving out of Brandon's reach. 'Goodbye, Hetty.'

'Here, take this.' Hetty passed her the cloth-covered Bible. 'Lord knows you'll be needing it out in the wild lands. You can read?'

'Poor to middling, but I'll try my best with it.' Maggie opened the book. 'Maybe I'll see you again.'

'Maybe,' said Hetty indifferently.

Brandon took Maggie's hand, feeling the calluses that told a story of their own. He wanted to take her in his arms one last time, to beg her not to leave, but he saw the determination that lay behind her wide, bright eyes and he knew that nothing he could say would alter her decision, and he had no right to ask. 'You will try to send word to me once you've arrived? I won't sleep until you do.'

'Have a good life, Brandon,' she said.

'Don't say that, Maggie. We'll see each other again.' He clutched at her hands but she drew free of his grasp. Then she was stepping away, into a beginning he was not to be part of.

'Be well, Brandon, and if you ever see Sean again, tell him goodbye.' Maggie nodded at Mr Truby, smiled at Hetty, and was lifted into the rear of the wagon by one of the horsemen, where she sat on a crate near the opening.

About them, men tightened surcingles and closed flaps on saddlebags. They placed boots in stirrups and heaved themselves up into newly greased saddles. The horses started off and then the bullocky cracked a whip and the wagon lurched forwards, dust rising under the creak of the wheels.

Brandon started to walk after the wagon, his pace increasing, his stomach churning.

'Brandon,' said Mr Truby. 'Brandon.'

He stopped and stared at the departing convoy. Maggie kept her gaze fixed on him from the rear of the wagon. He lifted a hand and waved, hoping that she'd reciprocate, to give a sign that they were still friends at least.

'It's a hard thing knowing you might never see your family again,' said Mr Truby thoughtfully.

'Where's she going?'

'Kirooma Station. It'll be an adventure for her. Not many can say they've travelled into the interior.'

'Kirooma Station,' repeated Brandon, pronouncing the name as if it were a foreign territory. The riders and wagon completed a half circle and turned towards the main track. 'Is it very far?'

'Very. I'll expect to see you in a half hour. We have much to discuss. I'm investigating the recruitment of Islanders to work in the cane fields.' Mr Truby walked towards the homestead.

Brandon watched as the overlanders kept up a steady pace. Before them lay the hills, a final landfall before Maggie's proper journey commenced. There would be virgin ground to cross and trails to blaze and, beyond it all, a homestead carved out of nothing in the middle of nowhere that would be her home. A new start that he would not share in. All Brandon could see was an eternity of space and light stretching into emptiness ahead.

'She wasn't so bad in the end. Had she stayed, we might even have been friends,' said Hetty.

He'd not realised that she was still there. 'You didn't tell me she was going to leave.'

'She said nothing to me until this morning.'

'You told me Maggie wanted to go home to Ireland. Isn't that what you said?'

'That's exactly what she told me. And I'm sure she will one day, like all of us, one way or another,' said Hetty wistfully, before leaving.

'One way or another,' repeated Brandon. It was inexcusable to feel the way he did, and his moral failing now fixed itself like an axe in a tree, forever branding itself into his life. Yet, he couldn't help himself. He'd spent the entire night awake, wondering how he and Maggie could ever move past what had transpired yesterday afternoon. It never crossed his mind that she might leave and he'd never see her again. He stood on the flat outside his master's homestead and watched as all that mattered to him was driven away.

⫷ Chapter 51 ⫸

Late that evening, Brandon left the men's quarters and walked aimlessly across the paddock. He was in no mood for the lighthearted banter amongst the men, nor was he keen to have his life dissected by McCauley, who'd recently returned from the tallow works, his slaughtering duties at an end until the new year. McCauley had been observing him most of the evening and more than once had tried to draw him aside. Brandon supposed his sadness at Maggie's leaving was written across his face and so he'd escaped into the quiet of the night, unwilling for others to learn what he himself had taken so long to admit.

For a few brief seconds he had held Maggie in his arms and now she was gone. He was no longer whole. Maggie's absence haunted him, for with her leaving, all of his family were now gone. He dragged his axe across the ground, finding solace in the weight of the tool. Every now and then he would lift it and thrust the blade needlessly into the soil, chipping unrelentingly at the earth's crust until his shoulders pained from the effort. Eventually, habit led him to Hetty's cottage. He stared at the outline of the dwelling and then quietly made his way towards it, where he sat on the edge of the veranda, scraping the heel of his boot in the dirt and thinking of Ireland. The gentle mists and trickling streams appeared before him as if in a dream and he saw himself as a boy, racing across the fields with Sean, throwing rocks and laughing as Maggie chastised them for their childish ways.

'Brandon?' said Hetty. Stepping outside, she emptied a bucket of water over the edge of the veranda and then stood before him. 'What are you doing here?'

'I'm sorry. I needed somewhere quiet. I was thinking about home. About Ireland,' he said.

'Feeling sorry for yourself, are you? Some lose their families sooner than others, but just because we're alone at the beginning of our lives and at the end, it doesn't have to be that way in the middle.' Hetty knelt before him and placed her hands on his knees. 'I'd care for you if you'd let me.'

'Even with what you know?'

'That you were infatuated with your stepsister.' Hetty gave a huff. 'I blame your father for giving a boy a man's job. If all of us were perfect it would be a piddling world, and anyway, she's gone now. There's only the two of us left.'

'That's true enough,' said Brandon.

'Don't you care even a little?' asked Hetty, moving closer.

'I care that you think so kindly towards me when you know the type of man that I am and the things that I've done,' replied Brandon.

She reached for him, stroking his cheek. Brandon concentrated on the warmth of her skin. It was such a simple gesture, and yet it made his chest heavy with loneliness. He heard the catch of her skirt on twigs as she moved nearer, the warmth of her sweet and untainted. Hetty pressed against him, resting her cheek against his.

'Let me care for you, Brandon,' she whispered, close to his ear. 'Like only a woman can. Let me love you and feed you and support you. Let me have your children and work beside you. I promise you'll never be sorry having me for a wife.'

He listened to the gentle intake of air into Hetty's lungs. The pause in the rise of her chest as she waited for his response. He could give her no answer because he feared it might burden them both. He doubted he would ever accept what Hetty offered, but he knew what he wanted and, at that moment, feeding his desire was enough. He ran a finger around the plain round collar of her gown, felt the rough weave of material slip away as the butterfly shape of her shoulders was bared.

Hetty was quick to free him of his trousers and lift her skirts. It was not what Brandon expected. She wore nothing except God's grace beneath. The roundness of her breasts and the hardened nipples were his to explore, her hips anchoring him, though she swayed like a tree caught in the drift of a gathering storm. With each movement, the angle of her hips grew closer to his. He leant back to take her weight as each thrust grew more forceful, until he began to forget who he was and where he'd come from. The gasps that came from his mouth were like those of a stranger and he fell back onto the timber boards, unmade.

Brandon woke on the cramped cot, Hetty sprawled next to him. One of her arms pinned his chest, a leg rested on his thigh. He rather thought he was like a fish caught in a moon-spun net and he straightened his aching body, extricating himself from the woman who'd finally managed to bring him to bed. He ran fingers through sweaty hair. The fire burnt steadily. Directly in front of him, Tommy sat on the floor, awake and watchful. Though the boy was too young to fully understand the scene before him, Brandon felt a son's judgement. He stepped around the boy and moved to the pot kept warm by the fire and spooned mouthfuls of the meaty stew into his mouth, ensuring to leave a portion for Hetty. He was reckoning on her being starving as well, for one couldn't say that she lacked enthusiasm.

Hetty stirred herself with a gentle snore. She rolled on one side, her back towards him, her spine passive and knobbly. He observed the length of it, the way it snaked from her neck to dip at the indentation of her waist before drawing his gaze to her buttocks and the dimples that centred his thoughts. Her skin was the colour of clotted cream. The taste of her was still on his tongue. There was no love, but there was desire. Perhaps one could grow from the other. The idea that love could be tended from passion seemed an impossibility. He saw love as a commitment, but it was certain fact that not everyone married for love and many, his father included, fashioned a life from need. For the moment, it was enough that Hetty fancied him and, in return, he had found solace in what she offered.

The little boy startled and glanced about the room, suddenly anxious.

'What is it, Tommy?' whispered Brandon. Shrugging on his trousers and shirt, he turned the knob on the door, opening it to voices calling into the night. Flames were coming from the men's quarters, the oblong building a wall of sparks and licking fire.

Hetty joined him, a shawl concealing her nakedness, a knuckle rubbing at an eye.

'Stay inside,' said Brandon, as the baby began to cry. She nodded obediently and he heard the latch drop behind him.

Brandon pulled on his boots, worrying for the men inside the quarters and the smoke that might send a man to sleep unaware of the danger. He searched for his axe, reassured by the familiarity of its handle and then spun on his heel, noting the destruction. Great orange-red plumes traced the timber walls of the stable and the mill, sucking upwards into the sky. Horses were whinnying in fright. Brandon broke into a run, cold sweat seeping through his clothes. The homestead remained intact. The burning was reflected in the glass windows, flickering terror across the face of the great house. He reached the front door and knocked loudly.

'Who is it?' said Mr Truby, his voice uncertain with fear.

'It's me, Brandon.'

The Englishman was quick to draw him indoors. 'We're under attack.'

'There are fires everywhere,' replied Brandon, taking in the pistol his employer held.

'The men will have scattered,' Mr Truby said. 'McCauley can probably be relied on, and a couple of the others. As for the rest . . .' Mr Truby shrugged. 'Here take this.' He handed Brandon a pistol.

'No,' said Brandon warily, displaying the axe. 'This will be enough of a weapon for me. Let's hope we won't be needing it.'

'Amen to that. We're defending this property, so don't be afraid. No ill can come to those who believe in God's righteousness.'

They waited on either side of the front entrance, peering through the windows for a sign of the intruders.

'Maybe they won't come,' said Brandon as the minutes passed.

'It's possible,' said Mr Truby. 'Most likely they'll burn the rest of the outbuildings first.'

'Then I can't stay here.' There was Hetty to consider, left alone in the cottage with her children, and McCauley, who was bunked down in the quarters with the other workers.

Brandon ignored Mr Truby's warnings and, crouching low, ran to the cover of the paling fence that ringed the homestead. Hetty's cottage was still safe but the rest of the lit buildings were nearly collapsed, their fire-wasted frames jagged piles of burning, protruding beams. Men still called through the darkness but it was impossible to guess who was friend or foe. He tightened his grasp on the axe.

Flickers of light gathered in the distance. Like air-blown embers they drew apart and then came together again, forming a cluster of growing brightness that increased in shape and form. The group of men approached at a fast walk, their flares held high in proud determination, as if they were on some great mission. They set one of the outbuildings alight and then another, heading in the direction of Hetty's cottage.

'He could be in there!' yelled a man.

'Don't hurt my cousin Maggie or the servant girl.'

Brandon recognised the second voice as Sean's. He sat heavily in the dirt, unable to believe that his cousin was involved in the attack. But it was true. Sean was here and he was unaware of Maggie's leaving. Brandon should have known Hackett wouldn't take kindly to being bested by Mr Truby. They were here to send a strong message of what they thought of his illegal squatting on vast tracts of land. In that same instant, Brandon understood that it was him that they ultimately wanted. As far as Hackett was concerned, Brandon was to blame. He began to run the short distance towards Hetty's home but was not fast enough to avoid the gang of men, who caught sight of him and bore down with speed.

The men gathered in front of Brandon. There were eight of them; people he'd once felled timber with and others he recognised from the Brotherhood meeting, men involved in the attacks in the village. He saw their heaving chests, the delight at destruction that shone in their glassy eyes and the anger that could only come from a people stripped of dignity, partly through circumstance, but also through longstanding hate. In the centre of the group, Hackett's face was grimly firm, the firelight emphasising the weathered creases of his skin.

'I was right about you. From the very beginning I knew you weren't to be trusted.' Hackett spat on the ground, as if sealing his opinion. 'I gave you the benefit of the doubt because of your cousin, thinking that a little waywardness could be beaten out of you, but you've gone far beyond redemption, Brandon O'Riain. You've gone to the other side, converted and changed your name. There is no coming back from what you've done.'

'I'm just an excuse for you to get at Mr Truby. And what I may or may not have done is none of your damn business,' said Brandon.

'None of our business, eh?' Sean tossed a rock into the air and caught it.

Brandon stared at his cousin in the torchlight. At the rock he held. Thought of what the stone represented. Of Macklin dead on the ground. 'Sean,' he said in disbelief.

'We're Irishmen, born into poverty, forced to leave the old country and exist here in this land, though the English would squash us with their boots if they could,' Sean sneered. 'I thought you had the makings of an eagle that might soar high one day, but I was wrong. You're just a pigeon, one who shits on everyone below.'

'Take him,' Hackett said to the men at his side. 'A belting might make him see sense.'

Three men moved towards him. Brandon swung the axe in a half circle. They scattered and regrouped, more men attacking from all sides. A bloodcurdling scream shrank the air, and Brandon turned to see McCauley running into the group from the rear, swinging a lump of timber and clobbering the unsuspecting men on the head. One man fell immediately, then a second. A third. The mob grew wary. The men about Brandon broke free and ran, unwilling to risk their lives. Hackett lifted a cleaver and fronted McCauley, goading the slaughterer to fight, drawing McCauley's blood with a choppy strike to his body.

Brandon saw his friend under attack and drew his concentration back to the lone man who was still attacking him with a torch. He reversed the axe, swooping it low, and struck the man's thigh with the blunt end so that the assailant unbalanced and fell.

'Fight on, fight on for the cause!' yelled Sean, as he tried to stop his friends from retreating.

Brandon watched as Hackett sliced again at McCauley. The two men were sidestepping and lunging at each other. He dropped the blade over his head, feeling the balance of it anchored between his shoulders. The instrument hung patiently as he focused on Hackett, a bitter taste filling his mouth. The chance of a direct strike was low, for his target was moving, slashing the cleaver, intent on causing McCauley more harm. The calmness required for a steady hand was beyond Brandon at that point. He swiftly tested the wind, felt his arms tense, and then flung the axe forwards. Simultaneously, a warning shot echoed from the direction of the main house and the few men left scattered in all directions, running off into the scrub as first light turned the horizon grey.

Brandon's heart slowed with the abrupt end to the fight. He caught sight of Mr Truby approaching, a pistol in his grasp, and then he walked to where Hackett lay motionless on the ground. McCauley stood over the body, swinging a piece of wood, a foolish grin easing the harshness of his features. The axe was nowhere to be seen.

Brandon frowned. '*You* killed him?'

'All I need now is a vat,' replied McCauley. 'Your axe is over there.'

Brandon swung around, expecting to find his weapon embedded in the ground. Instead, he saw Sean lying collapsed in the dirt, close to the men felled by McCauley. Brandon ran forwards and then stopped sharply, not believing what he was seeing. The axe blade had struck his cousin on the knee. Blood poured from the wound.

'But how . . .' Brandon said, as McCauley came to his side. 'I was aiming for Hackett.'

'Lucky for me, then,' said McCauley, lifting a shaggy eyebrow. 'Light and shade. A chance wind. Men moving in different directions. The wrong direction.' He made a cutting motion across his throat.

Brandon kneeled at his cousin's side. Sean's face was grey. Dots of sweat covered his skin. Dreading what was coming next, he took hold of the axe's handle and pulled the blade free. Sean screamed.

'We can walk away and leave him to his maker. Give him time to join his friends,' said McCauley, obviously keen for this idea. 'The heart is a mighty pump when left unattended.'

Brandon thought of McCauley's life, one lived in partial shadows. His friend searched the fallen men's pockets, shaking his head at their emptiness.

'You tried to kill me,' said Sean, gasping.

'It was an accident, I swear,' said Brandon. 'I was aiming for Hackett.'

Mr Truby arrived, his progression slowing as he took in the sight of the battle.

Brandon spoke quietly to McCauley. 'He's my cousin. Let me explain things to Mr Truby.'

The slaughterer lifted his head to the sky and mumbled, 'God's drawers, if it ain't a curse to be an honourable man. All right then.'

'What happened?' asked Mr Truby, taking in the wrecked skulls of the four men.

'That's Hackett.' Brandon pointed to the man's body.

'And this one. He's your cousin,' said Mr Truby sharply. 'I told you he was a troublemaker.'

'He was only pretending to be one of Hackett's men. He turned on them when they attacked me and was wounded for his efforts,' Brandon said quickly.

'And did he also try to stop them from burning my property?' His employer waited, taking the opportunity to search Brandon and McCauley for traces of deceit. Brandon dropped his head. Mr Truby was within his rights to set the law on Sean. That was, if his cousin survived. Cutting timber in the Big Scrub had given Brandon plenty of opportunity to witness the ailments that came from open wounds.

'He needs tending, boss,' said McCauley. He gave Sean's injury a brief inspection, which involved prodding shattered flesh and bone. 'You'll lose it. There's no way I can save that leg and keep you alive,' he told Sean.

'Don't you take my leg. Don't let him take my leg, Brandon. Please God, don't let him!' yelled Sean. 'I'll never forgive you if you let him take it, Brandon.'

'Be a man – if there is such a thing within that fanatical body you inhabit,' Mr Truby replied to Sean's ravings. 'What about you, McCauley? I see you're not unscathed.' He gestured at the blood staining his shirt. 'I'd rather you tend to your own injury first before worrying about that criminal.'

'I've done worse to myself, Mr Truby.' McCauley lifted Sean and threw him over a bony shoulder. Sean moaned.

'I'll be needing your table, lass, and some boiling water,' said McCauley as he walked towards Hetty's cottage, where she waited at the door.

A white-faced Hetty stood back as he entered and lay a now-unconscious Sean on the table. Taking a gutting knife from a sheath at his waist McCauley cut the material of Sean's trousers, revealing the bloody mass. 'Best get him tied down while he's passed out. And this ain't no place for young'uns.'

Hetty took the children outside and then returned to stoke the fire.

McCauley turned to Brandon. 'He won't hate you any less for you lying to the squatter. In fact, after I've finished, he'll probably hate you more. And you understand that even if I take his leg, he might not survive.'

Brandon rubbed at his forehead. 'If we can't save him without taking his leg, then we have no choice.'

'There's always a choice, boy. It's making the right one that counts. And I'm afraid he'll cause you more trouble than your kindness is worth. If he survives.'

'Do it,' Brandon told him.

'Well then, you best hurry to the mill and see if you can salvage a saw,' said McCauley.

Brandon went outside. Everything around him seemed so large and he so small. Men were trawling through the smoking buildings and the bodies of the four men still lay on the ground. And there was his axe, his kin's blood on the blade. He vomited in the dirt. Then went in search of a saw.

343

⋘ Chapter 52 ⋙

Richmond Valley, 1949

Stella was tempted to dismiss the tale that Brandon told her of his early life. It was so dense with intrigue and uncertainty that to pick it apart would have taken a finer seamstress than she. Instead, she found herself wanting to retrace the journey of the two cousins from Ireland, to sift the falsehoods from fact and gather the remaining strands. But all she had were the utterances of a very old man.

She was exhausted by what had been described to her. The steely machinations for land. The conflicting values that had set two cousins against each other. The opposing faiths that destroyed love and, ultimately, friendship. And the grievous injury that Brandon had caused his cousin. She was certain it was this maiming that had torn the two families apart. Religion and name-changing were simply further proof of Brandon's unreliable character, as far as Sean's descendants were concerned.

It was late afternoon. Light struck the statue of the woman in the garden. Ants crawled over sandwich crumbs on the table between them. And still, Brandon was unrepentant. Not once had he said the word 'sorry' regarding his cousin's injury.

'You'll tell Harry some of this?' said Brandon.

'I imagine that the version of events that Sean told him are very different from your recollections.'

Brandon gave a weary nod of his head. 'That's the problem with stories. We bring our preconceived ideas and values to the heart of the issue, and within seconds we've altered the substance of a thing entirely. What is good becomes bad. What should be joyous becomes plagued with doubt and disbelief. We are an anxious people at times. And it seems that we're doomed to repeat our mistakes.'

'Sean was very bitter,' said Stella.

'My dear girl, after that day he was like a black snake for most of his life. It wasn't all my doing. I was caught up in circumstances I had no idea how to deal with.'

'And yet many people suffered because of you and Sean,' said Stella.

'Yes, they did,' Brandon agreed.

'Why didn't you apologise to Sean after the accident?'

'He wasn't my target. Hackett was,' Brandon protested. 'But the wind was changeable that morning. If there'd been more time, if Mr Truby had not been so quick to fire his pistol . . . The last of the men scattered when they heard that shot, including Sean. He ran into the path of the blade. And they were the ones who attacked me. It wasn't the other way around.'

'But you still threw an axe at another human being.'

'Was I supposed to let Hackett kill McCauley? That man was my friend.' His voice rose, his mouth twitching in agitation.

So that was how he'd managed to survive for all these years. He'd refused to acknowledge what he'd done by fashioning his guilt into excuses. Her own behaviour at Kirooma sprung to mind.

'You never said how you came to own this farm,' she said, quickly changing the topic.

'Mr Truby willed the house and contents and the eight thousand acres to me on his death in 1874. Miss Schaefer died of the sweating fever in Sydney a few years before her uncle so there was no one left to contest the will. He'd already lost most of his holding by then. The Lands Department caught up with him eventually.'

'And Sean?' asked Stella.

'It took a long time for him to get over the infections. By the time the gangrene had finished with him, McCauley had cut off another three inches.' Brandon blanched at the memory. 'He lived at the men's quarters while he recovered. I rarely saw him during that time and when I tried to, he refused to speak to me. Hetty cared for him until he was capable of hobbling about on a stick and he left soon after. Mr Truby refused to have him on the property any longer and Sean was desperate to leave. He ended up being employed as a sailmaker in Wirra and eventually took over the business. I heard he kept to himself for many years until he eventually married a much younger girl. He made a good living in those early days. I used to ride by his house when I was in the village, hoping I'd catch a glimpse of him, find a reason to say hello, but the few times I chanced on him, he ignored me,' he said sadly.

'Their first four children never made it past childhood. Then I learnt that Sean and his wife had been forced to sell their home to pay their debts and were living in a hovel on the edge of town. It was the same year Harry was born, 1891. I never really knew what happened. Perhaps the paddle-steamers lessened the need for sailmakers on the river, but there was also a whisper that Sean overspent, pandering to a young wife. I couldn't blame him for wanting to see Edwina happy.'

'You met her?' asked Stella.

'Eventually, yes. I wrote to Sean, offering him a place here. I figured that enough time had passed. Nearly twenty-four years to be exact. I reminded him that it would be selfish to deprive his baby boy of a decent home and, more importantly, land, for I promised to gift acreage to Harry. It was a good couple of months before I received a response. However eventually Sean replied, agreeing to my offer for his family's sake.'

'And that's when they moved here? To the same spot where Ann and Harry live now?' said Stella.

'The very same.' He rose stiffly, using the arm of the chair for support. When he walked to the timber pillar on the veranda it was with a slight shuffle, as if he couldn't quite trust his feet to move on command. He steadied his body against the pole. 'When Sean died, Harry blamed me. He stood at the boundary fence and cursed me for an hour. Yelling at the top of his lungs. Sean had been burning one of the cane fields. It was a damn fool thing to put a crippled man in a fired field. But you never could tell Sean anything – his son either, it seems.' He turned to her. '*That* wasn't my fault.'

'No. It wasn't,' she agreed. Brandon wasn't responsible for Sean's disposition.

Brandon appeared satisfied by her answer and he returned to the chair, extending his legs and flexing his feet. The bones cracked.

'And you married Hetty,' said Stella.

The mention of her name made him smile fondly. 'No. We never married. Never had children. Though we lived together for a long time. We moved into this house when Mr Truby died. Tommy grew up here. It was his motorbike that Joe used to ride.'

'Tommy, Hetty's little boy?' queried Stella.

'Yes,' said Brandon. 'And Geoffrey, Clinton's father. Geoff was Hetty's baby too.'

'Can I ask why you and Hetty never married?' Stella knew she was prying but having discovered so much else it seemed that the story of Brandon and Hetty offered an element of optimism. Not so much for the man who'd shared his life story, but for her own understanding of relationships and the difficult place her marriage had inhabited.

'Hetty understood that although I cared, I wasn't capable of devoting myself to her. It was an unusual arrangement, however the two of us had come from poor beginnings, and in the end, companionship was more valuable to us than anything else. She died not long before Sean and Edwina moved here. I still miss her. There's an album under the table. Can you pass it to me?'

Reaching for a rattan stool, Brandon positioned it under the backs of his knees. He sat the book on his lap and ran his fingers around the edge of it. It was stuffed full of photographs and clippings.

'I rarely need this now. My head is full of pictures. I can still see Mr Truby the very first day we met. The man's amiable face. The trust in his eyes. Trust for a stranger. I was so very young. Overeager. Willing to please. Gullible, that's the word. I thought he considered me better than others, and that I was deserving. Still, he left me all this. The land. This house. My albatross. A millstone to keep me shackled to Sean and his family.'

'You could have sold and left the district,' said Stella.

'So could he,' replied Brandon. 'Here.'

Stella accepted the grainy black-and-white photograph. It was a picture of a young woman. 'Is this Hetty?'

'No. That's my stepsister, Maggie. She wrote to me from Sydney to tell me that it was her time. A time of wine and roses. We'd talked about it once, how our lives would improve. What we'd do in the future. Oh, you should have seen that letter, it was written in the finest copperplate. I scarcely believed it was from her. I read the damn thing so much that eventually it fell apart. I would sit at a table and fit the four pieces together along the original fold lines and wonder at her life.' He ran a bony finger across the surface of the photo. 'That dress was brown. With blue ribboned edging. She told me of it. The plainness of it would have made her eyes sparkle. The colour. It had a particular name. The Sargasso Sea. That's what she'd called it. We were blown off course and ended up there on our way south to Australia. A sea with no land borders. Not a trace of country anywhere and certainly no glimpse of the old one we'd left. We were stranded for a week. Becalmed. Circled by stories of ships forever mired in the brown seaweed that threaded the ocean's surface. The younger passengers grew fearsome. Not Maggie. She was spellbound by the blueness of the water and she'd stare into its depths, her arms dangling over the railing. Lost in her Sargasso Sea. She pined for it once the winds finally came, and the sails billowed, and a new ocean was reached.'

An insect had long ago decided to end its life on the photograph so that a dark blotch marked the image. Stella returned the picture to Brandon and he tucked it back inside the scrapbook.

'You would think that age would have blunted an old man like me, but I can still recall those brown eyes. Sweet and fierce. If I could wish for anything, it would be to stand on the land that I'd travelled from all those years earlier. Her hand in mine. That last day was so crisp and clear. The land steaming with the heating of the sun. Blue-tinged mountains and the curls of smoke streaming from the farmhouses that stretched across the valley. It wasn't to be. Maggie eventually left Kirooma and returned to Ireland and I never saw or heard from her again.'

'It was your stepsister you wrote to at Kirooma,' said Stella, recalling the contents of the letter in the Bible. 'You were in love with your stepsister?'

'Judge me if you choose to, girl, but I have loved her all my life. I can't tell you why or how, only that from the age of ten or eleven I began to feel a special tenderness towards her. My stepmother was harsh and in those early years her expectations of Maggie as child-rearer and cook were high. There were lashings with a corded rope.' He broke off at this memory, clearly finding it difficult to continue. 'Her leaving for Kirooma fairly winded me, but what a thing to do, eh? Travel out through the wilderness with strangers to strangers. Ten years she stayed there. Ten whole years. She started a fine orchard. Helped birth children. Became a dressmaker to the lady of the house. I heard later from Mr Truby that the Handalays took Maggie under their wing, schooling her properly, so that by the time of her leaving the contents of the library at Kirooma was embedded in her brain. My Maggie, an educated woman.'

Stella thought of those books that she too had read. 'And you never visited her.'

'I considered it. Every day. But the thought of seeing Maggie, knowing that her feelings would be unchanged, stopped me.'

Brandon had reached an age where every emotion showed itself in the smallest of ways. He rubbed at a knuckle, slowly, pensively. 'I was shocked she returned to the old country, but that was her place, that's what called to her. So, she answered, and went home. Maggie was stronger than me. Stronger than the lot of us. And I have no doubt she lived well and fully. Believing that has given me some satisfaction. We lost so much saving her, my dear Stella. None of it would have been worth it if she'd stayed here with me under sufferance.'

'So, Sean moved here with his family, accepted your generosity but you and he never reconciled?'

Brandon's attention diverted to the garden. 'We might have, except for that one afternoon beneath the cedar tree.'

'Are you telling me that something *else* happened?' asked Stella.

From the rear of the scrapbook Brandon pulled out a folded paper, which he handed to her. Stella took it, their eyes meeting briefly and then she opened the parchment. It was cracked and weathered, however the diagram of the house was quite clear. It was a roomy home with wide windows and high ceilings. The construction measurements were intricately noted and even the materials were listed: pine timber, kiln-fired bricks for the fireplaces, and pressed-metal ceilings.

'Whose house is this?' she asked.

'I designed it for Sean.' Brandon lowered his chin and closed his eyes.

⋙ Chapter 53 ⋙

Richmond Valley, 1891

Sean hobbled down the hill early one morning, knocked on the door and then moved to stand in the middle of the garden. Brandon wasn't surprised by his cousin's aloof manner. It remained unaltered from the day of his arrival on the property a week earlier when they'd said each other's name in greeting, and then acknowledged over two decades of estrangement with a brief handshake. Harry, the heir apparent of the land, had been duly presented: a swaddled, chubby-faced baby cradled in the arms of his careworn mother, Edwina, a woman of few words but whose grateful smile more than compensated for Sean's unreadable expression. At the sound of Sean calling him, Brandon walked out onto the veranda, slipping his arms into his coat.

'I've come about the house,' said Sean.

'Morning,' Brandon replied cheerfully. 'It won't take Tommy and Geoff long to complete the frame.'

Sean had initially complained that the location of his home was too close to Brandon's. He didn't want to be living on the ridge overlooking the main homestead, however Brandon stuck fast to this single condition that came with the gifting of the land.

He hoped for a reconciliation and having Sean close by was the one way he could ensure that they saw each other regularly.

'Hetty's old cottage is probably a bit cramped. You could move in with us while the house is being built,' Brandon offered, not for the first time. 'It's up to you. The cottage is yours now. I have no use for it.'

Sean ignored him and, turning awkwardly, commenced walking back up the rise. For a cripple he moved efficiently, making the best of a leather-and-wood leg, which, combined with a walking stick, propelled him across the sloping ground. 'Come with me.'

'Should I bring the building plans?'

'No need for that,' called Sean.

Brandon followed, wondering what problem Sean had discovered with his new home. Maybe the rooms were too small, or another fireplace was needed, although he'd done his best to consider his cousin's needs, even ensuring that the veranda was built flat on the ground so that Sean wouldn't be troubled by steps. They made their way to where the lone cedar tree marked the boundary between their two properties, and it was here that Sean stopped.

'I noticed that there's a stack of unused cedar planks stored in the shed next to the steam engine,' said Sean, slightly breathless.

'There is,' said Brandon, trying not to be offended by his cousin's brisk tone. 'They're left over from Mr Truby's time.' He didn't mention that the best ones had been burnt during Hackett's attack, twenty-four years earlier.

'I want to use that wood for my home,' stated Sean.

Brandon thought of the labour involved in felling the pine and then carting it back by dray to the site. 'But the pine is already cut,' he reminded his cousin.

'Yes. *Pine*. I can't see why my boy has to have a second-rate house.' Sean's attention was centred on Brandon's two-storey cedar homestead below. 'Especially when there's spare cedar lying about.'

'Firstly, there's not enough of it for the job and secondly, don't you think it's a waste, using it for another house? Why don't *we* sell it and split the proceeds? There's still excellent money about for decent timber.' Brandon emphasised the joint aspect of the venture, hopeful of easing his cousin's agitation with the offer.

'I'm amazed you haven't done that already, but then I suppose you've never had to worry about a lack of coin,' challenged Sean.

Brandon chose to ignore his cousin's attempt to rile him. 'The boards aren't in very good condition. Quite a few of them are cracked. Mr Truby was very particular about the quality of the timber that was used in the renovations.'

'That man had such a high opinion of himself that I wonder he even deigned to use wood that us Irish cut.' Sean leant on his stick, his eyes blazing as they had when they'd both been younger men.

To see Sean that way, still ready for a fight, unchanged in disposition, came as a deep disappointment to Brandon. 'Mr Truby's dead now,' he replied. His deferential air provoked a grunt from his cousin.

'I've checked those boards myself. There would be enough to build the house, if we cut down this tree.' Sean lifted his walking stick and tapped one of the roots that twisted out across the ground like a massive tentacle. 'This would finish the place off nicely. And once it's gone we can erect a boundary fence.'

Brandon rested his palm reverently on the trunk 'You want to cut this tree down?'

'Yes,' confirmed Sean. 'I can't understand why you didn't get rid of it with the rest of the timber years ago. I don't see the point of keeping a lone tree.'

They stood there for the slightest of moments, gazing up into the branches.

'When Mr Truby eventually had the rest of the cedars felled, I literally went cap in hand to him and asked him to keep this one. It's a fine specimen,' said Brandon.

'It's had its time. Lasted longer than most in these parts,' replied Sean dismissively.

Brandon couldn't believe what Sean was suggesting. The tree had stood for well over a century, witnessing the settlement of

353

Truby's property, surviving droughts and fires and the coming and going of those people who were dear to him. He'd sat beneath it after Maggie headed west and following Sean's amputation and his eventual leaving. At Mr Truby's death and the reading of the will, which left him a wealthy man, he'd spent many hours simply gazing up into the crown of the tree, contemplating his changed life. And finally, the day Hetty was buried, the tree stood guard at her wake. He knew the shade it provided, the birds that sheltered in its branches. More than that, the tree had watched him grow into a man of means, entrusted with acres, livestock, crops and labourers. If there was a shred of faith left within him, it was centred in the cedar tree. For it still stood. A silent observer to the folly of man.

'It's just a tree,' said Sean tightly.

'Maybe to you.' Brandon placed his palms on the trunk. 'We spent nearly three years of our lives destroying the timber in the Big Scrub. We're finished cutting down trees. This one stays.'

They regarded each other with unflinching stares.

It was Sean who broke away first. He coughed and repositioned the walking stick in the grass. 'I engraved my initials into it,' he said. 'Branded it. The day we moved into the house. So by law it's mine.'

They walked around the base of the tree and Brandon followed his cousin's gaze. A little above head height, in clear deep cuts, were Sean's initials.

'I can't let you have it. I'm sorry. If you want to use the leftover cedar, you can, but this tree stays,' said Brandon adamantly.

'Oh, I see. We can't have the poor cousin building anything that even remotely resembles your mansion.' Sean's face grew hard. A fan of wrinkles spread out from the corners of his eyes. 'And here I was, thinking that you'd changed. That you were prepared to make amends for everything you'd done in the past. I should have known better.'

'Sean, please. If you're so desperate to build your house with cedar, we'll go out and find another. There are still a few stands left on the property.'

'No. I'm claiming a cedar-feller's rights. It's branded and I'll be cutting it tomorrow. It's the least you can do, considering everything that's happened,' said Sean more loudly.

Brandon was stunned. 'You'd still be destitute if it wasn't for me, Sean, so don't stand there talking about what you intend to claim. I branded this tree the first year we came here. 1867.' He stalked to the opposite side of the trunk and pointed to his own initials. They were large and clear. 'If it's the law of the axeman you're keen to abide by then I'll tell you straight. The tree is mine and it stands in the middle of the boundary between our two properties, so you best keep your axe away from it. I can kick you off this land just as easily as I've allowed you onto it. Don't forget that.'

'You bastard.' Sean smacked his stick forcefully across Brandon's shoulders and then drove hard and fast into his body so that Brandon unbalanced and rolled down the hill.

He sat up as the dizziness cleared from his head. On the rise above, Sean was waving his stick. 'Don't you dare cross this boundary ever again. Do you hear me, Brandon Ryan? You can keep your blasted tree, but I'll be keeping Harry's land. Maybe you've forgotten but possession is nine-tenths of the law.'

❦ Chapter 54 ❧

Richmond Valley, 1949

They were in the kitchen waiting for her; Harry and Ann sitting at the table, and John and Bill leaning on the bench together. Stella noticed the way the twins fidgeted, and their proximity to the door, as if they were hoping for the possibility of a quick escape. She lingered in the doorway, the diagram in her hand. Being stared at was far from pleasant, but then silence was a state that she'd grown used to. She thought of Kirooma and the still air of the homestead. The surrounding, ceaseless dunes. If the O'Riain family hoped to intimidate, there would be disappointment. They were yet to realise that she could summon the hardness that came with desertion.

Dirty plates were stacked on the sink. The rings from the tea and coffee mugs stained the surface of a table that usually shone from the daily rubbing she gave it. They were an untidy lot. Used to being cared for. It was the first time she'd seen these four members of the family together and the differences were plain. Bill, stout and broad-faced like Harry, had stayed clear of the house since her arrival. His brother John favoured his mother, but while Ann was pleasant but prone to argument, he'd proved to be open and interested. She hoped John might offer reassurance. A nod, perhaps. Some gesture of solidarity, for he had been aware of her visits beyond the fence before she'd told Ann about them. Across the room, John rubbed a socked foot on the rear of his calf. Like Bill, he was concentrating on his father's profile. Waiting.

Ann noticed Stella's arrival and reached for her husband, lightly touching the back of his hand. Harry barely registered her gesture, concentrating instead on ignoring Stella completely. It was a wasted exercise, for the family had obviously gathered for her benefit. It was late afternoon. A whole day had passed since Stella had told Ann that she'd been visiting Brandon and that she was partially packed and ready to leave.

'It's difficult to understand why you've purposely gone against my wishes,' said Harry finally, folding his large hands and resting them on the tabletop.

Stella had to stifle a laugh. It was not what he said, but the condescension that laced his speech that made the situation so absurd.

'You think it's funny,' said Harry. 'We invite you into this house and the one thing I ask you not to do . . .'

Stella leant against the cupboards, closing her mind to the words tumbling out of her brother-in-law's mouth. She was so weary of this family, with their resentments and cloistered existence. Even the Valley with its sweet greenery and chain of hills had lost its allure. It was no longer a safe haven. It had become like Kirooma – small and stifling.

At some stage, Harry noticed that she wasn't listening, and he stood rather abruptly. Stella imagined the fury Harry yearned to wield. He was Joe's brother, after all. There was only so much backing away he could withstand before his need to assert superiority would present.

'You think you know a story, but you have to go back to the beginning to truly understand it. Now I do, and you should make the effort to as well,' said Stella.

Harry gave her a withering gaze. He'd obviously not expected her to speak so plainly. Not when she was a guest in his home.

Ann and the boys were like circus clowns, mouths open, swivelling from left to right.

'I'm sure there are differences between Brandon's version of events and that of your father's, however regardless of Sean's Fenian leanings or Brandon's involvement with Mr Truby, the fact remains that the loss of your father's leg was an accident.'

'Grandfather was a Fenian?' said Bill.

'Shh.' Ann glared at her son.

Harry's eyes grew as small as currants.

Stella knew it was a mistake to show contempt, although perhaps it wasn't contempt, more disappointment at Harry's steadfast refusal to budge from the past. 'It was Ann who made me curious about your neighbour. She was the one who told me that Joe had visited his house. And, as none of you wanted to talk about Joe, I needed to speak to someone who'd known him. Someone who might have been able to explain his personality. You can't blame me for that.'

'I knew it would upset you.' Ann's attention was directed at her husband, who refused to meet her gaze.

'Well, that's the reason I visited him. Anyway, as far as the disagreement between the two families, it was between Brandon and Sean. One that was based on a stupid argument. Surely after all these years it's time to let go and move on,' argued Stella.

'You're talking about things that are none of your business,' said Harry.

'They became my business when I married into this family.' Stella realised her voice had grown loud and waspish.

In one fluid movement, Harry's expression altered. 'Brandon Ryan went against everything my father believed in and then ended up maiming him and ruining his livelihood. A man can live with that, I suppose. Come to terms with it even. But denying my father his pride, that's something else entirely. Brandon invited my father here. Offered him land. Then he ensured he could keep an eye on him by erecting a house in direct view of his own. There was stockpiled cedar in one of the sheds, but no, Brandon wanted to make sure our family always played the part of the poor relations. It was a small house of shoddy pine for us.'

'Your father could have had his grand cedar home, Harry. Brandon said he offered to fell more timber for that very purpose, to supplement the timber in the shed, however Sean demanded one tree be cut down. And one tree only. He wanted no other. The lone cedar on your boundary fence. Brandon said no. Your father was trying to make a point, I suppose. Maybe he knew how much Brandon liked that tree. Perhaps he simply wanted to assert what little authority he had left. I don't know. They were both determined men. What I do have is this.' She handed Harry the rolled parchment she'd been clutching since entering the kitchen. 'That's the original plan for Sean's house, designed and drawn by Brandon. After their argument over the tree, your father decided against using this blueprint or any cedar in its construction. He built this house instead.'

Harry unrolled the paper and studied the diagram. Stella watched as Harry's face lost all colour. His Adam's apple bobbed as he swallowed, then he passed the document to John. Ann watched her husband intently, her rounded shoulders straightening in attention.

When Harry finally spoke it was to no one. He may well have been standing out in one of the cane fields, speaking to the plants he'd dedicated his life to. 'It was all over that bloody tree?'

'In the end, yes,' said Stella.

Harry rubbed at the bristles on his chin. 'A damn tree. I can't believe it.'

John passed the map to his brother. 'It would have been a good house by the looks of it.'

'It's twice the size of this one,' said Bill.

'The past seems to have affected everyone in this family. Including Joe,' said Stella.

'Do we have to keep harping on about Joe?' said Ann. She rearranged the cushion on the chair.

'I liked Uncle Joe,' said John. Bill nudged him in the ribs.

Stella threw her nephew a grateful smile.

'Anything else?' asked Harry. He positioned himself midway between the table and the stove, placing distance between his errant wife and his sons, whose expressions alternated between concern and fascination.

Stella was aware that the O'Riains were not the type of people who would suffer her interference for long. There was an apartness about them, as if they were imprisoned by the very history that they were so intent on holding tight to. And yet, if there were a time to say exactly how she felt, this was it.

'Joe was a young boy and you expected too much of him, Harry. You were happy for him to sleep in that run-down cottage and then complained when he decided to better his life. You were the one who sent Joe away and made him a loner. Maybe not intentionally, but you refused to consider his ideas for this farm and in the end you succeeded in cutting him off from his family. No wonder he was impossible to live with. It was his upbringing that made a normal life for him so difficult.'

'And, in turn, your life was ruined. That is what you're trying to say, isn't it?' said Harry.

Her brother-in-law's statement made Stella crumble inside. He made her sound ridiculous, immature, and she realised with a start that she was both those things and more. In the month spent on the farm she'd come to blame Harry for Joe's peculiarities while she searched for excuses about how their life at Kirooma had unravelled. That's why she'd agreed to come to the Valley. To uncover a little of the workings of Joe's family in the hope it might make her own situation clearer and somehow atone for what she'd done. It was a much easier path to take, making others accountable for her disastrous marriage rather than to take responsibility herself. But it was also wrong.

'Harry, Joe told me once that he wanted to do something important with his life as you had during the war. He admired you. He wanted to be like you. He loved you.'

Harry met her gaze. 'Joe liked taking things apart and putting them back together. I was never good at stuff like that. I never had the knack for it,' he said quietly.

He left the kitchen and walked outside, the door slamming behind him. The twins watched through the window as he began to stride towards the ramp, his pace gathering with every step. Stella observed him through the screen door.

'What's he doing?' asked Ann.

'Walking,' said Bill. He glanced briefly at Stella.

The shoulder that was slightly lower than the other grew more pronounced. Harry was two-thirds of the way from the house to the grid when he slowed and turned around. He might have been a new settler to the area, the way he studied the length and breadth of his home. Stella imagined what it was that Harry saw. The long, low structure. The neat, nondescript garden. The trees that ringed the perimeter. The electricity line that led from the house to a pole near the tilting clothesline and on through the trees to the derelict cottage, which she now realised once belonged to Hetty.

When Harry moved again, it was with obvious effort. He made his way home slowly and stopped just shy of the veranda. He kicked at the dirt, making piles of soil and flattening out the mounds. Then he nodded his head as if finishing a long conversation. He returned to the kitchen and stamped on the mat at the door to clean his boots and then drew the door closed. It clicked softly.

'Thank you for telling me that,' he said to Stella. 'All of it.'

'I should have told you how Joe felt before,' she replied.

He took an envelope from a shirt pocket and set it on the kitchen table, sliding it towards Stella. 'That's a cheque for two thousand pounds.'

'I don't expect anything. I told Ann that,' said Stella.

'Maybe not, but legally you're entitled to it.' Harry went to his wife's side and, taking her by the elbow, helped her from the chair. 'Bill, take your mother to her bedroom so she can lie down, she's been sitting far too long.'

'Righto.' Bill moved quickly, assisting his mother.

Ann straightened slowly. Unexpectedly she took Stella's hand and squeezed it and, in the gesture, Stella felt their shared bond. Her sister-in-law's world appeared perfect but she too had her burdens. Ann was married to Joe's brother, after all.

'Come on, Mum. Let's get you into bed,' said Bill, leading her away.

Harry waited until Ann left. 'We've already loaded your furniture into the station wagon and trailer,' he explained apologetically. 'Bit of a rush of blood to the head, I suppose. I don't expect you to leave immediately. In fact, you could stay until the end of the month.'

'Ann's better. There's not much point staying on.'

'But where will you go?' asked John.

'Sydney. I *do* have my own family,' Stella replied.

'You'll stay for dinner at least, Aunty Stella?' said John.

'No, I don't think so,' she replied.

'But it will be dark soon.'

'Yes, it will be.'

The three of them stared at each other.

'Well, once you're settled, write me your address and I'll start sending you monthly amounts to pay out Joe's share of the farm.' Harry took the cheque from the table, holding it mid-air until she accepted it.

'Thank you,' she said.

≪ Chapter 55 ≫

Stella opened the driver's-side door of the idling car as John slid Watson's travelling cage onto the back seat. The cockatoo ruffled his feathers as her nephew wound down the rear window, the bird quickly scuttling along the perch to poke his beak through the wire bars.

'You don't have to leave straight away, Aunty Stella. At least wait until the morning,' said John as he walked around the vehicle to join her.

'It's best I go now,' said Stella. Harry's silhouette was visible through the kitchen window. 'Your family has a lot to talk about.'

'Do you really believe the story about the cedar tree?' asked John.

'Well, those house plans are proof that Brandon was trying to do something nice for your grandfather.'

'He doesn't have a reputation for being trustworthy. I mean, he did convert and change his name and he stole Mr Truby's land.'

'That land was willed to him, John. If it wasn't, don't you think the authorities would have caught up with him by now? I very much doubt Brandon ever stole anything,' Stella told him.

'He doesn't seem like the type to me.' She studied her nephew's features. The boy could only be accused of behaving like a dutiful son, mindful of his father's opinion. 'You should speak to Brandon. He was friends with your grandfather and once he's gone, a whole chunk of your family history will be lost.'

'Maybe.' John appeared unconvinced.

'You only have to visit him once, and if after that you're not comfortable returning, you don't have to,' said Stella.

'I'll think about it.'

It might have been the sugarcane caramel of the twilight air but for the briefest of moments, it was as if Joe were before her – young, hopeful, confident, caring. Stella grew wistful. 'Take care, John.'

He hugged her briefly but tightly. 'Don't be a stranger, Aunty Stella.'

The screen door creaked. Harry waited on the top step. Her nephew returned to stand by his father's side.

Watson jumped up and down in the cage as Stella sat behind the steering wheel.

'*Pretty boy, pretty boy,*' screeched Watson out the car window.

'Bloody bird,' replied Harry, walking back inside the house with his son.

At the crossroad, Stella slowed and turned down the road that led to the Ryan house. She parked out the front and pulled the terrestrial globe from the back of the car. It was heavy and her arms strained as she walked up the path to the stairs and onto the homestead's veranda. It was the first time she'd seen the front of the building. It was a pretty structure and well kept, with curling fretwork and freshly painted timber. A pair of fine windows complemented the narrow entrance to the house, which featured a tarnished doorknob. Stella thought of Brandon's arrival on the property. He may have waited at this very spot as a young man, filled with expectation, unaware that his coming to this place would alter his life in ways he could never have imagined. She shifted the globe from a hip, wedging the ornament on the bone of the other and then walked to the rear of the house.

The side veranda was bare and leaf-littered. Peeling lattice had been wired to the garden fence and a vine clung to sections of it. It formed a screen that ran perpendicular to the corner of the homestead. Ahead was the statue of the woman. It was strange to see the figure in the failing light. Up close, the sculpture was streaked with bird droppings. The corners of the pedestal chipped. The stone woman looked as Stella felt, eroded by events.

'You came back,' said Brandon. 'I thought I must have waffled on far too long. Young people don't take to waffling. What have you got there?'

He was still sitting in the rattan chair on the veranda.

'Your globe.' Stella placed it on the timber boards at his feet and then took up the vacant seat.

Brandon leant forwards, spinning it softly. 'It's been a long time since I last saw this.' He stroked the earth as if it were the contours of a loved one's face.

'The heat out west has melted the glue. It needs some repairing,' said Stella.

'Don't we all.' Brandon patted the orb affectionately and then lit the kerosene lamp on the table between them. The yellowish light fluctuated and then steadied.

'Have you eaten? Can I make you something?' offered Stella.

'Clinton dropped in. He brought a casserole. In the old days we called it stew. Usually we had it straight out of the cooking pot with a lump of bread on the side. Back then, anything we ate was delicious, however I have to admit this one was pretty good.'

Across from them the dog rolled on the lawn, twisting one way and then another before lying on his back, his four legs bent and floppy.

'I came to say goodbye,' said Stella, not wanting to draw out their parting.

'I figured as much. That car of yours sounds like it needs a service. They throw you out?' Brandon moved stiffly until his hand rested on the globe once more.

'Not exactly, it was my decision. My nephew John knew I'd visited you and it seemed ridiculous keeping it a secret, so I told Ann,' admitted Stella. 'Word travelled quickly.'

Brandon stopped trailing the mountain ranges of America. 'You just came out and said it, eh? Well, good for you. Who would have thought it? Joe's widow stepping where others fear to tread.'

'No promises, however you might find that you have at least one visitor from across the fence in the weeks to come. They had no idea about the argument over the cedar tree.' The possibility of some form of reconciliation, however slight, occurring between the Ryans and the O'Riains stirred hope within her. It was an unfamiliar sensation.

'After all these years,' mulled Brandon, staring into the twilight.

'Well, you know what they say about things being better late,' replied Stella.

Brandon coughed and then reached into his pocket for a handkerchief and blew his nose. She'd not given much thought to how this news might affect the old man but as he wiped his eyes Stella began to realise that the years of festering animosity were beginning to break down. It was a small but significant beginning.

'You can stay here tonight, if you want. There's no shortage of beds although I can't speak for the state of the rooms. I live downstairs mostly and sleep on the sleigh bed. I'm like one of those medieval people. I have to sleep partially sitting up.'

Stella hesitated. 'I don't want to impose.'

'You won't be. But there's something I need to tell you first. I wasn't going to but you've given an old man more than you can imagine and it's only fair that I return the sentiment.'

She'd grown fond of Brandon, so the implication that he'd not been totally honest with her during their discussions brought the pleasantness of this, their last meeting, to a halt.

'I thought that Joe might have explained the arrangement,' Brandon began hesitantly. 'Actually, it's one of the reasons I thought you came to the Valley. To see if there was a chance of any money.'

It was Stella's turn to fumble in answering. 'Money? You mean from Joe's share of the farm?' She hated discussing finance. It made her uncomfortable, particularly as it was not the reason for her visit. However here she was, close to leaving the Valley, her every possession heaped in a station wagon and rickety trailer. There was little point letting pride overrule honesty.

'Money was the very last thing on my mind when I came here, but yes, Harry has offered to pay me out Joe's share and I accepted.'

'A young woman like you, recently widowed, it won't take long for you to get tangled up with another fellow. Still, you were right to take the money if only because every time Harry checks his bank statement it will remind him of his brother. He was hard on Joe. Too hard. But that's not what I was referring to. I'm talking about Kirooma.'

'What about Kirooma?'

The old man made no attempt to explain himself immediately, choosing instead to let the seconds spread out until more than a minute had passed. Stella sensed that Brandon had not quite the resolve to finish the sentence he'd begun. Part of her was pleased. Through careful persistence, she'd relegated the property to a fringe world, a place located on the very edges of her mind, although at times the land trailed her like a homeless dog. Yet she sat patiently waiting for Brandon to speak, a morbid curiosity swelling within her.

'The arrangement wasn't a secret, however Joe told me in one of his letters that he thought it was better to keep the past separate from his new life. That wasn't the real reason, of course, but I knew Joe well enough not to query his decision. I've never seen someone receive so much personal satisfaction as Joe did with the purchase of Kirooma Station. It was the fulfillment of a dream and his pride simply wouldn't allow anything to tarnish the achievement.'

'I'm really not following you,' replied Stella.

'Joe was adamant that no one be told that he'd received assistance to buy the property. It was important to him that people believed he'd done it all on his own merit,' explained Brandon.

'Assistance? From whom?'

'Mr Truby owned half of Kirooma Station in partnership with the Handalay family. The original owners. When he died, he left his share to me.'

It was as if some greater force were controlling her, pushing her one way and the other, as she came to realise that all the parts she'd played – an unwanted relation, an errant daughter, a deserted wife, the woman who'd watched her husband ride away on a motorbike never to set eyes on him again – were all distinct personalities pushed upon her by the attitudes and manipulations of other people.

'You own half of Kirooma Station?'

'I used to, yes.'

Bewildered, Stella sat in the rattan chair, the kerosene lantern flickering like a lighthouse.

'The Handalays were big pastoralists and canny managers. It was a good business partnership for many years. However, when the grandsons of the original owners decided to sell, I agreed with their decision. I had no interest in buying them out, and we were starting to lose money. Unfortunately, the property stayed on the market for years, firstly due to the Depression and then, of course, war broke out. That's when I thought of Joe, and the promise that I'd made to him when he was young. We talked about Kirooma. The possibilities. The money to be made from sheep. He was older by then. A man. I said he'd need a wife if he was going out to the far west. The deal hinged on that. I wasn't sending him out there alone. A few months later he rang to tell me that he'd found one.'

Stella remained quite still, feeling the truth of her marriage begin to emerge.

'We sat on this very veranda and he told me that he believed that you were the one,' said Brandon.

Believed. It was not an absolute. There was no certainty in it. If anything, the word invoked fairytales, conveniently ignoring the messy reality of what might transpire after the prince had captured his bride. Stella hadn't realised that her fingers were digging into

368

the cane of the chair until a splinter lodged itself in a nail bed and she jerked her hand free, blaming the hurt for the gathering tears.

'Don't be angry with him. It's difficult for a man to quantify love. We can't add up columns where it's concerned and always come to a satisfying conclusion. And I wasn't so insensitive as to not consider his intended bride, so I asked him a simple question,' said Brandon.

'Which was?' Stella tried to stifle her sniffing.

'Could he imagine himself with any other woman.'

'And could he?' she asked.

'He said no, and I had to be satisfied with that.'

'But you weren't,' said Stella.

The dog walked towards Brandon, resting his muzzle on his master's knee. 'Can a person ever be sure of another's motives? Joe had a mighty desire to better himself and prove his capability and he needed a wife to achieve his dream of becoming a landholder. Of course, I'm just an old man with too much time on my hands so I may well be wrong, but I think his priorities were a little skewed.'

'You weren't wrong,' said Stella.

'I'm sorry,' said Brandon.

'So am I.'

There it was. An answer to what she'd long been searching to understand. It was not her fault that their relationship had deteriorated. More than a partner, a lover, a helper, or even a woman to ward off the nothingness he'd brought them to, he'd needed a wife because it was the only way he'd get the property.

'I gifted Joe my half share of Kirooma and then paid the deposit on the Handalays' portion, ensuring the banks would lend him the money to buy them out. It's because of me that you went to live on the fringes of the Strzelecki Desert, and I'm sorry for that.'

'You did it for Joe.'

'Yes,' Brandon said tentatively, 'and also to spite Harry for his treatment of his little brother. But if I'm honest, I did it for myself. I already had one albatross: this farm. I refused to be stuck with another sitting empty in the desert.'

Stella got up slowly and walked out into the garden. The lawn was soft underfoot. The night air filled with the chirping of crickets. The dog brushed against her leg and she absently patted the animal.

'You're angry with me, no doubt, as well as Joe,' said Brandon from the veranda. 'Well, I'm angry with him as well. He was a good man, but I would have been better off mothballing Kirooma for another eight years than handing it over to him. For all his talk and plans, the reports he sent me, the boy had no idea about business. I'll never get my deposit back and neither one of us will ever have anything to show for our investment in that property.'

Stella thought of all the things Brandon had shared with her. His love for Joe. The early years in the Valley. The bitterness between family. She'd grown to care for this old man, even defending him to Harry. And yet, in the end, it was because he'd been desperate to rid himself of a piece of real estate that she'd lost seven years of her life to the desert. Perhaps Brandon Ryan was not quite the wounded party he presented.

Stella walked back to the car in the dark and leant on the bonnet. A slim crescent moon drifted overhead as she slid down the side of the vehicle to sit in the dirt. She cried until she grew bleary-eyed. She felt used by Brandon and Joe, and was also angry with herself. She hadn't needed an old man to tell her what she'd understood for years. Joe had never loved her. And yet that simple fact distressed her terribly. She was ashamed about an ending she'd orchestrated, and tormented by what could have been, who she had become and by what Joe had driven her to do. Except that she wasn't solely to blame. Not anymore. It may have been unintentional, however it occurred to her that if anyone had caused Joe's death, it was Brandon.

She opened the back door of the station wagon and retrieved the cage. Watson scattered seed as he scrambled from the perch to the floor, fluffing his feathers in annoyance. Stella set the enclosure on the ground and opened the cage door, then she returned to the vehicle, started it and reversed. For a few seconds, the cockatoo was spotlighted, still inside the cage, then she drove away.

As she drove, Stella thought of Watson with his proud sulphur crest, the new world he was about to set foot into and what he might make of his changed circumstances when there was no one to feed or water him. That was the problem with freedom. No matter the century, it came at a cost.

⚔ Chapter 56 ⚔

Kirooma Station, 1949

Stella shone the torch on the motorbike. The light flickered across the handlebars, the ripped leather seat, the crate that held water and fuel.

Earlier that afternoon, she'd been sitting cross-legged in the dirt talking to Watson in his cage near the back gate when she saw Joe fill the jerry can with petrol. He stood at the bowser, pushing and pulling the hand-pump until the container was full and then he lugged the can back towards the house and the parked motorbike.

That's how she knew he was leaving.

It was six months since her return from hospital. So many weeks spreading out like the ceaseless sand dunes. Hours spent waiting for Joe to depart. Since her return to Kirooma, he had limited his adventures to overnight affairs. Brief trips to check watering points and to muster sheep, dragging the job out over several days as he moved mobs steadily from one paddock to another, ensuring he was home most nights, until eventually they reached the yards. These short expeditions left him thudding through the homestead or yelling at the dog. Like her, he was desperate to be free.

The wait to see how long Joe would last before the need to go bush struck him had begun to test them both. Each day was the same. Tea, breakfast, morning tea, lunch, afternoon tea, dinner. And sherry in the library on Friday nights. Her husband fetched her at each appointed time like a lamb on the bottle, prepared their meals and made her sit across the table and listen to his endless chatter. Which she did. Quietly. Unaccustomed to continual speech, his words cluttered her. They filled up the spaces of the building they now both inhabited, scaring away the whispers of the past, making her reach more frequently than she should have for the pills the doctor had prescribed. Eventually Joe would leave her alone and head off to potter in one of the sheds, reclassify his fossicking collection or ride about the homestead on the motorbike. He raced the bike around the house, loop after loop. Red dust flying. Engine screeching. The dog giving chase and barking in pursuit. Stella wasn't sure which of them was madder.

She did however know what was behind his absurdly intense concern. Not her health, but that she might still pack her bags and leave. Their circle of acquaintances was now bigger. There were doctors and nurses, tea-ladies and a particular Catholic priest, all of whom represented yet more reasons to keep their marriage intact. He'd already lost face with the bank and he wasn't going to be humiliated by an uncontrollable wife. He hid the keys for the station wagon and the work truck.

Patience and femininity became her weapons. The first she was well practised in, the second only required the unpacking of the softness that once overshadowed all other aspects of her personality. And now she was being rewarded.

It was pitch-black and the torch was shining on the motorbike, which was packed and ready for his next adventure. Stella lay the light on the ground. She lifted the full container of petrol from the crate on the rear of the bike and replaced it with one of the empty jerry cans near the garage. Then she filled the can with the precious water from the bottle next to it so that the liquid was undrinkable, and the bike remained weighted down by its load.

Finally she placed an empty water bottle in the crate. She shone the torch on her handiwork, the light catching the dog's eyes in the dark as he padded towards her.

'I'm sorry,' she said to the animal. She flicked off the torch and returned to the house.

❖

Stella woke at daylight, feeling the tightness of the sheet across her toes. She kicked at the covering and then swung her legs over the side of the bed. There was a jug of water sitting next to a glass on the dressing table and she went to it and upended the lukewarm contents of the vessel on top of her head. The water splashed over her head and shoulders, running in streams along her naked body before landing with a splatter on the floorboards, bedsheets and her discarded nightgown. She brushed wet strands of hair from her face and walked out onto the veranda. The red dust clung to the dribbles of water on her feet. She looked at them, absently lifting her soles from the dirt. Then at the wedding band on her finger.

'I brought you some tea and toast.' Joe set a tray down on the bed. 'What are you doing out there? You've nothing on.' He came to her side, draping the nightgown about her shoulders. 'You're wet. How did all this water get on the floor?'

She allowed Joe to lead her back indoors. He drew the night-dress over her head. Then he made her sit. 'Did you sleep last night? Have you been taking your tablets?' he said.

'I've only just woken up,' she told him.

'Oh,' he said, as if that explained everything. 'Here, I made you some tea.' He passed her the cup.

'When are you going?' she asked him.

He was immediately wary. 'I'm not going anywhere.'

'Joe,' she said playfully, 'I'm feeling better and I do sleep during the day. I'm worried that you haven't been out to check on the sheep more thoroughly. Don't we start shearing soon?'

He leant against the dressing table. Curling grey hairs were visible above the vee of his blue shirt. 'Yes, but I need to know that you'll be okay. The doctor said you weren't to be left alone.'

She reached for his arm, stroking it. There had been little contact between them since the day he removed her from the hospital. Joe appeared to be deciding whether to reciprocate, then patted her, briefly.

'I was pretty worried about you,' he admitted.

'It takes a while to get over some things.'

'We've had a bit of a rough trot,' he said.

'We have,' she agreed. 'And I do appreciate the effort that you've made to stay with me the last few months.' She saw it then, the breaking down of the barrier he'd constructed long ago. It was almost as if she were breaching his stony walls, removing blocks of granite until the prize revealed itself. Joe was pleased by her gratitude, delighted by her recognition of what had been a difficult six months for *him*.

Stella drank the tea. 'Just how I like it. Black and strong. You should go, Joe. I'll feel bad if you stay any longer.'

'Really? Well, if you're sure. I might be gone at least a week. It's a hike out to the north-west of the run,' he told her.

'I'll walk you out,' she offered.

Perhaps she was being a little too amenable, for Joe halted in the doorway. 'You haven't done that for years.'

'Haven't I?' She made a fuss of scrunching her brow and sounding vague. She could feel how torn her husband was. He was desperate to leave and yet still unsure of doing so. But it was too much for him. He had to go.

'Come on,' said Joe.

Together they walked through the homestead as the sun rose.

'It's a beautiful morning. An egg-yolk dawn,' he said. In the kitchen he placed a loaf of bread and a chunk of salted meat in his lunchbox container and tucked his notebook under his arm. 'Well, I'm off.'

She rinsed her cup in the sink, conscious of not appearing too eager.

'Stella?' Joe called from the back door where he was pulling on his boots.

'Coming.'

Together they walked down the back path and through the gate to where the motorbike was parked.

'You'll take care of yourself while I'm gone?' said Joe.

Stella nodded. Her mouth was dry.

'I *do* care for you,' he told her.

Joe tied rope around the lunchbox to secure the lid and then wired it to the crate on the rear of the bike. Next he patted the jerry can and checked the water bottle was secure before throwing his leg over the motorbike. He straddled the machine and then turned to wink at her.

'See you, Stella.' He struck the bike's starter with his boot.

'See you,' she replied.

The bike's engine sputtered as it started. Joe gave a long whistle and the dog jumped up onto his thighs. He waved absently as the animal rested its head on his shoulder, watching her as they rode away. Stella closed the gate on the reddening horizon.

In the weeks to come, when the authorities had been and gone, and she had played the grieving widow, she would note down the location they found his body and write about his heroic end in the desert, in much the way he had described the death of his beloved ram, KR10. It would be a final grand entry in Joe's leather-bound volume, one worthy of a man who lived for the land and nothing else. He would have liked that. Stella was sure of it.

⋘ Author's Note ⋙

The Cedar Tree is a work of fiction, however historical fact lies at the heart of the narrative. The Big Scrub, located between Byron Bay, Ballina and Lismore in northern New South Wales, once covered 75,000 hectares prior to European settlement. By 1900 less than one per cent of it remained. It was once the largest expanse of lowland subtropical rainforest in Australia, containing a prized possession: cedar. The term 'red gold' was coined because of its value, which at the time made it equal in many eyes to those seeking actual gold, but far more attainable for hardened timber-cutters and merchants who were only too willing to fill the demand for the timber, which was sought after by the likes of furniture-makers, and ship- and housebuilders. Cedar-getters were true pioneers, venturing far into the unknown, often exploring country before the arrival of farmers. Unfortunately, their endeavours came at a huge environmental cost.

The Marquis de Rays was a French nobleman who attempted to start a colony on an island now referred to as New Ireland near Papua New Guinea. Three hundred and forty Italian colonists from Veneto, Italy set sail for this colony from Barcelona in 1880.

One hundred and twenty-three died en route before the survivors were rescued from Noumea by Australian authorities. Some of these immigrants formed a community at New Italy on the Richmond River near Woodburn in 1882. The settlement is now deserted.

Edith O'Gorman, the 'escaped nun' mentioned in *The Cedar Tree*, was a real person. A woman of Irish birth, she emigrated to America and joined the Sisters of Charity in 1862. In 1868, O'Gorman escaped from this convent, and in 1871 she wrote *Trials and Persecutions of Miss Edith O'Gorman*, which described the cruelty she endured. To fit in with the novel's timeline, I have placed O'Gorman's anti-Catholic lecture tour in Australia in 1867. It actually took place between 1886 and 1887. Her life was threatened many times and riots occurred between Catholics and Protestants, including in Lismore, New South Wales. This further stirred the animosities that already existed between the Green and the Orange in some parts of Australia at that time.

The 1861 Robertson Lands Act (also known as the *Crown Lands Acts 1861*) changed the lives of many. Vast areas of grazing lands previously under the control of pastoralists were offered for sale, thereby addressing the imbalance of land ownership. New settlers flooded into rural areas ready to stake their claim. Attempts by selectors, whether honest settlers or speculators, to obtain land led to open conflict with pastoralists.

I would like to thank the following organisations: Ballina Naval and Maritime Museum; the Mid-Richmond Historical Society and Museum at Coraki, which provided access to early pastoral lease maps of the Richmond Valley as well as pioneer settler accounts; and the Richmond River Historical Society, Lismore, for their guidance. My thanks also to Christine Porter, who is not only a gifted artist, but a great Lismore tour guide.

Kirooma Station is fictitious. I especially wish to thank the generosity of Mark and Jenny Lacey and family, who kindly took me into their home, allowing me to explore the extraordinary environment of the Strzelecki Desert as well as immerse myself in

378

the history of their property through access to journals and other material.

Thank you to everyone at Penguin Random House, especially my publisher, Beverley Cousins, whose guidance is invaluable, Emily Cook, Genevieve Buzo and my agent, Tara Wynne at Curtis Brown. To my family – hugs. Readers, booksellers and libraries – thank you. *The Cedar Tree* is my tenth novel. I would not have made it this far without everyone's support.

I am indebted to many works and recommend a selection for further reading: *A New History of the Irish in Australia* by Elizabeth Malcolm and Dianne Hall; *Irish Women in Colonial Australia* by Trevor McClaughlin (editor); *The Oxford History of Ireland* by R. F. Foster (editor); *Turmoil – Tragedy to Triumph: The story of New Italy* by Anne-Gabrielle Thompson; *They Were Expeditioners: The chronicle of Northern Italian farmers – pioneer settlers of New Italy with documentation of the Marquis de Ray's four expeditions to New Ireland between 1879 and 1881* by Rosemary Harrigan; *Red Cedar in Australia* by John A. McPhee (editor); *Red Gold: The tree that built a nation* by John Vader; *Red Cedar, Our Heritage: A personal account of the lives and times of the men and women who worked in the red cedar industry* by Alex S. Gaddes; *Men and a River: Richmond River District 1828–1895* by Louise Tiffany Daley; *Squatters on the Richmond: Runs, owners and boundaries, from settlement to dissolution 1840–1900* by W. J. Olley; *Australia's Outback Heritage: Frontier country (vol. 1)* by Sheena Coupe (general editor); *Fence People: Yarns from the dingo fence* by Dinah Percival and Candida Westney; *Regolith and Landscape Evolution of Far Western NSW* by S. M. Hill.

Discover a
new favourite